THE

BEAST

IN THE

FIELD

The Beast in the Field is published under Reverie, a sectionalized division under Di Angelo Publications, Inc.

Reverie is an imprint of Di Angelo Publications.
Copyright 2024.
All rights reserved.
Printed in the United States of America.

Di Angelo Publications
Los Angeles, California

Library of Congress
The Beast in the Field
ISBN: 978-1-955690-52-2
Paperback

Words: D.J. Graystone
Cover Design: D.J. Graystone
Interior Design: Kimberly James
Editors: Willy Rowberry

Downloadable via www.dapbooks.shop and other e-book retailers.

For educational, business, and bulk orders, contact distribution@diangelopublications.com.

1. Fiction --- Thrillers --- Crime
2. Fiction --- Crime
3. Fiction --- Mystery & Detective --- Women Sleuths

THE
BEAST
IN THE
FIELD

D.J. GRAYSTONE

CONTENTS

INTRODUCTION

Yes, hello, hi.

My name is D.J. Graystone, but you can call me "D.G." Most of my friends do, and we *are* friends now, aren't we?

The book you are holding in your hot little hands came about as many other books, songs, and movies have in the past: personal experience. Look at it as a fictional memoir—as a timeline of events that could have been, but never were, but maybe, almost . . .

This book came together over the timespan of a year and a half. It was written in three different countries, on two continents. Now if that doesn't make it hot shit right off the bat, I don't know what does.

Fancy.

The funny part about this book is that it didn't start off as a book at all. I was merely pecking out my feelings—or better yet, verbally vomiting emotions into the notepad of my iPhone. I was just trying to make sense of the Universe's often cruel, and usually darkly wicked sense of humor—or rather, what some people would believe is called "Karma."

I was stuck looking for a silver lining in a deep, dark place.

The first "chapter" was originally over sixty pages. But remember, it wasn't a chapter; this wasn't a book. It was only a collapsing string of mad ramblings on my phone that was so incredibly wordy and pretentious that even Lovecraft himself would have blushed, and probably told me to go fuck myself.

In other words: It was real garbage.

Through the wonders of modern technology, I sent the note to a dear friend, who is the inspiration for the main female character of this book. After an hour or so, she replied and said something along the lines of:

"Wow, this is a great story . . . What happens next?"

I stopped crying long enough to respond to her text:

"Oh, these are just my fucked up feelings. This isn't a book or anything."

At this point, I wasn't sure if she was being kind or lying, or maybe a combination of the two, but she replied:

"This should totally be a book. People would read this!"

All of a sudden, I found the silver lining in this whole shitty-train-wreck-cluster-fuck of a situation.

I went to work. I created a cast of characters—some inspired by real people I have known, still know, or maybe met once or twice. Others are composites of people based off characters from popular culture.

Keep an eye out for nerdy Easter eggs while you read. I can assure you, I have hidden a plethora of brightly colored surprises like piñatas in the pages that follow. (That was one just now, from Three Amigos! Caught you slipping, didn't I?)

A lot of this book reflects completely fictional memories and situations throughout many years. Or, at least, the way I saw things. Names, locations, and identifying characteristics have been changed, and any resulting resemblance to any person, living or dead, is entirely coincidental and unintentional. The same goes for all dialogue, events, happenstance, and timelines. It's all a bunch of mumbo-jumbo. So don't read too much into it.

And no, this book isn't about you.

So, after being encouraged to turn this into a proper book, I got to work and wrote the first twenty-two chapters on my iPhone—and I still have the notepad docs to prove it.

I decided to invest in a laptop and spent the better part of six months holed up in a dim room, with my dog, and finished the rest.

What a long, strange trip it's been.

I hope that some sections of this book will give you the same feelings you might expect to have after taking copious amounts of LSD while staring at a mirror in a darkened room. On the opposite end of the spectrum, I hope that you will also laugh, cry, and maybe even fall in love with some of the characters that reside in the long-dead trees that laid their lives on the altar to produce the pulp that made the pages this ink is printed on.

"Cool, you're writing a novel; what's it about?" was a question that many people have asked me throughout the last year and a half, and it's still one that is puzzling for me to answer.

So, I came up with this bullshit answer that happened to be true: "It's a horror story that works part-time as a thriller, and on weekends, pretends to be a love story. But really, deep down, it's a story about mental illness."

My own . . .

So, my advice to you, my awesome new friend, is to grab your favorite adult beverage and perhaps something to smoke, crank up the sounds, dim down the lights, and make sure the doors are locked.

Buckle up, new friend, we are expecting turbulence.

Enjoy the show.

—D.J. Graystone

P.S. For one more bit for extra credit: Put on some Cryochamber while you read. My favorites are Hastur 1 & 2. On YouTube, they have a twenty-four-hour-a-day live stream of great dark ambient music. It sets the mood for the book, and I wrote much of the book while listening to them.

TAILSPIN

"But I don't want to go among mad people," Alice remarked. "Oh, you can't help that," said the Cat: "we're all mad here. I'm mad. You're mad." "How do you know I'm mad?" said Alice. "You must be," said the Cat, "or you wouldn't have come here."

—Lewis Carroll, Alice in Wonderland

"Babe? I'm starting to worry."

Another text bubble went green on Jesse's iPhone as he sat anxiously at the table of his mandatory work dinner.

It had been over two hours since he had heard from his wife, Katia, which wasn't like her at all.

He sat staring at his phone. His crisp, white-collared dress shirt that was tucked into his dark jeans almost hid the colorful tattoos poking out from the bottom of his sleeves.

Jesse was in, what some would call, the best part of a man's life. He was forty years old and in good shape, and he made good money. Sure, he had a little bit of a tummy now, and his beard had gone from a dark brown to a mix of distinguished salt and pepper, but Jesse was okay with that. His hairline had receded to the point of no return, so now he kept his head shaved, and he was just fine with that too. He always thought the shaved head with beard combination was "strong like bull." Although some would say Jesse looked intimidating, he never thought so.

"Hey, Jesse, have you ordered yet?" his coworker and friend Yvette asked him from across the table. "I got the filet mignon and baked Alaska."

"No, not yet. I'm still deciding," Jesse replied, forcing a smile. He could feel the anxiety start to deepen as he sent out another text to Katia: *"Kat?"*

The text bubble once again went green.

Jesse's inner monologue tried to reassure him: *Maybe her phone died, or maybe she has it turned off while she's at therapy. Yes, that's typical of her—it's happened before.*

Just as that thought rounded off, another voice slithered into Jesse's mind: *Maybe, but not for this long, has it, Jesse?*

A violent image of twisted metal and flashing red and blue emergency lights scratched its way into his mind's eye. The stink of oil and gasoline on the pavement. The smoking, warm skid marks from an awful and sudden swerve that caused that strangle-like tightening of a seatbelt, coupled with the terrible, high-pitched chirping of the ABS engaging. The deafening *CRHUSAH!* of two automobiles colliding and the appalling silence immediately after. Jesse shook that thought off as paranoia, but that ominous, scratchy voice grew a bit louder.

She's been in a terrible car accident, you know.

Jesse looked at his phone again and grimaced.

She's most likely dead, the raspy voice echoed through his mind, but this time it tied his guts up into knots, growing tighter with every moment that passed. Still no response.

She has been complaining about her phone charger this week, Jesse tried to reason. *Maybe it finally blew? That sounds plausible, doesn't it?*

"Sir?"

Jesse smiled as he imagined Katia trying to find her way home from her therapy session in Pasadena without the aid of navigation. Katia and Jesse had been married and living in the same house for nearly two years, and she's been making the same drive to her psychologist's office for several months now, but Katia still got lost going around town. Jesse found her lack of directional ability endearing and adorable in a funny sort of way.

"Sir?"

Jesse opened the messaging app on his phone and clicked on a favorited contact. He quickly typed out a text and sent it. *"Hello Lynn, is Katia still with you? I haven't heard from her in a couple of hours. Please let me know ASAP, thanks! Jesse."* The text bubble went through as blue.

"SIR?"

"Jesse, wake up man. The waitress is trying to take your order. We're all starving." Yvette reached over the table and swatted at Jesse with her menu.

It was true. The team had already been at the bar for an hour, and before that, they'd been working all day. High-pressure sales. They were "road dogs"—commission only, boiler room, Glengarry Glen Ross, door-knocking, dick-deep in the trenches, high-pressure salespeople. So yes, they were starving.

And this was a special night for the entire team.

The month prior, Jesse and a couple others in the team had broken some sales records at their regional office. Tonight was their night. Employees only—just the team. Although the company did have work events where people could bring their families, tonight wasn't one of those nights, which was fine with Katia. She loathed going to Jesse's work dinners. They would start out fine, but after a couple of glasses of wine, she'd have trouble controlling herself around the buffets and would start binge eating, only to lament her impulses on the way home.

As far as Jesse was concerned, though, Katia would always be flawless. She was, aesthetically speaking, the kind of woman who could stop time just by passing by. When she'd enter a room, the lights would seem to dim because she'd shine so brightly. Even the tone of her voice was beautiful, and was enough to charm even the most savage of beasts. After all, she had charmed Jesse. "JESSE! FOOD, NOW!"

Yvette playfully threw a half-eaten dinner roll at Jesse from across the table. Jesse picked up the menu and stuttered out the first item he saw. "I'll have the shrimp and pasta." The setting of the restaurant was beautiful. It was a perfect night. The waves were gently lapping against the rocky shore of Manhattan Beach, and the restaurant was perched at the end of the pier. The weather was bliss—68 degrees and clear. The sun had just dipped below the horizon of the Pacific Ocean, casting a dancing glow of orange- and violet-feathered kisses on the vanishing point far, far away.

Although the sea was calm and glassy, Jesse could feel currents of emotion starting to churn inside him. What started off as a ripple of amusement at Katia's typical irresponsibility had now turned into a swell of anxiety that brought savage images to Jesse's head. Seatbelts being cut off with safety scissors, and the sickly smell of the airbag deploying in the cockpit of her little white SUV.

That single drop of anxiety had morphed and swelled into a tidal wave of panic, growing as each moment slipped by, thick and slow, the way honey drips from a spoon into a hot cup of tea.

Jesse flipped his phone over and tapped the screen, bringing the device to life. Still no reply from Katia, still no response from Lynn. Jesse unlocked the phone. It had full bars of service, but just to be safe, he flipped it to airplane mode and back again. He opened the messaging app, selected the conversation with Katia, and tapped out another quick message: *"Kat? Please, I'm terrified."*

The text bubble popped up green.

"I have to go make a call."

Jesse walked briskly to the parking lot of the restaurant and ran into one of the other salespeople from his company.

"Hey, Josh, can I bum one of those?" Jesse asked, nodding at the cigarette Josh had hanging from his lips.

Katia loathed smokers. One of the conditions of her moving in was that Jesse quit those filthy shit sticks, as she so pleasantly referred to them. It had been over two years since Jesse had bought a pack of his own, but he would still bum the odd smoke from a coworker from time to time. To help ease the pangs of quitting, Jesse had started vaping, which was just as disgusting—but now instead of smelling like those filthy shit sticks, he always smelled of sticky sweet vape juice.

Katia also hated vaping, but she tolerated it as long as it kept her man from smoking. She'd say, "I'm proud of you for quitting smoking, but I will not have you doing it in our house!"

Jesse took another drag off the cigarette. They tasted foul to him now, and he was trying to remember how he had ever smoked two packs a day in the first place.

Jesse would give anything right now to get an annoyed phone call from Katia, saying he had woken her up with his obnoxious, worried texts. Or, even better, to have Katia call, upset that he forgot to take the trash cans out. After all, it was Tuesday, trash day, and Jesse often forgot the little things while he was focused on work. They would lie in bed together tonight, and Jesse would whisper in Katia's ear, "For five years, I work, I slave, we save up, cut corners, and then we move to Europe. We live our dream. We start our lives." The plan was so simple.

Jesse did indeed put in hours—long hours. It wasn't rare for him to leave the house at 7:00 a.m. and to get home after 10:00 p.m. He'd have three sales appointments—with 300 miles of driving and a paycheck of $4,500 for the day's work—then come home to a house lit only with candles, the sounds of soft French music playing in the background, and the aroma of an elaborate gourmet meal that his gorgeous twenty-nine-year-old wife had prepared for him.

Katia would be dressed only in Agent Provocateur lingerie and the sexiest of high heels, her athletic five-foot-four frame looking graceful and almost feline as she waited for him to cross the threshold.

Upon entering, Jesse would put down his bags and embrace her. He would coo into Katia's ear, just slightly more than a whisper, "I missed you so much, my Kat. Thank you for everything you do for us. I am grateful for you."

She would melt into him, her hands on his chest and her cheek resting on his neck, then slowly, with her big blue eyes, she'd look up to the man she adored and whisper back, "I missed you, my love.

Thank you for everything you do for us. I am grateful for you."

The two would embrace again and kiss as if Jesse had just gotten home from war; they'd exchange energy in a delicate dance of delicious, familiar intimacy.

Katia had made that house into a home.

She's dead, you know.

Jesse turned around to enter the restaurant again and ran into Hunter, who was the only other person in the company in the same age bracket as Jesse.

"What's up, man?" Hunter said, extending his heavily tattooed arm for his customary fist bump.

"No word from Katia for a couple hours," Jesse said, pulling out his overly orange and fancy digital vape mod. Hunter gave Jesse a crooked smile and pulled out his own vape.

"Walk with me," Hunter said as he gave Jesse a nudge with his elbow and headed back into the parking lot. Hunter took a long, loud draw from his vape and exhaled smoke that smelled of sweet melons and strawberry. Jesse often wondered if he looked like that much of an asshole when he was vaping, too. After emitting the vaporized vegetable glycerin, Hunter smiled, winked, and said, "She's probably getting fucked right now, as we speak."

Jesse glared at Hunter, then took another drag off his vape. While exhaling, eyes still fixed on the man in front of him, Jesse cracked a smile at Hunter and chuckled.

"Go fuck yourself, asshole."

Hunter was one of Jesse's best friends. They had been close for years. They knew all of each other's bullshit. They both had enough dirt on the other that if one of them decided to go rogue and write a tell-all, it would be mutually assured destruction. Hunter was about five-foot-seven, heavyset, covered in tattoos, and a generally good-looking guy. The self-proclaimed "whitest Mexican you know." And Hunter, like Jesse, also had a sordid, colorful past.

"Don't worry about anything. Let's go back inside and have some fun. I can assure you that she's more than fine. She's sleeping off her therapy session, no doubt. Let's go, c'mon!"

Jesse and Hunter were so close that Hunter even knew Katia's therapy schedule.

"Yeah, let me text her again." *"You're the love of my life."*

The text bubble went green once again.

Jesse looked up at Hunter and watched him take another hit.

"Dude, relax. Quit being a bitch, and let's get back to the dinner. I bet the food is there already."

Hunter put his arm around Jesse, and together they walked back in through the large glass doors of the restaurant to their party on the patio that overlooked the ocean.

The hearty laughter and conversations from the intoxicated group echoed off the splintered planks of wood that were cobbled together to make up the boardwalk of the old pier. The sound that wasn't absorbed by the wood bounced off and quickly dissipated into the rolling black waves of the sea below. The smell of food, booze, old growth wood, and salt water perfumed the air.

As Jesse got back to the table, he pulled out his chair. Yvette, who at this point had been over-served, glanced up at Jesse with a *where-the-fuck-have-you-been?* face, accompanied by a *WTF?* hand gesture.

Hunter sat down beside Jesse and pulled out his phone. "I'm sending you a new audiobook; you have to give it a listen. Good shit."

Jesse and Hunter always shared books, audio and otherwise. Spending as much time in traffic as they did, they figured it was the best use of their time.

"Download it right now, fucker. I heard the dude on Rogan. His name is David Goggins. That dude is a GOD!"

Hunter looked up with a smile as the waiter brought a still-sizzling plate up to the table and placed it in front of him. Jesse just stared at the blackened cut of beef.

Looks like a ribeye, Jesse thought enviously. *Fuck, why didn't I order steak?* Jesse felt horribly cheated as he looked down at his pale heap of pasta.

Your wife is dead.

That little voice in the back of his head started whispering to him again from a dark, damp corner. Jesse stared at Hunter's plate, waging a silent internal battle with that whispering voice. He flipped over his phone. There was a text notification. He unlocked it and frantically went to the messaging app.

One text message from Lynn Shrink: *"No, she didn't make it in today. Is everything okay?"*Moments later, a second text came through: *"I have to bill you anyway - the usual card?"*Jesse gave her a quick response, but he could feel his blood pressure rise.

A hot neon pink panic crashed into him like an avalanche. The anxiety pumped through his veins and pounded in his temples like kettledrums. It was as if he had been envenomated by a serpent, its fangs plunged deep and true. The reptile's forked tongue recessed completely as it pumped what Jesse could imagine was a pale yellow, syrupy, semi-clotted substance into his veins that flowed to every cell of his body, collecting and pooling in his mind, forming puddles behind his eyes.

"Thank You for the Venom," Jesse thought—his wife's favorite song by her favorite band. He would have loved to take her to see them, but they had broken up years ago. Katia also loved French culture. Her childhood dream was to go to Paris, and Jesse helped make that wish come true for her. He took her there for her birthday two years ago. On her birthday, on the Eiffel Tower, they got engaged. It was a real-life fairytale.

That trip taught him that storybook endings were possible, but tonight was looking more and more Grimm.

"Was that her?"

Jesse couldn't hear Hunter's question. As a matter of fact, Jesse couldn't hear anything other than the pounding of his heart and the almost tambourine-like jingle of his watch shaking on his wrist.

"Dude, was that her?"

Jesse just stared at his phone. Only six or seven seconds had gone by since Lynn had sent her last text.

Hunter gave him a nudge with his elbow, and Jesse snapped back into the present moment.

"I . . . I have to go," Jesse said as he stood from the table and nearly stumbled over Hunter.

"I'll walk you out." Hunter immediately got up and helped Jesse to the parking lot.

"What's the deal, man? What's happening?" Hunter asked as soon as they got outside.

"It . . . That was Lynn," Jesse said, still looking at the message on his phone.

"How's Katia? Is she still with her?" Hunter knew it wasn't unusual for Katia to be with Lynn for two or three hours at a time. Trudging through the years of childhood abuse, neglect, and abandonment that made Katia into the woman she was today took time. Katia was a beautiful disaster of issues, the perfect storm of maladies. She had a childhood that looked perfect to the people passing by. An upper-class upbringing filled with dance recitals and ballet classes. But there, just below the surface, something dark had always lurked. Something was very wrong in the house where Katia had grown up.

"She . . . never showed up to her appointment."

"Get out of here, man. I'll cover for you. Go!"

Jesse was expected to stand up in front of the company and give a speech tonight, but that wasn't happening now. It didn't matter. Nothing mattered. Nothing mattered except Katia. Jesse jogged to his car and wasted no time in bringing the Prius to life. Jesse's phone connected to the car's stereo, and he immediately silenced the music that began blasting. As he began driving, he called out loud, "Hey, Siri, call Katia!"

"Calling Katia," Siri's pleasant monotone replied.

"You have reached the voice mailbox for 818—"

Jesse clicked the hang-up button on the steering wheel and hastily repeated, "Hey, Siri, call Katia."

"Calling Katia."

"You have reached the voi—"

Jesse hung up the call again.

"Fuck!" Jesse yelled as his pulse quickened. His mind started screaming, *Her phone must be off, or broken, or maybe she was up all night again.*

Katia suffered from night terrors and would sometimes wake up screaming in a panic, not knowing where she was. That was something she and Lynn were working on in therapy.

Maybe last night was one of those nights, Jesse thought as the little black Prius zoomed its way to the freeway. *Maybe she was up all night again, passed out for a nap this afternoon, and forgot to set the alarm. Yeah, that's it. That must be it.*

That had happened more than once, but this time felt different. This time felt sticky, like a thick, green, hot summer in Indiana, right before an evening thunderstorm.

She's dead. Your wife is dead.

That raspy voice rattled through Jesse's mind again.

Jesse slammed his foot on the gas, and the four cylinders of the Prius came to life. He raced to the intersection, hoping to beat the signal, but ended up getting stuck at a red light.

"FUCK!" Jesse screamed again as his hands tightened their grip on the steering wheel. He asked Siri to call again, only to get the same result: voicemail.

Jesse hung up and manually dialed Katia's number. The call went directly to voicemail. He repeated that action until the light turned green. When it did, he mashed the pedal to the floor. The Prius lurched forward, and in less than a minute, Jesse was racing to the on-ramp of the 110 Freeway, heading towards their home in Montrose.

When Katia moved into his cozy two-bedroom Spanish-style bungalow, she was horrified when she found out that Jesse typically didn't lock the doors when he left to run errands. That was the first of many things on which Katia had put her foot down.

"Hey, Siri, call Katia."

"Calling Katia."

"You have reached the voi—"

Although it was nearly 9:30 p.m., it was still the typical never-ending rush hour traffic of Los Angeles. Jesse approached the 110/105 interchange. The bumper-to-bumper traffic was already starting to back up, and Jesse continued calling Katia, to no avail. As he slowly passed the 105 Freeway, the traffic started to let up. He floored it again, and the Prius accelerated to forty miles per hour. Jesse figured if he kept up this pace, he would be home in about an hour. He started speaking out loud, trying to manifest the outcome he wanted in this situation.

"Okay, here is how it's going to be. I'm going to pull into the driveway. Her car will be there. I'll open the door, and she will be asleep on the couch with a book in her hand. This whole thing will just be another funny story to tell our friends."

Jesse and Katia had hundreds of stories. Magical shit just seemed to happen to them. Ever since Jesse got the courage to tell her how he felt about her, everything just seemed to fall into place. The cosmic dominos all lined up—the universal puzzle pieces all came together effortlessly, magically, spontaneously, miraculously. Even events that some would consider mundane were perfect to the two of them, and Jesse let his mind wander to an evening just a couple months prior.

Katia's dream was to have a husky. Ever since she was a little girl, she'd wanted one. Sadly, no amount of begging or pleading with her parents would make them see reason on the husky agenda. However, Jesse had plans to make that dream come true for her. He had called her on his way home from work and told her to wait for him in the kitchen, close her eyes, and be patient. Katia had obviously been annoyed as she sighed and hung up the phone, and Jesse could almost hear her eyes roll when she terminated the call. Little did she know, he had a twelve-pound ball of gray and white fluff in his lap.

When he got home, he called again. "You in the kitchen, Kat?"

"Ugh, yes."

Now she was a bit more than annoyed—Jesse could hear it in her voice.

"Close your eyes, babe. I'll be right there."

"Fine."

Jesse had hung up the phone and picked up the puppy, gently tucking him under his arm. He walked up to the front door and unlocked it.

"Babe, you in the kitchen?" Jesse called out into the house.

"Yes," replied Katia, the impatience of her tone now clearly audible over the dark piano music she had streaming from the TV in the living room. Jesse poked his head into the kitchen and there she was, eyes closed, arms folded, leaning against the kitchen sink. No lingerie tonight; instead, she wore sweats and a hoodie, her second-favorite house outfit. To Jesse, she looked every bit as alluring in the sweats as she did in silk. He approached her slowly, back turned to her.

"Keep 'em closed, babe."

"Ugh, okay." Katia was now cracking a smile. She knew he was up to something, and this something wasn't the typical flowers he would show up with randomly. Jesse plopped the clumsy pup down on his velveteen paws and held him.

"Okay, open your eyes."

As Katia opened her eyes, Jesse released the puppy, and off he went! A streak of gray and white bounded clumsily toward her. Katia's hands instinctively covered her mouth as she gasped in delight and as tears welled up in her eyes.

"What?! What?! Who is this?!" Katia cried out in joy.

"He's a sweet baby, and he's yours," exclaimed Jesse, who was filming the moment on his cellphone. The puppy jumped into her arms and covered her smiling face with kisses, his tiny tongue wiping away the tears flowing freely down her cheeks. Jesse had to choke back his own tears. Another check on her bucket list. These were the moments he lived for. The look of joy in her eyes was intoxicating to him. This was the man Jesse always knew he could be. The light inside her made his light burn brighter. Her calming energy extinguished the fires of rage he had held inside since he was a child. He was set free.

"Hey, Siri," Jesse demanded again, shaking the memory from his mind. "Call Katia."

"Calling Katia."

"You have reached the voi—"

She's dead, Jesse! the voice hissed again. That voice inside him that had been tormenting him since, well, since as long as he could remember. He had a mental image of the thing that produced the voice. It was a sickly, skinny, pitch-black creature. Skin and bones, ribs and spine protruding against its coal flesh, like a jagged skeleton wrapped up tightly in black trash bags.

Jesse was now at the 110/5 Freeway interchange. Traffic came to a halt again, just as it always did on the 5 Freeway. When he moved onto the 2 Freeway heading north, he tried calling Katia again with the same result.

Only fifteen minutes and he would be home with her. It was entirely possible that she was in bed with her neon green sleep mask, noise-canceling headphones on tight, passed out from one of her guided meditation sessions.

"Please, God, please let that be it," Jesse whispered to himself as he flew up the 2 Freeway, passing under the 134 interchange. He looked up at the monolithic overpass and smiled.

"Katia hates that fucking on-ramp."

It was a couple hundred feet up in the air and had a sharp bank, and she would request he get off the 134 at Harvey and go a couple blocks north on surface streets to avoid it. Jesse never did mind doing those little things for her. It became routine. So routine, in fact, that she didn't even have to ask anymore. He filed it away in the Rolodex in his mind he kept for her. Her favorite music, food, scents—clean laundry and vanilla, but her number one was lavender—were all stored in his memory.

Jesse floored the accelerator, hitting nearly ninety on the interchange.

"Hey, Siri, call Katia."

"Calling Katia."

"You have reached the voi—"

"I'm almost home. Almost there. Almost there."

He couldn't help but think of Garven Dreis in *Star Wars Episode IV*. Poor bastard. Blown up by Darth Vader while making a run in his X-Wing in the battle of Yavin.

I wonder if it was the initial explosion, or if the vacuum of space killed him? Jesse smirked. *Jesus, it's a wonder I've ever been laid.*

Jesse pushed the steering to the right and headed off the Ocean View exit. Off the freeway, two sharp rights, followed by a third, and finally a left onto Piedmont. Jesse pulled onto his street into the driveway of their little house. Katia's car was parked in its usual place, and the lights in the house were on.

Jesse let out a deep, well-earned sigh of relief.

"She's cooking or sleeping."

He parked the car but left it running.

"Hey, Siri, call Hunter."

"Calling Hunter."

After two rings, Hunter answered the call. Jesse could hear the loud party in the background.

"Yo, man, you okay?"

Hunter's voice was concerned, but Jesse could tell he was hopeful from the uptick of his inflection.

"Yeah, man, she's home. Just pulled up. Thanks for having my back."

"Cool, man, talk in the a.m.? Say hi to Katia for me."

"Will do."

"Love you, bro!"

Hunter disconnected the call. Jesse opened the car door, stepped out, and looked up at the night sky.

"Thank you, God," Jesse whispered. The relief he felt was palpable. All the pent-up tension of the last several hours was draining out of him. He felt a lightness returning that he hadn't felt all night.

About ten steps to the front door of his home and all he could think about was getting into the house and sliding into bed next to his sleeping wife, giving her a kiss on her forehead, and gently whispering, "I'm home, love. I'm so grateful for you."

"I'm gwatefo to yu too, my lov. I luv you so," Katia would reply with her oh-so-famous sleep talk.

Jesse unhinged the eye ring keychain he kept attached to his belt loop. On it was the solid silver charm that Katia had gotten for him when they'd first started dating. The keys slipped from Jesse's hand right before he was about to insert it into the lock.

Jesse bent down to get them, and on his way up, he reached and checked the front door. It was locked.

He smiled. *She always locks the doors.*

He slid the key into the lock, turned it clockwise, and heard the deadbolt retract from the doorjamb. He gave the big door a push, and it started to open but with more resistance than usual, like pushing an oar through water.

Jesse looked down to see the weather stripping of the door was sweeping away a pool of blood from the threshold, leaving an almost-clean quarter circle, like a windshield wiper, and exposing the Douglas Fir flooring underneath.

Six feet from the door lay the disconnected form of Katia. Her body, dismembered, pieces laid out neatly, on display, like a naked jigsaw puzzle, a mannequin waiting to be put back together.

I told you she was dead.

The voice inside Jesse's head cackled louder and louder and kept laughing until it turned into a shrill, siren-like scream. The raspy, slithery voice kept screaming until Jesse hit the floor.

ASTROLOGY AND GASOLINE

A person often meets his destiny on the road he took to avoid it.

—Jean de La Fontaine

Jesse and Ben walked through the showroom of Wood Bridge Motors, the number-one selling Mercedes dealership in the world. They were making small talk and joking after having lunch at the dealership's on-property restaurant. As they walked across the main showroom's gleaming marble floors on their way back to their offices, Jesse glanced over his right shoulder to the receptionist desk. At that exact moment, time stopped.

There was Katia.

This was the first time Jesse had laid eyes on her, and he froze. She had her near waist-length red hair back in a tight ponytail. She was wearing a white blouse with a charcoal-gray pencil skirt. Even though it would be six long years until they were officially together, Jesse still remembered exactly what she was wearing that day. And on the day they were married, he told that story at the reception, tears rolling down his face.

As far as Jesse was concerned, this was the day his life really began.

Ben paused from the silly story he was telling and watched Jesse stare at Katia.

"Who's that new ginger girl?" Jesse managed to sputter out after what seemed like an eternity.

"I don't know. Some hot new girl," Ben said passively.

Jesse turned to Ben and gave him a grin. "No, Ben, I'll tell you exactly who that is. That's the woman I'm going to marry."

Jesse walked straight up to the receptionist desk and just stood and stared stupidly. He had never laid eyes on a woman as beautiful as Katia, who, of course, was oblivious to his presence for the thirty seconds he stood there as she finished her phone call. She dispatched the customer to the appropriate department, and after typing a note on her computer, Katia looked up and saw the man standing in front of her desk.

Jesse locked eyes with Katia for the first time.

He was sure that he looked wholly ridiculous or creepy while standing there, staring at a woman he had never even met before. Ben gave him a nudge, and it quickly broke him out of the hypnotic spell that he was under. Jesse awkwardly thrust out his right hand at Katia, fingers spread wide as if he was trying to palm a basketball.

"Hi, yes. I'm, um, hi, Jesse Silver . . . Hello!"

Jesse spit the words out in a collapsing tangle of fragmented vowels and consonants that barely sounded like English.

Katia reached out with a dainty manicured hand, took one of Jesse's outstretched fingers, and shook it.

"Hi," she said meekly, obviously creeped out. "I'm Katia."

Jesse just continued to stare. He could tell that Katia was getting noticeably uncomfortable with this interaction and was probably thinking something along the lines of, "Who is this awkward creep?"

Ben shoved Jesse in the back again, jarring him into the present moment. "Let's get back to our office, man."

Ben took Jesse by the arm and walked him away from the receptionist desk.

The sheriff cruiser that was first on the scene illuminated the quiet street with its flashing lights, giving the quiet suburb the appearance of some sort of nightmare carnival. The sandpaper-like scratch of the chatter on Deputy Amador's walkie-talkie sounded like dead leaves blowing across the pavement. Jesse didn't remember calling 911, nor did he remember sitting in the pool of Katia's blood, like a child during bath time playing with a broken Barbie doll, trying to put the pieces of Katia back together.

He also couldn't recall exactly when or who had pulled him off Katia's remains, or how or when he was strapped down to the gurney, or which deputy had handcuffed him to the rails of the stretcher.

The plastic of the oxygen mask had an almost sweet odor. It reminded him of the injection molded animal figurines he used to get at the zoo when he was a child. He loved those machines. Put in a quarter, and the hot liquid plastic would flow like molten lava into the mold of whatever animal he chose.

The EMT that was checking his vitals shone a flashlight in his eyes, spreading his eyelids open and frantically waving the bright LED in front of his face.

"Pupillary response, mydriasis. Pulse elevated 140 bpm and climbing. Blood pressure 86/50. Sir, stay with me. Sir!" The EMT spoke calmly while patting Jesse over and inspecting him, looking for wounds.

"He's in shock. Heated blanket, now!"

Jesse squinted his eyes and tried to focus on the ceiling of the ambulance, watching the EMTs frantically go back and forth. He didn't feel the IV needle go into his arm, or the icy fluid creeping into his circulatory system.

He was viewing the scene from a new perspective, watching himself from above. The shiny, sterile plastic of the instruments, the machines monitoring him, the two EMTs hovering over him like battlefield surgeons. One, the female, was shouting orders to the obvious rookie, a boy no older than twenty-three, who was overseeing and assessing the patient.

The 911 call that Jesse had made had no words, only his screaming. The 911 operator tried to get Jesse to calm down for the sixteen-second phone call, but it was no use. When the line went dead, the operator hesitated for a moment, gathered herself, then radioed to dispatch the sheriff's department to the GPS location.

"We need a unit to 2455 Piedmont Avenue, Montrose. Code 3, Possible 415 in progress."

There was a brief pause, then the snap-like, crackled response. "Ten-four. Unit 2 responding." That residential address was only one and a half miles from the local sheriff's station. A unit would be on the scene in minutes.

The first unit to respond to the scene that night was driven by deputy Amador. Amador had joined the Marines at nineteen. After Boot Camp and three tours in Afghanistan, this job was a cakewalk. Once Amador was out of the academy, he spent time working in the jails, which was customary for new sheriffs, then it was out to the field.

The first year, Amador was on patrol with his field training officer, then he was put under direct command of Sergeant Durazo. The two had hit it off instantly. Durazo, a retired Marine who had served in Vietnam, immediately won Amador's respect and admiration.

Durazo had shown Amador the ins and outs and the everyday bullshit that working in a quiet suburb of Los Angeles entailed: traffic stops, minor fender benders, the occasional break-in of some blue-haired old lady's house—where the homeowner would cluck her tongue and roll her eyes as the deputies asked her questions and tried to explain, "No, ma'am, we don't have a database of everyone's DNA on file like you see on TV," or, Amador's personal favorite, "No ma'am, I don't think Donald Trump had anything to do with this."

Amador had forged a strong bond with Sergeant Durazo. Durazo's wisdom and experience were indispensable for a young deputy who was newly married with his first child on the way. All this gave Amador a greater appreciation for life than he had had before, when he was back in Afghanistan.

As Amador pulled up to the house, his code 3 lights and sirens were still flashing and blaring in a panicked frenzy. He cut the siren off but left the lights on. Amador reached for his flashlight and hesitated, then tilted his head toward the open window of his cruiser. Amador could swear he heard screaming coming from the little house.

Deputy Amador had seen some shit in Afghanistan and knew what screaming like that meant. During his time there, he was a combat operator. He was on point. The tip of the spear. He became squad leader after proving himself over and over to the men in his unit. He loved being the first one in. As soon as the door was breached on whatever shit-hole mud-hut they were going into that day, after the sizzling *hiss* and deafening *crack* of the flashbang went off, Amador always led the charge

A quick button hook entry was Amador's go-to maneuver. After all, he was calling the shots on the missions, and it was his responsibility to not only eliminate the targets with extreme prejudice but also to ensure that the same number of Marines came back to base that had left that morning. He'd be in first, sweeping immediately to the left. The second operator would follow in shortly after him and sweep to the right. They would clear both the corners of the room, making sure to stay out of the dreaded fatal funnel: the hallways, doorways, or stairwells that offered no cover and were the most obvious kill zones in any building.

Amador's eye would stay glued to the green dot of his reflex sight as he moved from room to room. He'd shout as he swept, "Clear! Next room, in!"

The team would follow the room-by-room clearing method, systematically going from one to the next, eliminating any and every threat until the building was secure.

Amador had loved it. He'd lived for it. He, like many millennials, had grown up playing ultra-violent video games like "Call of Duty" and "Counter-Strike." And those days in Afghanistan gave him major wood. Nothing made his blood pump like that. There was no other feeling like it in the world.

The intoxication of adrenaline became his drug of choice, and now, like most junkies, he had to tie off daily to get his fix.

The real fucked up part, what you wouldn't ever see on the mainstream media in America, was that by the time Amador had gotten there, most of the "Taliban" was already crushed . . . and the only "insurgents" left were kids. Most of the people he would have to engage were under the age of seventeen.

That used to bother him, until he lost a member of his team to a thirteen-year-old with a Kalashnikov. Amador got over his bleeding heart real fast after that.

After Afghanistan, the volume on everything else in life seemed to get turned down. This was the only thing that brought Amador's life back into that crystal-clear, 4K, razor-sharp focus. The way combat could. This was the only way he could find to feel alive.

Still in his cruiser outside the house, Amador clicked on his flashlight. Many of the neighbors had come outside and were standing in their bathrobes and nightgowns, frozen on their doorsteps like statues.

Amador's pulse quickened as he slowly got out of his unit. His Smith and Wesson M&P 9 was already free from its holster and drawn. His flashlight and weapon intertwined in the "Harries Hold" position.

He ascended the steep driveway and slowly made his way to the steps of the little house. His training kicked in. His mind was cataloging everything: Weather: 65--75 degrees. Visibility: clear. Time: just after 2300 hours. House lights: on.

As he went up the steps to the landing at the entry of the house, he noted that the screaming didn't sound human. It sounded like some desperate animal that had gotten caught in a bear trap. It had been years since Amador felt his blood run cold, and he felt the icy fingers of fear grip his heart.

This exhilarated him.

His heartbeat raged, and he shook off the newly formed icicles in his chest as he stepped to the threshold and was overwhelmed with the thick, tangy-sweet smell of copper. He looked into the doorway, and all he could see at first was the blood that had congealed to the consistency of maple syrup. It had turned from crimson to a deep purple-maroon. *The color of royalty,* Amador mused for a moment as his eyes fixated on the Rorschach-esque patterns on the hardwood floor, then the nearly surgical clean sweep caused by the weather-stripping of the door.

Amador looked up. His eyes finally landed on the source of that awful screaming.

It was only a man, a man cradling the torso of a woman, her head in his left hand clutched firmly to his chest. One of her arms—Amador couldn't tell which—lay limp and lifeless in the man's lap.

For a moment, the man froze when the bright LED beam of Amador's flashlight hit him in the face. The man in the puddle slowly turned and looked up to the source of the light. He started trying to pick up the pieces of the girl. He was fumbling with them, juggling them. He almost looked like someone carrying too many grocery bags while trying to get the key into the front door of their walk-up apartment.

He held the woman's severed head up and was trying to open her eyes. The man in the puddle was caressing the head's lips. Raising the head to his, he started kissing her, all the while babbling and screaming, sounding animalistic. His eyes were halfway closed, still blinded by the flashlight. It looked like he was trying desperately to reanimate the shattered, disconnected bits and pieces of the girl.

"Kat? My sweet baby. Kat . . . Kat, answer me! Get up, let's go to bed! Kat, get up! Please, get up!"

Amador stood frozen, listening to the guttural, muttered, one-sided conversation, trying to take in the absolute horror of it all. He pointed the flashlight at the puddle, and the light bounced off the crimson pool the frantic man was sitting in.

"Freeze!"

The man in the puddle complied. The babble stopped, and slowly, the man turned in the mess he was kneeling in, a wide wild-eyed expression on his face.

"I need help, there is something wrong with my wife . . . Please! I need help!" the man started screaming and pleading to the young deputy. "I NEED HELP!"

Amador stood frozen, his mind trying to process what he was witnessing.

The man in the puddle held up the woman's severed hand, looked at it, and dropped it into the abyss of black and red. A sickening, sloppy thud of meat splashing into plasma on the hardwood echoed through the room. Then, in a smooth, almost graceful movement, the man in the puddle curled into a fetal position, the decapitated head of a woman still cradled in his arms. He gently, almost rhythmically, started rocking while still sobbing and stroking the severed head.

Amador strained to hear the words the man in the puddle was repeating over and over, cooing in the woman's ear that was right up to his lips.

"Kat it up, Kat it up, Kat it up!"

Amador reached for the speaker on his Motorola Astro Spectra radio and yelled, "Unit 2! 918V! Repeat! 918V! 187! 187! 999! 999! 999!"

And there Amador stood, watching the broken man until the singsong sound of sirens and flashing lights joined his cruiser—his cruiser that was still idling in front of the cute bungalow on the middle of the quiet street in the center of the sleepy little town. The town that was host to mom-and-pop businesses, charming cafes, and the famous Sunday morning farmers market. It was a time capsule nestled in the balcony of the foothills, only minutes from downtown Los Angeles, but during moments like this, it was a world away.

THANK YOU FOR THE VENOM

The boundaries which divide Life from Death are at best shadowy and vague. Who shall say where the one ends, and where the other begins?

—Edgar Allan Poe

Jesse's consciousness was observing the scene from outside the ambulance. He watched from above as the deputies put the bright yellow police tape around his property and started placing little-numbered evidence markers around his yard, on his stairs, and inside his and Katia's house. He could clearly see them inside his home, sweeping around with their flashlights, being careful not to disturb the neatly organized shelves with all of Katia's personal treasures.

The sheriffs set up a mobile command station in front of his neighbor's house and had established a perimeter around the scene. They were only allowing the people who were crucial to the investigation anywhere near the crime scene, so as not to contaminate any evidence. The rhythmic beating of a helicopter could be heard overhead as an air unit swept around the neighborhood.

Jesse floated back into his house. He circled around the pieces of Katia, still trying to make sense of what was going on, trying to find order in the chaos, an answer in the storm.

He floated into the bedroom, and there, standing in the corner, was Katia. She was looking out the window, standing next to the still lit and flickering scented candles she kept on her nightstand.

A slight luminescence danced on her skin, and she was dressed in a beautiful white silk robe, its long tail flowing past her feet and cascading onto the floor.

As Jesse entered the room, she turned slowly to face him. Her face lit up with that smile—her smile. In her eyes was a look of peace that Jesse had never seen before, when she was alive. It was as if she had finally found the serenity that she had been thirsting for her entire life.

She floated toward him, arms outstretched, and they passed through each other, their souls mingling in the cold night air.

Jesse, confused, turned around to see her, but she was gone. He floated into the living room, and there she was, standing over the pieces of her discarded body. She looked up from the bloody horror that was strewn out on the hardwood floor of the living room, then turned to Jesse and smiled again, as if the mess of her mortal coil didn't bother her in the slightest. She made a silent gasp, as if there were something that excited her, then walked over to the front door, looked at it, studied it, reached out and touched the back of it, then looked to Jesse, her mouth pulled back to a huge grin. She ran towards him, arms outstretched as if she were going to jump into his arms—but when she reached him, her phantom evaporated, leaving Jesse floating there. Her spirit was now just a lingering memory, or perhaps just a spark of the imagination and energy returning home to its source in the universe.

Jesse heard the sound of bells ringing, felt a hard, cold jolt, and suddenly he was back in his body. *This feels heavy, clumsy, unnecessary,* Jesse thought as the weight of his mortal shell sank in around him.

A young EMT was sitting beside him, his supervisor driving the ambulance toward Verdugo Hills Hospital, just a couple of miles up the street. The ambulance was followed closely by a deputy in his patrol unit.

"May I walk you to your car?"

Katia looked up from her workstation as she packed her personal belongings into her oversized Coach purse behind the receptionist desk.

It was nearly 10:00 p.m., and this neighborhood looked more like a demilitarized zone than a residential block.

The once beautiful streets of the San Fernando Valley had now been turned into a hive of non-rent controlled Section Eight concrete apartment buildings that played host to all manner of unsavory characters: the standard drug dealers, pimps, prostitutes, and local gang bangers that milled around the once lovely, tree-lined suburban streets—streets that had apartments that housed good families, too. Families who, as soon as the sun went down, stayed safely indoors.

"I don't think that's necessary," Katia said while packing up her belongings. "I'm only parked a few blocks away." She hardly glanced up from her bag.

"I'd feel better about it, and it's no hassle. This is a terrible neighborhood, and it's late. Please, allow me this favor," Jesse said while leaning on the reception desk, trying to put on his best Tyler Durden impression.

Katia paused. "This isn't a good neighborhood?"

She had finished packing up her bag and finally looked up at Jesse.

"Are you serious? This place is awful."

Katia was from a small Indiana farming town, fresh to Los Angeles to pursue her dream of being an actress.

"I didn't know this neighborhood was bad."

"Oh yeah. You have gangs on this block, and two blocks down, you have a homeless camp. Not a good place for a young lady to be walking at night."

Katia grimaced while throwing her large bag over her shoulder and grabbing her keys.

"I would feel much better if I could walk you to your car." Jesse smiled while looking over his shoulder, trying to be nonchalant.

Katia shrugged her shoulders and looked down at her high heels. "Okay, sure . . . fine."

Jesse held the heavy glass door open for her and escorted her down the moonlit street. The company parking lot was only two blocks away, but it was still home to vagrants, junkies, and, of course, the occasional aggressive stray that tended to roam the dark corners of these types of neighborhoods.

"So, what are you into?" asked Jesse awkwardly as he walked next to Katia, his hands in his pockets, his head on a swivel.

Stay frosty, Jesse, he thought to himself. His street-smart Spidey-sense was going off the charts.

Paranoid? Yes. Paranoid enough? Probably not . . .

"I love to act, sing, and dance."

"Dance?" asked Jesse, genuinely interested.

"Yes, I've been dancing since I was a girl. It's my world."

"That's so cool. What kind of dance?" asked Jesse as if he knew the difference between the styles.

"Well, I started with ballet, of course, then I went to Madison for acting."

"Mega!" said Jesse while glancing over his shoulder, as a group of large men walked swiftly out from an alley, followed them for a moment, then crossed the street.

Almost to the car lot, thank Christ, thought Jesse as they rounded the last corner.

"Are you into . . . Do you like music?" Jesse spit out the words. He hated small talk. However, this was an opportunity for him to have the first conversation with his soon-to-be girlfriend, soon-to-be fiancée, soon-to-be wife.

Sure, Katia wasn't aware of his plan and obviously had zero interest in him, but that was a minor technicality, a detail he could figure out later. Now was all about her, learning about her.

"My favorite band is My Chemical Romance." Katia sounded almost embarrassed about having just admitted a burning passion for the mainstream staple of emo bands.

"Holy shit! I love My Chem!"

"Really? O-M-G! I thought you would be, like, too old to like them!" replied Katia, surprised.

"Too old? I'm thirty-two." said Jesse. "'Three Cheers for Sweet Revenge' came out in 2004." Jesse felt a sinking feeling in the pit of his stomach. "How old are you?"

"I'm twenty-two."

Jesse did an internal facepalm. *Fuck, goddammit!* His mind was reeling. *Twenty-two? She's just a kid. How the hell? How can I make this work?*

Numbers were racing in Jesse's head as he tried to figure out the angle he could take on this to make him look a little less like a creep.

What's the bright side? When I'm forty, she'll be thirty. That's not bad. When I'm fifty, she's forty. Much better. But right now? . . . Bullocks.

Jesse realized that there was a long silence as he was running the internal calculations, so he tried to conjure up something interesting to say. "I play guitar in a band, and I wear makeup when we play shows." Well, he really did try.

"Wow, that's . . . that's cool," Katia said, sarcasm intended. Jesse could almost hear her eyes roll.

As the two approached her Ford Escape, Katia turned and looked at Jesse. "Thanks for walking me to my car."

She immediately grabbed her keys from her bag, and without saying another word, she clicked the remote, hopped in her car, gave a wave, and off she went, leaving Jesse standing there alone in the moonlight.

"Bye, Katia," he said under his breath as he turned to walk alone back to the dealership.

In the background, he could hear people arguing in their Section Eight apartments, some random dogs barking, the faint sounds of the throbbing bass of ranchero music, and the gentle sigh of a warm breeze as the Santa Ana winds blew in from the west, churning up the leaves and trash that littered the streets. To the east, the moon peeked through the clouds overlooking the Angeles Forest mountain range.

THE BLACK PARADE

When you lose a person you love so much, surviving the loss is difficult.

—Cristiano Ronaldo

There was chaos on the scene in the middle of the now not-so-quiet street in the apparently not-so-safe neighborhood with the permanently stained reputation. Every neighbor that was curious about the carnage unfolding on their block, every deputy on the scene, and the detectives that had just arrived to investigate turned to watch the two full-size black SUV's that pulled up and parked in front of the makeshift command center. Out of the first SUV, two men emerged wearing dark slacks and windbreakers. One turned to look down the street; the other walked around to join his partner. They leaned in and spoke in hushed tones, nodding their heads as they looked up to the little house on Piedmont.

On the back of their windbreakers, screen printed and clear as day, were the three letters every local law enforcement officer hated to see: FBI.

The second black SUV sat there idling. The thudding bass of the truck's stereo was almost muffled, but still clearly audible to everyone on the block. The driver killed the ignition, and the music stopped; all that could be heard was the clicking of the cooling engine. The glossy black driver's door opened, and out of the second SUV emerged another figure, her long blonde hair and small feminine form a stark contrast to the two other agents.

Her white blouse was tucked neatly into her dark fitted jeans that tapered down to her black high heels.

The woman gave a nod to the other two agents, and they walked briskly over to her.

The deputies on the scene watched with curiosity as the two agents who towered over the young woman nodded their heads as she spoke slowly and quietly to them. They were obviously giving her their complete and undivided respect and attention.

After a moment, the young woman gave the two agents a smile and a nod. The two men got straight to work. The first headed over to the sheriff's forensics team, and the second walked from house to house down the street to interview the neighbors that, by now, had formed into small, huddled groups, talking and gossiping in hushed and fearful tones.

The woman turned her attention to the bustling action in front of the makeshift command center. She confidently approached the deputies who had been curiously eavesdropping a moment ago, but were now parted like the Red Sea as she strode between them. All five foot, three inches of her focused, a predatory look in her eye, a woman fixated on her mission.

With badge in hand and heels clicking on the pavement, she approached the sergeant and paused. She looked him up and down, and with a crooked grin and the sweetest tone heard on that dark little street that night, she exclaimed loud and clear so everyone on the street could hear, "Good evening, gentleman. I'm Special Agent Eastman with the FBI. From this moment forward, we are taking over the scene and the investigation. We appreciate your department's cooperation, and I look forward to working with you. But as of right now, I'm in charge."

The deputies stood frozen like a herd of deer caught in the headlights of a semi-truck screaming toward them.

Eastman's pale blue eyes scanned the crowd of men, each of whom were at least seven inches taller than her. She could tell they were trying to figure out whether or not to take this "girl" seriously.

Eastman was used to this stage of the game. As a matter of fact, this was her favorite part. After all, she had started college at the age of fourteen, and was recruited by the FBI at seventeen. Not only did she ace every test they could throw at her, but because of her outstanding forensic psychology expertise and her almost psychic-like profiling techniques, she was a shoo-in for the work. She was a natural.

Now at the ripe age of twenty-five, Eastman was already a seasoned agent, having cracked some of the most significant serial killer cases in recent history. Not to mention—and "no big deal"—she was also a psychologist, and one of the top in her field as the youngest person ever honored by the APA. She was used to being underestimated, so this was not her first rodeo.

One by one, the men staring at her opened mouthed-averted their eyes and looked down at the concrete.

Special Agent Eastman scanned the crowd, her eyes turning back on the little house that was surrounded with yellow tape. "Get me everything you have right now," she barked. "Get your team out of the scene immediately! Assemble your CSI team; I want them all in front of me with what they have found in three minutes. Get me the first person on the scene; I need to interview them personally." Eastman paused and raised an eyebrow. "A cup of coffee wouldn't hurt either."

The deputies on the street stared blankly at her for a long moment. She noticed one of the men's jaws drop slightly, a deadpan expression on his face. She smiled, and in a sweet but assertive tone, roared into the crowd of still dumbfounded officers, "NOW!"

All at once, the sheriffs sprang to action, calling out their CSI team for debriefing and awaiting new orders. Durazo walked up to the FBI agent that was still staring at the little house, taking in the scene.

"Get her a cup of coffee!" he called out gruffly at one of the young, fresh-out-of-the-academy deputies on the scene, who scurried off to the command center.

Durazo then yelled out to nobody in particular, "And for Christ's sake, can someone please find Amador?" He walked over to Eastman and nodded to her as he rested his hands on his utility belt.

"Hello, Agent Eastman, I'm Sergeant Durazo. We were not expecting you to—"

"Nice to meet you, Durazo," the young agent interrupted with a smile and an almost-warm tone. "I wish it were under better circumstances. Now, if you would please get me the information—and coffee—I requested, that'd be great. Thank you."

Durazo nodded and walked away at that.

Eastman could tell the sergeant was annoyed with her intrusion on his case, but that suited her just fine. Soon enough, she had a hot cup of coffee in one hand and the CSI findings in the other. She was ready to work.

She took a sip of her coffee while thumbing through the investigation's initial findings.

"Durazo, what are we looking at here?"

Eastman glanced quickly over to Durazo as he surveyed the scene, his hands resting on his gun belt.

"Well, Agent Eastman, it's a pretty open-and-shut case. Husband went crazy, murdered his wife, called 911, and waited for us to arrive. Deputy Amador found him literally on top of the body. I'm not sure why you're here or what else you need. As a matter of fact, I have two deputies outside the suspect's room in the ER right now with strict orders to read him his rights as soon as he decides to snap out of whatever lunacy he has thrown himself into, or when the drugs he's wigged himself out on wear off—whichever comes first."

Special Agent Eastman didn't even glance up from the report she was reading as Durazo hovered over her and awaited her response.

"Tell me, sergeant, what was the murder weapon? And where is it now?"

"We believe it to be a bladed weapon. The wounds on the vic are consistent with a saw or a large serrated blade."

Durazo paused and then said, "With all due respect, Agent Eastman, you haven't even walked the scene yet. Were you planning on doing that while you're here?"

Eastman took another sip of her coffee. "Where is your first responding officer? What was his name? Amador?"

Durazo glanced down at his wristwatch. "He's on his way. I sent him back to the station to cool off. He's a good man, but this . . . rattled him a little. Understandably. I've worked with him for two years now, helped field train him myself. He's one of the best I have."

"I need to talk with him as soon as he arrives."

"He will be here in less than two minutes, Agent Eastman. What is your plan here now?"

Eastman, still staring down at her Styrofoam coffee cup, gave a slight smirk, paused, and said, "Can you feel it, sergeant? The energy here? It's heavy, oppressive, dark . . . Something bad happened here tonight, and not just to our victim." She paused while looking at the initial report, then sighed and continued. "Something happened to that man, too." She glanced back down at the paperwork in her hand, scanning for a name. "Jesse. Jesse Silver."

Eastman closed her eyes, drew a deep breath, and held it.

Sergeant Durazo rolled his eyes and looked up at the house. He'd had enough of this "woo-woo bullshit." He turned and started to walk away, but Eastman grabbed his arm without opening her eyes. On her outbreath, she said in just above a whisper, "Katia wasn't the only one left here in pieces tonight."

Her blue eyes opened and fixated on Durazo. She let go of his arm, looked down at her coffee, drew in another sharp breath, and in a low tone, said, "Radio your deputies at the hospital, sergeant. You're going to tell them they are now on special duty to protect Jesse, and they are not to leave his side until I get there. Is that clear, sergeant?"

"Yes, ma'am."

Eastman and Durazo both turned when they noticed the lights of a sheriff cruiser illuminate the street as it pulled up and parked half a block down.

"That's Amador," Durazo said. He leaned down to Eastman, and in a low tone of voice so that the other deputies couldn't hear, whispered to the young FBI agent, "Have you heard of anything like this before?"

"Yes," replied Eastman as she tucked the CSI folder under her arm and looked down the street at the now parked patrol car.

"Are you going to tell me anything, Agent Eastman?" Durazo hissed, clearly aggravated.

He could have sworn he saw the little girl smirk as she answered, "No."

Eastman finished her cup of coffee, handing Durazo the empty cup.

Durazo leaned down close to the agent's ear and glanced at the neighbors that were still posted on their front porches. He looked at the young deputies milling around the command post. Just above a whisper, so that none of his men could hear, Durazo spilled his worries to the young agent, "Listen, Agent Eastman . . . I have heard the rumors about you. Good things. Great things. But I don't feel right with you making assumptions about the husband before you even walk the scene. This whole thing is a nightmare of a clusterfuck, and we are lucky that the press isn't elbow-deep up our asses already—God only knows how long it will stay that way. But none of that matters right now. What matters is the fact that we have a young woman in there that has been butchered. We have her husband, covered in blood, blabbering gibberish, and strapped to a bed in the ER. And I have you and the rest of the Feds up my ass. Now don't get me wrong, agent, I'm glad you're here." Durazo hesitated and looked back to the house. "And I'm happy to follow your lead. But I need you to give me something to feel good about. Give me something to hang my hat on here."

Eastman looked up to Durazo, locking eyes with the big man as he continued. "So, what is it? What are you going to say to me to assure me that the husband didn't do this? If he isn't the one who slaughtered that young woman in there—and believe me, I have seen some shit in my twenty-eight years on the job, but I have never seen anything close to the brutality that I saw in that house—then who is?" Durazo pointed angrily at the little Spanish style house. "What are you going to tell me so I can let my deputies, my community, and for Christ's sake, the goddammed media know, so that they don't go on some kind of speculation spree saying that we have some sort of psycho serial killer on our hands here?"

Special Agent Eastman was still locked onto Durazo with her unblinking pale blue eyes. She shook her head and paused, like she was about to say something, then thought better of it. She started walking toward Amador, but after a couple of steps, she turned and faced Durazo again. Her voice was no longer sweet.

"I wish I could tell you that isn't what I'm afraid of, sergeant. I really, really wish I could tell you that. But yes, I have seen this before, and I was expecting this to happen. But now you have a bigger problem on your hands than a 'husband that snapped,' or some random 'crime of passion' or even some sort of 'home invasion turned deadly.' No . . . I've seen this before, sergeant, and all the signs are telling me one thing: You have a beast in your field, Sergeant Durazo. You have a beast in your field."

THE BROKEN KIND OF PRETTY

I don't think of all the misery, but of the beauty that still remains.
—Anne Frank

Amador watched as the attractive young woman approached him, her silhouette briskly advancing up the darkened street. He couldn't help but notice her sleek athletic form as she strode up to his still warm patrol vehicle.

What sort of FBI agent wears skinny jeans and heels? Amador thought as the woman walked up to him, coming only up to his mid-chest as she got within speaking distance.

"Deputy Amador?"

"Yes, ma'am," Amador replied in his standard issue flat but respectful military tone.

"You were the first on the scene, yes?"

"Yes, ma'am."

"And you were the one that placed Mr. Silver under arrest?"

"Yes, ma'am."

"And you were the one that called in for backup?"

"Yes, ma'am."

Amador knew that the special agent already knew the answers to all these questions. He found it puzzling, almost rude, that she would be so redundant. But that's how the chain of command is most of the time; Lord knows he was used to it.

"Good job tonight, deputy. Let's go for a walk around the block. I want to talk about how you're feeling after what you saw here tonight."

Eastman motioned to the house, which was now cocooned in police tape.

This was new, unfamiliar territory for Amador. The agent's statement took him a little off guard. He muttered his concern out loud. "How . . . How I'm feeling . . . ma'am?"

"Yes, deputy, how you're feeling. Let's go for a walk. It is, after all, a beautiful night in spite of everything else going on around here, and I want to make sure that you're okay."

She started walking past Amador, motioning him to follow her.

"I'm fine, ma'am. I . . ."

Eastman took Amador by the arm and started walking.

"It's not a request, deputy," Eastman sang as they continued walking past the motorcade of sheriff vehicles and down the moonlit street.

"Yes, ma'am," replied Amador. He followed, although he was still confused as to what she wanted with him. After all, the crime scene was in the house, not around the block. Certainly, the answers to this murder wouldn't be found in walking and talking. Nevertheless, Amador walked beside her, quickening his pace until he was in lockstep with Eastman.

"Ma'am?" Amador said, with an inflection that indicated that he was ready to answer any questions that the agent was prepared to throw at him.

Eastman was right about one thing: it was indeed beautiful outside. The April air was a tepid 70 degrees. The night was clear, and the moon hung fat and full in the sky overhead, bright enough to cast pale blue shadows on the tree-lined street below.

"Tell me about yourself, deputy. What year were you discharged from the Marines? And how were your deployments?"

"Did Durazo tell you I was in the Marines, ma'am?"

"No, deputy. Your walk, posture, and the way you got out of your vehicle told me that—you favored your left leg a bit more than someone that is just sore from the gym, so my guess is wounded in combat. And there's your haircut—standard issue for a man who has been in the military long enough to come to appreciate having things a certain way. The way you address me is also a dead giveaway. You had no problem in recognizing the chain of command, and even less of a problem respecting it." Eastman paused and smiled. "Good on you."

Eastman looked Amador up and down once more.

"Your boots . . . are too well shined for someone who wasn't in the military. You're clearly not a kid that just wanted to follow the family tradition of law enforcement. You have had some serious rituals and protocols drilled into you, so you live by them now. It's a lifestyle for you; it's a good thing. It makes you feel safe . . . in control."

Eastman paused but continued walking.

"You have a wedding band on your left hand," she continued. "Most officers don't wear them on duty, even if they are married, so as not to allow anyone they arrest to be able to lash out at their relationship as a way to get under the arresting officer's skin—causing the officer to mess up and possibly cause an issue in court if the officer plays into their game. But that doesn't rattle you at all, does it? What that tells me, deputy, is that you're recently married, and you are proud of your wife and your marriage, no matter the risk wearing that ring might bring while on the job.

"Also, on your right hand, you have a Marine combat veteran ring," Eastman pointed out the obvious with a smirk, and continued on.

"What that tells me is, much like your marriage, you're proud of what you did in your deployments, of what you did in combat. You felt you made a difference. Either that or the memories from those times keep you awake at night. And when you do manage to find sleep, deputy, it's shallow, broken. You have almost gotten used to waking, jolting up, covered in sweat, crying out into the darkness, reaching for your wife for help, but never wanting to wake her. And since you wear your ring so proudly, I'm sure she's happy and there to hold you tight on the nights you do wake her . . . Does that sound about right, deputy?"

Amador paused, taking in his entire life story told to him by a total stranger on a moonlit street. "Ma'am?" was all he could think of to say.

"So . . . do you like to read?"

Katia looked up from her receptionist desk and phone bank to see Jesse had once again materialized at her workstation.

Katia held up one finger to Jesse, still while looking at her phone bank as she transferred the caller to the appropriate department. Katia slid off her Cisco headset and placed it gently onto her desk. She looked up to Jesse, a *what do you want now?* look on her face.

"I'm sorry, what?"

"Do . . . do you like to read?" Jesse asked, with not even half of the confidence he had been able to conjure up the first time the question passed his lips. Katia just stared at him, keeping the blank expression on her face. It didn't even look like she was breathing.

"Y'know . . . books?" Jesse sputtered out again, but this time in an entirely sheepish, shaky tone. Katia stared at Jesse with a look he found quite challenging to read, somewhere between contemplative and offended, with maybe a dash of amusement and a pinch of disgust.

"Yes, I know how to read," Katia replied with an eye roll.

"Cool, me . . . me too," Jesse responded with a chuckle, choosing to ignore her obvious annoyance.

"I'm reading a new book. It's actually fascinating; it's about indigo children." Jesse looked nonchalantly across the showroom, at the gleaming new vehicles and the customers—or, rather, potential customers—milling about, avoiding the salespeople like swimmers avoiding a sharp coral reef.

"Indigo children?" said Katia, trying her best not to sound the least bit interested.

"Yeah, indigo children. It's a new-age concept, a theory that some people possess special, unusual, and sometimes even supernatural traits they're born with. They have a problem fitting into normal society, and never really feel like they belong."

"That sounds . . . actually, sort of amazing," said Katia, for the first time seeming like she really saw Jesse, really saw the man that stood in front of her.

"Oh, yeah? I'm almost finished with it. I'd be happy to lend it to you tomorrow. Are you working?"

Katia flashed a big smile, then looked down at her lap. "Nobody has ever wanted to give me a book before," she said as she looked back up at Jesse. Her smile went from her mouth up to her eyes, now aglow with interest and inquiry.

"Great, I'll drop it by tomorrow when I see you."

Jesse smiled back at Katia with a wink. Without saying another word, he turned and walked away.

Durazo waited impatiently for the deputy to get back to him with a fresh cup of coffee. There was a Coffee Bean and Starbucks right down the street from the scene on Piedmont,

but Durazo had requested the deputy go to the Black Cow Café, a local family-owned restaurant and coffee bar.

It was the best coffee in town for his money, and they made it extra strong.

As Durazo saw the lights of the unit turn the corner of Sunset and Piedmont, he whispered a silent prayer of gratitude, and, of course, the prayer was laced with profanity.

In the headlights of the approaching cruiser, he could see the silhouettes of Amador and Special Agent Eastman slowly walking up the street.

"It's about goddamn time," Durazo muttered as the patrol car passed. The car pulled up the one hundred and fifty or so yards to the makeshift command station that was, up until an hour or so ago, actually working on gathering evidence and trying to solve a grisly murder that happened on this cute little street.

But since those two black SUVs pulled up, not a goddamned thing had been accomplished. No questions had been answered and no progress made whatsoever.

Durazo started getting hot. He hadn't been angry on the job since he could remember. But there, standing in the moonlight, his heart was pounding, his blood was boiling, and his temples were throbbing. He thought about Jesse Silver, who, apparently, was now not the murder suspect, according to the little girl who had just shown up to play "special agent." She hadn't even taken the time to look at the scene yet. She had just sat there and "felt the energy." That burned his ass the most, these fucking millennials and their "woo-woo" bullshit.

She might be hot shit back in Quantico, but out here, she was just a kid.

Durazo muttered under his breath, "I was arresting shit-bags before you were even born, you little bitch."

The deputy, fresh from his coffee run, got out of his cruiser and briskly approached Durazo.

"Your coffee, sir," the young deputy said as he handed Durazo his precious coffee.

Durazo was grateful that they sent the young recruits here. Montrose was a great training ground. Usually, nothing of note happened here, and that was just the way he liked it.

Durazo thanked the deputy, grabbed his coffee, and took a big sip. Damn, it was perfect—bittersweet with a nutty aftertaste.

"Can't get shit like this at Starbucks," Durazo mused as he glanced at the cup with the cute, cartoon-like cow printed on it.

One block south on Hermosa Street, away from the blood and flashing lights, away from the nosy neighbors and deputies, Eastman and Amador were quietly talking. Up and down the street they walked together in the moonlight. After several minutes, Eastman hugged Amador, assuring him that it was all going to be okay. Amador let go of his long embrace with Eastman, turned, took two steps forward then crumbled to the ground.

Eastman flew to his side in one cat-like movement. She knelt beside him on the sidewalk, one hand on his head, the other patting his back, while still whispering in Amador's ear.

Eastman could hear Amador, in between his sloppy sobs and shallow, ugly breaths, whisper over and over, "Thank you, thank you, thank you."

Eastman stroked his head and ever-so-gently whispered to the big deputy, "C'mon, honey, let's get you up."

Eastman helped the six-foot-three, two-hundred-plus-pound deputy to his feet. Amador, who was still sobbing, embraced her again, and, almost like a child, leaned down and buried his head into her bosom.

She held him, tenderly rocking him back and forth, swaying with him, patting his back.

Eastman cooed to him in a singsong tone, "You've done good, Amador. You are good."

Amador raised his head. Eastman wiped the tears from his face, and with a big smile on hers, said to the man, now towering over her, "You're going to be okay, Amador. You're going to be okay." Eastman couldn't see Amador's expression under the orange-yellow glow of the streetlamp overhead, but she could feel the shift—a shift that told her that he was processing, doing a complete and total personal inventory of his life in a matter of milliseconds there in the moonlight.

"C'mon, deputy, let's get you cleaned up and get you some coffee." Eastman smiled as she put her arm around Amador. Together, they walked back to the command station on Piedmont.

Durazo watched as his deputy and the agent rounded the corner. He noticed Amador looked shaken, like he had been crying. Agent Eastman walked up to the young deputy that was handing out coffee and took one to Amador. She then turned, walked back to Durazo, and gave him a nod.

"Gather your team, Sergeant Durazo. It's time to get to work."

BOOKS, CAFFEINE, HOPES, AND DREAMS

"Hope is being able to see that there is light despite all of the darkness."

—Desmond Tutu

"Here's that book I told you about yesterday," Jesse said as he handed Katia a slim, colorful paperback. She looked down at the brightly colored book and flipped it over. "This is the one about indigos. I have the feeling you may just be one."

Katia cradled the book gently in her delicate hands, reading the description on the back cover.

"Why . . . why do you think I might be one?" Katia asked, eyes still scanning over the back.

"Well, I just have a feeling about you. I could be wrong . . . but probably not."

Jesse then placed a venti iced coffee from Starbucks on top of the receptioni desk, giving Katia a sly wink as he pulled the paper wrapper off the straw and plunged it through the lid and into the dark brown cold brew. "I noticed you had one of these on your desk the other day, and I know how hard they work you guys, so I figured you could use a little recharge."

Katia stared at the ice coffee, then looked up at Jesse with a smile.

"Working late again tonight?" Jesse asked.

"Yes, but I'm off at ten."

"Great, I'll be here at ten to walk you to your car again, if that's okay with you," Jesse said casually, as he turned and started walking away from the desk, not giving Katia a chance to respond. As he started back off to his office, he turned back and saw that Katia had already cracked open the book and was flipping through it, smiling broadly. His heart filled with joy seeing her so happy by such a simple gesture.

He saw her take a sip of the iced coffee and start to read the introduction.

She's the one, Jesse thought with a smile. *She's the one.*

"So, now you're ready to get to work, doctor?" Durazo said snidely as Eastman went through the trunk of her SUV and got out her own camera and notebook.

"Yes, sergeant, now I'm ready to go inside the house. I already have a pretty good idea what I'm going to see in there," Eastman replied as she loaded a fresh memory card into her camera, checked the batteries, and pulled her long mane of blonde hair back into a tight ponytail.

"What the hell did you do to Amador? He's a goddamned mess."

"We had a nice talk, is all, sergeant. I wanted to know exactly what was happening on the scene when he first arrived." Eastman slipped the camera strap around her neck.

"Amador's going to be okay. He just needs some time to process."

"I've known Amador for years. I spent six months with him after his training. He doesn't have any issues or trauma; he's as solid as a piece of oak."

Eastman paused and looked over at Durazo. She gave him a quick shrug, then turned back to the trunk of her SUV.

"Whatever you say, sergeant."

Durazo rolled his eyes and stared at the young woman who now had on horned-rimmed glasses. She pulled out her own dark FBI windbreaker and put it on over her white blouse.

"Are you ready now, Agent Eastman?"

"One last thing, sergeant." Eastman went to her purse and pulled out some dark scarlet lipstick and applied it using the side view mirror of her SUV.

Durazo stared in disbelief as she took her time getting ready, meticulously gathering her pens, highlighters, and moleskin notepad. She then grabbed a small stone from her bag and kissed it, then quietly slipped it into the back pocket of her jeans.

"Okay, let's go," she said.

Durazo led Special Agent Eastman for the first time up the steep driveway to the steps of the small bungalow on the dark street.

Eastman quickly slid in front of Durazo and made her way up the steps. She paused at the open front door, closed her eyes, took a deep breath, and exhaled while she extended her hand over the threshold and into the living room, as if she were testing the temperature of the water flowing out of the spigot while running a bath.

She whispered under her breath, "This is bad, sergeant. This is very, very bad." She pulled her hand back as if the temperature had suddenly and unexpectedly turned too hot, then shook her hand like she was trying to cool it off.

Eastman released a slight whimper as she exhaled slowly once again, stepped over the threshold of the modest house, and opened her eyes. The scene flooded her senses like a tsunami that pushed and penetrated her consciousness.

The abstract macabre beauty of it all overwhelmed her.

The pieces of Katia were strewn about the floor like toys scattered randomly in a child's messy room, the grisly puzzle pieces entangled and meshed in the now-gelatinized pool of plasma.

Durazo stood back to observe the observer, while Special Agent Eastman's pale blue eyes darted rapidly back and forth, analyzing and interpreting everything in the room, taking in every minute detail as her inner voice catalogued and calculated everything.

She surveyed the dismembered body, her eyes going to every loose, unbruised limb and up to the fingertips of the severed hands. *A French manicure, but with . . . gloss black tips?* "Great aesthetic," Eastman mused, near silent, before moving her gaze to the blood on the floor that seemed to pool deeper near the front door—uneven floorboards, or maybe a problem with the foundation. "Gravity doesn't lie," Eastman quietly remarked, eyes staying fixed downwards.

The floor itself was hardwood—no, *softwood. Douglas fir. Original to the house, but refinished more than once. Feels thin, but well-sealed. No blood is seeping between the slats, and the blood has pooled perfectly . . .*

Her eyes flicked to the sofa, leather and hardly used—but one of the arms has been worn down, or . . . chewed on. *They have a puppy. Big, most likely a high-energy breed. Border collie? Husky? Golden? Where is it now?*

She turned her attention to the décor. *Walls: a vibrant dark yellow, almost an ochre with a trim of a dark blue, Spanish influenced.* Her eyes darted to the art that covered the walls, taking in the Diego Rivera painting hung above the bookcase.

That's what they based the color theme of the house off, the colors in that painting. Nice, Eastman noted.

She then moved on to the bookcase: five shelves, roughly thirty books per shelf, about one hundred and fifty books in this one bookcase, and none of them had dust on them. *They were treasured.* Eastman scanned the titles: *You can Heal your Life, Radical Forgiveness, Care of the Soul, Leaving the Body, The Hero with a Thousand Faces, Maps of Meaning.* Mostly all self-help.

The spines of the books are well creased, indicating that they have been read and reread, Eastman would bet that they were highlighted, too. *Someone here has a history of trauma, early childhood, maybe adolescence.* Her eyes darted back to the disconnected pieces of Katia on the floor. She silently felt for anything, *Was it the mom, the dad, or both?*

Eastman's mind swam and pondered, her eyes darting back to the books, then back to Katia's disconnected body. *Both.*

Eastman let out a sad sigh and whispered to the pile in front of her, "What did they do to you, honey?"

She slowly raised her camera and snapped photos of the scene. Her eyes went back to the bookcase.

On the shelves in front of the books was a large piece of smooth and weathered beechwood—something likely sourced from Oregon or Washington.

Beside the smooth hunk of wood were some flat rocks. *A river? No . . . The ocean. Definitely the ocean.* On the ends of the bookcase were several scented candles, still burning, now only pools of liquid wax. They had been burning for a while. *She always lit them as soon as the sun went down . . . she loved the ambiance.*

Eastman put her nose into the air and inhaled deeply. Over the coppery smell of blood, she picked up the aroma emanating from the scented wax. Lavender, vanilla, and more lavender.

Next to the candles were an Eiffel Tower statuette and photographs. None were from local places. There were several postcards from Paris, and several other trinkets and treasures— nothing particularly expensive or valuable, but things you buy at little shops, or even find while out exploring. *Typically, it's the little things that make up life's best memories,* Eastman thought, echoing the sentiment that was displayed.

There was also a large selection of incense, both cone and stick, and a toy sonic screwdriver.

Eastman smiled sadly as she waded through the shelves, picking up on the energy and echoes of laughter from the good times that were long since passed. She looked closer at the items on the shelf. There she saw coins and currency from all over the world: Iceland, Cuba, Europe, Mexico.

They lived to travel together. He wanted to give her the whole wide world, and he had every intention of doing so.

Eastman smiled again to herself, thinking of the smell of jet fuel, the screech of airplane tires landing on the runway, and the sound of a rubber stamp bouncing off passports.

But her smile quickly faded. *They were just getting started.*

Her eyes darted to the art on the opposite wall—a large acrylic painting of a woman. She then looked at the head of the woman on the floor, then back to the painting, and back again to the head. *It's her,* she concluded. *The painting is of her.*

There was another painting of a woman on the wall beside Eastman—it was the same woman. Same style, same artist, same pallet knife strokes, same love poured onto the canvas. Far too much emotion to be just a commission. It was too close. It felt personal. It felt alive.

He painted these of her.

Her eyes went back to the couch. On the soft black leather sat a coarse burlap pillow. On the pillow, written in black typewriter font was, "'We shall not cease from exploration, and the end of all our exploring will be to arrive where we started and know the place for the first time.' —T.S. Elliot."

She looked to the corner of the bookcase, next to it was a large wicker basket overflowing with neatly folded comforters. Eastman walked over to the basket and carefully picked through it, examining the contents. *One, two, three, four.* Four large comforters.

She studied the scene and pondered. Her eyes swept to the right, where next to the basket was a wall heater. *They're not for warmth. This place is small, cozy, wouldn't take much to heat.* She scanned the corner of the room, where there were four large, colorful Moroccan-style floor pillows that made things click. They would build forts on the floor—they'd watch movies there.

Eastman moved from the living room down the narrow hallway into the kitchen, Durazo following closely behind.

Eastman stepped into the kitchen and started surveying the scene. It was large, but not at all fancy.

Tile countertops, linoleum floors, but nice appliances.

Her heels clicked on the old linoleum as she walked up to the sink. She noted that there were no dirty dishes anywhere in the kitchen, even though the one appliance the kitchen was missing was a dishwasher. To her right was a Davenport where a side-by-side washer and dryer sat, and a laundry basket of freshly laundered and folded clothes on top of it.

Eastman walked over to the stainless steel fridge and opened the door. As the cool LED light of the fridge illuminated, she could see perfectly organized rows of organic, healthy food. What was the message, what was she seeing? No soda, nothing at all with sugar, nothing processed, not at all your typical American diet. *She showed him love by feeding him well. She wanted Jesse to be around for a long time.* The whole bottom of the rack was stuffed with fresh vegetables—not the store-bought kind, but the larger, greener, and more imperfect-looking variety. *The type you find at the famous Sunday farmers market*, she thought as she closed the refrigerator door.

Eastman opened the freezer: lean protein, chicken, ninety-percent grass-fed lean ground beef, frozen homemade soup, and bags of chicken bones. She looked over to the juicer, and to the slow cooker sitting beside it. *She makes bone broth. Who gets sick? Who has the stomach issues?* Eastman wondered as she closed the freezer.

She turned to see the shelving that held all the usual suspects: spices, herbs, a microwave that—thanks to a thin layer of dust covering the number pad—you could tell didn't get used very often.

Eastman scanned the twenty or so boxes of assorted teas, as well as Mason jars filled with homemade, hand-labeled concoctions. Witch's brews ready for the bubble bubble toil and trouble of steaming water. A large jar of home-harvested local honey.

No doubt for the tea and also bought at the farmers market.

Eastman walked from the kitchen to the only bathroom of the house. It was small but clean. The tub was just big enough for soaking in, and it was spotless.

The *Doctor Who* shower curtain confirmed her suspicions that one of them, but most likely both, were somewhat nerdy. The bathmats had dog prints on them. *The puppy is big enough to drink from the toilet, and dribbles water onto the floor, then steps in it, then onto the mats.* Eastman smiled. *They have given up trying to keep those mats clean.* Eastman looked around the house. *But where is it?*

As if on cue, Eastman heard a yelp from the backyard.

She walked back through the kitchen and looked out the kitchen window that overlooked the backyard. There, sitting in the moonlight, appeared to be a large white wolfdog.

"Hello, beautiful," Eastman whispered under her breath. The wolf, who turned out to be a monster-sized husky, cocked his head to one side and bounded to the back door.

"Want to read his aura? Maybe take a statement from him?" Eastman hadn't even realized that Durazo was behind her, shadowing her this entire time, until he finally spoke.

"Maybe later, after I'm done with the house," Eastman replied, paying no attention to Durazo's sad attempt at snark as she walked quickly to the bedroom. She paused at the doorway, then slowly extended her hand over the threshold.

"Oh, honey, you're still here, aren't you?" Eastman closed her eyes again and felt the energy in the room.

It was small but large enough to fit an eastern king-sized bed, along with chunky wood furniture. That, along with the art on the walls, added to the Spanish feel of the house. Eastman smiled as she sensed the energy. She could hear the echoes of the books being read aloud to Katia at night and the soft sigh that Katia would let out just before she fell asleep.

"Yes, you're still here. I'm sorry this had to happen. I'm sorry it had to go this way," she said quietly into the empty bedroom. One of the still-lit candles on the nightstand flickered and crackled. She paused and smiled at it, as if acknowledging the message.

She walked over to the closet and slid the door to the side. An avalanche of vintage dresses filled the space.

Sorted by color, they looked like a rainbow, and all were custom-tailored to perfectly fit Katia's form. On the floor of the closet were two dozen pairs of high heels: Louis Vuitton, Manolo Blahnik, and several pairs of Pleasers.

Agent Eastman closed that half of the closet and slowly slid open the other side. There, like a split personality, was a sea of shiny black latex—a stark contrast to the sundresses and flowy dresses. Eastman was starting to get a feel for whom Katia had been. *Perfect and precise, graceful and elegant, mindful and meticulous . . . to a fault.*

Eastman glanced down to a large suitcase on the floor of the closet, then pulled it out and placed it on the bed. The bag was much heavier than anticipated and almost startled her. Carefully, she unzipped the bag and opened the lid. The rich smell of leather filled the bedroom. She peered into the bag as her heart pounded. Her eyes scanned the contents: Floggers, canes, single tails, hemp rope, dragons' tongues, leather bird, clothespins, wartenberg wheel, vampire gloves. All neatly organized, and in their proper place, clean and ready for use.

"Still think the husband didn't do this? Looks to me like he is a real sick freak," Durazo said from over Eastman's shoulder.

Eastman flinched as the man's gruff voice broke the leather-induced spell she was under. The energy in the room was enough, but the energy pouring out of this bag was almost too much for her to deal with.

"There is no correlation between BDSM and domestic violence. Or, for that matter, murder, sergeant. As a matter of fact, it can be quite cathartic for some people." Eastman zipped the bag shut and put it back to its home in the closet, then carefully closed the closet door.

"What are we missing here, sergeant?"

Durazo paused, folded his arms, and said, "The murder weapon, Agent Eastman?"

"Exactly. But what else?"

"You tell me, special agent," answered Durazo snidely, arms still folded tightly. Eastman didn't need a degree in psychology to see his guarded, churlish attitude. It dripped from him.

"Follow me." Eastman walked Durazo from room to room,

pointing out the multiple photos of Katia and Jesse.

"What do you see in these photos that you don't see here?"

"A woman that's alive and breathing . . . and in one piece?" said Durazo with an obvious eyeroll.

Eastman, without skipping a beat, smiled. "Well, that. And this." She handed Durazo a photo from the bookcase and pointed out a necklace Katia was wearing in a picture of her and Jesse on the Eiffel Tower. The necklace appeared to be an antique key with a small diamond in it. "I'll bet that's the first real—the first expensive—gift that Jesse ever bought her."

She walked Durazo over to a picture of Katia and Jesse on a dark, gloomy beach somewhere on the Oregon coast.

"Here," she said, pointing to the same necklace in the photo. She grabbed another picture off the bookcase of the couple in a snow-filled winter scene at a cabin and pointed to Katia's necklace in that photo. "And here."

Eastman held the picture and studied the young couple embracing in it. She whispered so low that Durazo couldn't hear, "You were loved, Katia, loved more and harder in the last couple of years than most women get in an entire lifetime."

"Here!" Eastman took a photo off the bookcase of Jesse and Katia's wedding. "She was wearing it on the day they were married, Durazo. My guess is she never took it off."

"That's a good observation, agent," Durazo said as he jotted a note in his case file, trying hard to hide any tone that he was impressed. "Anything else we are missing?"

Eastman froze and held up a single finger. She cocked her head and looked as if she were straining to hear something far away.

Durazo stared as Eastman seemed to be listening to an inaudible conversation. She nodded her head and whispered, "Okay." Then in a louder voice, she said, "Yes, sergeant, there is something."

Eastman looked around the room, at the couch, the entertainment center, and back to the bookcase. Then, finally, her eyes landed on Katia. She stared at the pieces of Katia for what seemed like a long minute. "We won't let you down, Katia. We won't let you or Jesse down. I promise you that."

Eastman paused, then turned. She took in a deep breath and exhaled. She stood perfectly still, as if she were again listening to a hushed whisper that only she could hear.

"It's in here?" She paused, and listened, and whispered again into the air, "Okay. I understand."

She slowly walked over to the front door and turned to face Durazo. Reaching into the back pocket of her skinny jeans, she produced a pair of latex gloves. Never taking her eyes off of the sergeant, she slipped the latex gloves over her slender, beautiful hands.

"Earlier tonight, sergeant, you asked me if I had seen this before, and I told you I had. Now, you've asked me if there was anything that we were missing, and I said there is." With her eyes steady on Durazo, Eastman reached for the front door and slowly closed it, producing the sickening sound of thick blood as it was scraped again across the floor. The creak of the old brass hardware made the singsong-like tone of a baby's cry. As the door came to its full stop in its frame, there, on the back of the door in Katia's blood, was a sigil, an odd design painted eloquently, expertly onto the back of the door. There was a hodgepodge of shapes put together in blood. The shapes alone would be meaningless, but when intertwined, they looked almost evil.

Durazo didn't recognize the design, but nonetheless stood there in awe as Eastman turned to face him.

"We may not know the name of the beast in the field yet, sergeant, but now . . . now we know his footprint."

SO THIS IS WHAT IT IS TO BURN

Love is a sacred reserve of energy; it is like the blood of spiritual evolution.

—Pierre Teilhard de Chardin

"How are you feeling, deputy?"

Amador looked up from his phone. His brown eyes were still bloodshot from the torrent of emotions he released on the pavement only an hour before.

"I feel . . . at peace, ma'am. I was just texting my wife. I was telling her how much I love her and how grateful I am that she is in my life. She puts up with a lot, you know?"

Amador lowered his head. Tears once again started rolling down his cheeks.

"You did great tonight, Amador. I'm very proud of you. And yes, I am sure she knows how much you love her and how lucky she is to have you." Eastman gave Amador a squeeze on his thick, muscular shoulder. "I have a private practice in Pasadena. I specialize in PTSD & CPTSD and only work with people I encounter on my full-time job. Call me. And if you like, we can meet maybe once or twice a month and just talk. Does that sound okay, Amador?"

Eastman handed Amador a matte, off-white business card with only a phone number, an address, and a watermark. Amador noted the tasteful thickness of the card stock as he held it in his hand.

"Thank you, ma'am. I think I'd like that." He put the card in the breast pocket of his uniform and gave it a pat.

"I look forward to it, Amador. I look forward to it."

"How you doing, deputy?"

Eastman spun on her heels as Durazo, once again, startled her from behind.

"I'm good, sir. I'm good," replied Amador as he switched off his iPhone.

"You did good tonight, deputy. Did you write your report while you were at the station?"

"Yes, sir."

"Take the rest of the night off, Amador, and we will see you at the station tomorrow."

"Yes, sir. Thank you, sir."

Durazo tapped the roof of Amador's car three times before he turned and started walking back to the mobile command center. As he passed Eastman, he gave her a tap on her shoulder. "Walk with me, agent."

Eastman raised an eyebrow. This is when he was planning to tell her off, and put her in her place, the finale of the bullshit that she was used to dealing with on every case she took over. Goody.

She stood fast.

"Listen, agent, I don't like—"

"Doctor, thank you. You may continue," Eastman cut Durazo off at the pass. She wasn't about to tolerate an inch of bullshit from a man she could read like a freeway sign from a mile away.

"I'm sorry, Doctor Special Agent Eastman," Durazo rattled back at her in a sarcastic tone before his common sense got the better of him. "Listen, agent . . ."

Durazo turned to see that Eastman had not taken a single step to follow him. She was still ten feet behind him at the line of cars that were parked like a funeral procession along the once quiet street.

Even ten feet behind Durazo, she heard every word he muttered. Every note of his condescending tone echoed in her ears. As Durazo's eyes met hers, she smiled. She opened the door and reached into her SUV, rifled through her purse, and produced her Too Faced Melted Latex Liquified High Shine Lipstick.

The name of the shade was "Bite Me." Eastman had been hankering to sink her fangs into Durazo. She had been waiting for this moment with wet anticipation.

She unscrewed the lid off the tube, and with four clean, even, perfect strokes, freshened the pigment on her pouty, full lips. She then screwed the cap back onto the tube and slid it into the back pocket of her skinny black jeans, all the while never taking her eyes off of her reflection in the side view mirror of her SUV. She flicked her long blonde curly locks over her shoulder, pursed her lips, and gave her reflection a wink. She turned and squared up to Durazo.

Like a metronome, the rhythmic clicking of Eastman's Louboutin heels could be heard reverberating off the natural river rock walls that lined the curbsides and sidewalks of Piedmont Avenue.

She walked confidently yet slowly up to Durazo, her hips working like the muscular shoulders of a jungle cat, every movement calculated, every step precise. Every sweet moment tasted, savored like a sip of wine. She closed the gap quickly, and happily penetrated the American version of personal space. This was her version of Manifest Destiny, her own personal Declaration of Independence from the nonsensical, patriarchal "old boys club."

Now, only inches apart, she rose her head to lock eyes with Durazo.

Eastman imagined that if ever there were a man who wished he could travel back in time and pull his foot out of his own mouth at this very moment, in this universe, in this galaxy, his name would've been Durazo.

"Sergeant, have I said something to offended you?" Eastman calmly cooed, her words flowing off her glossy red lips like soap suds off a freshly waxed Ferrari.

Durazo instinctively tried to fold his arms, probably in hopes of creating just a bit more space between him and the well-curved, five-foot-three predator standing in front of him.

But the predator just stepped into him closer, preventing his arms from folding, and now this jungle cat was nearly chest to chest with him.

"No, agent, but—"

Eastman cut him off sharply. "Good. I would hate to think I have offended you, because if I did, that would mean we couldn't be friends anymore. And, well, sergeant . . . that would really hurt my feelings." Her lips pursed together momentarily in a mock pout, but her eyes bore holes into Durazo. "I'm not sure you've noticed, sergeant, but there is the mutilated, butchered corpse of a young lady in that house. And her husband, who is madly in love with that chopped-up girl, is now catatonic and most likely handcuffed to a hospital bed, with no idea of what has happened. But don't worry, sergeant. I can assure you that 'Doctor Special Agent Eastman' will attend to him soon."

"I'm sorry, agent, but—"

Eastman, as fast as a hummingbird, placed her finger on Durazo's lips in a *shooshing* motion.

"Excuse me, sergeant. The doctor is speaking, and when the doctor is speaking, boys need to listen." Eastman paused, smiled, and continued. "I'm not sure if it's ageism, sexism, chauvinism, or a lovely, blended potpourri of all three that you hold against me, sergeant, and frankly, I don't really care. I could run circles around you mentally, even in my Louboutins, which I saw you noticed. Well . . . not just noticed, sergeant, but stared at several times, stealing a peek every chance you could. So, how's that shoe fetish working out for you?"

"I—"

Eastman, her finger still pressed on the sergeant's lips, reapplied pressure, derailing Durazo's train of thought, leaving the locomotive, boxcars, and caboose crumpled and burning like logs on a bonfire."You know, sergeant, men typically have shoe fetishes because they associate the imagery of women's footwear from their earliest days of childhood, while they were babies on the floor. They say the first memories one has are of one's mother . . .

What year were you born, Durazo? 1956? Or was it '57?"

Durazo just stared down at the smoldering, sparking phoenix in front of him.

"You may answer now, sergeant."

"'58," Durazo whispered.

"So, your mother, I can see her now . . . a typical 1950's housewife, her full-time job taking care of you and your younger . . . sister, who, as soon as you were old enough, you were given the responsibility of raising."

Eastman paused and watched Durazo's pupils, which dilated, telling her she was correct. "Yes . . . a sister. The responsibility fell on you because of the alcoholism that ran—excuse me . . ." Eastman leaned forward and got a quick sniff of Durazo, picking up the faint bitter smell of old number seven.

" *—runs*" she corrected, "in your family. So, taking care of your baby sister became your burden to bear, which gave you your first initial resentment of women. But as a baby—before your sister was born, when you were the only one, the love of your mother's life— your mother would put you on the floor to play while she cleaned the house. Your father, a World War II veteran, a member of the 'greatest generation,' expected nothing less from her than to stay home, cook, and clean, and to always be dolled up in dresses, heels, and makeup as she did. You loved watching me put on my lipstick, didn't you, sergeant? I saw your longing eyes, how you unconsciously licked your lips. It's okay, sweetie," she said with a quick wink. "I liked that you noticed."

Eastman continued, "And there you were, on the floor, your perspective and point of view always focused on those shoes. That lovely *click-clack* of her heels on the linoleum, like what you heard when I walked into the kitchen on our crime scene. Do you think I didn't hear you gasp when I stepped foot on that first linoleum tile? Did you really think I would miss that, you silly boy?" She smiled.

"Without even knowing it, you formed the perception of an ideal woman: the giant Amazonian goddess in heels. You saw her as perfect, and you idolized the man who was able to have her— your father. So, for your whole life, you've tried to be the most masculine, macho, tough guy you could. Trying to be your father on the battlefields of France, fighting for the noblest of noble causes. But you never could find that validation, could you? Even your tours while a Marine in Vietnam, and your bashing of 'hippies' in your early days on the police force weren't enough to make your father proud, were they? And all these years, with all your might and mental fortitude, you have been stuffing deep down who you really are, haven't you?"

Durazo swallowed hard.

"Hiding what you really want, what you really need in the dark corners of your mind, doing your very best to subdue your urge to be a baby again . . . or better yet, a little bitch, choking and drooling on a ball-gag, your hands and feet bound with leather, a plug deep in your ass—a big one—and you, on the floor, looking up at those shiny heels, those muscular calves, those thick thighs, and that hot, wet pussy that you won't ever be able to touch . . . because you're an unworthy little bitch, aren't you?"

Eastman saw Durazo's pupils contract and swell. She noticed the veins in his neck start pounding faster.

She smiled, batted her eyes, and tapped her finger against his lips as she asked again, "Aren't you?"

"Yes, ma'am," whispered Durazo, his eyes turned down to the pavement.

"Now we both know where we stand, sergeant, so we can be friends again!" Eastman beamed. "And doesn't that just feel better?"

Durazo swallowed hard. He turned his eyes up and again was held in Eastman's gaze.

"Yes, ma'am."

"Good! Now if you don't mind, I'm going to go visit our second victim in the hospital. I've got it all under control, Durazo."

Eastman pulled her finger away from Durazo's lips and motioned to the little house on Piedmont. "Now run along and have this place cataloged. I have faith in your team . . . and maybe, now that we're friends again, I have some faith in you." She took a step back, out of Durazo's space. Instantly, she could see the pressure leave his body, like letting a bit of air out of an overfilled balloon. "I want everything scanned and sent to me by eleven hundred tomorrow. Are we crystal, sergeant?"

Durazo, still frozen and staring off thousands of yards in the distance with his mouth slightly open, nodded dumbly.

"Good boy. Thank you for taking the time to listen to me. I really do appreciate it. Now if you will pardon me, Doctor Special Agent Eastman has someone special to visit in the hospital." Eastman gave Durazo another wink. "I look forward to seeing you tomorrow, sergeant. Be sure to enjoy the rest of your night." Eastman's smile never broke through the whole exchange. But Durazo did break, and he broke beautifully.

Eastman got into her SUV. The engine roared to life. She was off to the Verdugo Hills Hospital to see about a man—also in pieces, also broken, but handcuffed to a bed.

"Ready for our nightly 'walk to your car' date?" Jesse said to Katia as she was finishing straightening her workstation, organizing and wiping down the phones and desktop for the morning crew.

"You scared me!" Katia said with a smile. "I didn't think you were actually going to show up."

"I always do what I say I'm going to do," replied Jesse with a smirk as he turned and motioned to Katia to follow him. "C'mon, kiddo, let's get out of here."

Jesse walked over to the heavy glass door, swung it open for

Katia, and held it as she passed through. Always the gentleman, but the added benefit to this particular act of chivalry was he could steal a quick glimpse of Katia's backside as she slinked by him. As she passed, Jesse inhaled deeply, taking in the primal concoction of her pheromones; the smell of her perfume mixed with the oils of her skin and the smell of her hair was a bouquet for the olfactory system. The glow of her flawless skin bounced off the inside of his retinas. Everything interwove to make an intoxicating amalgamation for his senses.

"So, have you started the book yet?" Jesse asked as they walked through the parking lot.

"I read a little on my break. I love it so far," Katia answered.

"Good, I thought it would be meaningful to you."

"So . . . why did you decide on that particular book for me?" asked Katia while looking down at her shoes.

"Well, I just get a special vibe from you. I can't really explain it," Jesse said as he grazed the small of her back, turning her as they rounded the corner, making their way up to the employee parking lot. The night was crisp and clear. It was the only time of year that Jesse liked living in Los Angeles, one of the four months a year that the weather was actually bearable for him. "Pardon me . . . I didn't mean to touch you," Jesse mumbled as he pulled his hand from the gentle curve of her form.

Katia knew his statement was total bullshit. She knew that he knew exactly what he was doing—and Jesse knew that she knew that he knew. But nonetheless, he had put the bullshit statement out there and let it hang, ripening on the vine, and Jesse waited for her response—whether it be good or bad.

"It's okay, I don't mind," Katia said, trying to hide her smile as they crossed the street and entered the employee parking lot.

"Oh, okay, cool, I just don't want you to think I'm trying to get . . . 'handsy' with you or anything like that," Jesse said, throwing out a baited line, hoping for her to take a bite.

And bite she did.

"Just don't make a habit of it," Katia said with a giggle as she pulled her keys out of her purse and unlocked her Ford Escape. The vehicle's headlights came on and illuminated the parking lot with a blue and amber glow.

"Thanks for walking to my car again," said Katia as she opened the door and threw her bag into the passenger's seat. She reached up and started to slide herself into the little white SUV.

"Katia, wait."

Katia paused and turned to face Jesse.

"What's up?" she said nonchalantly, as if she were expecting Jesse to trouble her with a question.

"I . . . I was wondering if you would like to go out on an actual date sometime . . . maybe something a bit nicer than our 'walking to the car' dates?"

Katia stared at Jesse with that same blank expression she had become famous to him for, and after what seemed like minutes had passed—which, in reality, was less than five seconds—Katia's expression turned into that wide smile.

She simply said, "Aw, thanks . . . maybe someday."

Katia then turned and hopped into the driver seat of her car, started the ignition, turned to Jesse, waved, and was gone—leaving Jesse standing there in the cool night air wondering what the fuck had just happened.

"Bye, Katia," Jesse said aloud as he turned to walk back to the dealership to finish his nightly work duties.

After several steps, he stopped and smiled to himself. "Maybe someday? That wasn't a no."

Jesse smiled again. "Curiouser and curiouser. Curiouser and curiouser." He walked down the dark street, just he and his moonlit shadow.

"Jesse? Mr. Silver? Jesse Silver? Wake up, Sweetie. It's okay . . . I'm here. Wake up."

"Sweet baby?" Jesse whispered, not knowing why his throat was so raw. His mouth was as dry as an ashtray, his body covered in dried blood and sweat from the drugs and the fever dreams. "Sweet baby?"

Jesse repeated as he opened his eyes. The blinding overhead lighting was shifting, waving, and making it hard to see. He closed his eyes.

"Babe, where are you?" Jesse tried reaching out to the soft, soothing voice of Katia that was calling out to him, but was shocked when the cuffs pulled tight on this still throbbing but now nicely bandaged wrists.

"Katia!" Jesse sat up with a start and realized he had no idea where he was.

"It's okay. You're okay."

Jesse turned to see the blurry form of a woman seated next to him.

"Wh-where am I?"

"You're in the emergency room of the Verdugo Hills Hospital, sweetie."

Jesse blinked hard, trying to bring his eyes into focus.

"Where's Katia? Where's my Katia? Wha . . . Who are you? Where's my Katia?"

The woman snapped into focus.

"Jesse, my name is Doctor Melantha Eastman. We have to have a talk."

THE BLOCKED CALLER

Only those who will risk going too far can possibly find out how far one can go.

—T. S. Eliot

"How are you doing, Jesse?"

Jesse looked across the large executive desk. There sat a man in his late 60s with short gray hair, in a very hip style for a man his age.

The man's kind face was framed by his thick black Dior glasses.

His crisp white shirt was perfectly fitted, and his lightweight, custom-made navy blue blazer was finished with a white pocket square.

Around his wrist hung a red Buddhist prayer bracelet.

"It's been a lot . . ." Jesse said, now looking down at his shoes.

"All of us here know what has happened, but none of us could possibly understand what you have been through."

"Thank you, Lance. I appreciate that."

Lance sat back in his big leather chair and glanced over at his Tibetan singing bowl. He gently reached for the small wooden mallet with the felt tip and gave it a gentle tap.

"You have lost quite a bit of weight. How much?"

"About forty pounds since that night."

Ever since—since Katia, his sales have understandably been in the toilet. Jesse, who was used to making $10,000 on a slow month, had had to resort to digging into his savings to make ends meet.

He had plenty saved up, but that wasn't the point. That was the Europe money.

Jesse trusted Lance. He adored Lance and often referred to the gray-haired president of his company as "the Jewish Yoda" because he always had something insightful and impactful to offer.

"Have you been eating at all? How about sleeping?"

"I . . . try and eat . . . I still have a problem keeping much of anything down. Apples seem to be okay for me, though, and bone broth."

Lance just stared at Jesse.

Jesse could tell he was calculating his words carefully.

"As far as sleep goes, maybe an hour here or there, but that's pretty much it . . . I typically wake up screaming and covered in sweat. I try to get to bed around 11:30 p.m., but I'm up several times through the night, and I usually just get out of bed by 4:00 a.m. because I can't sleep."

"We are here to help and support you through this thing," Lance said while giving his gray goatee a quick stroke. He reached over his desk and tapped his singing bowl once again.

"You know, the things that happened to you, aren't you. They are just things that happened to you." Lance leaned back in his chair again and cracked his famous Zen smile. "And they're over now. What's most important is that we realize that they don't make us who we are. We must consider them, then move on in our lives."

Jesse stared at Lance, trying to make sense of the deeper meaning.

"You see, I believe that, ultimately, the things that happen to us are empty and meaningless. Now, that's not to diminish your situation, or how you feel about the situation . . . Because, Jesse, in a cosmic sense, it's fucked, brother. It's fucked. But you have a choice now: you can keep reliving that night, and keep punishing yourself over what happened, or you can *choose* to keep moving forward. And this may sound funny, but there is a blessing or a lesson somewhere to be found in all this."

Jesse's phone started buzzing with a call.

"Get that if you need to."

Jesse pulled the phone out of his pocket and looked at the screen.

"Blocked ID"

He grimaced and sent the caller to voicemail.

"Telemarketing call," Jesse said as he slipped the iPhone back into his pocket.

Lance gave Jesse a smile, leaned back in his big chair, and softly asked, "Have you heard the First Nations story of the two wolves"?

"No, sir." *Here comes the impactful takeaway,* Jesse thought, glad the topic had shifted. The speech Lance had given about his experience not mattering was starting to annoy Jesse. If anyone but Lance had said that, Jesse probably would have highly considered putting a few of their teeth down their throat. However, after years with Lance, Jesse held him in high regard. He'd learned to let Lance's words marinate while he looked for the deeper meaning. It was like opening a bottle of wine, you had to let it breathe.

"I love this story," Lance said with a smirk. "I'll probably butcher it, but it goes like this . . .

"The grandson came to his old grandfather. He was angry at a friend who had done him an injustice. The grandfather listened to his grandson yell and scream about the outrage that had befallen him. After his grandson had finished, the grandfather just smiled and said, 'Let me tell you a story. I, too, at times have felt a great hate for those that have taken so much, with no sorrow for what they do.

"But hate wears you down and does not hurt your enemy. It is like taking poison and wishing your enemy would die. I have struggled with these feelings many times. It is as if there are two wolves inside me. One is good and does no harm. He lives in harmony with all around him and does not take offense when no offense was intended. He will only fight when it is right to do so and in the right way.

"But the other wolf, ah, he is so full of anger. The littlest thing will set him into a fit of temper. He fights everyone, all the time, and for no reason. He cannot think because his anger and hate are so great. It is helpless anger, for his anger will change nothing . . . Sometimes, it is hard to live with these two wolves inside me, for both of them try to dominate my spirit.'

"The young man looked intently into his grandfather's eyes and asked, 'Which wolf wins, Grandfather?' The grandfather smiled and quietly said, 'The one I feed.'"

Jesse nodded, and sensing that the exchange was over, got up from his chair and started out of the office.

"Keep feeding the right one, Jess, and if you ever need anything, I'm right here."

Jesse paused at the threshold . . .

"Thanks, Lance . . . for everything."

Lance had been there for Jesse through everything.

As soon as word reached him that Jesse was in trouble, he was at the hospital, sitting by Jesse's bedside, and trying his best to console the man. At the funeral, he was there, standing right behind Jesse to offer some kind of solace.

Lance did, after all, marry Katia and Jesse—having been an ordained Gnostic minister for years, he was the first choice for the happy couple.

The wedding had been small—just immediate friends and family. Jesse and Katia agreed not to have a big wedding; they both decided to spend the money on travel, rather than throwing a huge party for one hundred-fifty people. Most of who were just there for the food, and of course, the open bar.

Jesse walked down the hallway, head down, passing some of the other sales reps that he hadn't seen since that night. He had a lot of guilt that he hadn't been home that night. If he hadn't gone to the work dinner would any of this have happened?

If he had faked having not felt well, and stayed home, would

Katia still be alive?

Would he be dead also?

This scenario had run through Jesse's head more than a few times.

He imagined himself coming home from work to find Katia struggling with the killer.

Jesse leaping upon him, pulling him off her, and just going to work on him.

Even if Jesse hadn't survived the encounter, that would have been fine with him. It would have given Katia the precious seconds she would have needed to escape—to run, to sprint down the street screaming for help.

Even while Jesse was bleeding out on the floor, the beast standing over him, he would have died happy knowing Katia was safe.

But Jesse wouldn't fall to the beast. In Jesse's fantasy, that's not how it went . . .

All the anger, all the rage, all the pain Jesse had ever felt throughout his life would have been focused, multiplied, and aimed, like the tip of a Tomahawk cruise missile at the man threatening his woman, his wife, his world . . .

The beast would have found no quarter with Jesse.

The beast would, on that day, have been met with forty years of pain and suffering. An apex predator. Forty years of unbelievable burning anger, that had, for the most part, been suppressed and bottled up, but still lurked just below the waves . . .

Slowly circling . . .

Waiting . . .

Thirsting . . .

Starving . . .

Like a Great White Shark, looking for a chance to break through the façade of the cellophane-thin viscose of the surface, and let loose all the rage, the black grudge that had grown strong over the years. Its large moon-shaped tail fighting against the currents and undertows and lies of the 'I'm fines,' the 'No worries,' and the 'Sure, no problems.'

All the shit that Jesse had let slide. All the shit he had to chew and swallow.

The shark would have torn the beast to pieces. His jaws closing around the beast, thrashing and ripping side to side, his serrated triangle-shaped dentition going through the dermis, muscle, bone, and cartilage like a chainsaw through gelatin and chopsticks. Gulping down fist-size chunks of flesh, the warmth of the tangy blood cloud flowing over his tongue and passing through his gills—

Jesse startled from his thoughts as he bumped into Jeremy on the way out to the parking lot.

Jeremy was one of the other sales reps at the company, and Jesse considered him a friend. Jeremy was tall, mid 30s with dark caramel skin, and a shaved head. He looked more like a Calvin Kline model than a sales rep.

"Hey, man, how have you been? I miss seeing you around."

"I'm okay. I'm doing better."

Jeremy put one of his hands on Jesse's shoulder. "If you ever need to talk, I'm here for you."

"Ttsick the next day after going out with Jeremy. And in the worst-case scenario, nobody went to work because they were still in jail.

"Oh?" Jesse responded cautiously. *Here it comes.*

"I got passes to an underground strip club, really nice place. It's time to get you out there, back in the saddle, man!"

Jesse, for once, was speechless. Then out of his mouth, after a few seconds of calculating, came the first words he could think of. "Are you serious? First off, not my get down; I'm not into strip clubs. Second off, Katia would kill me if she found out."

And all at once, Jesse was back at the scene.

Cradling the pieces of Katia.

Screaming. Frothing. Flailing.

Jesse's hand had instinctively covered his mouth as he started hyperventilating. He lost his balance and fell to a knee.

In a heartbeat, Jeremy was on him and pulled him to his feet. "Dude, what the fuck?"

Jesse snapped back to present. "I've . . . I've got to go."

He pushed past Jeremy and bolted out the doors of his office building, jogged through the parking lot, got into his Prius, and started sobbing and screaming, all while pounding the steering wheel with his fists. The Toyota emblem cracked under the force of his blows as he attacked his car in a blind black outrage.

He stopped and looked down at his steering wheel. Only then, he noticed his coworkers and boss standing around the car.

Of course, they all came outside to see what the random, constant honking was.

Lance went up to his window and gave it a gentle tap with his fingers. "Jesse, take the rest of the day off. We will see tomorrow."

"I'm okay, just . . . a little upset," Jesse said while wiping away the tears and trying to force a smile.

"That's not a request, Jesse. We will see you in the morning. Go get some rest."

Jesse turned on his Prius and the Bluetooth automatically connected.

And as soon as it did, his phone started ringing again. The image displayed on the car's screen read: "Blocked Caller"

This had been going on for weeks—every couple of hours it seemed.

"Blocked caller" in the morning. "Blocked caller" before he attempted to sleep. He had never answered, but the "Blocked caller" was beginning to haunt him as much as his memories did. He finally gave in.

"What?" He screamed into the car's microphone as he accepted the call.

There was a short pause, then a woman's voice flowed from the car's speakers.

"Jesse . . . Jesse Silver?"

Jesse, now feeling a bit embarrassed for being an asshole to what apparently wasn't anyone trying to sell him anything, straightened his posture in his car, as if the woman could see him correct himself. "This is Jesse. How may I assist you?"

"Hi, Jesse, I'm not sure if you remember me . . . this is Doctor Eastman, from the FBI."

"Hello, Doctor Eastman. Any . . . any word?"

"No, Jesse, we are still investigating, as soon as I hear anything, you will be the first to know."

"Oh, okay, thank you for calling." Jesse reached to disconnect the call.

"Jesse, Jesse, wait."

There was a pregnant pause as Doctor Eastman continued, "I want to get together with you. And talk . . ."

"Thank you, doctor, but I'm fine."

"Are you?"

Something about the rise in the inflection of her tone pulled Jesse in. "No. No, I'm really not."

"Listen, Jesse, let's get together. I want to see how you are, talk to you, share some feelings with you. And maybe you can help me with some insights . . . to help me solve the case."

"When?" . .

"How's . . . this afternoon?"

Jesse paused. He was frozen. He waited a moment before slowly answering, "Okay."

"My office is in Pasadena. May I text the address to this number?"

"Yes."

"I'm here now. Just take your time and I'll see you when you get here. I'm looking forward to this, Jesse. Thank you."

Before Jesse could respond, the call was terminated. As soon as the call was cut, "Time to waste" started blaring through the stereo. Jesse turned down the knob and sat, staying in his car, unmoving from his position as the seconds passed by.

His phone buzzed, snapping him from his trance. It was a text from a 310 area code number:

"1334 Green street.

Pasadena Ca, 91101

See you soon.

Dr. E. ☺"

Jesse copied the address from the text message and pasted it into maps. The drive time was one hour and thirty-two minutes. Jesse tapped the faux shift knob on his Prius, put the car into reverse, and backed out of the parking space.

He pulled the knob down, putting the Prius into drive.

And Jesse . . . Jesse started moving forward.

FACEPLANT

If you knew that your life was merely a phase or short, short segment of your entire existence, how would you live? Knowing nothing "real" was at risk, what would you do?

You'd live a gigantic, bold, fun, dazzling life. You know you would. That's what the ghosts want us to do — all the exciting things they no longer can.

—Chuck Palahniuk

Katia waved to Jesse as he approached the reception desk at Wood Bridge Mercedes.

"Gooooood morning, kiddo!"

"Good morning!" Katia beamed back, showing her perfect smile.

Jesse closed the distance between him on the desk, much more casual now than he had been in the past. She was beginning to look happy to see him on these daily check-ins."What do you think about the book so far?"

Katia lit up at the question, immediately pulling the book from her bag. It was filled with colored post-it notes with thoughts and comments written on them.

"I absolutely loved this book! Like, it was amazing. It . . . really spoke to me."

"What was your biggest takeaway?" Jesse asked, trying not to look incredibly impressed at Katia's far superior, methodical system of comprehensive study.

"Well, first off, it explained . . . like . . . perfectly why I have always felt like I don't fit in—anywhere." Katia paused and smiled while gently thumbing through the pages. "It was, really, just nice to read. Thank you."

"You're most welcome."

"Hey, are you on the Facebook?" Jesse asked while pulling out his iPhone. "Because, you see, I'm on the Facebook, and if you're on the Facebook as well, I thought we could be friends together."

Jesse knew damn well Katia was on Facebook. He had already gone through the last couple weeks of her feed, looking at the things she liked, and of course, her photos.

But the best part? The icing on the cake?

Relationship status: Single.

Now, Jesse, of course, realized that some people might call this sort of thing "stalking." Such an ugly word, "stalking." Jesse preferred the term: "Noninvasive conversation enablers" or "N.I.C.E."

"Yes, I'm on Facebook"

"Cool, what's your last name?"

"Berlin."

Katia Berlin. What a great fucking name. Jesse typed in her name into the search bar, and immediately it populated with a couple different girls' profiles.

"Which one are you?" As if he didn't already know.

"That one, with the black and white photo," Katia said while pointing at the image on Jesse's screen.

"Cool, just sent you a request."

Katia picked up her phone and swiped the Facebook notification to the right. "Accepted." Katia smiled. Her nose crinkled.

"Thank you, now that we are officially friends, I was wondering if you thought about what I asked you the other night in the parking lot?"

Katia just stared at him, Jesse could tell the wheels in her head were spinning.

"About going out sometime?"

"Oh!" Katia bit her lower lip, "I'm kinda . . . seeing someone right now, but maybe next time?"

Jesse's heart sank. Seeing someone? Next time? What in the bloody hell does that mean? Why would she have "single" on her profile if she were "seeing someone"?

"No problem. Thanks for the consideration," Jesse said, putting on the most vinyl fake smile he could muster.

"Walk you to your car later?"

"Sure!" Katia took another sip from her iced coffee, then as she slipped her headset on, the phone at her desk started ringing.

Jesse turned and started back to his office.

Jesse parked on the tree-lined street and double checked the address that Doctor Eastman had sent him. He looked up at the 1910 craftsman style house that sat raised above the level of the sidewalk. The drought-resistant, manicured landscaping, the stones that lined the walkway—it all was picture perfect in every way.

The freshly painted house, that was once a residence and was now zoned a C1 office, gleamed in the sun.

It was a delicious palate of dark green and brick red—very traditional for the homes of the era. Jesse had an outright fetish for everything craftsman and Victorian: the look, feel, and smell of old wood, of walking into a room that holds the stored energy of one hundred shared Christmases, long forgotten birthday wishes, New Year's Eve parties, and wedding anniversaries. He loved to imagine them all taking place at once.

As Jesse looked up the steps to Eastman's office, he noticed the extra wide front door had delicate stained glass in it, as well as ancient looking, clearly original, brass hardware. The overhang that framed the front door was shrouded in lavender vines, and a wind chime hung to the right of the door off the porch, lazily singing its operatic dissonance.

Jesse made his way up the front steps. The mailbox next to the door simply read: "Dr. M. Eastman."

Inside the waiting room, the usual suspects: a coffee table with neatly assorted *Life*, *People*, even *Highlights* magazines, for kids no doubt; a comfy leather loveseat and matching chair sat opposite each other; and all of the above sat on top of the Persian rug—the colors of the carpet matching the room.

In the corner, a small table with a salt lamp, and on the floor beneath, a little Buddha fountain with recirculating water that flowed over and over, creating a soothing, bubbling sound.

New age music softly played in the background.

Jesse plopped down on the sofa and sat for a second, and as he started flipping through one of the magazines, he could hear muffled voices behind the closed door of the other room. Jesse assumed that was the room with the rubber walls and the straightjackets—and at that thought, he knew he was in the right place

The door opened and out walked a woman—in her late 20s and obviously pregnant. She glowed with happiness and the radiance that only a pregnant woman could.

She was followed by a stocky, taller-than-average man, hand in hers. Behind him, there was the woman that had called Jesse earlier that day: Doctor Eastman.

"Thank you, Mel. I can't tell you how much you have done for us!" the pregnant woman beamed, now hugging the petite blonde doctor.

"May I?" asked Doctor Eastman as she glanced down at the woman's round tummy.

"Of course—you're basically family!"

The pregnant woman took the doctor's hand and placed it on her belly.

"I'm so excited for you both. This is the start of your lives together.

This is your happily forever after."

"Thanks again, Mel. I couldn't ever have imagined that we would be where we are today. Martin is a new man thanks to you . . . He's kinder, sweeter, and just . . . happier."

"How's the sleeping?" Dr. Eastman asked with a wink.

"Like a log! That's the best part!"

The pregnant woman laughed as her husband stood behind them, silent, but starting to blush.

"Okay, sweetie, let's get out of here so she can get back to work."

The man turned, and as soon he noticed Jesse sitting in the loveseat, his posture immediately stiffened. He stepped between the man in the chair and his wife.

Jesse sat there, pretending to look at his phone and wondering what the big deal was. Jesse could feel the man's eyes burning a hole into him. And when he glanced up again, their eyes locked for more than enough seconds to make the situation uncomfortable. The tension was thick.

All at once, that frozen moment was broken as Doctor Eastman's soothing voice floated in the air like a feather in the breeze. "Hello, Jesse. Thank you for making it in today."

The man's gaze never left Jesse's as he hurriedly walked his wife to the front door. The man paused at the door and turned. "Thank you again, Dr. Eastman, for everything."

"No problem, Amador! That's what I'm here for. Now you guys go have a great day!"

Jesse watched as they exited the room through the big red door.

As the door closed, Jesse shrugged his shoulders.

"Hi, Jess!" Doctor Eastman gave Jesse a wave as she walked back into her office. "Have a seat here." She motioned to the large white seat against a wall, framed with tasteful abstract art. "Or do you prefer Jesse?"

Jesse tried to sit, negotiating with three throw pillows on the chair, but after some awkward fidgeting, he just placed them on the floor. On his right, there was a small table with a box of Kleenex and a dimly lit lamp. Underneath the stand was a small litter basket, filled with used tissues.

"Either is fine. I respond to both," said Jesse as he pulled out the throw blanket he was sitting on, folded it, and placed it next to the pillows on the floor.

He leaned back and finally sank into the deep, comfortable chair.

Doctor Eastman sat in a large chestnut-colored leather executive chair opposite of him, but only about six feet away.

"Jesse, thank you for taking the time to meet with me. I know I already said that to you, but I wanted to reinforce it. It's a big deal to come see me after, well . . . after everything that's happened." Eastman paused and closely observed Jesse.

His breathing pattern hasn't changed. Pupils are stable. He's looking around the room, observing, taking inventory of everything I have in here.

Eastman watched as Jesse scanned her bookcase, her desk, her diplomas, the multiple framed news clippings of her achievements— even the little glass bowl of peanut butter cups on her desk—all the little things that, at least in this room, add up to make her feel at home.

She allowed Jesse the extra three or four seconds to finish his scan of the room, and when his eyes met hers, she began, "Talk to me, Jesse. How are you? What's going on?"

"I'm doing much better," said Jesse with his best "sales smile." Eastman stared at him, notepad on her lap, pen tapping on the pad, not breaking the gaze she held with him for a single moment.

"Bullshit," Eastman said with a smirk. "How could you possibly be doing 'better'? Explain that to me, please, so I can take this to the APA . . . I'll win a Nobel prize for this! I'll be the next Jung!"

Jesse and Eastman sat in several seconds of silence, reading each other, studying each other.

The tension was broken when Jesse smiled, let out an organic chuckle, and looked over to the window.

Eastman chased after his attention when it strayed, speaking evenly. "We spent some time together after Katia was killed. I did my best to piece you together that night, and the next morning. I cleared your name and worked the case to try to give you some closure. Do you remember any of that, Jesse? Do you remember our talk in the hospital?"

Jesse stared blankly, and though Eastman could tell he was doing his best to recall the happenings of the night so long ago, he came up with nothing. "No, I don't remember any of that."

"That's okay, Jess." Eastman gave Jesse a kind smile to reassure him that he wasn't "wrong" for not remembering anything, then she continued. "After the dust settled, you just vanished on me—robotically going about your daily rituals and routines like nothing had ever happened, living life like you're the same person you were five months ago. But you're not, are you?"

Eastman paused, and let the silence hang in the air until it turned stale. "You have a hole in you: a void—*le vide*—an empty space that can't be filled. Not with work, not with friends, not with your art, not with anything. It's a ravenous sucking crack in your soul . . . and I'd be willing to bet you don't want it filled. I'd be willing to bet that you're torturing yourself every day. Flogging yourself with guilt and beating yourself down with the never-ending trains of 'what ifs,' and 'could haves' and 'should haves.'

"Your clothes, although clean, are not crisp. Your shoes are tied, but loosely. Your belt has two new notches—looks like you used a knife, and just stabbed at it, sloppy. This is unlike you—or should I say, unlike the old you. I'm sure you can't sleep, either, but you don't worry about that because it's the least of your issues."

Jesse sat as still as a statue in the chair, his eyes fixed coldly on Eastman.

"You're starving yourself and denying yourself sleep because that is the only way you can punish yourself that won't be glaring and obvious to all those around you. You can't stand how everyone puts on a show for you when they see you. You don't want their pity—all it does is remind you of what happened. And how can they empathize anyway?" Eastman's expression turned to pure, dripping sympathy. "Who could empathize with you, Jesse? How many people come home to find the love of their life butchered and in pieces on the floor of their house? A house that you two made into a home. Who could empathize with that? Who could even begin to understand what you went through that night?"

Jesse stared, still silent and stoic, at the petite blonde across from him. Eastman could see his fingernails turning white as he gripped his knees.

"But it didn't start on that night, did it, Jesse?" She paused. "Did it?"

No response.

"When did it start?" She continued, "It's always been like this. It's always been hard. Hasn't it? When did it start? When did the pain really start?

"I would bet that you look at your life as a series of dominoes falling, each event triggering the next, one big chain reaction of bad luck. Tell me, Jess, what was the first domino to fall?"

Eastman saw the tension in Jesse's fingers relax, and in a monotone voice, he muttered, "I've never felt *right*. I've never really *fit in*."

"How do you mean?"

"I was adopted. I was always told I was adopted. It was never kept a secret from me. Ever since I was little, I could remember my mom telling me that I was adopted." Jesse paused, squeezing his legs again, digging his nails into his jeans.

He relaxed his hands, interlaced his fingers, and placed them gently on his lap. "I was born in Hawaii . . . I was supposed to have a very nice life." Jesse glanced around the room as he spoke. "Both my parents were teachers. My mom taught phys ed, and my dad was a wrestling coach and also taught statistics. I was supposed to grow up in Hawaii. I was supposed to go to good schools. I was supposed to be . . . different than how I was. Than how I am."

"And . . . how are you?" Eastman interjected, breaking the long pause Jesse left hanging in the room.

"Fucked."

"How do you mean, 'fucked'?" asked Eastman, biting the end of her pen between her teeth.

"I was supposed to have a really nice, normal life, I was supposed to have had a chance."

"But something happened, didn't it?"

"My dad wanted to get his Ph.D. So . . . he moved us to the mainland. Santa Barbara."

"And how was that?"

"It was good. I have early memories of running around with the other kids in 'married student housing' off the UCSB campus. Catching polliwogs, and ya know, just being a kid. My mom and dad made fast friends with the family that lived next door. They had three little kids—all older than me, but we became like family. It was . . . It was good."

"And then what?" asked Eastman, slightly leaning forward in her chair. She crossed her legs and squeezed them tightly. She could smell the trauma coming. This was the best part of the trip—the *best* part. Trauma had an odor like bleach and ammonia mixed together in a big plastic bottle that had been shaken into a frothy, bubbling concoction of deep orange and yellow-colored sludge.

She could feel his anxiety and pain building. She could smell it, taste it, drink it, bathe in it. She wanted to breathe it in like smoke—this was her opiate.

"Then, everything changed."

"What changed?" Her legs squeezed tighter. Eastman leaned in toward Jesse as she continued to nibble the end of her pen.

"My dad left us. He left me."

"How old were you when this happened?" She held the pen to her notepad.

"Two, almost three . . ."

"You remember that?"

"Yes. He left us on Christmas morning."

"Excuse me?" Eastman looked up from her notepad and again laid her eyes on Jesse.

"On Christmas morning, after we opened presents, he took my mom outside and told her that he was leaving. He had fallen in love with one of his grad students, and he was leaving us. Then he got in his car, and he just left."

"Then what happened?"

"I can remember my mom coming in and picking up the scraps of wrapping paper, trying not to cry. I tried to get her to pick me up, but she was too upset. She just sat there in the pile of torn up wrapping paper—using the brightly colored bits and pieces of it to wipe up her tears."

"How did that make you feel?"

"Helpless . . . like I couldn't help her, like I wasn't enough for her."

Eastman let Jesse's words sit within the room, finding a place within the silence between them. After a pause, she said, "That's not your fault, Jess. You know that, right?"

Jesse looked again to the window. "Sure."

"Really. That had nothing to do with you."

"I guess."

Eastman felt Jesse's pain. She knew this was only the tip of the iceberg of who he was and how he viewed his worth. This was the scene that had set the stage for the rest of his life.

The rest of him, the rest of that iceberg, was a leviathan of betrayal, abandonment, abuse, and suffering that plunged miles below the surface. Eastman could feel his inner child scratching, clawing, clinging to her bosom.

She could be his life raft. She could right his compass and help him re-chart his destiny. She could save him. Eastman uncrossed her legs. She had been squeezing them so tightly, she could feel the blood rush down her thighs. She'd gotten her fix.

"Thank you for sharing that with me, Jess, that's a lot."

"Yeah."

"I want to try something with you, it's kind of new and experimental . . . Would that be all right?"

"Sure, why not."

"It's called 'Havening.' It was developed by a man named Ronald Ruben. It's a new technique. I'll read the description to you, and you can decide if you want to give it a try. Okay?"

"Yeah, that's fine."

Doctor Eastman got up from her big leather chair, walked to her bookcase, and after grabbing a sheet of parapet from a red folder, she returned to her chair. "This is how it works for trauma therapy."

She read the sheet to Jesse.

"First is activation of the emotional content of the traumatic event by imagining, recalling. A gentle and soothing touch is then applied to the upper arms, palms, and around the eyes. It produces an extrasensory response of safety that arises from the evolutionary equivalent of what a mother's touch does at the time of birth. It is innately wired, concurrently with a havening touch. The therapist distracts the individual, since the mind cannot hold two thoughts simultaneously. The use of distraction displaces the recalled event from working memory and prevents it from re-activating the amygdala." She paused. "Does that sound okay with you? And do you mind if we try this?"

"Sounds fine," Jesse assured.

"Is it okay if I touch you on your face, arms, and hands?"

"Sure."

Jesse stood and removed his work shirt. Underneath his shirt, Jesse had a white form-fitting v-neck undershirt.

Doctor Eastman was a bit pleasantly taken back by the tapestry of tattoos that covered Jesse's arms and chest. Eastman was also a bit surprised by the amount of muscle Jesse carried on his frame for a guy who spent most of his day driving in his car from appointment to appointment.

"Okay, Jesse . . . Let's get to this."

Doctor Eastman walked over to Jesse and kneeled on the floor in front of him. She locked eyes with him and took a deep, slow breath.

"Close your eyes and try to relax the best you can."

Jesse closed his hazel eyes and sat motionless in the big white chair.

"Breathe with me, Jesse. Deep breath in . . ."

Jesse inhaled sharp and deep, oxygen filling his lungs.

"Hold it, Jess. Hold . . . and out . . . Now deep breath in . . ."

Eastman noted that Jesse allowed a more relaxed inhale, and she watched as his shoulders relaxed into their natural position.

"I'm going to reach out for your hands. Is that okay?"

"Yes," Jesse said, just above a whisper.

Doctor Eastman, still kneeling, slowly took his hands into hers. She looked down at his fingers and saw the story of a man that used his hands to create beauty. Hands of a man that played music for the woman he loved, each note ingrained in the calluses on his fingertips. She noted the small scars on his knuckles, from beating the canvas with a palette knife, bringing her image to life.

His hands were warm. She felt like she could fall asleep in them.

"Tell me . . . Tell me about the day your father left."

Jesse recounted the story of his early childhood abandonment, and as he did, Eastman caressed around Jesse's eyes, upper arms, and the palms of his hands.

"Outstanding, Jess," Eastman coaxed, "now tell me the story again please."

Jesse told the story again, and Eastman's tapered fingers traced around Jesse's flesh, drawing longitude and latitude lines— searching for the pain. Her eyes explored Jesse's body while he spoke. She tried her best to memorize the tattoos that covered his arms and chest. The colors danced on his skin while her fingers played a symphony on his body.

As Jesse finished the story, Eastman, still kneeling, whispered to him, "Now open your eyes."

Jesse's eyes slowly opened, and for the first time, the woman in front of him saw more than just trauma. She saw the depths of kindness in those hazel eyes—and that kindness flowed like a vein of gold from his eyes directly into his heart.

"How do you feel, Jess? Are you okay?"

Jesse took a deep breath in and let it out. "Better, actually. Much better."

"Good, it looked like you were about to follow the white rabbit."

In a split second, Jesse reached for Eastman and buried his head into her shoulder. She held him as he poured out years of anguish and suffering. Years of not being good enough for his father to stick around for him. Years of not being enough to console his mother. Years of the primal wound of his first betrayal, the abandonment and shattering loss of his biological parents just being able to walk away from their newborn baby boy—like he was nothing . . . Just a bag of bones . . . Worthless.

For the first time since Katia's death, Jesse allowed himself to feel. To feel the release of that pain, if only for a moment, and having that burden lifted was intoxicating.

Eastman held him close. She let him pull at her as he sobbed. She helped him off the deep white chair, and onto his knees, and there he wept himself into joyful abandon.

She whispered as softly as she could, as she rocked him slowly like a mother cradling her newborn after taking its first breath of life, "Shhh, baby. Shhh, it's okay . . . It's all okay. I'm here. I care about you. I'm not going to let you go."

Jesse pulled her in tighter as he let it all go, unashamed.

This was the beginning of his rebirth.

This was the birth of the phoenix.

This was the start of his life, after it had been taken from him again, and for the first time, he felt deserving of this new start.

~~THE DEAD WIVES CLUB~~

The most loving parents and relatives commit murder with smiles on their faces. They force us to destroy the person we really are: a subtle kind of murder.

—Jim Morrison

A thick haze of sage smoke permeated Doctor Eastman's private back office. She had carefully, ritualistically, lit the dried plant and let it sit in a bronze bowl on her desk after Jesse left his session. She sat in the thick, a dense haze, in silence. Breathing in the rich earthy smoke and allowing it to flow deep within her.

She was replaying the events of the session over and over in her mind—analyzing and breaking down every word Jesse spoke, every meaning behind every move he made. *The outright wrong this man has endured in his life is never-ending . . . In his first three years of life, he went through more abandonment and suffering than most people in the Western World face in a lifetime.*

She inhaled, held her breath, and released, looking for answers in the silence. She was taught that if you sit in silence and ask the right questions, the answers will always come. The silence always answers. Always.

Who is he?

What is he?

What can he be made into?

Eastman's mind wandered back to the image of Jesse's hands

unbuttoning the buttons on his white collared shirt. She breathed in again deeply. In slow motion, she saw him removing the garment. His deltoids flexing and stretching, showing his tattoos. His hands moving slowly, deliberately, and with purpose.

She breathed in again, closed her eyes, and was transported to a small living room.

There she watched Jesse's Christmas morning unfold.

She watched as the toddler went to console his mother, and his mother turning her back and walking away from his reaching arms and grasping hands.

Tears rolled down her face as she watched the scene in her mind's eye.

She watched the child sit in the shreds of wrapping paper, picking up the shiny cellophane pieces and holding them in his tiny, innocent hands, just to try to hold onto anything tangible, anything that was a living piece of the recent past before his whole world was turned upside down. And he was left, again, abandoned brutally, for the second time in his young life.

She looked to see Jesse's mother, sitting at the modest kitchen table, also crying.

This moment set the tone for the rest of his life. This has to end . . . and it has to end now.

Eastman felt a hand on her shoulder, and she turned to see Jesse standing there, staring at her.

I'm going to set you free; I promise.

Eastman threw herself into Jesse's arms and held him, her face pressed firmly into his chest.

I'm going to show you who you really are. I swear to you, I'm going to set you free.

Eastman sat there in the lingering haze of sage smoke, the tracks of her tears still fresh on her cheeks. She went over the questions she had asked her guides again as she glanced over to a sword that was mounted on her wall. *Who is he? What is he? What can he be made into?* Then, she added after a pause, *Can he be the one?*

She sat in silence, floating in the sweet brine of her own energy.

All at once, a smile came over her face as a feeling washed over her. It was the silence, and it answered: "Yes, he is the one I've been waiting for . . ."

Slowly, she got up, walked over to her desk, and picked up her phone. She took it off of 'do not disturb.'

One missed call from Sergeant Durazo, just moments ago. She took a moment to compose herself and dry her eyes, then tapped the name in red.

"Doctor Eastman, ma'am? Thank you for returning my call so quickly. I was just leaving you a voicemail, ma'am."

"How can I help you, sergeant?"

"There has been another killing. How long until you can get here? I need your help."

"Where are you now, sergeant?"

"1456 Journeys End Drive, La Cañada."

Eastman jotted down the address in her moleskin book and grabbed her oversized bag. "Got it, I'm on my way. Oh, and sergeant?"

"Yes, ma'am?"

"Don't touch anything."

"Yes. Yes, ma'am."

Eastman hung up the phone with a smile and looked at her reflection in the now black screen of her iPhone.

"Well, girl, it's time to go and save the day again."

Jesse sat in traffic in silence. He hadn't thought about his childhood in years.

He imagined passing a bloody car wreck on the highway and watching the events unfold in his rearview mirror.

Yeah, it would be sort of like that: nothing but carnage, chaos, and pain. Why bother?

Then Jesse did something he hadn't done in months. He called a friend.

"Hey, Siri, call Andy."

"Calling Andy."

The phone rang five times, and Jesse contemplated hanging up after each ring, and nearly did when a male voice answered.

"Hey, man, what's up? You busy?"

There was a brief pause. Then Andy answered, "No, just getting off work . . . You . . . you wanna do something?"

"Yeah, let's hit a hike and have some dinner. Sound good?"

"Yeah, sounds fine. Meet you at your place?"

"Sure." Jesse paused and looked at the clock on the Prius' dashboard. "Six thirty? Seven?"

"Yeah, see you there."

Jesse made it home about twenty minutes later. Every time he pulled in, his driveway was an exercise in mindfulness. Every time, he imagined Katia looking out the window the way she used to. Her smile spread so wide, her hands frantically waving at him, her embrace when he crossed the threshold. But those were the good memories.

All too often, the images that came flooding back to Jesse were from that night. The night. The slow opening of the door. The scattered, mutilated pieces of his wife. The sickly-sweet smell of it.

Since that night, Jesse would wake up from some awful fever dream to notice she wasn't beside him. He would call out for her into the thick, empty darkness of their home. When his conscious mind would finally snap back to the cruel reality of what was now his life, Jesse would break all over again.

And this happened almost nightly in that little house on Piedmont Avenue. Jesse hadn't really slept in months.

People had been urging Jesse to move since it all happened, but this was his and Katia's house. This was their home, and sometimes—just sometimes—he could still feel her there. Sometimes when he turned a corner in the house, out of the corner of his eye, just for an instant, he would see Katia sitting in her favorite chair and reading one of her favorite books.

One night, when he passed the bathroom, he could have sworn he saw her standing at the sink, putting on her makeup—only stopping to glance at him and smile. If he moved or breathed or blinked, she would be gone. But those milliseconds of lingering images, her apparition, his misplaced memories, were all that Jesse had left.

It was those fragments of their life that Jesse missed the most.

Jesse unlocked the door and was happily greeted by Loki—the once tiny, now giant white and gray husky that he gave to Katia on that cold February night.

Jesse smiled as the nearly-eighty-pound pupper did cartwheels around the room, singing the song of his people.

"Okay, buddy. Settle down. Let's settle down." The giant wolfdog sat and awkwardly begged for a high five. Jesse gave in.

"C'mon, buddy, let's go outside." Jesse walked through the kitchen to the laundry room that led to the backyard. Upon opening the back door, the husky bounded outside and immediately relieved himself on the dirt that made up the lion's share of the yard.

It was funny how little time it took Jesse to go completely feral. The once sparkling kitchen was now dark, cold, and dingy; the laundry room, where clothes once sat neatly folded, now had a basket overflowing with soiled garments; the living room, once alive with the warm glow of candles and the soothing sound of classical music was now just a room that was the furthest thing from "living." And the bedroom that used to be a haven for them—a place of stories being read at night, of laughter, and the sounds of love that spilled out into the streets through the single pane wood windows—was now just a room with a bed.

Their home was now just a house.

You don't realize how much someone brings to the table until their seat is empty.

A knocking at the door startled Jesse. He glanced at the stove to the right of the fridge and saw the time: 6:42 p.m.

Jesse just remembered that he had made plans with Andy. Gathering his thoughts, he opened the front door to see a tall, slender man standing there.

"Hey, man, come on in."

"How was your day?" Andy asked as he walked into the room and sat in Jesse's chair.

"Interesting," Jesse said as he sat on the couch next to his friend. "Yours?"

"Dead." Andy was a funeral director and a twenty-six-year friend of Jesse. They lost touch for several years after their teens, but when they were kids, they had been attached at the hip. Now having rekindled their friendship after all these years, it had a nice familiarity that only long-term dynamics can bring.

"So . . . the haunted forest?" Jesse asked while rechecking the time on his phone.

"Yes, the haunted forest," Andy echoed back while also looking at his phone.

"Great. Let me get changed and we can get out of here."

Jesse walked into the room with a bed and put on a pair of cargo shorts, heavy socks, and cross trainers. He then walked over to his nightstand and opened the drawer to grab one of the small LED flashlights he kept there in case of a power outage.

In the drawer, Jesse was confronted with the Valentine's Day card Katia had given him. He hadn't gone in the drawer in months, and he wasn't prepared for this. He froze and stared at the card with the picture of the silly cat on it, then slowly took the card out of the drawer and opened it:

"My dearest hubby,

Valentine's Day is pretty lame, but I wanted to take the time to honor our relationship and our connection. Thank you for awakening in me a love I didn't know was possible. And next year, Europe!

—your adoring wife,

Katia

Xoxoxo"

Jesse read and reread the card, studying her handwriting. The swishing swoops of every S, the perfect circles of her Os, the loops in her Ks that looked like ribbons and bows.

"You ready?" Andy's voice shook Jesse. He dropped the card. He bent down and picked it up, kissed it, and placed it back in the drawer. Jesse grabbed the two small flashlights that he kept in the nightstand, as well as a small tactical folding knife, and turned to Andy, who was standing in the doorway.

"Let's go. I'll drive."

They got in the black Prius and backed out of the driveway.

"My Blue Heaven," one of Jesse's favorite Taking Back Sunday songs, played softly in the background as he rounded the corner of Piedmont onto Rosemont Ave. Neither man talked until Jesse pulled onto the freeway.

"So, how are you?" Andy muttered robotically as he stared out the passenger side window of the accelerating car, as if he was counting the apartment buildings and palm trees they passed while the vehicle picked up speed.

"Fucked. You?"

"Fucked."

The men sat in silence for another minute as Jesse navigated the ever-flowing traffic on the 210 freeway heading east. Aside from being childhood friends and having the comfort that comes with familiarity, the two men also shared a brokenness that only comes from extreme loss.

Jesse took a puff from his vape. "How long has it been now?"

Andy, still staring out the window, responded, "Fourteen months, three days . . ." He paused momentarily as he glanced at the time on his phone. ". . . eleven hours."

It was a typical Wednesday.

But on that typical, not so special Wednesday, Mr. John Muster, Jr. had a little too much to drink for breakfast. And he decided to get behind the wheel of his blue 1996 Chevy Blazer—something that Mr. John Muster, Jr. did on a daily basis. Then he blew a red light, killing Andy's wife, Carmen, as she was walking through a crosswalk.

Mr. John Muster, Jr. didn't even stop.

Later that afternoon, the police knocked on Mr. John Muster, Jr.'s door, only having found him because the license plate on the front of his blue 1996 Chevy Blazer had been left on the scene from the impact on Carmen's body.

Mr. John Muster, Jr. had still been drunk and didn't even seem to care about what had happened hours ago. As a matter of fact, Mr. John Muster, Jr. had forgotten entirely about it.

But Andy hadn't . . . Andy hadn't forgotten anything about that Wednesday.

"So, the haunted forest, then Everest?" Jesse said.

"Remember when we used to go there, the haunted forest, when we were kids?" Andy asked, still staring at the buildings passing by in rapid succession.

"Oh yeah."

"Remember when we saw the ghost of the little girl?"

"Yes, I remember." Jesse let out a chuckle.

One night, when Jesse and Andy were maybe both sixteen, perhaps seventeen, they were up there walking around in the darkness, and they happened across what appeared to be a little girl sitting on a stump in the forest.

Although, the peculiar thing about this little girl was that she dressed in clothing typical to the turn of the last century. That and the fact that she was sitting alone in the woods at midnight, illuminated only by the moonlight. If it weren't for those things, they wouldn't have thought anything when passing by her.

The two boys approached her, and she looked up at them and vanished.

Jesse and Andy set a new land speed record running out of the forest and back to the car that night.

Jesse hadn't thought about that night in years. The memory brought a smile to his face.

The land where the forest stood used to belong to a gentleman by the name of Mr. Cobb. Mr. Cobb and his wife, Carrie, were in the lumber business. They built a mansion in the mountains of Pasadena in 1918. Over the next years, the estate survived multiple brush fires before it was ultimately transformed into public parkland.

Some claim that there was also a sanitarium on the property that used to house tuberculosis patients—"Lungers," as they were called. Word was that it burned down, or rather, was set ablaze in an act of arson, killing the poor souls trapped inside, too sick to escape. Others claimed that old Los Angeles gangland-style executions have taken place in the forest, along with Satanic rituals, and the obligatory few sasquatch sightings.

Charles Cobb, the tortured ghost of the man who once owned the land, was said to still walk the grounds at night. It was claimed that he didn't like it when people stood on the ruins of the old house.

Basically, the place was a veritable cornucopia of awesomeness for drunk, goth teenagers like Jesse and Andy back in the day.

"Great album," Jesse said while turning up the frantic, bipolar, manic screeching of the sonic masterpiece "Louder Now."

"Yep," Andy said, who was now looking at the long northern stretch of Lake Avenue, which led up to the haunted forest. They continued up the road in silence with only the sounds of the radio.

And that was enough.

JOURNEYS END DRIVE

Love is an adventure and a conquest. It survives and develops, like the universe itself, only by perpetual discovery.

—Pierre Teilhard de Chardin

"Need a light?"

Katia, who was frantically digging through her oversized purse, looked up to see Jesse standing in front of her. "Yes, please! I only have a couple minutes before my shift starts, and I'm dying for a smoke!"

Jesse took three steps toward the girl, her cigarette hanging loosely from her ruby red lips. Her long red hair was pulled back into her customary work ponytail. Her scarlet mane nearly reached down to the small of her back.

More than once—actually, more than a few times, Jesse had imagined grabbing a fist full of that long red hair. Hair damp from sweat, he would grab it and roll his wrist, bringing his fistfull of her locks tight against the back of her head, and giving her a good yank, forcing her head back. Her mouth would open into a silent moan as he gently forced her up against the wall. Her body pressed like a puzzle piece against his.

His free hand would be on her hip, slowly pushing and pulling, moving her form against his in a musical rhythmic passion—like a concert cellist playing her favorite piece of music.

Flick!

Jesse's lighter ignited on the first try, and he, a mere eight inches from her, the closest he had ever been but still farther than he wanted to be, sparked a flame on the end of her Camel.

Katia sucked and inhaled deeply. "Thank you so much. You're always here to save the day for me!"

"I know," said Jesse with his signature wink and grin. "Oh, hey, I brought you another book. I was going to just drop it off at your desk, but since you're here . . ."

Katia watched wide-eyed as Jesse opened his backpack and produced a green and white paperback that was a bit thicker than the last book he had gifted her.

"I'm excited, what is it?"

"One of my favorite books. It's called, *The Power of Now* by Elkhart Tolle. I think—actually I know you'll like it."

Jesse handed Katia the book, and she immediately started thumbing through it.

"It's about being present. The dude has a total mental breakdown and comes out the other side a totally different person. I think it will be meaningful for you."

"Wow, thank you. Really, Jesse . . . Thank you."

"My pleasure."

They locked eyes and really, honestly saw each other.

Jesse glanced down at his phone.

"You had better go . . . You're almost late."

"Shit. See you later?" Katia asked while taking the last drag off her cigarette and stepping on it with the toe of her high heel.

"If I'm lucky," Jesse said with a smile.

"Okay, byeee!"

"Bye, Katia." Jesse finished his cigarette and took the long way around the building to his office, letting his mind wander back to the swelling sounds of a cello and a fist full of that long red hair . . .

Sergeant Durazo watched as the big black SUV pulled past the sheriff line that was blocking the local news reporters and their cameramen. Durazo shook his head with a smile as he could hear the young blonde doctor singing along at the top of her lungs to "Better than Revenge" by Taylor Swift.

Eastman parked her SUV next to Durazo's cruiser, finished singing the last chorus while checking her lipstick, and got out of her truck.

"Good afternoon, sergeant. What are we looking at here?"

"Afternoon, ma'am." Durazo motioned Eastman to the front door of the large, almost palatial home on Journeys End Drive. "Looks similar to the Katia Silver murder, so I called as soon as I got here. I wanted to give you the first look at the scene."

"Has anyone been inside yet?" asked Eastman as she observed the perfectly manicured lawn and the little porcelain ducks and rabbits surrounding the front door.

"Just the responding officer who called it in and myself."

"Has anything been touched or moved yet?"

"No, ma'am."

"Good boy," Eastman said with a wink.

Durazo followed her as she walked up the cobblestone driveway to the front door. There, she hesitated for a moment. Eastman scanned the entry door: bright brass knob, doormat, the brickwork surrounding it. Eastman noted how everything was *just so* and had a place.

"Who called 911?"

"The mother. She's a mess."

"Age and sex of victim?"

"Twenty-one, female."

"Where was Mother when this happened?"

"She has been gone for the last two weeks on vacation. Came home this morning, discovered her daughter, called us from outside."

"Assumed time of death?" Eastman asked, glancing at the time on her phone.

"A . . . a couple days, I would imagine."

Eastman paused and looked up to Durazo as he shook his head and looked down at the little statues by the front door. She knew it must be a mess inside.

"I see," Eastman sighed as she slipped her phone into her bag.

***

Jesse parked his Prius at the top of Lake Avenue. Both men exited the car without saying a word. He tossed one of the flashlights to Andy, who put it in the pocket of his jeans.

Even though it had been public use land for decades, the entrance to the Cobb Estate was still somewhat intimidating. Two huge rock pillars loomed, supporting an old, intricate, beautiful rot iron gate. To the right of the old gate was the entrance. A wood-composite forest service sign warning of snakes and fire hazards marked the start of the public land.

"Ready?" asked Jesse as he knelt and tied the laces of his ratty old Nikes.

"Sure . . . Might as well," Andy said while checking to see if he had any notifications on his iPhone. There were none.

Jesse started up the trail with Andy flanking him. The two men walked up the long-decrepit remains of the old driveway that led to the once grand Spanish-style estate. The ancient California Oaks created a natural canopy in some spots over the men as they walked.

After a couple minutes of walking in silence, Jesse simply said, "Fucked."

"Yep," replied Andy.

After a several hundred yards, they reached the head of the trail.

The old trail became a narrow switchback of crisscrossing loose dirt that took hikers deep up into the San Gabriel mountains. Beset on one side by narrow cliff faces, and on the other, steep ascending slopes of granite that looked like, at any moment, it could come crashing and sliding in a dry avalanche—taking the loose shrubs and any unlucky hikers down into the cavern with it. Not to mention the tarantulas, rattlesnakes, mountain lions, and, of course, ghosts that inhabited the area.

As the men started to gain elevation, the hike started getting more treacherous. Jesse could feel Andy's frustration beginning to build.

They reached the first switchback and paused to catch their breath. The view over the San Gabriel Valley was quite striking, really. An ocean of trees and buildings filled the ring-shaped valley, which was flanked by more large mountain ranges to the west and south. Beyond that, they could see the skyline of downtown Los Angeles, and south from there, the port of Long Beach.

The funny thing was at street level, Jesse found the city to be dirty, savage, foul, and ugly. A filthy mix of orange and yellow hues, cracked decaying concrete, bars on windows, concrete ghettos and graffiti . . . But from up here, the city had the appearance of a shining utopia.

I guess that most things in life are merely a matter of perspective.

"You know . . ." Andy said aloud, but then he hesitated.

Jesse walked over to Andy and looked over the valley with him. Jesse stood in silence, waiting for Andy to speak.

"Under normal circumstances, the person . . . the person is there. You get to have the discussion of, 'You're not giving me what I need. This relationship isn't working for me anymore,' all that petty bullshit that people worry about. The things that feel like big deals and are big upsets in their relationships. I had a friend call me up crying a couple weeks ago. He was bitching to me about his wife running up his credit cards on a shopping spree, like . . . like it was the end of the fucking world. That's not the end of the world."

Andy paused. He was still looking over the valley. "They don't know . . ." He let out an exhale through his nose, head tilting as he gathered himself. "They don't know what the end of the world feels like. When your world is taken from you in an instant, and you have no reason why. When your world is somebody else, and all at once they're gone . . . and there's nothing you can do about it . . . That's it. That's the end of the world—the end of you.

"When you share a life with someone, and you're with them every day, and night. You have cars and a home . . . Memories of a thousand road trips and . . . and the special places you go together, your favorite restaurants. When everywhere you go—everywhere— you have a memory associated . . . with them . . ." There was a look in Andy's eyes that Jesse would recognize all too well, but he kept his eyes towards the skyline. "You can't even walk in the goddamned grocery story without trying not to break down. You walk down the same aisles that you did with them and remember every conversation you had there. All of a sudden, you would give everything—everything in the world—just to be able to do that with them one more time . . . And a fucking credit card is your biggest problem?" Andy paused and took a deep breath.

"When one day it's all gone . . . You wake up wondering when things will get easier. Some days, you wake up and it feels like it just happened yesterday, and that old familiar panic comes back . . . The panic of your world ending. I know the date my world ended. I know the date of my apocalypse: One-sixteen, two-thousand-sixteen . . . And now. And every day since . . . "

Andy stared at the now nearly complete sunset dipping deep in the western sky, an explosion of reds, oranges, yellows, and the far deep blue surrounded it.

"Fucked," Andy stated plainly, then continued. "Normal people will never understand this. And that's good—that's a good thing. They don't want to know what this is like. I . . . I wish I didn't know what this is like. I wish I could flip a switch and be back to normal, be okay again."

Jesse put his arm around Andy's shoulder, but didn't say a word.

The two men stayed for a few moments longer, before they turned and started back up the steep and narrow trail in silence, the sound of the loose granite and sand crunching underneath their shoes.

Jesse started talking as they rounded the first corner, heading up the next switchback. "I can't even sleep anymore . . . I don't even remember what it's like to naturally wake up. Every time I wake up, it's from some god-awful nightmare."

"Yeah."

Jesse continued, "Last night, I had a dream, if you want to call it that."

Jesse thought about his statement and amended it, "Last night I had a nightmare that she was alive. Katia was alive, but living with someone else. I didn't recognize the house or where I was. But she was there and I was trying to talk to her. I was pleading, begging her to come home . . ."

They rounded another switchback and quickened their pace up the mountain.

"Please . . . just please come home."

"That's fucked up, man, but I feel you."

Jesse laughed. "That's not the most fucked up part though."

"What do you mean?"

"What I mean is . . . It was like I was a ghost."

Andy grimaced and looked over to Jesse. "What do you mean?"

"It was like I was invisible, like it wasn't that she was ignoring me on purpose, but like I was a fucking ghost. A spirit . . . A poltergeist. But I was still pleading with her to come home. The more I realized she couldn't see me, the more I begged and screamed and cried, the angrier and angrier I got . . ." Jesse paused and looked over the canyon below. "I woke up sobbing."

Andy was silent.

"Then I got to thinking that maybe ghosts don't start out being scary and mean. Maybe ghosts start out happy and optimistic.

Perhaps they're just driven insane by the fact that they are right there in front of us, in front of the people that they love the most, and we can't see them. They scream for us, but we can't hear them. They reach out for us, but we can't feel them. And, after a while, they just stop screaming, stop trying to hold our hands . . . top trying to comfort us at night. And all that's left is resentment, anger, even hate. And maybe, just maybe, that's what turns a home into a haunted house."

Andy and Jesse rounded the last switchback that led to the summit.

They had reached the top of the mountain. The sky was now full of stars, and the horizon was no longer glowing. It was just an infinite pool of black. The lights of the freeways and streets crisscrossed, slicing across the terrain as far as the eyes could see.

"You want to ring the bell?" Jesse pointed to an old bell that someone had put on the top of the mountain God knows when.

"Sure."

They both took turns ringing the old bell and listening to its percussive *ding* echo through the canyon below. There they stood, drinking in the majesty of creation and all that was laid before them.

"How did the press get here so fast?" Eastman quietly asked Durazo while opening the trunk to her SUV.

"No clue. Maybe a neighbor called. It's anyone's guess at this point. Not much happens up here—nothing like this at least."

"Interesting," replied Eastman. She reached into the back of the SUV and pulled out the bag she kept her work supplies in.

"I'm not going to wear my windbreaker if you don't mind, sergeant. I don't want to give the press anything more to speculate about," Eastman said as she glanced at the two news trucks parked up the street next to the waiting coroner's van.

"Good call, agent."

Special Agent Eastman grabbed her kit containing her latex gloves, camera, and moleskin. She reached into a little bag and withdrew a small dark blue vile. She took the lid off and covered the lip of the bottle with a finger, turned the bottle upside down and placed a finger in one nostril, then repeated the same action with the next, then added a dab to the top of her head, the center of her forehead, on her throat, her sternum, and finally on her belly.

Durazo watched silently as Eastman reached into her kit again and removed a small wooden box. It was covered with intricate engravings. She opened it, and inside was a pile of different colored rocks and crystals.

Eastman slowly picked through the dozen or so treasures, carefully picking out the two she was hunting for, and placed them carefully on the bed of the SUV's trunk. She then closed the box and set it back into the bag.

"Ma'am?" Durazo asked with genuine curiosity, not a single ounce of snark in his voice.

"Smokey quartz and black tourmaline," replied Eastman as she took the crystals and held them close to her heart. She closed her eyes, her lips moving as she said something silently to herself. Then after a few moments of silence, standing with her eyes closed in total serenity, Eastman continued packing up her kit as if nothing had just happened.

"What do those do, agent?"

"I believe they ward off negative energy, sergeant. And if you were wondering, the blue bottle contains essential oils for cleansing, but the heavy aroma will also mask the smell of the scene. You did mention you believe the time of death to be a couple days ago. Yes, sergeant?"

"Yes, ma'am."

"Well, then . . . would you like some?" Agent Eastman offered the bottle of liquid to Durazo.

"No, ma'am. I'm fine."

"Suit yourself, sergeant." Eastman gave Durazo a wink as she zipped up the bag containing her scene investigation kit. She stood on her tippy toes, grabbed the handle of the SUV's trunk, and pulled. It came down with a muffled *whoosh*.

She pulled her liquid lipstick from her pocket, and using her reflection in the big GM's rear window, she freshened her look. She stopped to look beyond her own reflection and watched as a third news truck pulled up and parked on Journeys End Drive.

"Let's do this, sergeant." Eastman screwed the cap of her lipstick back on and slid the slim tube into the pocket of her jeans. She grabbed her kit and started toward the front door of the house on Journeys End Drive.

GARLIC AND ROSES

The joy of life consists in the exercise of one's energies,
continual growth, constant change, the enjoyment of every new
experience. To stop means simply to die. The eternal mistake of
mankind is to set up an attainable ideal.

—Aleister Crowley

"What's good here?" Andy asked while staring up at the menu of the little family-owned Mediterranean restaurant in Downtown Montrose.

"Everything," replied Jesse, looking down at his phone.

"What are you getting?"

"The number six."

Jesse stepped up to the register where the eager-eyed teen was waiting to take their orders. They both got the number six, and the two men went and sat outside, the cool blue glow of their phones illuminating their blank expressions.

Jesse scrolled through his camera roll, and Andy was reading the news.

"Look at this." Jesse handed his iPhone across the little stainless-steel table to Andy. "That's our trip to Paris."

Andy studied the picture of Jesse and Katia, on top of the Eiffel Tower at sunset. An obvious selfie, but still a great photo. Andy stared at the photo for more than a few seconds, then handed the phone back to Jesse. "How many photos of her do you have on your phone?"

"Just photos, or photos and videos?"

"Both."

"One thousand seven hundred and twenty-seven." Jesse paused. "And I have about ten gigs of high-resolution photos on SD cards from my camera, so who knows, another four thousand there?"

Andy just shook his head while scrolling down the news feed on his iPhone.

"Fucked."

Jesse sighed in return. "Fucked."

The men again sat in silence until a young girl materialized at the table with two black trays.

"Isn't it nice to watch all the happy couples walking their dogs and eating?" Andy said while stabbing at the chicken on his plate with his fork.

"Yeah, it's super," Jesse chuckled. "We used to come here a couple times a week. She loved it."

"Food's good," Andy said while chewing his first bite.

"We used to sit at this table and plan our escape to Europe."

Jesse took his fork and scooped a healthy portion of the garlic sauce and mixed it in with the chicken on his plate.

"You know what I miss the most?"

"What?"

"The unpredictable consistency of our relationship."

"What?" Andy asked, looking up from his plate.

"The unpredictable consistency. It was like everything we did together was magical. We would come up with an idea for an adventure late one night, and boom, the next morning, we would be on the road. Of course, we had our daily routines and rituals, the things we had to do, but we never felt 'locked in' to anything."

Jesse took another bite of his chicken. "It was like we were really and truly free. I could set my watch to her patterns, and she could do the same for me. Other than my erratic work schedule,

119

of course. But we knew each other. We really knew each other. The best was when we would be in the living room. She would be reading a book and taking notes or writing in her journal, and I would be working on a painting, listening to Classical music. We wouldn't say a word for hours.

"We were alone. But together . . . That was our time. Some of our best adventures happened without ever leaving the house."

Doctor Eastman slowly turned the doorknob of the big house on Journeys End Drive. She hesitated when she heard the click of the lock.

She released the knob, and with a single gloved finger, gently pushed the door open. The big, heavy door swung open slowly and came to rest at the end of its radius.

Eastman stood at the threshold and waited.

She took in a deep breath and could smell the lingering stench of decay. She stood in silence and read the energy that spilled out of the house. It felt still, empty—it felt dead.

She took another deep breath as she reached out with all of her senses.

She's not here anymore.

Eastman opened her eyes. *She's gone already.*

"Let's go," said Eastman, looking down at her heels and stepping over the threshold.

Just inside the door, directly in front of her was a large brown leather sectional sofa. There was an entertainment center to her right. She paused. "Who died right here, in this room?" Eastman whispered while slowly turning to Durazo.

"The husband. But that was about fifteen years ago. I was here on the 911 call. Natural causes, heart attack, but how did you—"

"Shhh!" Eastman closed her eyes and held a finger to her lips as she swayed gently in place, like a limb of a tree caught in a soft breeze.

"Okay, let's keep moving." Eastman looked to her right and saw what seemed like an office, clutter and paperwork all over the desk. She looked at the sectional and noticed heavy creases in one of the seats.

The seat that gets used most: Mom's seat.

Her eyes further scanned the room. On the table sat a huge stack of mail, mostly junk mail, with a couple of bills mixed in.

Must have been from the daughter collecting it while Mom was on holiday.

Eastman gathered data as her eyes went to the several large windows that provided a view to the backyard, complete with outdoor living room and kitchen. *Nice plantation shutters.*, Eastman mused to herself as her eyes darted to all the other windows on the first floor.

These blinds are open. All the rest on this floor are closed. Doesn't make any sense, having these closed would cut the glare on the TV.

Her eyes shot to the large flat screen TV opposite the windows, then went back to the living room, and the several large windows that flanked the sides of the north and south elevations of the house. *All the shutters are closed, interesting.* Eastman tapped her lips with her finger as her mind labored.

She walked over to the shutters facing the north side of the house, the elevation facing toward the street, and opened them slowly, peeking out and onto the driveway. *Can't see the street from here, nor can the street see us. It wasn't our bad guy that closed them.*

She raised an eyebrow. *A young girl had the house to herself for two weeks. What would I be doing if my mom was on vacation? What would I be doing if I still lived at home?* Eastman walked back to the shutters facing the backyard. She couldn't see any of the other houses directly, total privacy. *No neighbors could get close to see anything going on in here.*

Eastman smirked as her mind conjured up the answer. *She liked walking around the house naked—that's exactly what I would be doing if I had the house to myself for two weeks. It would be one big no pants party.*

Durazo walked up behind Eastman. He shuffled his feet, not wanting to startle her again.

"Think she was down here watching TV when the perpetrator entered the house?" asked Durazo. Eastman turned and shook her head.

"Not a chance, sergeant. She's young; she wouldn't have been watching cable on TV. At most, she would have been in her room on her laptop or on an iPad, maybe on her phone."

Durazo's face had a blank expression, then he furled his brow. "Oh . . . why not just watch it on the TV?"

Eastman sighed. It was a good thing Durazo wasn't facing her, because the ferocity of her eyeroll would have split him right down the middle.

Eastman's eyes went to the center of the large open floor plan. An exotic wood rocking chair sat on a Persian rug in front of the large river rock fireplace. *Those came from the Arroyo quarry no doubt. The house was built between 1918–1922, judging off the rocks. The same time they were building the rose bowl. I guess they had to do something with all those extra stones.*

Her eyes traveled to the beams that ran across the center of the ceiling. *Old growth redwood—the tree was at least three hundred years old when it was cut down. Can't find that stuff anymore.*

Eastman looked back to the office, then back to the living room. Where the Persian rug ended, the dining room began. A ten-foot formal dining table sat there covered in a tablecloth, with ten chairs surrounding it.

Eastman took a deep breath in and closed her eyes.

The smell of death was growing stronger as she neared the narrow staircase that led to the second story of the large house. She reached out her gloved hand and gripped the old wood rail that flowed up the stairs to the second floor.

She paused and squeezed the railing, feeling the grain of the redwood through her latex gloves.With a slight jog, she quickly made her way up the stairs and paused at the landing. There was a hallway.

On the right, a closed door. Halfway down the hall, another door, slightly open. At the end of the hallway, another closed door.

The stench of death and decay was now overpowering.

"Door number one, two, or three?" Eastman pointed at the doors in rapid succession. Tiny words escaped her lips just above a whisper. "Eeny-meeny-miny, moe, catch a psycho by his toe, when we catch him, we won't let him go, my mother told me to pick the best one, and you are it." She landed on the middle door. She turned again to Durazo and smiled. "Let's see what's behind door number two, shall we?"

Eastman pushed the solid core wood door, and it swung with a barely audible squeak. It was a huge, beautiful master bathroom.

Sparkling Granite floors flowed up into a Jacuzzi tub, and into a dual-headed walk-in shower. Around the tub, there were large candles and little soaps shaped like seashells. Above the tub on a floating rack were six neatly folded fluffy towels—but what was hanging above the tub wasn't so pretty: a girl's nude body, suspended by her ankles from heavy eye-screws that were freshly wound into the ceiling.

Her legs were spread wide.

The ropes that suspended her lowered what was left of her into the bathtub, just to the level of her belly button. Her body was severed, sawed in half from her crotch to the waterline, just above her navel.

The water was a thick, murky soup of congealed blood, flesh, and decay. Floating in the soup were the innards and organs of a once beautiful young woman.

Eastman looked over to Durazo, who was covering his nose and mouth, trying to stop the unavoidable stench that had soaked into the paint, the drywall, and the studs underneath.

"A couple days, sergeant?"

"That's my best guess, ma'am. Nobody has been in here other than the vic, the killer, the mom, and us."

"I am putting my money on at least five days."

"Yes, ma'am."

Eastman walked over to the far side of the tub and flipped the trip lever for the drain.

The concoction of murky brine churned and bubbled as the standard residential plumbing choked and gagged, trying to gulp down the thick soupy mixture of blood, bits of flesh, a pile of bloated organs, and bone. Not to mention the jelly-like skin that had formed on the surface of the curdled milk-textured semi-liquid.

Eastman and Durazo watched in silence as the bloated lower half of the girl materialized before their eyes while gravity did its grim duty.

"Most of her wasn't floating anymore, agent."

"No . . . No, Durazo, it wasn't." Eastman shook her head. "Five days," she sighed as she pulled out her camera and started taking photos of the body—or rather, what remained of it.

"Just like the Katia Silver murder," Durazo mumbled, his hand over his mouth and nose, trying to avoid the overpowering greasy stench.

Eastman observed the scene, taking in the horrible beauty of this insanity.

"We couldn't see this from the murk of the water, Durazo, but her head and arms have been taken clean off. Her arms have been severed at the shoulders. These cuts were clean at the time, just like at the Silver house, but now, due to advanced bloating and decay, they look sloppy."

Eastman pointed at the dismembered body. "Decapitation occurred right above the hyoid bone in a diagonal sawing motion here . . . The weapon that was used was sharp, sergeant, precise.

I'm guessing it was made for this. It was made for butchering."

Eastman used her pen to point out the low-to-high cut that ran from front to back of what was the girl's throat. "Our boy has been practicing this for a while."

Eastman poked her head into the tub, looking over, and trying to put all the pieces together.

"One of her hands is missing, sergeant."

"Maybe it's underneath her?"

Eastman craned her neck, trying to see underneath the decomposed lump of flesh. "I don't think so, sergeant. I don't think so."

Durazo pondered out loud, "Maybe he took it as a trophy?"

Eastman paused, closed her eyes, and shook her head.

"No, it's here . . . somewhere."

Eastman stood up and scanned the room. Every nook and cranny analyzed and interpreted—even the tiny crack on one of the pieces of the quarter round that went around the stool of the window above the tub.

There was nothing.

She looked up at the two eye-screws that were tapped into the ceiling, the precise ropework that flowed down and tied around the girl's ankles, the blue-green veins that weaved like spiderwebs over the girl's decaying legs, and the blotchy black of the infected dead blood that pooled from gravity at the bottom of the tub.

Eastman looked back to the ropes tied around the girl's ankles, and whispered, "Rope burns."

Durazo stepped beside Eastman to see from her perspective. "Ma'am?"

Eastman pointed. "She has rope burns around her ankles, sergeant."

Durazo looked closely at the feet that were about eye level to him. The skin under the ropes was raw, lacerated away. He muttered in horror, "What does that mean?"

Eastman's voice was quivering. "It means she was alive when he suspended her up there. She was alive when he started cutting through her pelvis and pulled out her organs. He filled up the tub after he did the work." Eastman closed her eyes hard. "He's a monster, sergeant."

Durazo looked down to Eastman. "Have any leads, agent?"

Eastman looked around the room as she spoke. "I have some ideas."

As the last of the muck slid down the drain, the tub made a sickening belching sound. Durazo coughed and swallowed hard, his hand going back to cover his mouth.

Eastman glanced up to Durazo, and with a matter-of-fact tone said, "I did offer you the oil, sergeant."

Durazo nodded his head. "I'll take you up on it next time."

She gave Durazo a wink and shook her head while taking another look at the chunks in the tub.

"You poor thing," Eastman sighed as she put her hands on her hips and looked around the room. A smile slowly came over her face as her eyes darted back and forth.

"What's missing, sergeant?"

"Ma'am?"

"Look around the room, sergeant—what's not here?"

"I'm not sure what you're getting at, agent," Durazo said, looking slowly around the room.

"What does every millennial have in their hands or by their side twenty-four-seven?" Eastman turned to see Durazo shrug his shoulders, a blank, questioning expression on his face.

"You really are getting old, you know that, sergeant?" Eastman paused, waiting for Durazo to catch up.

He didn't.

"Where's her phone?"

Durazo looked around the bathroom again.

"Maybe she left it in her room?"

"Sergeant, she has a pile of bath bombs from Lush in that basket over there. She wouldn't dream of taking a bath without snapping or putting a video of the bomb going into her tub on her insta-story or TikTok."

Durazo's eyes glazed over. "Her what?"

Eastman stared at Durazo in disbelief.

"Wow, sergeant, Just . . . wow . . ." Eastman turned and went back into the hallway. "Let's see what else there is to see." Eastman walked down the hall to the closed door, opened it, and entered.

Although the victim was in her early twenties, her room still had the feel of a teenager. Posters of Lana Del Rey, RuPaul, and tattooed-faced mumble rappers hung on the walls. To the right of the bed were bookcases. On the bookcases were dozens of trinkets and bobbles the girl had collected or been given by her friends.

Pictures from a photo booth at a prom party were tacked on the wall. Her friends had on silly hats. The girl in the tub had giant oversized sunglasses. Eastman could almost hear the girls laughing and squealing with delight as they all five crammed into a booth meant for only three, at most. Duck faces and silly giggles were the order of the night—a night of memories made to last a lifetime. But this lifetime was cut short.

A small twin-sized bed was dwarfed by the large room. Eastman looked to the left of the bed: a small study desk with a lamp. On the desk were piles of scattered Sephora makeup and accessories. Eastman raised an eyebrow. *Oh shit, she has the new Kat Von D collection. I've been wanting to check that out.*

Eastman turned to the slim but tall dresser and carefully opened the top drawer. A sea of Victoria's Secret PINK panties and boy shorts were stuffed and crammed haphazardly into the cramped space. In the corner of the drawer, a slim chrome vibrator.

They say diamonds are a girl's best friend, but you and I know the truth. Don't we, sister? Eastman smirked as she gently closed the drawer and turned on her heel, going back to the bookcase.

Yearbooks and magazines, a novelty Polaroid camera, stuffed animals that were at one time a big deal in a little girl's life. When she was little, those stuffed animals were present at every princess tea party, but now, sadly, they were just bookends for her pleasure reading collection.

Eastman scanned the spines that lined the bookcase. *50 shades? Twilight? Sharp Objects?* Melantha smiled as she said out loud, "And all seven Harry Potter books? That's what I'm talking about!"

She shook her head as her eyes wandered and were now fixated on something else, something on the perfectly made bed.

There was a single stuffed animal.

A little tattered stuffed horse.

It was a little-known fact that all little girls have a favorite childhood toy that they will keep forever.

On that little bed was the horsey that was held tight through a dozen cases of flu and colds, cried into when the first boy she loved broke her heart, and hugged tightly at every horror movie sleepover pajama party.

Eastman smiled and turned to Durazo, who was staring at the poster of RuPaul.

"What are your thoughts, sergeant? What are we missing?"

Durazo looked around the room slowly and back to Eastman, then walked over and peeked at the back of the bedroom door. It was clean. "That design. What did you call it before, ma'am, the sign?"

Eastman smiled. "A sigil."

Durazo snapped his fingers as he was given the word his mind was chasing. "That's right. I haven't seen one here yet. Any chance there's one we are missing?"

Eastman walked to the center of the room. She placed her hand over her heart and closed her eyes to inhale deeply. She held her breath for what seemed like a full minute, then as she slowly opened her eyes, she took in every minute detail of the room.

"What am I not seeing? What's out of place?"

Her eyes fell back on the bed: the perfectly made bed.

The bed with an exact four-inch crease on the turndown of the covers.

The bed with the perfectly fluffed pillows.

The bed was burning. It was screaming.

Eastman walked up to the head of the bed and took a corner of the sheet and comforter in her hand and held it close. She took in a deep breath, and in one fluid movement, she pulled the comforter and sheet off the perfectly made bed.

And there, in the nine hundred thread count white cotton sheets, was the missing hand, holding an iPhone, laying in the middle of the sigil, that was once again painted with the blood of the victim.

"Sweet Jesus," Durazo whispered in sharp red horror.

Eastman stared at the sigil stained into the sheets, the sigil that had soaked through into the mattress pad.

Eastman turned to Durazo, a forest fire burning in her eyes. "Our beast has come out of the woods and into the field to hunt, sergeant, and he's not going to stop. He's not going to stop until we stop him."

Durazo shook his head. "We are going to get him soon. Aren't we, agent?"

Melantha sneered. "I think it's time that the hunter becomes the hunted. And I do believe it's time for us to declare open season on beasts. Would you agree, sergeant?"

ANTI-SOCIAL MEDIA

You must not lose faith in humanity. Humanity is an ocean; if a few drops of the ocean are dirty, the ocean does not become dirty.

—Mahatma Gandhi

Bzzzzz. Bzzzzz. Bzzzz.

Jesse was awakened by the sound of his phone buzzing on his nightstand.

With eyes still closed, he reached for the device, groping blindly in the dark. He forced one eye open and looked at the time and the notifications: 3:14 a.m.

Facebook messenger: three notifications from Katia Berlin.

Jesse rolled onto his back, cradling his phone in his hand. With some considerable effort, he willed his other eye open and swiped right on the notification.

3:10 a.m. Katia Berlin: *"are you up?"*

3:10 a.m. Katia Berlin: *"I'm freaking out!"*

3:11 a.m. Katia Berlin: *"nvm."*

Jesse typed his reply: *"I'm here, what's up?"* He sat and watched the message go from 'sent' to 'read.'

The "they're typing" bubble popped up, then disappeared, appeared, and went away again. Two minutes passed, and there was still no reply. *"Katia?"*

She immediately responded: *"I'm freaking out!"*

Jesse's brow furrowed as he typed his response: *"What's up? I'm here."*

Katia: *"I don't know. I'm freaking out!"*

Jesse raised an eyebrow as he read the frantic text. *"What happened?"*

Katia: *"I don't know, I'm freaking out."*

Jesse grimaced at his glowing screen and chose his next words carefully. *"Whatever it is, you can talk to me, I won't judge you."*

The "they're typing" bubble came up, then disappeared, then came up, and disappeared for a second time.

She's trying to express herself, but she's scared. Jesse knew a thing or two about anxiety and how sometimes finding the right words or trying to piece the fractured mosaic of emotions together in a cognitive, coherent, meaningful way wasn't as easy as we had hoped.

Jesse: *"Are you home? Are you safe?"*

Katia: *"yes and yes."*

Jesse: *"Did anything happen, or are you just freaking out?"*

Katia: *"just freaking out."*

Jesse: *"Oh, that's great news! :)"*

Katia: *"????"*

Jesse: *"Congratulations, you're a human being, and you're totally allowed to freak out and have breakdowns. I do all the time. :)"*

The last message sat and marinated in the chat about two minutes before it was marked as 'read.'

Katia: *"really?"*

Jesse: *"Oh totally, I freak the fuck out and have anxiety attacks constantly. It never ends. That's one of the drawbacks to being awake."*

Katia: *"awake?"*

Jesse shook his head, because he knew she would get it—he knew she was like him. *"Yeah, you know. Plugged in, outside of the matrix . . . The creeping feeling like there is something very wrong with the world, but you can't quite put your finger on it. Feeling like, I'm here for something more, something bigger, but I don't know what. And sometimes I feel like it's slipping through my fingers, and I'll never know what I'm supposed to be doing, or why I'm really here."*

Katia's response came only moments after Jesse sent his message: *"KSJFBDIWIUEJE!!!!!!!! EXACTLY!"*

Jesse: *"There is no spoon."*

Katia: *"OMG."*

Jesse: *"So that's why I freak out. Tell me, why are YOU freaking out right now?"*

Katia: *"I feel like I'm not in my body right now. I feel like I'm not doing enough. I feel . . . stuck."*

Jesse: *"Hmmm tell me more, padawan."*

Katia: *"I feel like, I don't know, like I'm . . ."*

Jesse: *"Like you're just going through the motions?"*

Katia: *"EXACTLY!"*

Jesse: *"Good."*

Katia: *"how is that good?"*

Jesse: *"because that means you're growing."*

Katia: *"?"*

Jesse was sitting fully upright in his bed now, his fingers tapping away at his keyboard. *"You know, before a snake sheds its skin, it's temporarily blind. It can't really see where it's going, and it gets very uncomfortable. But after some discomfort, the snake sheds its old skin and is more beautiful than ever. That's the only way it can grow. Maybe that's what's happening to you right now, and perhaps, it's a wonderful thing."*

The message was instantly read, and it sat for over five minutes before Katia responded: *"wow, just . . . wow."*

Jesse looked at the time, 4:25 a.m. He responded: *"You okay?"*

Katia: *"thank you, I feel much better, seriously. thank you."*

Jesse: *"Anytime, and I mean that."*

Katia: *"see you at work?"*

Jesse: *"Absolutely."*

Katia: *"thank you again."*

Jesse: *"Always."*

Jesse woke from his nap covered in sweat and jumped for the phone resting on his nightstand. There were no notifications from Katia—it was just another cruel nightmare. A trick the subconscious mind played on him every day.

He rolled onto his right side and grabbed the pillow she slept on. It was the pillow Katia last slept on, the pillowcase still unchanged, unwashed.

Jesse held the pillow close and sobbed into it.

"Okay, sergeant. Call your team in. I'm good here." Eastman took off her latex gloves and put them into the back pocket of her dark blue jeans.

Durazo grabbed the transmitter of his Motorola radio that was attached to the upper right shoulder of his body armor. "Forensics? You can come in. Over."

There was an immediate reply over his walkie-talkie. "Copy that. Over."

Durazo looked around the room, then back to Eastman. "What's next, ma'am?" Durazo asked Eastman as she scrolled through her Instagram feed on her phone.

Eastman was humming to herself as she scrolled. "Where's Mom now?" Eastman asked without looking up from her feed.

"She's at the station. She asked to stay there for a while. She didn't feel safe anywhere else."

"Well, I suppose we should go have a word with her. I have a feeling she will be able to give some insight to some patterns and behaviors that—" Eastman's eyes scanned the room and landed on a postcard that was addressed and sent to the victim. "—Dani may have been exhibiting in the last few weeks that may have something to do with this."

"You already have a good idea who's doing this, don't you, agent?"

Eastman looked to Durazo. "I have a gut feeling. Let's go see Mom." As Eastman walked out the front door with Durazo by her side, the forensics team started to catalog and categorize the house.

"Ready for some fun, Durazo?" Eastman said as she made a bee-line toward the waiting news vans and crowd of reporters still being held behind the yellow lines of police tape by the deputies.

Durazo shook his head and huffed. "Oh shit, here we go."

She turned to Durazo and with a raised eyebrow whispered back, "You trust me, don't you, sergeant?"

Durazo didn't hesitate. "Yes, ma'am!"

Eastman smirked. "Then let's have some fun!"

A dozen waiting reporters started firing questions at the petite blonde as she approached the makeshift barricade the sheriff's department had set up.

Eastman opened the back of her SUV, reached into her kit. and produced her FBI badge. She leaned in and whispered to Durazo, who was now standing stiffly beside her, looking at the dozen or so reporters that were waiting with bated breath for any statement the sheriff's department would be willing to give.

Eastman gave Durazo a playful nudge with her elbow. "This is my favorite part, Durazo. Ready from some X-Files shit?"

Before Durazo knew what was happening, Eastman's voice boomed above the murmuring crowd of reporters.

"Ladies and gentlemen. my name is Special Agent Eastman with the FBI!"

The hush that fell over the crowd was only broken by the sounds of pens scribbling on notepads and cameramen scrambling to start recording.

"A terrible crime was committed here. Myself, along with Sergeant Durazo, will be giving a formal press conference at the Briggs station in exactly one hour. Thank you, that is all."

As soon as she punctuated her sentence, the crowd of reporters erupted into another frenzied fury of questions.

Eastman turned her back and, with the cocksure stride of an old west gunslinger, started back to her SUV. "You like that, Durazo?"

Durazo winced. "You're going to be on every news station in Los Angeles, maybe even the whole country! What do you plan on saying?"

"I think it's time we catch this beast. Don't you, sergeant?"

"Yes, ma'am!"

"Well, how do you catch a beast, sergeant?"

Durazo cracked a smile as he looked at Eastman. "Set a trap?"

She smiled back while nodding her head. "And Bingo was his name-o. Let's see if we can stir the pot and fluster him a little."

Durazo nodded back. "Yes, Ma'am!"

Fifteen minutes later, the black SUV pulled into the entryway of the employee only section of the sheriff's station.

Eastman parked, rolled up the limo-tinted windows, and pulled down the sun visor. She slowly put both hands on the steering wheel and started squeezing. Her fists shook and all color had drained out of them from the force she was exerting. All at once, she exploded in a scream of rage that turned into uncontrollable sobs.

To quickly gain back her composure, Eastman slapped herself and grabbed a tissue from her purse, wiped the smeared mascara from her cheeks, and gave herself a quick once over. As soon as she had finished, she noticed that Durazo had pulled in and parked next to her.

She looked into the mirror of her sun visor, making sure she had no signs of having just melted down, then got out of her truck and nodded to the big man as he closed the door to his cruiser.

"Hello, sergeant, are you ready for the spotlight?"

"Hello, agent. I hate the media. I hate these fucking press conference things. Total clusterfuck, dog and pony show."

"Well, then, Sergeant Sunshine, I have good news for you. I'm going to handle it. All you have to do is stand next to me and look official."

Durazo chuckled while shaking his head. "That's the best news I've heard all day."

Eastman's face took on a serious expression. "But first, let's go see Mom."

"Yes, ma'am. I already called ahead. She's waiting for us in my office."

Durazo led Eastman into the back of the sheriff's station, past the several jail cells they had on site, and into his private office. Eastman stopped Durazo before they opened the door. "What's the last name, sergeant?"

"Ackles."

Durazo opened the door and held it for Eastman.

There sat a woman in her mid-fifties, but still quite attractive by conventional beauty standards. She was just starting to show wisps of gray in her hair, but to Eastman's way of thinking, that made her even more beautiful.

"Hello, Mrs. Ackles? My name is Melantha Eastman. I'm a forensic psychologist and a special agent with the FBI. I know you have been through a lot today, but I was wondering if it would be okay with you if we could have a talk about Danielle. Maybe you could share some insight into her behavior over the last couple weeks that might help us in finding the monster that did this to her." Eastman paused. "If that's okay?"

Mrs. Ackles looked up at Eastman with a blank expression. Her hollow eyes were bloodshot from the torrent of tears she had let go that morning, tears that were still coming and going in waves, like a storm.

Her hands were wringing a tissue that was now disintegrating. It was shedding off microfibers into the air, that floated lazily to the floor beneath her feet.

The biggest fear any parent has is the loss of a child. But to find your only daughter, your legacy, like that?

Eastman slowly pulled up a chair and placed it next to Mrs. Ackles, beside her. She offered her hand to Mrs. Ackles.

The woman looked down at Eastman's outstretched hand. After a long moment, she slowly, gently took it into hers.

"I'm here for you, Mrs. Ackles. I'm here," Eastman whispered as she gave the woman's hand a squeeze.

"Please, call me Judy," the woman whispered back. She was still staring forward at the wall, or maybe at nothing.

"Thank you, Judy. Is it okay to talk for a couple of minutes?"

The woman drew in a slow stuttering breath. "Yes."

Eastman spoke to the woman in a hushed tone, slightly above a whisper. Her voice was calm yet soothing. "Tell me about Dani. Has she said or done anything in the last couple of weeks that was unusual? Or maybe . . . out of the ordinary for her?"

Judy just shook her head and whispered, "No. Well, not really. I have been gone for eleven days. I . . . I never should have left."

"Why? Why shouldn't you have left, Judy?"

"Dani was always a good girl. She was a kind girl . . . She had lots of friends. She . . . she was always popular and did well in school. Well, until about six months ago. That's when her grades fell apart, and she decided to drop out."

Eastman's eyebrows quirked. "Grades?"

"Yeah. She just . . . stopped caring. She stopped caring about everything she worked so hard for. She started changing everything."

"What changed?"

"She wouldn't open up to me anymore. We . . . we used to be

so close, like sisters. Ever since Steve, her father, died. We were a team. We were taking on the world together." Judy gathered herself. "What changed? Well, Dani started wearing a lot more black and writing really dark poems. I thought it was just a phase, you know? Dramatic college kid stuff. But . . . it was more than that. She started isolating herself from all her friends. They would call, and she would just ignore them—girls she was close with since elementary school. They would call the house phone and ask me if she was okay. I would lie to them and tell them she was just busy."

Judy shook her head. She let go of Eastman's hand and started tightly twisting the scraps of tissue again.

"She would stay up all hours of the night, locked in her room. She hardly ever left that room . . . She was on her phone constantly, and the music she used to love, what she grew up listening to, was gone. Replaced with the only thing she would listen to, which was this creepy classical music. She blocked me and the rest of her family on Facebook. But not before she deleted all her old pictures and replaced them with only black and white photos of herself . . . Like I said, I thought it was a phase. Something she would grow out of—at least I hoped that she would.

"I tried to talk to her, like how we used to talk. She would just get angry and ramble this incoherent nonsense back to me. About how she wanted to be 'a beacon' or something . . . No, I'm sure of it. She would tell me that she was working to become 'a beacon.' Something about having to be 'pure enough' . . . She would scream and cry because she wasn't 'pure enough.'"

Eastman's body became noticeably tense as those words escaped Judy's mouth. She glanced over to Durazo, who was scribbling down notes, but he paused as she caught his eye.

"She was always reading these, these books."

Eastman's ears perked up. "Books?" She thought back to the bookcase in Dani's room. She would have remembered seeing anything out of the ordinary.

"Yeah, about archangels. No, wait, that's not it . . . Arch . . . Arch . . . ." Judy was struggling to find the word.

Eastman offered an assist. "Archetypes?"

"Yes, archetypes! That's it. I hid those books from her in the garage, and . . . she had a fit. I . . . I was just trying to get the old Dani back."

"Is there anything else that jumps out at you, Judy? Anything at all you can remember?"

"Well, no, not really. Except . . ."

"Except?"

"Dani became obsessed with drinking tea."

Eastman's eyes went wide. "Tea?"

Judy nodded. "Yes, tea. She would come home with huge packages of it . . . She would spend all day at this tea shop."

"Tea shop?" Eastman glanced up to Durazo, who was still jotting down notes as fast as he could.

"Yes, she would go there and hang out all day. At least that's what she told me she was doing."

"Do you know where this tea shop is, Judy?"

Durazo froze.

"No, no, Dani never said. I was just happy to get that much out of her. "

"Thank you, Judy. Is it okay if I contact you in a couple days to see how you're doing?"

Judy nodded slowly.

Eastman put her hand on Judy's shoulder. "Do you have anyone you can call or stay with?"

Judy looked down at her hands.

"My sister lives in Eagle Rock. I'm going to go stay with her for a couple days."

"Okay, I think that is a good idea. Here is my card." Eastman took out her card and put it in Mrs. Ackles' hands, then she took Judy's hands in hers, and in a soft voice said, "I'm going to find the person that did this to Dani. I promise you, Judy, I'm going to find him."

Judy let out a gentle sob as she squeezed Eastman's hands. "Thank you, Doctor Eastman, thank you."

Eastman stood up out of the chair next to Judy and started to turn toward the door.

Judy reached out and grabbed her wrist as she started walking, stopping Eastman in her tracks.

"When you do find him, you make him pay for this. Make him pay for what he did to my Dani."

Eastman nodded and walked to the door of the office, paused, and turned back to Judy. "Mrs. Ackles, would you like one of our deputies to escort you to your sister's house?"

"Yes, please."

"Okay, please wait for just a moment, I'll find someone to go with you."

Durazo closed the door of his office where Judy Ackles was still sitting—alone again.

Eastman was already on her way to the pool of reporters that were set up in front of the sheriff's station on Briggs Avenue.

Durazo quickened his pace to catch up with the young agent. "A moment of your time, Ma'am?"

Eastman paused, turned to Durazo, and looked up at the big man.

"Did you get anything out of that line of questioning with Mrs. Ackles?" he asked.

"Yes." Eastman started to turn to continue to the main exit doors of the station.

"Ma'am, can you please share anything with me?" Durazo's question caused Eastman to stop and pause again. "We have had two similar murders, no clues, no real evidence—we have nothing. But something Mrs. Ackles said in there meant something to you. That thing about a . . ." Durazo glanced down at his scribbled notes. "Something she said about being a 'pure beacon' struck a nerve with you. And the tea house . . . Can you please tell me what your train of thought is here?"

Eastman turned to Durazo, not looking at him, but through him. She was off in her own realm of thoughts and possibilities, a million miles away. "Everything is everything, sergeant. Everything is connected. And all the pieces we have put together so far tell me one thing, and it's worse than you can possibly imagine."

Eastman looked up and focused on the big man who stood in front of her. "Durazo, do you remember Ramirez?"

"Yes, ma'am, I was a young deputy during the Night Stalker days in the mid-eighties."

"Do you remember how it was reported that he only went after people with yellow houses?"

Durazo nodded. "Yeah, people were so afraid, they were painting their homes. If they couldn't afford to paint, they would stay with friends or family."

Eastman sighed and shook her head. "You see, it's all a matter of perception, sergeant. You say there was a homicide, people say, 'that's a shame,' or 'that's strange for this area.' The people read about it in the local paper while drinking their wine at the local restaurant. Then they go on with their lives. But you say, 'We have a serial killer on the loose,' and you have a whole city living in fear . . ."

Eastman paused, letting her words sink in before continuing. "I have a pretty good idea of what we're looking at here, sergeant. This is going to be the case of your life. We aren't hunting some wannabe sloppy loser like Ramirez. We are tracking a monster. We are pursuing the beast, and to catch the beast, you must become that which you hunt. And everyone wants to be a beast. until it's time to do what beasts do . . ." Eastman sighed as she trailed off, and her eyes wandered past Durazo once again.

"It's press time," she declared simply. "After this, see how many tea houses are in the greater Los Angeles area . . . but that sounds like a story that Dani told her mom to make her feel better about where she was really going. What young girl would go hang out at a tea house?"

Durazo shrugged his shoulders. "Well, it's a start, agent. It's a start."

"I wouldn't waste too much of your time on the 'tea house,' sergeant."

Eastman turned to Durazo as they resumed their brisk pace toward the press conference waiting for them outside.

"It's time for our beast to feel some fear. He may be a monster, but I'm Queen fucking Kong."

And with that, the tiny blonde doctor pushed through the doors and dove into the ocean of bright news camera lights. Melantha stepped up to the podium that the deputies had set up in front of the station on Briggs Avenue and greeted the crowd.

WHAT'S LEFT OF JESSE

Death is not the greatest loss in life.

The greatest loss is what dies inside us while we live.

—Norman Cousins

PEARLS BEFORE SWINE

No act of kindness, no matter how small, is ever wasted.

—-Aesop

"Ladies and gentlemen, if I may have your attention, please. First, I would like to thank you all for your patience, and I would also like to thank you in advance for your cooperation in this ongoing investigation . . ."

Eastman looked out into the two-dozen people crowded into the small courtyard of the Briggs sheriff station, and she waited until all eyes were on her. The group of reporters hushed.

"My name is Melantha Eastman. I am a special agent with the FBI, and I am leading this investigation with the assistance of Sergeant Durazo and his team of local law enforcement professionals, as well as other local, state, and federal agencies." Eastman motioned to Durazo, who was standing like a mannequin beside her. Durazo looked at the crowd and gave the nod.

"This press conference is being held in hopes to ensure the peace, dignity, and tranquility of the citizens of this community."

The sounds of digital cameras clicking were music to Eastman's ears as she chose her words precisely to have the impact she desired. She wanted every word, every sentence to land as planned.

"This evening, as we advise you and the community of our findings, there have been three slayings that all seem to be connected in the last six months, all within the greater Los Angeles area. We have the families of the three victims in our hearts, and in our prayers."

"Three?" Eastman heard Durazo say in a surprised whisper under his breath.

Eastman didn't pause from her speech—did nothing to acknowledge his question.

"On behalf of those families and this community, we want to thank you again for your cooperation in this investigation. That being said, it should be noted that this investigation is still underway. Therefore, some of your questions may not be immediately answered. However, I do wish to grant you, the media, some brief time after this short conference for questions. We are committed to bringing you accurate and timely information as it becomes known to us and does not compromise the integrity of this investigation."

Eastman glanced over to Durazo. She could feel his eyes burning into her.

"Thank you. Now I will take time briefly to answer some of your questions."

A sea of hands shot up in the air as cameras clicked and flashbulbs flashed. Eastman pointed at a young man in the first row. "Yes, you?"

"Were all the victims female?"

"Yes."

Eastman scanned the crowd and pointed to another reporter.

"Why do you think the murders are related?"

"The patterns we have observed at the scene, and the way the victims were killed is indicative of the murders being conducted by the same individual. Next?"

"Do we have a serial killer on the loose?"

Eastman smiled and gave Durazo a sideways glance. "I am not at liberty to say . . . Next?"

"What are the names of the victims?"

"As I said, the investigation is ongoing. We are not prepared to release the victims' names at this time. Next?"

"Do we have a serial killer on our hands, agent? The people have a right to know if they are in danger."

"We are doing everything in our power right now to make sure the citizens here in the foothills, and throughout Los Angeles, are safe. Next and final question."

A young female reporter stepped forward and addressed Eastman with a smile. "Doctor Eastman, I have been following your career for the last couple of years. I respect your work very much. As a matter of fact, you're an inspiration to me. But the problem is, doctor, I know who you are, and I know what you do. If this wasn't a serial killer case, you wouldn't be here. Your investigations apprehended the Chicago Butcher earlier this year, and the Bus Stop Strangler in New York last year." The reporter paused as the others started murmuring around her.

"With all due respect, Doctor Eastman, if you don't mind, my question is two-fold."

Eastman smiled and nodded at the young reporter. She adored her chutzpah.

"First, do you have a profile of the killer? And second, do we have a serial killer loose in Los Angeles?"

Eastman looked out to the crowd and saw Judy Ackles and the deputy assigned to escort her to her sister's house stop. They both turned and waited for her reply. Eastman locked eyes with Judy, and Mrs. Ackles gave the young doctor a slight nod as if to say, *It's okay, do it!*

Eastman turned to the pool of reporters waiting in silence for her response. She looked at the young female reporter and gave her a wink.

"The suspect in question is most likely a white male in his mid-fifties to mid-sixties. He is calm and calculated when he commits these crimes. How he chooses his victims is still unknown. The victims have all been young women, alone in their homes, which to my way of thinking, makes him weak, makes him a coward."

Eastman focused in on a single camera, staring directly at it as if she was looking the killer in the eyes.

"That makes you weak. That makes you a coward. You may have planned and plotted each of your killings—you may think you have committed the perfect crime, that you will never be caught—but there was one thing you couldn't have planned for, one thing you could never have anticipated . . ."

Eastman looked into the camera and raised a single, perfectly shaped brow.

"Me."

With that final word, Eastman turned and walked back into the sheriff's station with Durazo following briskly to keep up.

The crowd of reporters erupted into a roar of questions as flashbulbs from every direction created a dance of the shadows over Eastman and Durazo as they neared the big double entry doors of the station.

Eastman turned again to the crowd and saw Judy Ackles, still standing with her deputy, and for the first time that day, Judy Ackles smiled.

Jesse sat in the big leather chair in his living room in silence.

The first light of dawn crept through the windows facing east behind him, casting his shadow faintly on the wood floor of the living room.

Jesse's mother had brought over a new area rug for the room after the place was cleaned and sanitized by a biohazard cleanup crew. She had hoped that it would change the room enough so that Jesse wouldn't still see Katia in pieces on the floor—the floor two feet in front of him right now.

It didn't.

Jesse looked around the room.

The television that hadn't been turned on since that night was nearly obscured by stacks of unopened letters. Some were condolence cards, but most were red-framed utility bills with the bold printing "FINAL NOTICE" across each envelope.

Piles of Loki's hair congregated in the corners of the room and bunched in piles on the area rug.

The bookcase was still filled with the photos of their life and the treasures and found-off-the-beaten-path keepsakes from their road trips and adventures together.

Remember when she was there on the floor in pieces? That voice in Jesse's mind hissed at him again. That little black and scratchy raspy voice. *You should have been here. It's your fault. It's all your fault.*

Jesse sat motionlessly, watching his shadow slowly stretch across the hardwood floor.

I wonder if she was calling out for you when she died?

Jesse sat, listening to that little voice grow louder.

Remember when you were calling her and it was going straight to voicemail?

Jesse took a deep breath in and held it.

That's when he was slitting her throat, Jesse. That's when he was draining her. Right there on that very spot.

Jesse slowly stood from his chair and walked into the room with the bed.

He sat down on his side of the bed and opened the drawer of his nightstand slowly and deliberately. He took out the Valentine's Day card from Katia.—the one he'd happened upon the other day before the hike with Andy. He held the heavy stock paper in his hands and read the card, then placed it back in the drawer.

Jesse got up and walked over to the big sliding closet doors and opened them. All of Katia's clothes were still hung in the closet. Her dozens of pairs of shoes were still arranged neatly in rows on the floor or placed in the hanging shoe rack.

Jesse closed the closet door and walked to the door of the room with the bed in it, and gently, gently he closed the door.

On the back of the door hung Katia's scarf rack. Jesse gently pulled one of her favorites down: a black, white, and red silk number she could pair with anything. He brought it to his nose, closed his eyes, and inhaled deeply. The scent was faint, but it was there—lingering like a ghost in the wool fibers of that scarf.

It was there.

The smell of her hair.

He inhaled again.

The natural oils of her skin. The sugar scrub body washes she would use every day.

Jesse's breaths became more rapid in succession. His hands turned into fists, pulling and twisting the silk into a savage wrinkled tapestry. His breathing was no longer deep and rooted, but it had escalated to the shallow, rapid, anxious breathing of a frightened animal.

Tears blurred his vision and streamed down his face, and his mind was a thunderstorm of violet, red, and white flashes. A short-circuiting high voltage charge of raw emotion, a hurricane of hate and rage.

There were no thoughts—just images. Just seething hate pointed outward.

The blast radius of this hurt and misery could have shifted the tectonic plates and been registered, studied, and measured on seismographs by scientists a continent away.

In this moment, his violent outpouring of this hate, this rage, this evil, it all rushed back to Jesse like a pack of ravenous wolves and tore Jesse's legs out from under him.

He dropped onto the floor, and on that floor, he screamed.

All that hate and rage now pointed inward—pointed at himself.

He tumbled off the precipice and into the abyss. The rage

engulfed him.

IT'S YOUR FAULT THIS HAPPENED! The voice, no longer a raspy whisper, but now a train whistle, an alarm, an air raid siren in his mind, screamed in his mind over and over: *YOUR FAULT! YOUR FAULT! YOUR FAULT!*

Vision blurred, ears ringing, and on his knees, Jesse looked down at the scarf, now a tourniquet choking his purple and red fingers.

And then, all at once . . . Silence.

Jesse jumped to his feet and ran to the nightstand by his side of the bed. He picked it up and hurled it, lamp and all, across the room. The heavy antique wood shattered and splintered, leaving a knuckle-deep gouge in the wall. He ran to the closet and flung the door open so hard it came off the rail and fell to the floor.

Jesse reached into the closet with both hands and grabbed the biggest armful of Katia's clothes that he could. He threw the sweaters, custom tailored dresses, and blouses against the wall, the clothes making a muffled thud, and the hangers sounding like the clattering of skeletons as they danced against the drywall.

He turned to her big antique dresser, and in one clothesline swoop of his arm, flung all of Katia's little knickknacks, her little treasures, her small altar against the wall. Her prized possessions ricocheted like stray bullets around the room.

He pulled each drawer out and upended it, dumping all Katia's favorite lingerie, Katia's socks, Katia's t-shirts, Katia's jeans, into a pile, like a burial mound in the center of the room with a bed.

In tears, Jesse tore the keys off his belt loop and made for his safe.

He fumbled and dropped them as he tried to unlock the standing locker safe in the corner of Katia's closet. He was successful getting it unlocked on the second try and flung the door open.

He reached in blindly and grabbed his Glock 19.

AH-HAHAHAH!

The voice that had still been shrieking this entire time was now laughing, taunting, and squealing with delight and joy. It had the sound of children's laughter mixed with the screams of pigs being slaughtered.

Jesse fell on his knees in the pile of his dead wife's belongings, the smell of her engulfing him.

Sobbing and suffering, Jesse put the loaded gun in his mouth.

The metal tasted almost pleasant. Jesse fought hard to pull that trigger.

He really did.

Everything inside of him wanted to. But his finger—his finger just wouldn't listen. He threw the Glock against the floor, and it bounced off the carpet and hit the closed door of the room.

There was nothing left of Jesse at that moment.

Nothing.

Exhausted, Jesse fell asleep there in the nest of Katia's clothes.

Jesse woke hours later to the pocket of his jeans vibrating. He looked around the room, at the chaos and the destruction—the spectacle of it all.

He looked at the window to see it was now nighttime, the sun having long since dipped into the western sky.

It took a couple seconds for Jesse to realize that his phone was still vibrating. He reached into his pocket and pulled it out. It took him another moment for his eyes to focus and be able to read the bright screen in the now darkened room: "Blocked ID."

Jesse swiped right and accepted the call.

"Hello?" Jesse managed to spit out, the back of his throat still sore from the scratching of his Glock's front sights.

"Hello, Jess, it's Melantha . . . It's Doctor Eastman."

"Hello, Doctor Eastman."

"Hi, I want to see you. If I lure you with some coffee, can I count on you to come by tomorrow morning?"

"Sure . . . I think that would be okay."

"Great. Does 8:00 a.m. work for you, Jess?"

There was a pause. "Sure, sounds good."

"Perfection."

There was a pause on the line again, then Eastman spoke. "You okay?"

Jesse looked around the destroyed mess of the room with a bed, the splintered furniture, the piles of clothes, the broken glass, the shattered memories.

"Yeah, same as always."

"Good. See you at eight!"

The phone disconnected.

Jesse curled back up in the nest of clothes went back to sleep—deep sleep, where for the first time in months, he was still and silent, immersed in dreamless, black oblivion.

"Three?"

Eastman looked up to Durazo as she put her phone back into her oversized purse. "Yes, sergeant, three." She threw her purse over her shoulder and started making her way toward the rear exit of the station.

"When were you planning on telling me this, agent?"

Eastman shook her head. "I had to be sure." She looked over to Durazo, not breaking stride on her way out into the parking lot.

"Sure of what? We are supposed to be a team. I need to be kept in the loop on the happenings of this case. I—I have a responsibility to my community!"

Eastman sighed; she could hear the desperation in Durazo's voice. "Believe me, I understand that, sergeant." As she unlocked her SUV, she threw her purse into the passenger seat.

"Ma'am, will you please wait a minute and speak to me!"

Eastman paused and turned to Durazo. She sighed again and looked up at the big man, who was clearly frustrated but still showing her the respect that she required of him.

"About six months ago, before the Silver murder, a body turned up in Santa Monica. The murder of a young girl, twenty-three years old . . . She was a student at FIDM found by her ex-boyfriend. Very similar to what we have here."

"Why didn't you tell me about this, agent?"

"Sometimes, Durazo, the hardest part of catching monsters is waiting for the beast to grow hungry again. We know there is a beast out there, sergeant. We know that he is hunting, but I had to be sure."

Eastman placed her hand on Durazo's shoulder. She gently squeezed. "In reality, sergeant, you and I both know that we are not in the crime prevention business. We seldom ever catch anyone in the act. We are the ones that pick up the pieces and clean up the mess after the damage has already been done.

"We are the ones who have to tell the families that after today, their lives will never be the same again. How many times have you had to do that, sergeant? How many times have you had to tell some worried parents that their son or daughter won't be coming home ever again because of some drunk driver? How many times have you seen those faces of shock, hurt, and disbelief?"

Durazo looked down at the ground as if he were fighting back memories.

"I'm sure you have had a bellyful of it. The breed of monster—the species of the beast I hunt isn't some drunk behind the wheel. It isn't some gangbanger looking to earn his stripes or some junky kid who accidentally gets walked in on by an old lady while he's burglarizing her house. The beast I hunt is a super predator, a killing machine . . . It lives for the hunt. This beast is efficient and patient. It can be gone in an instant and vanish forever back into the woods. And the families . . . the families of the victims will be left with nothing."

Eastman gave Durazo's shoulder another light squeeze. "That's why I didn't say anything to you, sergeant. I had to wait for the pattern, the spiral, the sequence to reveal itself."

"Do you think he's done, agent?" Durazo asked as he brought his gaze from the floor up to Eastman's.

"The beast has a taste for flesh now, and the hunt is just getting started, sergeant. He's looking for something. He's on the hunt for someone special. Remember when we were talking to Judy, and she mentioned that Dani was obsessed with becoming a 'beacon'? That reminded me of something I haven't thought about in years. I have a feeling our beast isn't going to stop until he finds this 'beacon' of his. I just hope that we can get to him before . . ." Eastman's words trailed off as she got lost in her own mind.

Durazo stared at her in anticipation of her next word. After a couple seconds of silence, he broke Eastman out of the spell she was under. "Before what, ma'am?"

Eastman snapped back to reality and looked up to Durazo. "Before he finds her," she states. "If he finds this beacon, I'm not sure if we, or anyone, will be able to stop him."

Eastman opened the door to her SUV, climbed in, and drove away without saying another word, leaving Durazo in the parking lot.

DIVING DEEP

Who controls the past controls the future. Who controls the present controls the past.

—George Orwell

Jesse catapulted up from yet another nightmare. The night terrors have become routine. The ritual of it all: the night sweats, the dizzying confusion, the throbbing temples—it had become almost comforting.

Almost.

Jesse was still lying in the pile of Katia's clothes. The nest he had slept in cocooned around him and a thin sticky layer of sweat covering his body.

He blindly pawed around in the dark for his phone. After feeling in the mess of sweaters, dresses, shoes, and shirts—success! He brought the screen up to his face, and the phone instantly illuminated: 5:51 a.m.

Jesse got up and out of the nest in the same clothes from yesterday, and he put on his ratty Nike cross trainers. As he opened the door, Loki looked up from his resting place on the floor. He came over straight away to lick his master's face.

"C'mon, big boy, let's go for a walk." Jesse put the leash on the now excited pup and walked the mile to The Black Cow Café. Jesse got his iced coffee, made small talk with the morning staff, and headed straight out the door with Loki. While he started back down the street, he glanced down at his phone. It was nearly 7:00 a.m. He had to be in Pasadena in an hour.

When Jesse got home, he started his typical lukewarm shower—something that had also become routine at this point. He would stare at the water running down the drain. He would get in the shower and just stand there like a statue, hoping the water would cleanse his soul from the constant blitzkrieg of nocturnal hauntings that cradled him while he "slept."

It was a constant life of just starting to fall asleep, and then being woken up by the jarring feeling of falling. That's what even the waking hours felt like now.

His usually well-kept, close-cut beard was now scraggly and a bit longer than it should be for business. He didn't even care at this point anymore. It was one more thing to add to the list of the ever-evolving shitshow that had become his life.

Jesse got out of the shower and stood there, dripping and staring at his reflection in the bathroom mirror.

Jesse observed his pupils constricting and retracting to the size of pinholes. Behind the black pools in the center of his big hazel eyes, there was a vacuum. He could feel every molecule of oxygen entering his lungs. He could hear his heart beating and the blood pumping through his veins. He felt nothing. He was an empty vessel. He was nothing.

He was staring at nothing.

And the nothing was starting to stare back at him.

Life wasn't supposed to be like this. Every day *was* an adventure, everything *was* unique.

Now, every day was the same.

Everything was empty and meaningless.

Nothing had a weight or purpose to it anymore.

He was a robot, programmed to eat, sleep, shower, repeat.

This isn't how it was supposed to be. Jesse glanced at his phone and wiped away the condensation that had formed on the screen: 7:35

a.m.

He went to the room with the bed and stepped over the mound of clothes that was still covering the majority of the floor. He took out a clean pair of boxer briefs and put on the same dark blue jeans with the black leather belt he had been wearing for—how many days now? He wasn't sure.

Not that it mattered at all anyway.

Jesse slipped on some socks and a pair of black leather sneakers, then put on a black V-neck t-shirt.

Jesse always used to look great, but now, he wore the same clothes every day. Day in and day out. He took Loki to the backyard, made sure he had ample food and water, grabbed his keys, and was out the door and on his way to his appointment.

Jesse said a silent prayer as he sent the text: *"Meet me at my lodge. I have to walk it and make sure it's secure, and it's just a couple blocks from your place. I'll give you the VIP tour."*

Katia: *"Lodge?"*

Jesse: *"Yes, the Masonic temple on Magnolia and Tujunga. You live in North Hollywood, right?"*

Jesse knew precisely where Katia lived—it had come up in conversation a couple times. The kind of small talk where you learn a lot about people. What they like to eat, where they live, their favorite things.

Now that Jesse and Katia had been friends for about two years, they had developed a familiar trust, a consistency of kindness, respect, and communication.

Katia was living with her boyfriend in North Hollywood. He was much older than she was; Jesse didn't know how much older, but Katia had told Jesse that her boyfriend was older than he was. And apparently, things were not going too well.

Trouble in paradise.

He typed out another text: *"It will take 15 minutes. it's creepy and haunted, and I'd love to show you some places women aren't typically allowed to see."*

Katia: *"I know where that is. I'll meet you there in a couple minutes."*

Jesse waited in the empty parking lot of the old historic building.

The temple was quite large. In fact, it was three stories. As creepy at night as you could expect a big, old, historic building to be when it was dark and deserted.

One of Jesse's duties, and the other Masons that were members there, was to, if convenient, stop by the lodge on nights when nothing was happening and walk the perimeter, then go inside and make sure that the building was secure: no lights were left on, and no plumbing was leaking or flooding—as it often did.

Jesse wasn't bullshitting when he said the building was haunted. A couple Masons had died on premises—not because of anything to do with Masonry; it just had to do with them being old.

Jesse wasn't scared of them though. They were his brothers, and he was there to protect the lodge. His lodge, their lodge, the lodge.

It wasn't unusual to hear footsteps in the big lodge room or whispers coming from the darkened corners.

The black and white checkered floors did play with the imagination, and it was hard to play off as coincidence or tricks of the mind when you're the only person in a five-thousand-square-foot pitch black room, and you clearly hear footsteps coming up behind you—echoing on the tiled floors.

Sometimes you could *feel* someone or something standing there.

Jesse loved it. He would have been happy to have anyone join him when he walked the lodge. But to have *Katia* there—well, that was a whole different situation. A fantasy he had played out many times in his mind, and the fantasy always started out just like how tonight was going.

Jesse looked up as the headlights of the white Ford Escape as it pulled into the parking lot, casting long shadows and temporarily ruining his natural night vision.

Katia pulled in and parked in the far corner of the lot next to where Jesse was leaning against his car. She turned off her car and started getting out.

"Leave your purse," Jesse said as she started to exit.

"Will it be okay?" asked Katia, looking up to Jesse with a smile.

"Of course. Let's get inside."

Katia got out of the car and was wearing a pair of baggy gray sweatpants and a baby-doll t-shirt.

"Thanks so much for coming. This place is creepy at night, and I wanted to share it with you."

Katia just stood there smiling.

"Let's go." Jesse led Katia to the big doors with a combo lock beside them and pressed in the code. A loud click could be heard as the doors unlocked. Jesse turned the handle, and the big doors swung open.

"You ready?" Jesse said, turning to Katia, who was staring into the dark abyss of the building.

The pale glow of the parking lot lamps cast an eerie amber light that bled into the threshold of the huge, dark room.

"Here we go . . ." Jesse reached out and took Katia's hand as he walked her into the building and closed the big door behind him. It was pitch black, and all that could be heard was their breathing. Somewhere in the darkness of the room was the sound of a strange tap, tap, tapping. Jesse, still holding Katia's hand, felt Katia squeeze back—hard.

Katia whispered to Jesse, "What was that sound?"

Jesse gave Katia's hand a squeeze back and whispered, "That's *them*. Come, the light switch is on the other side of the room. I'll lead the way."

Jesse walked Katia through what seemed to be an infinite room of inky blackness, the sound of their footsteps echoing and bouncing off the walls. All at once, they stopped.

"Okay, let there be light!" Jesse flipped an old switch, and the hall illuminated to show a grand ballroom.

Katia squinted and let out a faint gasp as she adjusted to the brightness and size of it all.

"This is an extraordinary place to me. I'm glad I get to share it with you, Katia."

"What is this place? Is it like, like, a church?"

"Not exactly. It's a Masonic temple. Have you heard of the Freemasons?"

"Like in *National Treasure?*"

Jesse smiled. "Yes, like in *National Treasure.*"

"O-M-G. And you're one?" asked Katia, looking up to Jesse with her blue eyes now wide and full of intrigue.

Jesse knew he just got a +1 on the cool points scale.

"Yep." Jesse started walking, and Katia followed. "I know you don't have much time, so I'll show you around real quick."

"Yeah, I told him I was just running out for a pack of smokes."

Jesse took Katia's hand and started leading her up a grand staircase to the second story. "We will be fast."

As they climbed the stairs, Jesse gave Katia a CliffsNotes version on Masonry.

"The Masons have been around for thousands of years." Jesse said. "We are not a secret society, but a society of secrets." The staircase turned to go to the third story. Jesse pointed at the huge paintings on the wall of some of the founding fathers. "Many great men of history have been Masons."

"Like in the movie and the Knights Templar . . . like, is that all true?"

Jesse smiled and looked over to Katia. "Sure is." Jesse turned as he opened a big set of wood doors that led to a small room with another set of wooden doors. Engraved on them was a huge square and compass.

"I've seen that before!"

Jesse walked up to the symbol and rested his hand on it. "We are everywhere," he remarked while turning the knob at the doors that led to the actual lodge room. He was glad to find that it was unlocked—he didn't want to lose his +1 so quickly after gaining it.

"We are the oldest fraternity in the world, and you get to see where we hold our rituals. Women typically aren't allowed in here, and I could get in big trouble for this, but I wanted you to see this. I know you will love it."

Jesse led Katia up to the grand doors. "Go ahead, open the doors."

Katia reached out and opened the great doors with the square and compass engraved on them. The nine-foot-tall doors swung open with a loud creak, and there, another vast, expansive dark room.

Jesse led Katia by the hand into the pitch-black room and closed the door behind them. He guided her in the darkness across the wall to the master light switch for the great lodge room, then gently placed Katia's hand on the switch.

"When you're ready, bring us from darkness to light." Jesse left Katia's hand on the switch.

He could hear her breathing, her heart pounding. He could sense her excitement. After a moment of hesitation, Katia flipped the switch, and the great lodge room lit up in all its glory.

The rich tapestries that hung from the walls of the thirty-foot-tall ceilings and enormous crystal chandelier dazzled the senses. The grand chair of the worshipful master in the east looked larger than life even sixty feet across the room.

Crimson velvet rows of chairs, like those of an old movie theater, lined the walls four rows deep, and in them, Jesse could feel the generations of Masons long dead sitting there, smiling as he, their brother, showed this young woman exactly how important she was to his world.

And in the center of the room: the grand oak altar

"Wow . . ." was the only word that could escape Katia's lips.

"This is my gift to you, Katia. This is what I wanted you to see."

"It's . . . amazing. Thank you . . . Wow, just—thank you, Jesse."

"Thank you, Katia. Let's get you home. Don't want you to get into trouble." Jesse didn't want to get into trouble either. In reality, there wouldn't be a penalty for taking a woman in there during off hours, but it did add to the allure of it all.

Jesse would still rather not be caught by another Mason with a twenty-four-year-old woman in their lodge room. He was an officer at the lodge, and could technically get away with it, but still, bad form is still bad form.

Jesse took Katia by the hand once more and turned off the lights. Hand in hand, they walked down the stairs to the great hall, then over to the light switch opposite the big doors that they came in just ten minutes before.

Jesse looked at Katia as he put his hand on the light switch.

"Ready?" Jesse said with a smile, squeezing the hand that he was still grasping. He didn't want to waste any moment he had to hold her.

"I'm ready," Katia whispered back.

Jesse flipped off the lights, and they were plunged once again into darkness.

Not a single word was spoken as Jesse led Katia back to the big doors that they used to enter the building.

Jesse could feel Katia's pulse-pounding through her hand as they walked. He could, for the first time, feel the heart beating that he hoped one day would beat only for him.

As they approached the big doors, the bleeding amber light from the parking lot still dimly illuminated the doorway, and Jesse paused at the threshold.

Their shadows were swallowed by the darkness of the room behind them, but when Jesse turned to face Katia, he was stricken by the familiar image of her dazzling blue eyes.

"Thank you, Katia."

"Thank you, Jesse."

A moment that seemed like an hour passed as they gazed at each other in the mix of streetlight and moonlight. Jesse continued to hold her hand, to feel her pulse through their touch, and he had made his decision when he felt the spike in her.

"Well, I had better get going," Katia said as she started to turn— but Jesse tugged her back towards him, pulling Katia into him.

And there, standing in the threshold, they embraced for the first time.

Jesse's hands were on her back, then on her hips, pulling Katia's petite frame against his, trying to get closer.

They had parted just enough to look at each other, and in an instant, their lips met. They met with the intensity of years of wanting, Years of patience. Years of friendship. Years of long talks. Years of walks to the car.

Years of, "Bye, Katia."

Years of prayers and years of dreams.

All in that moment, those years were worth it.

And the best part, the very best part?

She was kissing him back—hard.

Katia was the first to pull away—gently—and she looked up at Jesse.

"I . . . I have to go." Katia darted to her Ford Escape as Jesse locked up the big historic building.

She jumped in, and the headlights illuminated the parking lot once again.

As she drove past Jesse, she waved and smiled.

"Bye, Katia," Jesse said aloud as Katia left him once again, standing in the moonlight and starshine of the San Fernando Valley.

"I hope you like iced coffee, Jesse," Doctor Eastman said with a smile as Jesse walked in the big door with the brass hardware and stained glass.

"Iced coffee is the business," Jesse beamed, trying his best to sound upbeat to the petite blonde that approached him with coffee in hand.

"Then, it's perfection." Eastman smiled back as she handed Jesse the large plastic cup.

"Thank you for calling me," Jesse said while looking down at the drink in his hand. The end of the wrapper was still on the straw that was poking out of the lid. Jesse removed it and looked around the room for a wastebasket. Eastman reached out her hand instead, and Jesse placed the bit of crumpled paper into her palm. When she closed her hand around it, it showed off her newly manicured nails: matte black with gloss black tips.

Jesse followed Melantha into the room.

Jesse noticed that Doctor Eastman had already moved the pillows and throw from the big white comfy chair As he sat down, he sunk into it and let out a big sigh.

Eastman sat down in her chair opposite him and took a big sip of her own iced coffee.

"Talk to me, Jess. What's happening?"

"I want to die . . ."

Eastman looked up from the coffee she was stirring as Jesse spoke. She placed the coffee on the chunky antique desk beside her chair.

"What are you feeling, Jesse?"

"Nothing. I don't feel anything. There is . . . nothing left of me."

Eastman's face was now sober. Her tone was steady. "That's how grief and loss work, Jess. You—"

Jesse cut Doctor Eastman off. "No! This isn't just grief . . . This isn't just a loss; this is the end of me." Jesse took a second before continuing, "I'm not grieving, I'm not in mourning. There is nothing left of me. When Katia was killed . . . I died that night as well. That . . . that fucking monster didn't just take my love; he took my life from me. He scooped out all of my insides and laughed while licking the fucking spoon."

Perfection . . . Eastman thought as she listened to the man, before she asked her follow-up question. "Tell me, Jesse, what would you do if you were in a room with Katia's killer?"

The two locked eyes from across the room. She could fell the rage pouring out of him.

Jesse seethed, "I'd slaughter him. I'd slaughter him like a fucking animal."

Eastman smiled internally and felt a tickle deep inside her. But on the outside, her voice was still calm and steady. "Being able to express these emotions is a good place for healing to begin, you see—"

Jesse interrupted once again, "I'm sorry, doc, but don't give me your touchy-feely hippy bullshit. There is no place for healing. There is no place for shelter, no salvation. There is nothing. There is nothing left of me."

Jesse paused and weighed his next statement before blurting it out. "I was going to kill myself last night—put the gun to my mouth, but couldn't pull the trigger. I wasn't going to tell you; I know you have to report this, and maybe that's what I need, to be put away and forgotten about. I can't eat, I can't sleep, I can't work, I can't fucking live . . . there's nothing left." By the end of his rant, Jesse was in tears.

Eastman looked at Jesse and sipped her coffee calmly. "Tell me another story of your childhood. We left off on Christmas morning. What else happened to you?"

Jesse looked to Eastman through his tears. "A lot . . ."

"Share with me if you feel like it. It's safe here for you, Jesse. I'm safe for you."

"After my dad left, we moved to Los Angeles. My mom, knowing she couldn't support us alone on her teacher's salary, decided to work for the family business. She thought it would be nice for me to be around my grandparents—not to mention the extra help they would bring to the table."

"Were your grandparents good to you, Jesse?"

"Yes. They were wonderful."

Eastman smiled. "Okay, go on, sweetie. You're very interesting."

"Not long after we moved down here, she met a man, and they moved in together."

Eastman glanced up from her coffee. "Was he a good man to you?"

"He was okay. He drank a lot, and didn't care much for kids, but he was okay. They would go out a lot at night. He was a big deal in the government, so they would have big dinner parties at the house all the time. That, or they would go out . . . a couple nights a week."

Here it comes! Eastman sat in anticipation, taking another sip of her coffee.

"They always had the same babysitter for me."

"Male or female?"

"Female."

"What did she do to you?"

Jesse sat in silence, staring a thousand yards away, then he again locked eyes with the young doctor.

"She beat and tortured me repeatedly for years . . . every time she would babysit me, As soon as they left, she would start beating me, or trying to drown me in the bathtub, or burn me with cigarettes. Every single time, doc." Jesse wasn't crying anymore. His expression was hardened, like he was used to facing this with steel.

"What fucked me up about the whole thing was, sometimes, she would have boyfriends of hers come over. They would both take turns beating me or holding me under the water until I blacked out. Then they'd pull me out and hold me upside down until I started coughing. Then they'd do the whole business over again."

Jesse shook his head and smiled and let out a forced chuckle. "The fuck is wrong with people?"

As he continued, Jesse's walls started to crack. He started to talk very fast, pouring over years of hurt . . .

"Sometimes, she and her boyfriends would do other things in front of me—make me watch, or . . . join in." Jesse shook his head while he looked out the window. "So naturally, while this was all going on, I couldn't tell anyone. I felt so ashamed, like I was the one who was bad. So I started acting out at school, started being violent. My mom, not having the patience to deal with a full-time job and a 'hyperactive' kid, put me on Ritalin—that's what you did to kids in the eighties."

Jesse leaned back in the big white chair and started laughing out loud. "So, picture this, doc. Not only was I abandoned at birth, but then my adopted dad left me on Christmas morning. Then I was uprooted again and forced to a new city, into a house with an alcoholic man that couldn't stand kids, where he and my mom were too busy partying to notice that their six-year-old child is getting repeatedly beaten, nearly drowned to death, and molested every time they left him. They only notice anything when he starts acting out in school, and he gets labeled as 'bad.'"

Jesse started laughing even harder.

"Then, what happens next, doc? They put that fucked up kid—that *child*—on new, stronger doses of the drugs. Amphetamines. Hoping it would be the plastic fantastic 1980's cure-all that it was hyped up to be. But then what happened? This little kid got addicted. This little kid got even more violent and started lashing out even harder. The only fucking difference was now this kid was so spun out on meth all day that he had no appetite until he got home. Then this little kid started binge eating all afternoon and into the evening."

Jesse continued laughing hysterically.

"You wanna know what happened next, doc? Wouldn't you know it—the little kid wasn't so little anymore. The little kid became a fat fuck. So now—now he was an abandoned, adopted, uprooted, alcoholic, molested, pumped-full-of-drugs, violent, angry-at-the-world, fat fucking piece of shit."

Jesse was now laughing so hard he was crying. He got all of his words out, but his voice was constantly strained. "And all this—All this before the age of eight fucking years old. Good fucking times, doc, good fucking times!" By now, Jesse had progressed to actual sobbing, his words a high-pitched whine of barely distinguishable babble. "But don't worry, doc. I won't skip over the part of my teenage years where I graduated from prescribed meth to street meth. I mean, why fucking not? Since I was fed that shit as a goddamned fucking *child*!"

Jesse was now yelling. "I had to sell dope and guns to feed my fucking habit. I had to do what I had to do—terrible things. Things I can't tell you or anyone else about."

Eastman's even voice made Jesse pause and look at her through his tear-wrapped eyes. "What kinds of things, Jess?"

Jesse shrugged his shoulders as if to say, *Why not tell you everything?*

He didn't hesitate, but didn't rush into his words either. "I . . . I killed someone."

Eastman just looked at Jesse calmly. She didn't even so much as raise an eyebrow or tap with her pen.

Jesse sighed and drew in another big gulp of air.

"After all that shit, I was able to shake the addictions, doc. I was able to pick myself up out of that fucking gutter and start a new life. I reached out to other people suffering from addiction. I helped them out of the same gutter I was in." Jesse paused and shook his head. "Even after all that, I still got back up! I got a fucking job—a regular job. I never had the privilege to go to school, doc. Not me. I just worked my fucking ass off. And after all that shit, after all that mess, I met Katia." At his last three words, there was a visible relaxation that rushed through him—but only for a moment, before reality caught up with him again.

"She was my payoff. She was the universe giving me my reward for everything I had gone through up until that point. Then . . . she was taken from me too. She left me too!" Jesse started shaking uncontrollably, all of his muscles contracting.

He was no longer there in his body.

Eastman jumped out of her chair on top of Jesse. She held him through the screaming and the shaking. She straddled the big man with her tiny body, trying to keep him from harming himself while he spastically jerked and bucked in the chair.

"You're here with me now, Jesse," Eastman said as she cradled Jesse's head in her hands. "You're here with me now."

Jesse's hazel eyes locked on the pale blue of hers. Her face was no more than five inches from his. His pulse slowed, and Jesse started repeating, "I'm here. I'm here. I'm here."

The energy exchange between the two at that moment couldn't have been hacked through by a machete.

Jesse stood from the chair, easily taking Eastman's petite body with him.

Her legs still wrapped around his waist, her hands still cradling his face, the torrent of the river of energy continuing to flow.

"I'm going to give you what you want more than anything else in the world," Eastman said as she stroked Jesse's shaved head. Their eyes locked in an intense gaze. Noses nearly touching.

"Oh, and what's that, doc?" whispered Jesse, not breaking eye contact.

"I'm going to give you the beast. I'm going to give you the beast on a silver fucking platter. No more games. No more lies. You just have to follow the white rabbit." The tiny blonde plunged herself into Jesse, into his lips, his tongue, and into the void of his soul.

THE REASON

If you prick us do we not bleed?

If you tickle us do we not laugh?

If you poison us do we not die?

And if you wrong us shall we not revenge?

—William Shakespeare

Jesse stood frozen, still holding the petite, 115-pound woman by her hips, her legs still wrapped around his waist.

At barely five-foot-three, she was a full five inches shorter than Katia, and about twenty-five pounds lighter.

Holding her felt foreign—but familiar. Curious, yet comfortable.

And what disturbed Jesse the most in that frantic moment, was that it felt okay . . . It felt natural . . .

It felt good.

Jesse also noticed that he felt something he hadn't felt in over five months: a tightening in his jeans.

Since that night, he hadn't even thought about sex, or anything related to it. As a matter of fact, he hadn't even had an erection since that night.

He slowly slid Eastman down off of him. She brushed against him as she went.

Jesse wondered, almost embarrassed, if she would notice the bulge in his jeans as he lowered her back to earth. The sharp gasp she let out as she brushed against him told Jesse that she did. He gently placed the tiny blonde doctor back down on her heels.

And even though she had on four-inch stilettos, he still looked down and into her eyes.

"What exactly did you mean about giving me 'the beast on a silver platter?'"

Eastman looked up into his big hazel eyes, eyes that were now focused, and for the first time, she noticed they had a life in them, a fire in them.

She whispered up to the man, while his hands still held her hips, "That's enough for today, Jesse. I feel like you have made some good progress and really opened up to me. I want to meet with you again in a couple days, and we can pick up where we left off."

Jesse whispered back to her, still focused on her blue eyes and red lips,

"If you have any sort of information, you need to share it with me now. I need to know."

Eastman smiled at the man holding her. "I don't have to do anything, Jesse. But I guess you're going to have to put off killing yourself until you get all the answers you're looking for. Deal?" She gave Jesse a snide smirk and a wink.

There was a moment that froze in time between them as they drank in each other's energy.

"Don't forget your coffee on your way out, sweetie," Eastman whispered as she broke the stare and motioned with her eyes to his still full, but slightly watered-down iced coffee, on the floor to the right of the white chair.

She really wanted to steal a glance of what she felt brush against her as slid against Jesse on her way to her feet.

He's gifted . . . Perfection. she thought, trying not to blush.

"Okay, have a great day. If you need anything, please don't hesitate to reach out to me. I'm here for you. I'm always here for you, Jesse." Quickly and without another word, she escorted Jesse to the front door.

"When do I see you next?" Jesse turned and asked as he crossed the threshold.

"Sooner than you think, sweetie. Sooner than you think."

She closed the door behind Jesse and leaned her back against it.

Eastman closed her eyes while squeezing her legs together, getting just the right amount of pressure, and shifting her hips for just the right amount of friction. She soaked up the energy of that moment. The memory of the softness of Jesse's lips, the feeling of his hands on her hips, and of course, the gift in his jeans, just waiting for her to unwrap.

Drag me . . .

She walked back into her office, a sparkle in her eye, a swing in her hips, and the taste of the man still upon her lips.

"I'm freaking the fuck out again. Help!"

It was 8:15 a.m. Jesse was just getting his day going when the Facebook notification came across his screen.

It had been a couple years since that night at the lodge.

Jesse was dating a sweet girl—living together, actually, but he couldn't ever forget about the girl who loved to read and loved to sing, or about her milky-white freckled skin, her big blue eyes, and of course, that long red hair.

There had been a couple more dates with Katia—well, more like meetings, but nothing had come out of them. Jesse could tell that Katia didn't like sneaking around on the man she was still living with. Jesse didn't like putting her in that position anyway. Even though he wanted her more than anything, it wasn't fair to her, and it wasn't fair to the poor bastard she had to go home to.

There was never any sex when they got together, and they didn't often kiss. They had long conversations over Italian food in a small café, and walks around the famous Halloween Town costume store in downtown Burbank.

To Jesse, those couple of minutes—those precious moments spent with Katia—meant the world to him.

Jesse: *"I'm here, what's going on?"*

Katia: *"I'm leaving. I just wanted to say goodbye."*

Jesse: *"You're what? Call me."*

Katia: *"I don't like talking on the phone."*

Jesse: *"I understand, call me anyway."*

Katia: *"No, can't we just do this?"*

Jesse: *"I'm calling you."*

Katia: *"Please don't . . ."*

Jesse opened his contact list and scrolled down to Katia Berlin. He pressed the call button, and the phone instantly started ringing. It rang twice and went to voicemail.

Jesse frowned and hit redial. While the phone once again connected, he saw a Facebook message from Katia pop up: *"I'm not going to answer. I'm freaking out, and I don't like talking on the phone!"*

Jesse hung up the phone and replied. *"That's too bad, because you're important to me, and I'm going to keep calling you until you do pick up. :)"*

Jesse called the number for Katia again. It rang twice and connected.

"Hello?" Jesse said after a long silence on the line. "Katia, I can hear you breathing. No matter what's happening, I'm here. Talk to me, babes."

Jesse could hear some muffled sobbing and what sounded like the phone being dropped.

"Katia? You around, kiddo?"

"I'm here."

"Hey, there you are!" Jesse said with a huge smile in the cheesiest tone he could muster at 8:37 a.m. "Talk to me, girl. What's going on?"

There was a long pause of dead air. Jesse took the phone away from his ear and looked at it to make sure it was still connected.

"Please don't say anything to anyone at work, but I'm leaving. I'm leaving today."

"Where are you going?"

"Back to Indiana. My dad is flying in today, and we are driving back there tomorrow."

Jesse paused and considered what to say next. "Katia, are you all right?"

"I . . . I don't know. I'm freaking out."

"Whatever is going on, I'm here. I'm here for you, Katia. All that matters to me is that you're safe and you're okay. You know that, right?"

"I know, I know. You have always been there for me, and it really has meant a lot to me."

"Hey, that's a two-way street, Katia. You have been there for me also." Jesse paused as he deliberated what to say next. He just needed her to know the truth. "Listen, as long as you're safe and happy, I'm behind whatever you want to do in your life, no matter what."

"I—I just wanted to say goodbye. I'm not telling anyone else. I'm leaving. I just have to go."

"We can still talk and stuff, yes?" Jesse said hesitantly, dreading the response.

"Probably not for a while."

"Okay. Well, you're always in my thoughts, Katia."

"Thank you, Jesse . . . You're in mine."

The call disconnected, and Jesse sat there on the back patio of his house.

He pulled a Camel Crush out of the pack next to the ashtray on the little table beside him and lit it.

He inhaled deeply and sighed quietly.

"Bye, Katia . . ."

Somewhere in West Los Angeles, a man sat at his computer desk.

The desk was immaculate, barren, except for a bamboo placemat, a single white orchid in a crystal vase, a steeping cup of tea, and an unburned sage wand.

The man turned on his MacBook. Instantly, the screen came to life with a black and white nature image. After signing in, that image disappeared to reveal his desktop wallpaper, which was a black and white HD image of the crescent moon.

The man opened his music app and selected a carefully chosen playlist to set the theme and mood of the night.

The hauntingly beautiful sounds of Chopin's Nocturne No. 2 in E-Flat Major Op 9 float lazily out of the Bluetooth speakers behind the man. He swayed his hand in tempo with the music. His black tattoos poked out from his crisp and perfectly pressed white shirt. He closed his eyes and continued to flow with the music.

In his mind, a wave of peace washed over him as the movements of his soul flowed down his arm and into his wrist, still keeping perfect time with the hallowed, fetching sounds emanating from the perfectly placed speakers.

The man opened his eyes and clicked his browser, then typed in the URL: www.instagram.com

He was delighted to see several notifications for direct messages, thirty-four likes, and twenty-six new followers.

But the man did not check his messages yet. No, the man is a man of ritual and purpose.

And first things were first.

The first order of the night, which was the same as the first order of every night, was to cast the net; he never checked what was in yesterday's net until he set the bait for today.

The man smiled as he thought of the old axiom: "A bird in the hand is worth two in the bush."

The man started typing in hashtags. The hashtags he used were his equivalent to a wounded animal call. At sporting goods stores, anyone could buy a device that mimicked the sound of a wounded animal. When you used such a device while hunting, it would call and attract all manner of predators to investigate what they hope to be an easy meal.

The most popular device to use in most areas was "wounded rabbit."

When using the wounded rabbit call correctly and out in the wild, it would sound exactly like an injured rabbit, calling out for the other rabbits to come and help it. But sometimes—most times—it would call in the predators too.

The man laughed as he mused at the ease of which the internet has made it all too easy to find wounded creatures.

The wounded animal calls the man liked the most were: #depression #eatingdisorder #ED #mentalillness #giveup #depressionquotes #medication #cantcope #scared #worried #alone #help #insomnia #edsoldier #healthynotskinny #selfharm

The man hit enter on his computer, and instantly the screen populated with the quarry of tonight's hunt.

The man went through liking every pic that came up. 1,334 posts related to those hashtags. For that was his lure—his bait. Nothing more. Nothing less.

In twenty minutes, all the posts had been liked.

In twenty minutes, 1,334 individual lures had been cast.

The man's tea had perfectly steeped.

He mindfully lifted the mug to his lips and took a sip.

The man smiled as Scherzo No. 1 in B minor, OP. 20 violently started with a crescendo of clamoring ivory and tightly wound metal strings.

The man minimized his browser and opened one of the three folders on his desktop. In it, thousands of images. On the images, tens of thousands of words.

His words.

Each carefully crafted and chosen to sing only to the broken, to resonate only with the shattered.

The man selected his carefully premeditated post of the day. He clicked on the image, and it expanded. It was a stark black and white of a Greek statue. The words he chose for this image read: "To stand in the light, you must first stand in my shadow."

The man looked at the watch on his wrist and waited for three more minutes while sitting in the aroma of his tea and the reverberating frequency of Chopin.

The man uploaded the perfectly worded, stark black and white image with the perfectly phrased words at precisely the right time to Instagram.

The he took his tea and sat back in his black leather chair.

The man took a sip and waited.

Waited for the first tug on the 1,334 lures he cast out that night.

Perfectly still, the man waited.

He waited.

He waited for his beacon.

A SHADOW IN THE DARK

If you are not too long, I will wait here for you all my life.

—Oscar Wilde

Jesse put the key into the front door of his house, managing to get it in the first time. The door swung open, and he was immediately greeted by Loki. The huge puppy jumped and bounded on Jesse, did three circles in the middle of the living room, and bounced twice off the couch before rolling on his back in front of the man's feet and showing him his white belly.

"Hey, buddy, I missed you too." Jesse laughed, giving Loki a couple pats on his tummy.

Jesse walked through the hallway to the room with a bed in it and opened the door. He stood and stared at the pile of clothes—the nest—that he had slept in the night before.

Loki nosed by him, panting, and jumped onto the bed.

"What do you think, buddy?"

The big wolf pup looked up at Jesse, stopped panting, and tilted his massive head.

"That's exactly what I think. It's time to clean." Jesse connected his iPhone to his big jam box and put on his favorite emo playlist as he looked around the room and took inventory of everything on the floor: the broken nightstand in splintered pieces, Katia's treasures strewn about the room like shells laying on a beach, and of course,

178

the nest.

"Okay, buddy. Let's get on this."

Jesse walked through the hallway and into the kitchen. He opened up the cupboard and got out four big black trash bags. Jesse went back to the room with the bed in it and started picking up pieces of the shattered dresser and putting them into one of the bags.

When that bag was full, he placed it in the hallway. Jesse started picking up the dresses, the shirts, the socks, the jeans, and the shoes and placed them into another bag.

By the time the song "Vindicated" by Dashboard Confessional started playing, Jesse was nearly done.

The floors were clean, the bed sheets and pillowcases were stripped and in the laundry basket, and for the first time since that night, the room was purged of all trash and broken things.

Jesse found a sage smudge stick while he was picking up the items behind the dresser, where he had flung the treasures off Katia's altar. He lit the sage, and it ignited and started burning, and billowing, thick, creamy smoke.

Jesse picked up one of the ceramic bowls from the altar and put the now smoking smudge stick in it. He placed it on Katia's nightstand and watched the plumes and wisps of smoke dance and dissipate into the ceiling of the room with a bed.

He walked over to the big double-hung window next to Katia's side of the bed and opened the blackout curtains and pulled up the sash. Fresh sunshine flooded into the room with a bed. The rays made the billowing smoke from the sage look like the once worshiped and revered, but now long forgotten spirits of an inner sanctum of a temple of some long dead religion.

Jesse went to the closet. He gently placed the rest of Katia's belongings in bags and put the bags in the hallway.

He then took the bags and put everything of hers in the storage shed behind the garage.

Loki watched and played in the backyard as Jesse carried the bags to the rickety shed. When the last bag was filled and put into the shed, Jesse sat on the steps of the back porch of the little house on Piedmont.

Loki came and sat next to him.

Jesse put his arm around the giant puppy and looked into his faithful friend's milky blue eyes.

"Well, buddy, I know what I have to do. I know exactly what I have to do."

The big dog's tongue scraped across Jesse's beard as the big man laughed out loud and tussled Loki's coarse fur. He looked at the puppy, and doing his best *Scooby-doo* impression, asked himself, "Rutt do you have to roo, Raddy?"

Jesse chucked at his own stupid joke; he usually always did.

"I'm going to kill the beast, buddy," Jesse said while rubbing the big floppy head of his puppy.

"I'm going to kill the beast."

"OMG are you ok?!?"

Jesse looked down at the phone resting on the arm of his big leather chair. It had been a while since Katia and him last spoke—he had stopped expecting to see her name pop up on his phone. He knew she was okay, and that was enough for him. But every time a message from her came through, he still felt the same burn in his chest that he always has.

A couple of minutes ago, he had posted the Facebook status update: "Just got home from surgery, ugh."

A year prior, Jesse was in a minor hit and run car accident. His injuries were slightly serious and did require some minor outpatient surgery.

Jesse picked up the phone, opened the Facebook messaging app, and typed: *"Thanks for checking in. Long time no talk. I'm okay. How are you doing?"*

Katia: *"I'm good, I'm just worried about you!"*

Jesse: *"Hey, Katia?"*

Katia: *"yes?"*

Jesse: *"I don't know if it's the painkillers talking, or what's going on, but I have to tell you something."*

Jesse took a deep breath before typing: *"I love you. I'm in love with you. And I've been in love with you since the moment I saw you in the showroom six years ago."*

It was something he had typed out plenty of times before, though he had never actually sent it. His confession. Still, Jesse cringed as he finally hit 'send.'

The message instantly went to 'read.'

The "they're typing" bubble came up and vanished, then came up and vanished again.

Katia: *"I've been waiting six years for you to say that!"*

Katia: *"I love you too, Jesse."*

Jesse dropped his iPhone and nearly popped one of his fresh stitches.

Jesse: *"Let's make this happen, Katia."*

Katia: *"is it ok if I call you when I get off work?"*

Jesse: *"Please do, I'm going to take a nap, but I'm here."*

Katia: *"ok, I'll call you as soon as I'm off. <3"*

Jesse: *"Bye, Katia."*

Jesse put his phone over his heart and smiled.

Katia called Jesse that night, and the two talked into the wee hours of the morning.

From that day going forward, Jesse and Katia talked every day.

Every morning, Katia would send Jesse a good morning text.

Every night, they would talk and say their "I love yous" and "I miss yous."

Katia being two hours ahead of Jesse made their talks exhausting for her, but they were worth it.

Three weeks into their nightly FaceTime sessions about life, love, ghosts, and the universe, Jesse asked Katia a big question.

"I want to fly you out for a couple days. I need to see if this will work."

The great thing about FaceTime is you can see people's reactions in real time, and there was no hiding Katia's excitement on her face.

"I would like that. I would really like that!" Katia said, spreading that smile that couldn't be faked.

"When is good for you?" asked Jesse as he opened the Priceline app on his phone.

"Well, I have three days off in two weeks," said Katia as she opened the calendar on her iPhone, momentarily pausing the FaceTime video, but they could still talk over the audio stream.

"What days are those, love?" asked Jesse as he put in the outgoing airport and arrival destination on the app.

"Um, November second through the fourth, but I have to be back to work early on the fifth."

"Your dad wouldn't give you a couple days off?" asked Jesse in a tone more hopeful than reality governed.

"No way. He's pretty tough about that stuff."

"No problem. What time do you work 'til on the first?"

"About five."

"Great. Could you make a flight out of Indianapolis at around 8:00 p.m.?"

"Yes, I think so."

"Awesome, you will arrive in LA around 9:30 p.m. our time. Booked your tickets and sent a confirmation to your email!"

Jesse's image returned to Katia's screen as he closed his other apps and returned to the FaceTime call. He could see her beautiful smile once again.

"Like, O-M-G, we are really doing this!"

"Yes, we really are!" said Jesse with a smile and a wink.

"I can't wait to see you!" Katia was doing a little happy dance on her bed for Jesse.

"It's happening!" said Jesse, mirroring Katia's enthusiasm. "Get some good sleep, love. It's nearly 2:00 a.m. for you. I want you to have a good day tomorrow!"

"Thank you, Jesse. Thank you for everything," Katia beamed. Her voice was full of gratitude and love.

"I love you, Katia Berlin." Jesse sighed and looked into Katia's eyes over thousands of miles of fiber optics and satellite transmissions.

"I love you, Jesse Silver."

Jesse smiled and waved as he disconnected the call.

"Bye, Katia . . ."

THE END OF THE BEGINNING

A heavyset man knocked on the wooden door with stained glass and antique brass hardware.

He was in his late thirties, relatively tall, and had long, dark, tightly curled hair, and a long gray and brown beard. He wore gray slacks and a white button-up collared shirt with a vest.

He stood there waiting on that overcast winter morning.

The man knocked on the door once again, but paused when he heard the *click-clack* of heels approaching from inside the office suite. The door swung open, and there stood the young blonde doctor.

"Why didn't you just come in, Geo?"

The man looked at his iPhone and said, "I just wanted to make sure I wasn't rude."

Eastman motioned Geo into the once-house now-office and closed the door behind him.

"Oh please, Geo, we have known each other far too long for those kinds of pleasantries. But, I do appreciate the gesture. Always the gentleman." Eastman threw a smile at the man. "I do appreciate you showing up, and I do appreciate you keeping this discreet."

"Of course." Geo nodded while reaching into the pocket of his white collared shirt and producing a one terabyte thumb drive.

"Hold on, I have something for you." Eastman held up a finger as she went to her purse and produced an envelope. She walked back to Geo, who was still standing, holding out the thumb drive. "Perfection."

She handed over the envelope while she took the thumb drive from Geo. She then immediately walked over to her desk and plugged it into her MacBook Pro. "Feel free to count it," Eastman said while staring at the screen of her computer. Geo just laughed and slid the thick envelope into the back pocket of his baggy jeans.

"So, kickass job on catching The Butcher. How was Chicago?"

Eastman glanced up from her computer and smiled. "Cold. I got to tell you; I don't know how people live with that weather."

Geo sighed as he took a seat in the big comfy white chair. "Mel, this isn't the first time you had me get into this creep's business. But, every time you do, I wish it was the last. I hate looking at this filth."

Eastman shook her head. "That's funny, Geo. For all the after-hours off-the-books black-hat work I've had you do for me in the past, you have never asked me any questions. So, why now?"

Geo looked at his friend sitting at her desk and smiled. "You've had me dig up some dirt on some real shit bags in the past . . . The CSI blood splatter analyst that was killing people? The investment banker that loved to video tape himself while he murdered prostitutes? We took them all down, but . . . Melantha, I . . . I have never seen anything like this before."

Geo was, now, a mostly "white hat" hacker for the FBI. At seventeen years old, he managed to hack into the NSA and release some very compromising footage online from Project Blue Book and Evergreen Airlines. Of course, that was in the early days of the internet, way before things went viral and the media just spun it as "hoax videos" and "conspiracy theories"—just like they did with everything else that was somehow leaked but turned out later to be entirely accurate information.

At any rate, Geo's parents were surprised when an FBI SWAT

team broke down the door of their cute two-story suburban house, complete with the white picket fence, garden gnomes, and, of course, a golden retriever.

Geo was lucky though. Well, not really lucky—talented. The FBI gave him an offer he couldn't refuse: put his talent to work for Homeland security or go to prison forever. The choice was an easy one for Geo.

About three years ago, when Geo first met Eastman while working a case together, he, like most men, had developed a massive crush on her. It had dissipated as his crush was replaced with trust and respect for the young agent.

He looked forward to her calls now.

Flying under the radar and digging into other people's lives without the silly standards, protocols, and warrants that his security clearance demanded of him was invigorating, not to mention fun, for Geo.

The rule here was: "No warrants. No questions. No problems."

Geo hadn't asked a question, but he was skirting around one, and Eastman didn't plan on acknowledging it further than she has. She turned to smile at Geo. "Just call it a woman's intuition."

"I see . . ."

"How's everything at the office?" Eastman asked, obviously changing the subject.

"It's good. Getting busy. We are entering into another election cycle, so you know what that means," responded Geo, glancing at his iPhone.

"Let me guess, investigating every death threat that comes down the line from every whacked out blue or red extremist?"

"Basically." Geo paused and chuckled to himself. "The internet really has turned into a cesspool. I really miss the good ol' days of BBS and ICQ."

"Well, sounds like a good time to me." Eastman smiled with an eyeroll, pretending to remember what the mid-1990's web culture was like.

"Well, I'm going to get going. Always a pleasure to see you, Melantha, and as always, thank you for your business."

"Always the gentleman, Geo."

"But of course." Geo gave his friend a dramatic Shakespearian bow and walked to the front door of the building with Melantha following closely behind.

"Hey . . . Geo?" Eastman said as he reached for the antique doorknob.

Geo paused and turned.

"Is what's on that thumb drive as bad as I think it is?"

Geo sighed and shook his head. "Worse . . ."

He put on his aviator sunglasses, gave Eastman a nod, and walked out the brick red door with stained glass and antique hardware.

"Tell me, where and in which ways do you most need to grow, my child?"

The direct message lingered for a moment before a response was given.

"I don't know. I don't know what I'm doing, I just feel like I'm lost."

"That is nothing to be ashamed of, my child. We were all lost at one point. The question you need to ask yourself is, how far are you willing to travel to be found?" The man sat back in his black leather chair. His heavily starched, crisp white shirt sounded like the rustling of dried leaves as he reclined in thought. He leaned forward in his chair as he read the response to his question.

"I'm willing to do anything. I am at the end of my rope."

"The end of one rope is the beginning of another . . . for all is connected . . . All is one. You already know this deep inside, don't you, my child?"

"*Yes, you speak the truth. I can feel it inside. That is the truth.*"

"*Good, you have just taken your first step on your journey from darkness into light. For I am the light from which no shadows are cast. I am the sun and the moon. I am the alpha and the omega. I am the truth.*"

The man in the crisp white shirt smiled as he picked up his perfectly steeped tea and took a sip. The sounds of Chopin danced in the air as the man saw his message being responded to.

"*Can you save me?*"

"*Yes, my child.*"

"*How? I'm so fucked up. I feel like nothing will ever help me.*"

"*I will teach you to stand in your power. I will show you how to unleash the divine feminine energy that is locked inside you. The energy that you have had to deny and suppress for far too long. In my strength, you will find peace. In your obeying me. you will find your power. My child, are you ready to feel my strength?*"

The man got up from his desk and walked over to the window of his apartment that overlooked Los Angeles. As his focus shifted from the distant horizon of the skyscrapers of downtown Los Angeles to his reflection in the window, he smiled.

This has become all too easy, the man's inner voice echoed to him. *I am the way. I am the peace. I am the light.*

Over the sublime drifting sway of Chopin's Ballade No. 3 in A-Flat Major Op 47, the man heard the familiar sound of a direct message ping in his inbox.

The man sat again in his leather chair. Each movement he made was exact and calculated. The man slowly read the incoming message: "*I am ready, sir.*"

The man smiled and tented his fingers. "*I'm very proud of you, my child, very proud.*"

"*What shall I do next? What needs to be done, sir?*"

The man picked up his cup of tea and noticed it was nearly empty. After taking a final sip, he gently placed the cup back on the saucer.

The man reached for the Orchid in the glass vase on the bamboo placemat and gave one of the soft petals a gentle caress. The delicate velvety feel of the petal was a delight to his touch. The man once again turned his attention to the screen of his laptop.

"My child, there is no rush. For you see, we will intertwine in the manner of the great spiral that beckons all change in our universe."

"Yes, sir. I understand, sir."

The man lowered his right hand and put it to rest on the head of a young nude woman who, this whole time, was kneeling by his chair. The man drummed his fingers on the young woman's scalp.

Her eyes were cast downward, her hands resting palm-up on her bent knees.

"I am nearly ready for some more tea. In a couple minutes, you will go prepare some."

The young nude woman gave a slight nod, her eyes never leaving the floor in front of her.

The man gave her head a pat, the way you would pat the head of a dog you were fond of, and returned his hand to the keyboard of his MacBook Pro.

He whispered without turning his eyes away from his laptop, "I am ready for more tea."

Without saying a word, the nude blonde woman nodded once again. In one fluid, well-trained motion, she rose to her feet, and silently made her way to the kitchen to prepare more tea.

The man began typing a long-anticipated response.

"I will call you Orchid. You will grow in strength and beauty under my loving solicitude. Together, we will walk through the gates of the cards, and you will become whole in my light and in my strength. Do you like your new name, Orchid?"

"Yes, sir. Very much, sir. I am so honored to be an initiate of yours."

Her typing continued, *"I am deeply moved and grateful that you would even consider me, sir."*

The young woman came back into the room with a fresh and

steaming steeping cup of tea. She returned to the right side of the man, cast her eyes downward, and slowly lowered herself onto her knees.

Once at rest upon her knees, she raised the saucer and cup with both hands and presented them to the man. Without a word or acknowledgment, the man took the cup of tea from the young woman and placed it to the right of his MacBook Pro. Polonaise No. 6 in A-Flat Major OP. 53, "Heroic" started playing.

"As with all without, as so within. the timing of all is perfect."

The young woman on her knees gave a slight nod. Her eyes never dared leaving the upturned palms of her hands.

The man typed again: *"You have been carefully chosen. You are now on your path. You will soon feel my strength. And in my strength, you will find your salvation. Do you understand, Orchid?"*

"Yes, sir. I do."

"From now on, Orchid, you will refer to me by one name. and one name only."

"I understand. How shall I address you, sir?"

"You will call me, Pedagogue."

"Just Landed!"

Jesse passed the 405 interchanges and continued west. The Sepulveda exit took him to the arrivals terminal of LAX.

LAX was *always* a dirty, disgusting clusterfuck of a thousand people trying to merge into three lanes of traffic at the same time, every five minutes. It was miserable, and It gave him ample time to respond to Katia. *"I can't wait to see you. I'll be there soon!"*

Katia sent a flurry of heart and kissy face emojis, then a quick follow-up: *"I'm just getting off the plane! :)"*

Jesse: *"Okay, love, I'm here."*

Jesse had instructed Katia not to check any luggage—just bring a backpack and a carry-on bag—that way she wouldn't be stuck in the limbo that was the baggage claim. After all, she was only going to be here for three days and four nights, and he didn't want to waste any moment.

Jesse looked at the huge terminal numbers that were painted on the side of the pickup zones. Katia should be at number five. Jesse was passing the big number two.

Katia: *"I'm outside!!!"*

Jesse: *"Be there in just a minute!!!"*

Katia: *"like OMG!! I can't believe this!! <3"*

Jesse negotiated between two airport shuttles as he rounded the corner. He guided his Prius into the pick-up zone of the airport and the traffic slowed. He could see the big number five about two hundred yards away.

His heart was pounding like a drum as he sent Katia a text. *"Pulling up!"*

Jesse pulled up intentionally about fifty feet from the big number five.

He broke all of LAX's rules and left his car running at the curb, got out, and walked up onto the sidewalk of the arriving flights pick up zone.

And there, about forty feet away, was Katia.

Jesse paused as she turned and saw him.

They stared at each other for what seemed like an eternity, from the shortest distance apart they had been in nearly two years. Katia started running to Jesse. Jesse started running to Katia.

They closed the distance quickly.

Katia jumped into Jesse's arms, and just like a scene from a movie, they shared a loving, passionate kiss that seemed to last a lifetime. At that moment, time stopped as they embraced each other on that sidewalk.

Jesse took Katia by the hand and led her to his waiting Prius. He opened the door for Katia, and she slid inside the little black car.

Jesse took her bag, opened the back door of the car, and placed it in the back seat. He got in the Prius and put the car into drive.

Jesse presented his hand to Katia, and she took it.

As her fingers intertwined with his, Jesse felt a wave of peace rush over him. During the car ride home, barely any words were spoken.

Katia leaned across to Jesse's side of the car and put her head on his shoulder. He had his hand on Katia's bare thigh, her little black dress riding up just below her panty line.

Jesse could feel the heat emanating from Katia's pelvis as his hand slid slightly higher up her thigh. But he was in no rush to go higher. The way he saw it, he had waited six years for this, and he wanted to drag out the anticipation for as long as possible.

It was delicious.

The anticipation was the best part.

As they pulled into the driveway of the little house on Piedmont, Jesse exited the car, walked around to Katia's side, and opened the passenger door for her.

He walked Katia to the front door and opened it.

He escorted her, guided her, slowly, by her hips to the bedroom and opened the bedroom door. The room was pitch black. He walked over to the nightstand and grabbed a small remote control. With the push of a button, thirty-four tiny LED candles came to life.

Jesse took the lighter on the nightstand and lit the three lavender-scented candles he had bought and prepared for tonight—their night.

Katia stood in the doorway in amazement at the scene.

Jesse turned to Katia, and she looked up to the man that had been her friend, her confidant, her support for the last six years.

Jesse gently placed his hand on her collarbone and slowly moved it up to Katia's delicate neck, and she bent and flowed with his intention of movement. Jesse gave Katia's throat a gentle squeeze. He was careful not to squeeze her windpipe, but rather only constrict the blood flow, just for an instant.

Katia let out a sharp gasp and Jesse applied the gentle, yet firm pressure.

He backed her slim frame against the wall and leaned his weight against her.

Still holding her, Jesse gently kissed Katia's clavicle as he, with a single finger, pulled the spaghetti strap of her dress off her petite shoulder and let it slide down her arm.

Jesse's lips grazed and traced every centimeter of Katia's fragile neckline as he memorized every cell of her skin, the smell of her flesh, and the scent of her hair.

Katia's eyes were still closed, her mouth slightly open, waiting, anticipating, yearning to feel his kiss.

Jesse brushed his lips against hers, and she let out another sharp gasp.

He moved to the other delicate strap of her dress. As soon as he slid it off her shoulder, the dress shed off her skin and lay at her feet. Her black Victoria's Secret bra and panty set fit and hugged perfectly, complementing her athletic form.

With his hand still on her throat, Jesse gave Katia another, firmer squeeze. Jesse then took both of Katia's hands and placed them above her head, against the wall.

Jesse leaned in and whispered in Katia's ear, "Keep your hands right here. Do you understand?"

Katia's head nodded as Jesse's hands were now free to roam her body.

Her body made Jesse feel like an early explorer first stepping foot on new land. A voyage that took years was beset on all sides by rough and rugged roads. But upon dropping anchor and stepping foot on the shore for the first time, he knew the long hard trek was worth it.

Instinctively, Katia thrust her pelvis toward Jesse.

Jesse dropped to his knees and started with her thighs, kissing and caressing his way up to that perfect crease where her leg met her body.

But he didn't touch her—not where she was aching for him.

Not yet.

He moved up to her tummy and gave her extra attention there, taking time to subliminally let her know that he loved every inch of her. To show her that even the parts of her that she felt were unworthy, parts of herself where she felt were lacking, he found perfection in them.

Jesse slowly rose to his feet and took Katia by her hands, that were still in the exact same place he had left them, and spun her so she was facing the wall.

She pushed her round, supple ass against his jeans.

Jesse reached his hand into her red mane of hair and gave it a twist.

Her head shot up in a silent gasp toward the ceiling. In ecstasy, she whimpered. He gently pulled her head back and with his free hand, he undid her bra.

Her perfect C cup breasts heaved as she was pushed again against the wall. Jesse held her there and kissed the nape of her neck.

Only this time, Jesse gently sunk his teeth into her flesh—just the right amount of pressure—to let her know he was there. To make her understand, at that moment, she was his.

Jesse lowered Katia's arms to her sides, letting her bra fall to the floor.

He turned her and brought her chin up so she could see him, could feel the intensity in his eyes.

Jesse took Katia's hand and led her to their bed. He stood over her and took off his black collared shirt. He had on a black sleeveless undershirt that was tucked into his dark fitted jeans with his black leather belt and boots.

Katia looked up to her man, standing there over her.

His muscular frame was silhouetted by the lights of the candles and the many glimmering lights emitting diodes that were placed carefully around the room to give it the appearance of the shimmering starry night.

Jesse reached down and unbuckled his belt and unbuttoned his jeans. Katia sat silently in anticipation as he slowly, deliberately removed them.

Now standing there only in his undershirt and black boxer briefs, Jesse moved onto the bed, and onto Katia.

He slowly, sincerely, passionately kissed her.

This was the moment Jesse had been waiting for since the second he laid eyes on this woman in the showroom.

And. It. Was. Perfect.

Jesse rubbed himself on Katia, and she moved her hips into him.

They flowed. They danced.

Jesse once again started working his way down Katia's body—exploring, navigating, discovering.

When he got down to her panties, he paused and sat upon his knees.

Jesse gently reached down and took hold of the delicate garment. Katia lifted her ass off the bed, and Jesse slowly slid her panties off.

Jesse took Katia's left foot and raised it to his mouth, he kissed from her ankle, up to her calves, and again, up her thighs.

In one motion, Jesse spread Katia's legs wide.

Her limber, athletic body readily accepted and moved with his motion.

Jesse kissed from her inner thighs, and with his soft tongue, in one smooth movement, licked from the outside of Katia's ass, in the crease of her thigh, to gently brush her outer labia.

Katia squirmed with excitement and raised her pelvis to meet the tongue of her lover. Jesse pulled away right before her clit would have brushed his tongue.

He felt Katia silently gasp, then squirm in frustration.

Immediately, he grabbed Katia's other leg and started slowing kissing and caressing his way up it.

By the time he got to her pelvis, she was already soaked. He gently slid one finger inside her, and with a "come here" motion, found and started stimulating her g-spot. Jesse then started doing tiny circles around her clit with his soft tongue.

He made sure not to touch Katia's clit—not yet.

Katia let out a loud gasp of pleasure and bucked her pelvis toward Jesse.

He placed his free hand on Katia's belly, right below her belly button, and kept her rooted onto the bed with a gentle pressure.

Jesse took his time absorbing the taste and smell of her. He savored and cherished every moment of it.

Suddenly, Katia called out, "Is it—is it okay if I cum?"

Jesse kept his rhythm and took his hand off her belly and intertwined his fingers with hers.

"Cum . . . Cum for me, now."

Katia arched her back and moaned as jolting waves of orgasm pulsed from deep inside her, traveling like lightning bolts up her spine. As soon as her body stopped convulsing, Jesse slid back on top of Katia and kissed her deeply.

Katia's hands moved from Jesse's face, down over his arms, onto his chest, and down to his waist, where she was frantically tugging at his black boxer briefs—trying to get them off.

Jesse helped Katia pull his boxer briefs down, and she reached for his already hard cock. Jesse stopped her, taking her hands and placing them over her head again. She let out an involuntary whine.

Jesse took the head of his cock and slowly teased it around Katia's engorged clit.

Her hips gyrated and pushed against him, the succulent friction sending jolts of static electricity through her.

He slid just the tip of his cock inside her, so she could just barely feel the stretch of his girth. Then slowly, gently, centimeter by centimeter, he pushed inside her.

Katia moaned as Jesse slid just a little deeper, only then to return back to the original, shallow starting point.

Katia threw her legs around Jesse and tried to pull him in.

She bucked her hips, trying to give herself just a taste more of him.

Jesse held fast.

After what seemed like an hour of his teasing, Jesse put his lips to Katia's ear and whispered, "Tell me. Tell me what you want, my love."

"I-I want all of you."

"You already have all of me."

Jesse slid deep into Katia. She writhed and spasmed in utter, pure bliss.

Jesse alternated his strokes.

Shallow, shallow, shallow, shallow, shallow.

Deep.

Shallow, shallow, shallow, shallow, shallow.

Deep.

Katia soon cried out again in ecstasy.

"Fuck, may I please cum again?"

Jesse and Katia had a long chat before she came out, and in that conversation, Jesse made a straightforward request of Katia.

"You will always ask me permission before you cum. Do you understand?"

Katia nodded in excitement over the FaceTime video.

Jesse kept his tempo steady as he whispered in Katia's ear, "Yes, you may, my love."

Katia let out in a loud scream that Jesse was quite sure made the neighborhood jealous. Jesse kept thrusting at the same rhythm as he felt Katia's body contract and squeeze him tightly inside her.

Never pulling out, or breaking contact with her body, Jesse rolled Katia on top of him.

The sweat from her body condensed into mini beads of perspiration that dripped onto Jesse's chest as she rode and gyrated on top of him.

Katia put her hands behind her head as she bared her clit down on Jesse's pubic bone.

"I'm right on the edge—I'm right on the fucking edge."

"Breathe it in. Put it up your spine. Let it get closer."

Jesse and Katia would play over FaceTime for hours. He would have her get right on the edge of orgasm and make her keep it there for extended periods of time. Some nights, after having her in that space for some forty-five minutes or so . . . he would have her just stop.

Some nights . . . he wouldn't let her cum.

He had got Katia to the point where he could control her ability to orgasm in a matter of minutes—seconds if he could guide her to the right headspace.

"How close?" Jesse whispered, now moving the palm of his hand to Katia's tummy applying pressure that pushed and moved her G-Spot closer to his cock inside her. The pressure she felt made her need to cum increase. Increase to the edge.

"I'm about to cum!"

"Good girl. I want you to hold it. Hold it right there for me."

Katia didn't stop grinding; she started rubbing harder, sliding all of Jesse inside her.

"How close?" Jesse asked again as he could feel himself bottoming out inside Katia. Pushing deep inside her as she moved and gyrated her pelvis in different positions to alternate the pressure she felt building deep within.

"I'm right—I'm right fucking there!"

"Cum for me."

Katia immediately exploded in the throes of passion and ecstasy. And after what seemed to be a full minute of orgasm, Katia collapsed on top of Jesse with deep heaving breaths.

Jesse enveloped Katia in his arms and held her close, her heart pounding in unison against his, her body and spirit filled with him.

Jesse rolled Katia over and guided her onto her knees.

She arched her back and presented her full round ass to him.

Jesse got off the bed and stood at the corner of it. He grabbed Katia by her hips and pulled her to the corner, so her feet were dangling off the edge.

Jesse's bed wasn't on a frame. The mattress and box spring rested neatly on the floor and provided the perfect height and the ideal angle for nocturnal shenanigans.

Jesse dropped to his knees and buried his face in Katia's ass.

The taste of her cum was delightfully tangy, yet not overpowering.

He rose back to his feet, grabbed Katia's right hand, and placed it between her legs.

"I want you to keep working your clit. You're going to make me cum now. Do you understand?"

"Yes . . . Give it to me . . . I want it . . ."

Katia varied the speed and friction on her clit with her fingertip as she took all off Jesse inside of her.

"Stay on edge, and go nice and slow for me. Make me cum."

Katia hissed in temped excitement, "I'm going to cum. I'm going to cum if I don't stop!" Katia again cried out as she still feverishly rubbed and pulled on her clit.

"Not until I say," Jesse said calmly. "Understand?"

"Fuck, but—but I'm so close!" Katia continued sliding Jesse deep inside of her.

Jesse, breathing slowly, placed his hand on Katia's ass, and directed her.

"I'm getting close. Slow down for me. Make me cum."

Katia slowed her rhythm as Jesse had instructed.

"Stay close for me. Stay on edge for me."

"I'm still on edge!"

Jesse could feel his orgasm starting to quicken.

"I want you to cum inside me. Please, I want all of you. I need you to fill me up!" Katia gasped, still fighting off her urge to cum.

Staying on that edge was a challenge, but also a pleasure.

"I'm going to cum, be still." Jesse wanted her to be perfectly still when he came. He wanted her to feel every inch of him throbbing inside her.

He needed her to feel every spasm.

"Here it comes, my love."

As soon as Jesse let the first shot of cum inside Katia, she screamed as she felt the wholeness and warmth fill her. Katia pushed Jesse as deep as he would go. She didn't want a single drop to go to waste.

Katia then cried out, "May I cum?"

"Yes!" Jesse moaned in ecstasy, and he continued to fill her up.

And together they came.

The built-up tension of six years of love's patience expanding and exploding. Jesse collapsed on top of Katia. Their bodies both heaving.

Drowning in sweat and pleasure, Jesse rolled Katia over, and they kissed and embraced. Katia put her head on Jesse's chest, and he held her.

Their bodies wouldn't break contact until the light of dawn crept in the window the next morning.

For the rest of that night, he held her.

HOOK, LINE, AND 5INKER

Most people want to avoid pain, and discipline is usually painful.

—John C. Maxwell

The small office was filled with the sound of a LaserJet printer chugging through its rhythmic task as hundreds of pages of direct messages and images streamed out of the printer and onto the printing tray.

Eastman walked from her desk over to her filing cabinet and pulled out another ream of paper.

Geo, being as anal as anal gets, had filed all the folders on the flash drive as follows:

Continent

Country

State / Provence

City

Name

Eastman smiled at how easy Geo made it for her to find information quickly and how efficient and effective his filing system was.

She moused over the master folder and clicked.

North America—The United States—California—Los Angeles.

The subfolder opened to reveal ninety-eight names. Of course, all the folders were in alphabetical order.

She clicked on the first folder: "Veronica Aaronson"

In the folder was one text document and another folder that contained two images.

"Let's see what happened to you, Veronica."

Melantha opened the text document first.

01/03/2017 23:41

@VKAaronsen92: *"cool posts."*

@ThePedagogue: *"Thank you, my child. I salute your spirit guides for leading you to me."*

@VKAaronsen92: *"So, are you a poet or something?"*

@ThePedagogue: *"I am the messenger and the message. I am the one who brings light to those in darkness."*

@VKAaronsen92: *"wow, ok. Lol!"*

@ThePedagogue: *"Tell me, where and in which ways do you most need to grow, my child?"*

@VKAaronsen92: *"wow. I'm good for now, but thanks. Have a good night. Bye!"*

%End-of-transcript%

Eastman shook her head and smirked.

Nice to know Veronica didn't fall for that nonsensical bullshit babble. She just wasn't wounded enough for him. Eastman sighed as she closed the text file and double clicked the image folder.

There were two images. Both were stark black and white images with text on them, both sent in succession with a reply.

He was trying to pull her back in, but she didn't take the bait. Good on ya, Veronica. Good on ya. Eastman closed the image folder and clicked to go back to the Los Angeles folder.

The second folder came next: "Danielle Ackles"

There were again two files: a text document and an images folder.

This time, Eastman opened the images folder first. It was filled with hundreds of photos and videos.

"Perfection," Melantha whispered as she scrolled through the images, most of which were black and white—many being sexually graphic.

A young nude blonde woman against a wall, looking over her shoulder with her ass facing the camera.

Looks like a college dorm room, Melantha figured as she glanced at the concrete block wall with posters and photos taped to it.

She closed that image and opened another. This time, Danielle was spread eagle, only a feather covering her.

Eastman analyzed the image. *Always black and white. Same room. Same bed in the corner. Same block walls. Obviously, he made her send these to him.*

Eastman closed the image, scrolled to the bottom of the folder, and clicked the last one.

"What. The. Fuck," she said out loud as the image maximized onto the screen of her MacBook Air. She pulled the image to the side, scrolled back up to the top of the folder, and opened up the first image she saw.

"Jesus. It doesn't even look like the same girl." But it was. The curvy blonde from the first two images was gone, replaced by a much thinner, sickly-looking, raven-haired girl. Her heavy dark mascara and her black locks obscured her features. She posed again nude, but this time on her knees, holding a saucer with an empty teacup in her hands.

Eastman read the caption that Danielle had obviously put on the photo:

"I wait weak and empty for my Pedagogue to fill me with his strength and his light."

Eastman shook her head in utter disgust. "You poor thing. Someone has to save you from this monster."

Eastman closed the folder containing all the photos of Danielle and clicked on the text document.

Without reading the content, she scrolled to see the quantity of the communication.

Eastman aggressively scrolled and scrolled for at least two minutes before she finally got to the end of the messages.

"Seems like this monster spent his every waking hour working on her. Wearing her down. Breaking who she was and turning her into what he wanted her to be. Fuck this asshole," Eastman whispered out loud, her tone one of disgust blended with anger.

The printer finished spitting out the thousand-plus pages of text exchanges and photos that Geo had procured for her. The shock of the silence almost gave Eastman a start as she was so accustomed to the rhythmic sound of the printer and the depth of the rabbit hole she was tumbling down.

Geo always gave Eastman a master print file, sorted the same way as in the thumb drive:

He knew that she preferred to look at big data on paper. Between each name, there was a sheet with solid @ symbols and a cover sheet for each case. Eastman thumbed through the names and started pulling out the thickest ones she could find. Her reasoning was that the more text and photos exchanged, the more likely the opportunity for manipulation, damage, and trauma.

She started laying the thickest files from California on the floor of her office. It was easy because they were printed in alphabetical order.

There were three that immediately jumped out to Melantha due to the amount of communication.

1. Danielle Ackles

2. Katia Silver

3. Jaycee Niermeier

"You girls were in big trouble, and you didn't even know it yet." Eastman placed the phonebook-sized stack of the rest of the correspondence onto her desk. She turned back to the three other piles on the floor, crossed her arms, and leaned against her desk.

"This is going to be a long night, but first . . . coffee!" Eastman grabbed her purse and fished out her keys. On her way out of her office, she turned and looked at the heaped pile of freshly printed data that needed to be gone over with a fine-tooth comb.

"I hope there is still a chance for me to save you guys. I really hope there's still a chance."

Jesse briskly walked, almost jogged through the baggage claim of the Indianapolis international airport.

All he had with him was a backpack full of clothes and his wallet.

It was February in Indiana, and it was cold. Indiana cold. But the weather didn't matter because, on this day, he and Katia were starting their life together.

After a couple trips back and forth, they had made a choice to give this a shot and make it work.

They both knew it was real.

They both knew it was right.

They both knew it was what they wanted.

On the last trip out, Jesse had a sit down with Katia's father.

Jesse told Mr. Berlin exactly what his intentions were and what he had planned. Jesse wasn't nervous at all. He had been waiting to have this conversation with Gary for nearly six years.

They sat at a table in Gary's five-car garage, exchanging guy talk while Katia and Gary's girlfriend, Andrea, were busy cooking in the kitchen.

"Thanks again for all the hospitality, Gary. I really do appreciate it."

"No problem, Jess. It's fun to have you out to visit."

Gary was playing it cool. He wasn't stupid.

Jesse waited until Gary lit a cigarette before he started explaining his plan.

Gary sat and listened. Jesse had a hard time reading Gary's expression and body language while he was talking. Like Jesse, Gary had been in sales since he was a kid and had a good twenty-five years on Jesse. Jesse explained his plans and intentions with Katia as openly and honestly as he could.

"Gary, I am deeply, sincerely, and madly in love with Katia, and I have been for years. We plan to leave here in a couple days, for Katia to move to Los Angeles with me, and for us to start our life together."

Jesse took a pregnant pause, keeping his eyes on Gary's. "Hopefully, with your blessing, sir."

Gary stared beyond Jesse out into the many snow-covered trees and forest that surrounded his acres of property. He lit another cigarette and shook his head. "I don't know, Jess. I just don't know."

"I understand how you feel, sir, but I want you to know—"

Gary cut Jesse off. "I don't think it's a good idea *right now*. I'm not sure if Katia is stable enough."

Jesse interjected, summoning the calmest tone he could. "Yes, sir, I am aware of your concerns, but she really wants this, and so do I. I will do everything in my power to keep her safe and sound, I promise you that."

"I don't like it, and I don't feel good about it . . . But you're going to do what you're going to do. This conversation is over." Gary put out his cigarette and went inside, leaving Jesse sitting alone in the garage.

Shortly after Gary went inside, Katia and Andrea came into the garage.

"Sooo, how'd it go?" Andrea asked with a hopeful yet nervous expression on her face.

"Good, I think."

Andrea winced a bit. She knew what "good" meant when it came to conversations with Gary.

Katia ran over to Jesse and jumped on his lap.

"Thank you!" Katia said kissing Jesse emphatically.

"Welcome, my love." Jesse smiled while he was getting the barrage of Katia kisses.

"Well, we are in no rush to leave. We thought we would stay out here for a couple weeks while Katia finished up her duties for Gary at the dealership. I'm staying at the motel down the street, so—" Jesse was interrupted by Gary walking into the garage.

The man was visibly unhappy. "Katia, I don't need you at work tomorrow, or ever again. If you're going to leave, don't hang around, just go. I don't want you in this house another night." Gary turned and walked out of the garage.

Andrea, still standing next to the door, was now wringing her hands and had a real look of worry on her face. "Can you take me with you?" she whispered to Katia, who was nearly in tears.

Jesse stood up and tried to calm the two women down. "I'm sure after he cools off, it will—"

As if he were lingering behind the door to listen in, Gary entered the garage again. He looked first at Jesse with utter disdain, then over to Katia. "Leave, now."

Jesse looked to Katia with a *Is he serious?* look on his face. He could tell by Katia's expression, that not only was Gary serious, but this par for the course.

"Dad, we just want to—"

Gary, now nearly yelling, cut Katia off, "Get out of my house, and don't come back!" Gary stormed back into the house, slamming the garage door behind him as he left.

"Let me get my things," Katia said, wiping a tear from her cheek.

Katia followed behind Gary, and as soon as she went in the house, Jesse could hear Gary screaming at her. Jesse got up and started to go toward the door leading into the house, but Andrea stopped him.

"Don't. Just . . . trust me. Don't."

"But—" replied Jesse as the screaming was now coming from both Gary and Katia.

Andrea held up both her hands in a gentle 'stop' position. "Don't," she repeated softly.

There was another slamming of a door somewhere in the house, and Jesse could hear Katia running up the stairs to her bedroom that was above the garage. About two minutes later, Katia was back in the garage with large pre-packed suitcases. Tears were streaming down her face as she walked up and embraced Jesse. He held her tightly as she shook and sobbed.

He looked to Andrea, who offered a sympathetic, saddened smile, while Katia embraced him. He nodded, then whispered into Katia's ear, "Let's go, Katia. Let's go."

He put his arm around his sobbing partner and led her out into the snowy night and down the winding rural roads to Jesse's motel room on what was now an even colder winter evening in Indiana.

"It's time to wake up, my love." Jesse gently nudged Katia as she slept in the semi-comfortable motel bed.

It was nearly 10:36 a.m., and Jesse had already been up for over two hours. Katia stirred and opened up one big blue eye to see Jesse standing over her, holding a coffee.

"I brought you White Lightning!" Jesse said with a smile as he handed Katia a Venti-sized Starbucks cup. "White Lightning" wasn't something that was on the regular Starbucks drink menu, unless you go to a specific Starbucks that Katia frequented in Indiana. It had five shots of espresso, over ice, with three or four pumps of white mocha.

Katia eagerly accepted the large iced beverage and took a sip from it.

"O-M-G, I fucking love you!" Katia wrapped her free arm around Jesse and gave him a huge hug. She got out of the bed and took the bedsheet with her, wrapped around her like a big white cloak.

"Let's go see Mom," Jesse said as Katia took another sip of her drink and walked across the room of the chilly motel to the bathroom.

"Do we have to?" asked Katia, half-joking as she peed with the bathroom door open.

"I think it's a good idea. We talked to Dad, and we saw how good that went. Might as well go for a double," Jesse quipped as he sat in the chair at the little table of the motel room and flipped through his emails on his phone.

He smiled as he heard a loud huff and sigh come from the bathroom.

"Fine." Katia started the shower, and after a couple of minutes, she was out and started getting ready, brushing her still wet hair and putting on her makeup. Jesse came up from behind her and wrapped his arms around the beautiful woman that was wearing only a towel.

"Do you have any idea of how perfectly beautiful you are?"

Katia just smiled as she applied more mascara.

"Look at us, babe. Look at us."

Katia and Jesse looked at the reflection of themselves in the large mirror in the motel bathroom. After a moment, Katia cracked a big smile.

"This is us," said Jesse, giving Katia a squeeze.

"This is us." Katia looked into Jesse's eyes in the reflection in the mirror, and Jesse gazed into hers. She flashed him another blinding smile as she started back on her mascara, and Jesse giggled as he kissed her on the head.

"O-M-G," Katia exclaimed, placing her wand back into the tube. "I just remembered I have a surprise for you!" She ran to one of her big suitcase bags and unzipped it. She took out a little blue box and handed it to Jesse.

"This is for you. It's not much, but I think you will like it."

Jesse opened the little blue box, and in it was a sterling silver keychain with a Masonic square and compass on it.

"I love it," said Jesse, already unhooking his keys from his belt and attaching his new keychain to it. "Wow. thanks, babe!"

Katia just smiled and went back into the bathroom to finish putting on her makeup.

Jesse sat and stared at the silver keychain. *Thank you,* he said internally, not to Katia, but *for* Katia. At that moment, Jesse was grateful to the universe for gifting him his partner, his woman, his angel—his love.

Later that afternoon, they arrived at Katia's mom's house.

It was a simple brick house on a tree-lined street in central Indiana. It was not unlike the millions of homes in thousands of towns that sprung up throughout the Rust Belt during the massive building spree that went on in pre- and post-war America.

"I don't like the sound of this at all, Katia."

Jesse and Katia sat at the dining room table of her mother's house.

Kate looked over to her daughter and said in a voice that was just above a tremble. "We just got you back a little while ago, and now you're leaving us again?"

"Mom, I'm not leaving you, but I have to live my life."

The evening had turned from fun, light-hearted dinner conversation to this after Jesse grew tired of pussy footing around and ignoring the elephant in the room. He dropped the plan to Katia's mom after what he thought was enough preamble, but it didn't prepare Kate enough.

"Katia, sure, you met him six years ago, but how well do you even know this man?" Kate asked across the table, motioning to Jesse. Jesse felt like that comment should have been saved for when he went outside to have a smoke; he knew now wasn't the time to try and defend himself or their relationship—this was Katia's duty.

Katia got up to go sit beside Kate. She put her hand on her mother's and pulled out her iPhone.

"Mom, look." Katia opened her Facebook Messenger app and endlessly scrolled back six years of conversations.

Six years of Jesse being there for her, even when she was at her worst. Six years of her relying on Jesse through breakdowns and freak outs. Six years of Jesse's consistent love for her.

Even in her darkest hours, he was there.

Kate looked down at the iPhone in amazement, then back up to Katia. She blinked hard, and tears started going down her face as she embraced Katia. "You need to go do this. You need to go."

Kate got up from her chair and gave Jesse a huge hug.

After, she looked Jesse dead in the eyes. "You better take good care of my Katia."

"Ma'am, I have every intention of it."

Kate wrapped her arms around the big man again and squeezed him tightly.

Jesse looked over Kate's shoulder to Katia. She was crying again, only this time, they were a very different kind of tears.

The crinkling sound of an old doorbell echoed through the sparsely decorated apartment. On the other side of the door stood a young woman, no older then nineteen, with a small suitcase.

Her suitcase showed the scuffs and bruises from dozens of family vacations. Well, vacations that the family had taken before they donated the suitcase to the Goodwill, where the young girl had bought it.

She was nervous, excited, and a little scared. Her pulse quickened as she heard heavy footfalls coming to answer the door.

The door opened, and there a man stood. The dimly lit room illuminated only by two salt lamps and a dozen black candles.

He was in a black suit.

White shirt.

Black tie.

Black shoes and belt to match.

He was an older man in his mid-sixties, maybe. Quite tall, six-foot-five with broad, powerful shoulders and a cleanly shaved head. His angular face framed by an all-gray goatee.

His suit was custom tailored to cling perfectly to his lean muscular build.

The man whispered, staring down coldly at the young girl in his doorway, "What is it that you seek?"

The girl quietly, hesitantly responded, "Your strength and your light, my Pedagogue."

The man stepped to the side and motioned her into the apartment.

"Then . . . you may enter."

The girl crossed the threshold of the apartment door, rolling her suitcase behind her. The man closed and locked the multiple deadbolts after she passed, then he turned to the girl who was standing sheepishly in the darkened room.

"You have just taken your first step into a larger world," he said as he looked the girl up and down. "Tell me, Orchid, are you frightened?"

"No, Pedagogue."

The man brushed the young woman's naturally wavy hair away from her face and took her chin into his hand. Her brown eyes looked up to the man, his steely blue eyes fixed on hers.

"Then let us begin," the man said coldly. He stepped back from the young woman and turned his back to her.

He called out into a darkened room of the large penthouse apartment. "Andromeda, Orchid is ready for preparation."

Moments later, a beautiful woman, in her late twenties, entered the large living area. As the woman entered the room, the man slowly turned and exited. He disappeared into the darkened room of the penthouse.

Andromeda was nude, her long black hair flowing over her shoulders and down her back.

"Hello, Orchid. It's so good to finally meet you in person after all the chatting we have been doing!" Andromeda embraced the young woman warmly. "I'm so excited for you. We are going to be like family—your real family."

Orchid smiled. Her nose crinkled up into a cute pixie-like expression.

"It feels so good to be here. I . . . I have been waiting so long to have a real family. I can't believe I finally made it."

"Was your flight good?" Andromeda asked while taking the woman's suitcase from her.

"It was my first time on an airplane! It was a little bumpy, but it was fine. I was so excited I couldn't sleep."

"It's normal to be excited right before you're about to be born again. We all felt that way. I'm so excited for you. This is going to be the greatest thing that has ever happened to you! You're going to feel so at home here. I feel like we're already best friends, like, sisters!" Andromeda's smile and tone made Orchid feel much more at ease.

"Thank you so much for all the tea you sent me. I can really feel a difference in my health and in my body since I have started drinking it. Oh, and living our Pedagogue's protocols has really made a huge difference."

"You're so welcome, Orchid. The pleasure is all mine. We are a family now, and family takes care of each other. Together under the warm, loving light and guidance of our Pedagogue." Andromeda rolled Orchids bag to the corner of the room. "Now, speaking of your body, let's get you prepared."

Andromeda approached the young girl and embraced her again. "It's so good to have you here, Orchid. It's so good. You're so good.

Now, let's get you started."

Andromeda lifted Orchids arms over her head and pulled her shirt up and off her thin body. She circled behind the young woman and undid her bra. She helped it off her and carefully took it and her shirt and placed them next to her suitcase. Andromeda approached Orchid once again.

She smiled and dropped to her knees.

"Foot number one, please."

Orchid lifted her left foot off the floor, and Andromeda slipped off her Nike cross trainer.

"Foot number two, my love."

Orchid lifted her second foot, and her second shoe was removed.

Andromeda looked up at Orchid and smiled as she pulled off her yoga pants and panties. Andromeda gathered Orchid's clothes, folded them neatly, and placed them next to her shirt and bra beside her suitcase.

Andromeda stood nude beside Orchid.

"You're doing great, my love. Now do as I do."

Andromeda fell to her knees and placed her hands palm-up on her knees.

Orchid studied Andromeda's fluid, poetic movement and did her best to mimic it exactly.

Andromeda whispered excitedly to Orchid as they both knelt on the floor, "You did perfect, my love. You're so good; you're perfect. Now, look down at the floor; we are going to start. Are you ready?"

"Yes."

"Okay, this is going to be amazing for you."

Andromeda called out loudly and with pride into the darkened room, "My Pedagogue, the initiate is prepared and ready for you."

To the young woman, who was doing the best she could to not show the blend of nerves and excitement, Andromeda whispered, "Keep your eyes on the floor, my love."

The sound of heavy footsteps entered the room. Orchid could feel her pulse quicken as the footsteps got closer to her. From her view of the dimly lit floor, she could first see the man's shadow, then the man's feet coming into her vision. A floor-length black robe flowed and billowed as he stopped directly in front of her.

A man's steady voice pierced the darkness. "You may look upon me, my child."

Orchid slowly looked up to the man, who was also nude, aside from the black robes that hung loosely around his body.

The woman gasped as her eyes caught a glimpse of the savage tattoos that were all over his body. A patchwork of black symbols covered the man's lean muscular form. The tapestry of designs—their esoteric meanings long forgotten in the sleepwalk of modern society—at one time were the symbols representing the reason babies were sacrificed to ensure the next year's harvest would come in. These symbols were the reason that children were intuitively afraid of the dark.

As Orchid's eyes raised to meet the man's face, in the dark room, she could barely make out the mask the man was wearing. It had the appearance of some sort of horned animal skull.

The man reached his hand down to the young woman.

She took his hand, and he slowly brought her to her feet.

The man inspected the young woman's nude body.

He touched on the tic-tac-toe pattern of self-inflicted scars that covered her upper legs and arms from the cutting rituals she used to engage in before she started speaking to him—before she found hope.

"You have punished yourself enough, my child. All that you have done to yourself was a manifestation of your inner goddess trying to free itself from the lie you were living and the mask you were wearing."

"Yes, Pedagogue, that is true."

"You are now ready to stand in my shadow, for I am the light that will bring you from darkness, and you will ascend through me, into my strength."

Andromeda rose to her feet as if a rehearsed cue had been spoken. She stepped behind the girl and placed her hands on her shoulders.

"Now we begin your transformation. Your transformation into beauty."

Andromeda pushed the young girl back on her knees.

The man placed his hand on the woman's head and violently pulled her open mouth into his robes—into the darkness.

THE LONG RIDE HOME

Enjoy present pleasures in such a way as not to injure future ones.

—Seneca

Eastman stood back and admired her handy work.

The entire wall of her private office was now a web of printed sheets of paper and photographs of the Instagram posts of Katia Silver, Dani Ackles, and Jaycee Niermeier.

Under the photos were the messages exchanged between each of the girls and the Pedagogue.

As far as Eastman could figure, the women were in no way connected, at least directly. They didn't follow one another, and they didn't like any of each other's posts.

Eastman stared at the images. *The only thing they have in common . . . is him.*

Eastman tapped around her lips with her middle finger, it was a compulsion she had when she was thinking profoundly or drinking heavily.

He must have kept them separated from one another, because he uses the same canned lines of bullshit for everyone. If they all started talking, his little game would be over in short order.

Eastman sat down at her MacBook Air.

As she did her own cyber-sleuthing, she came to discover that these girls were all talking to the Pedagogue from a newer account than their everyday ones. These weren't the accounts where they posted pictures of their pets, food, boyfriends, or husbands.

She looked back at the three women's public profiles that she had printed out for comparison.

Jaycee. Recently single. Looks like she dumped her boyfriend. Maybe he wasn't okay with her . . . lifestyle change.

Dani. Single . . . Looks like a recluse. Dropped out of school. Entirely off the grid and over the rainbow with this bullshit.

Katia Silver. Married. Melantha looked at the multiple pictures that Katia had with her husband on her public account. *Cute guy. Tattoos. Looks like he really loves her . . . Poor bastard.* She looked down to his name. *Jesse.*

These public accounts are the ones they used as their masks. Their secret ones told a different story altogether.

Their secret Instagram accounts looked very different from their everyday Instagram feeds. They were dark, stark black and white. They were filled with imagery of paintings and statues of murder and death. Decapitation was the theme of most of the Renaissance paintings and Greek and Roman statues. The imagery of women cutting the heads off men. Romanesque statues engaged in mortal battle with the Pedagogue's quotes underneath the images:

"You must be willing to kill all those that will try to hold you back from the mastery of self."

"Do what must be done."

"My strength will set you free."

Eastman spun her leather chair around and looked at the wall of pictures and messages. She looked back and forth: messages, pictures, messages, pictures.

She went back to the big data dump that Geo had provided to her and thumbed through all the countries, states, and cities.

There was no other meaningful long-term communication.

Most of the other girls' interest seems to have dissipated or fallen off when they realized how much of a loser creep this guy is.

218

She tapped her lips with her fingers as her mind plunged even deeper into thought.

So . . . now he's focusing more local. He's gotten impatient and has grown sloppy. He's making mistakes. He needs his fix, and he needs it faster.

Eastman leaned back in her chair and stared at the piles of printed pages on the three young women. She sighed and shook her head.

He has to be stopped. This cycle has to be broken.

Jesse finished cramming the last of Katia's belongings into her white Ford Escape.

The little SUV was packed to the gills with clothes, bags of shoes, and her various other personal items. Jesse got into the car and laughed when he realized that the rearview mirror was now blocked by all of Katia's belongings, and wholly unusable.

He looked over to Katia as she opened the passenger door of the SUV after getting a huge hug and kiss from her mom. Kate walked up to Katia's window and knocked on it as Jesse started up the car.

"Check in with me, please. I love you, Katia. I miss you already!"

Kate leaned in the open window of the SUV and gave Katia another goodbye hug.

Kate looked over to Jesse and while shaking a finger and said, "Drive safe, and no speeding."

Katia laughed out loud because she knew how Jesse drove—like the oldest of old ladies.

"Yes, ma'am," replied Jesse as he gave Kate a military-style salute. "I'll make sure we check in when we stop for the night." Jesse put the car into drive, and slowly pulled away as Kate stood there, waving from her driveway until they rounded the first corner.

"Are you ready?" asked Jesse as he pulled onto the freeway on-ramp.

Katia curled up to him and purred, "I'm ready to go anywhere with you."

"Here we go." Jesse accelerated onto the freeway heading south.

It was exactly 2,054 miles from Katia's mom's doorstep to the little house on Piedmont.

And every mile was a mile closer to home.

Around 11:45 p.m. that night, Jesse pulled into a motel somewhere in Missouri. He got out of the car and walked around Katia's side and opened her door for her. She groaned as she got out of the Ford Escape.

"Ugh. Such a long drive."

"But it's been a fun one, hasn't it?" Jesse smiled and winked at Katia.

The two made a deal to stop and have sex somewhere adventurous in each state they drove through. Before leaving Indiana, after filling up at the gas station, they found a secluded cornfield, parked, and Jesse leaned Katia up against the side of the white Ford Escape and . . . filled her up, while surrounded by hundreds of empty, desolate fields. If it had been the summertime, there would be corn as far as the eye could see, but it being winter, they were flat, gray, and barren.

Several hours later, in Illinois, they found an outside gas station bathroom to play some games in.

It was a good day.

"Oh, look, free popcorn!" Jesse laughed as they walked into the lobby of the old but well-maintained motel somewhere in the middle of Missouri.

They got checked in and made their way to their room. As soon as Jesse opened the door, Katia immediately jumped into the shower. Jesse made his way to the bed and stretched his back out.

As soon as Katia was out, Jesse got in and did a quick rinse off.

The two slept all night soundly, their bodies intertwined.

The next four days were filled with off the beaten path attractions. The kind of Americana that was the lifeblood of Route 66 before the interstate came and killed all but the bitter clingers of the long-forgotten era: The world's biggest thermometer. The world's largest ball of twine. A visit to 'Gravity Hill' and other high-end, low-brow oddities.

And of course, the mom-and-pop gas stations where Jesse would harass the locals by interviewing them and asking if they had seen any 'werewolves' or 'UFOs' lately.

Katia would giggle in delight at her man's rapier wit and sly winks as they made their way across thousands of miles of open road, a mountain of empty 'White Lightning' cups, dozens of orgasms, and the most excellent shitty motel rooms across the great nation.

While in the Texas panhandle, a thunderstorm rolled in, and the sky danced and illuminated with electrical radiance. Jesse put on his favorite mix of Fall Out Boy, Brand New, Taking Back Sunday, and Dashboard Confessional. They sang every verse, screamed every word, and harmonized through the cascading flashes of light that pierced the blackened night. They squealed with glee as they crossed the border from Nevada to California.

On the interchange from the 15 South to the 210 West, Jesse grabbed Katia's hand.

"We're almost home, my love! We're almost home!"

And after 2,054 miles together, they pulled into the driveway.

Katia reached for the passenger side handle of her door, and Jesse stopped her. She turned to look into her man's hazel eyes, and Jesse took her hand.

"Thank you Thank you for being brave enough to make this choice for us."

"Of course. That's what—"

Jesse interrupted Katia, for the first time ever, and spoke soft and slow. "I want you to know, that I know you're not perfect, and I never expect you to be perfect. I want you to know that house right there—" Jesse pointed at the little Spanish style house on Piedmont. "That's not *my* house; that's *our* house. The things inside of it are not *my* things; they're *our* things."

Katia listened with tears welling in her eyes.

"From now on, your 'issues,' your 'problems'—from now on, those are *our* issues. They're *our* problems."

Jesse, keeping his eyes locked onto Katia's, gently kissed her hand. "We are in this together. No. Matter. What."

Tears started rolling down Katia's cheeks.

"Welcome to our house. Welcome to our life."

Jesse was awakened by a knock at the door.

He had fallen asleep on his reclining leather chair.

Loki sat by the front door of the living room, staring at Jesse, his tail wagging.

10:47 p.m. was the time as Jesse checked his phone.

Who the fuck could this be? Jesse thought as he leaned forward in the big chair. He was happy that all the lights were off in the living room; it provided him with some cover.

There was another knock at the door.

Jesse got up and walked into the room with a bed and grabbed his Glock 19. Ever since what happened, Jesse was extremely paranoid. Would that fucker come back for round two?

His wolf-husky, although enormous, was still a puppy and not very handy in the realm of home protection. So, Jesse stashed several weapons around the house . . . just in case.

I wish that fucker would show up here again. Jesse often thought about that scenario.

The daydream had changed in the last few months.

Beating the beast into submission. Loudly dragging him into the middle of Piedmont Avenue. Laughing and screaming until all the neighbors, those same neighbors who watched Jesse crumble on that April night, got another, very different show.

Jesse would put the beast on his knees. He'd start screaming to the neighborhood, "You all remember? You all remember my wife, Katia? Do you all remember how we would wave to you on our nightly walks? Do you all remember how she would decorate the house for holidays?"

The beast would try to rise. Jesse would kick him in the face, knocking him to the pavement, and then Jesse would bring him again to his knees.

"Do you all remember how she would always have something nice to say to everyone, no matter what? Well, friends, this is the man that took her from us. This is the piece of shit that took her from me!"

The sirens of the sheriff's cars racing to the show on Piedmont would be heard not so far away.

"This is for my wife. Her name was Katia. She was my world."

Jesse would hold the weapon to the beast's head as the sirens drew closer, maybe just two blocks away.

"When you took her from me, you took everything from me!"

The beast would look up to Jesse for some spark of mercy . . .

But the beast would find no shelter or sanctuary in Jesse's eyes.

"When you take everything from somebody, when you take away their whole world, they have nothing left to lose. Her name was Katia!" Jesse would yell as he lowered the gun from the beast's forehead and pumped two rounds into his groin.

"You feel that, asshole?"

The beast would roll into the fetal position, screaming. Jesse would kick him over, onto his back. The gasps and screams of the neighbors would be drowned out as the sirens were now on the next street up and approaching fast.

Jesse would unload two more rounds into the stomach of the beast, and blood would pour from the monster's mouth.

"What's that you say, bitch?" Jesse would scream while laughing maniacally.

"I can't hear you from you choking on your own blood."

The headlights from the first sheriff's cruiser would now illuminate the street.

"Good, good. I don't want them to miss a second of this!" Jesse would drop on the chest of the beast, pinning him flat on his back as he'd put his Glock into the beast's mouth, angled up to the back of the beast's head.

"Look at me, you pathetic piece of shit. Look at me!"

Jesse would now be nose-to-nose with the beast. In Jesse's eyes, a bonfire burning rage and bloodlust.

"Her name was Katia!"

Jesse would pull the trigger and watch with orgasmic glee as the beast's brain cavity sprayed in chunks and pieces thirty yards down the pavement on Piedmont.

"Her name was Katia, and now you know you don't fuck with someone's wife." Jesse would spit into the smoldering crater of a human skull and throw the Glock down the street.

The sheriffs would still tackle and cuff Jesse, but while in the jail—Jesse would have slept well for the first time in months.

Jesse walked up to the door and placed the Glock against it, where he figured whoever was knocking at his door's center mass would be.

"Who's there?" Jesse called out, speaking to whoever was behind the door.

A singsong female voice replied, "It's Melantha Eastman."

Jesse lowered the Glock and put it behind his back while, at the same time, opening the door.

Eastman looked into the pitch-black living room, unable to see anything from the contrast of the streetlights. "Jesse?"

Jesse flipped two switches next to the front door and the living room lights illuminated.

"There you are!" said Eastman with a big smile.

"Is everything okay?" Jesse asked, confused to why she was showing up at his house, unannounced at nearly 11:00 p.m.

"Everything is great. Just wanted to see your face," she said as she breezed into the house, carrying a red file folder. The petite blonde walked past Jesse before she gave him the chance to invite her in.

"Nice Glock," Eastman said, eyeing the pistol in Jesse's hand.

"Oh, th-thanks," Jesse stuttered out, a bit embarrassed by his paranoia as he put the weapon on the bookcase among the trinkets, treasures, and driftwood.

Jesse wasn't sure how he felt about Eastman just showing up at his house so late at night. It's not that he was unhappy to see her, but it felt strange to have a woman in the house.

"So, what's up?" asked Jesse, trying his best to not look awkward and uncomfortable in his own living room.

"Nothing, just got some dinner at Seasoning Alley down the street, and I thought I would pop by and surprise you. Have you tried that place?"

"Yeah. I go there often." And by often, Jesse meant five or six days a week.

"With all the garlic I ate tonight, I'll never get kissed again," she said with a smile as she glanced around the room. Was she taking note of the new rug or how Jesse had rearranged all the furniture to make it look different than the night that it happened?

"Jesus, Jesse, it's hot as balls in here!"

She unbuttoned her blouse and slid it off her shoulders. Underneath, she had on nothing more than a thin white tank top and no bra.

Jesse tried to ignore the form of the beautiful young woman in his living room.

"I don't know how you live like this, you savage animal. I'm sweating already." Eastman giggled as she looked at the heaps of unopened letters on the dust-covered entertainment center.

Jesse's eyes locked with hers, then slowly traveled down the subtle curves of her body to the red folder she had in her hands.

"Is that for me?" Jesse asked, reaching for the red folder. She quickly spun the folder behind her back and stepped into Jesse. Her breasts were now brushing against his torso as she looked up into his deep hazel eyes.

"Not yet. I'll let you see it in a second, if you're a good boy."

"Oh really?" whispered Jesse, stepping in even closer to her.

"Yes, really," she whispered back while leaning into the man, so she could feel his body against hers.

"But first, I wanna play a little game with you," whispered the petite blonde as she raised on her tippy toes so her pouty red lips were just about to touch Jesse's.

"Oh, what sort of game is that?" Jesse said under his breath, leaning into her waiting crimson lips.

"Show and tell," said Eastman, dropping off her tippy toes, turning, and walking into the room with a bed, leaving Jesse half standing alone in the living room.

Before Jesse could even get out, "What are you doing?" he heard the big closet doors slide open.

He quickly walked into the room with a bed and saw the tiny blonde pulling, with both hands, his suitcase out of the closet.

The heavy suitcase made a loud thud on the floor as Eastman had forgotten how heavy it was from the night she first discovered it over five months ago.

"Tell me about what's in this bag, Jesse."

"Someday, I promise, but not tonight."

She smiled. "Here, take a peek at this." Eastman handed Jesse the folder that was resting on her hip.

"What's this now?"

"Open it and see."

Jesse opened the cover of the neatly bound red folder to see a cover page that read: Katia Silver.

"What's this all about, Doctor Eastman?"

She giggled. "Read it and see."

Jesse flipped to the first page. It was a transcription of Instagram direct messages.

"I don't understand. Wha-what is this?"

"Just keep reading, sweetie."

Jesse flipped through the pages and saw line after line of conversations between his wife and this man known as the "Pedagogue." He flipped back to the first page. The date of the first conversation was 3/4/2014, which was right before she left to Indiana.

He kept flipping through the pages and saw images that Katia had sent him.

Images of herself.

Nude.

In their house.

On their bed.

The little voice in Jesse's head woke up to see what all the excitement was.

She was cheating on you the whole time you were together? I knew it!

Jesse's heart began to pound, his mind began to race, and the room started closing in on him.

The voice started screaming at him from a now not so far away corner of his mind.

I told you, you weren't good enough for her! I said you wouldn't ever be enough for her!

The air he drew into his lungs felt like boiling water.

There were pictures—pictures of them together?

Jesse kept flipping and saw images of Katia with this man.

See, Jesse, no amount of money you could have made, no amount of dreams you fulfilled for her, could ever be enough. They weren't enough! You weren't enough!

There were messages from Katia telling this man that she . . . she loved him?

You weren't good enough for her! Just like how you weren't good enough for your biological parents or for your adopted father—that's why they all left you!

There was another image of Katia kneeling nude before this man, dated 03/28/2018. That was . . . less than a week before . . .

"What the fuck is this?" Jesse shrieked, sobbing. "What the fuck am I looking at?"

That voice. That voice was screaming with laughter, shrieking with glee.

AHHAHAHAHAHAHAHAHAHHAHHAHAHAHAHA!

Jesse stated hyperventilating.

The voice was now chanting: *NOT ENOUGH! NOT ENOUGH! NOT ENOUGH!*

Jesse was now screaming, "Sweet baby, no!"

He started dry heaving and made a break for the bathroom, but didn't make it.

NOT ENOUGH! NOT ENOUGH! NOT ENOUGH!

Still screaming, sobbing, clutching the red folder that was now tightly rolled into a tube. His knuckles turned the color of sun-bleached ivory.

NOT ENOUGH! NOT ENOUGH! NOT ENOUGH!

Eastman was on Jesse in an instant. Immediately, the voice stopped chanting and went silent.

All at once. There was silence.

Eastman grabbed the comforter off the bed and wrapped it like a cocoon around the man lying in a puddle of his tears and sweat. She gently rocked the man with a tender kindness usually reserved for a newborn baby.

She put his face into her bosom and shooshed him gently. Eastman whispered in Jesse's ear as she stroked his shorn head. "I've got you. I'm here. I'll never leave you. I'll never abandon you. I'd never do that to you," she cooed. "He's the one that did this."

Jesse nuzzled into Eastman, trying to swim inside of her.

"It's all his fault, Jesse." She shooshed and continued in a singsong like tone, "He took her from you." Like a lullaby, "It was him."

Jesse wept into Eastman's breasts, and he looked up to her and clutched her by her upper arms.

"Give him to me. You have to give him to me, now!"

Eastman patted Jesse's back. "I promised you I would give you the beast on a silver platter, Jesse, and I wouldn't ever lie to you."

Jesse loosened his grip on her arms. He could see the prints and indentations where his hands had been squeezing her skin, as if contemplating a bruise. Eastman hadn't even so much as flinched.

"I'm here now, Jesse. I've got you. I'll never abandon you."

Jesse whispered, what was more of a growl, "Give him to me."

Eastman smiled and stroked Jesse's beard. "He will be yours, but it's not just him. It's everyone in his family—his cult—all of them took her from you. We have a lot of work to do. You're going to have to follow the white rabbit down the rabbit hole to catch them."

Jesse put his head back into Eastman's bosom, and there he sobbed until his eyes were dry as raisins, until he had not another tear to squeeze out.

Everything he ever thought about his Katia was a lie.

The last shred, that last alive thing in Jesse, died that night in the arms of Eastman.

But now his purpose was clear.

THERE WAS ONLY SUPPOSED TO BE ONE

He is the best man who, when making his plans, fears and reflects on everything that can happen to him. But in the moment, the action is bold.

—Herodotus

"Okay, so we have two custom holistic tea blends, and one infuser spoon. Your total is $13.34."

The register dinged and hummed as Andromeda completed the transaction at Her Majesty's Teahouse and Supply, a cute little boutique tea house and new age supply store on the west side of Los Angeles.

"Would you like a bag today?" Andromeda asked the customer with a beaming and almost cheesy smile.

As the customer shuffled out the door, Andromeda turned to the young woman standing next to her.

"See, it's just that easy, Orchid. I'm sure you're going to be awesome at this!"

Orchid just nodded and reflected back her own, almost too big and too happy smile.

"You did so great last night. You did so well. I'm so proud of you," Andromeda said as she gave the young woman a big hug.

"Thank you. I felt our Pedagogue's strength flow into me. It felt so . . . so empowering."

Andromeda closed her eyes and put her hands into a reverse prayer position.

"In our darkness, the light of our Pedagogue is blinding."

Orchid attempted a reverse prayer, and her frustration was evident when she couldn't get her hands to touch behind her back.

Andromeda smiled. "Don't worry, Orchid. As our Pedagogue works to cleanse your body and awaken the divine feminine that dwells within you, you will be able to do things you never thought possible. Give it time, my love."

Orchid looked nervously at the floor. "Andromeda, do you think I can have my phone back later tonight? I would like to text my friend and let her know I'm okay."

"Of course, my love, that's no problem at all. But you do feel safe and at home with us, don't you?"

"Of course, I just don't want her to worry."

"I understand, and of course that's okay. We don't want them to worry either. But tonight, you get the honor of being introduced to the rest of our family. Do you have any idea of how special you are and how excited they are all to meet you, Orchid?"

Andromeda pulled Orchid in for another big hug, only this time, she squeezed her even harder.

"You're so good, Orchid. You're just perfect. You're coming along so fast, much faster than I did at first. You're going to be big." Andromeda released her grip on the young woman and looked deep into her eyes.

"You really think so, Andromeda?"

"Oh, yes. Our Pedagogue was telling me this morning before you got up, how he sees you becoming extremely powerful in short order. He even consulted the bones last night. The bones said you may be more than even we could have imagined. You might be someone very special to the family! That is what you want, isn't it, Orchid?"

The young woman's eyes lit up. "Of course it is! Is that really what he said?"

Andromeda's tone went from light and cheery to quite severe in a millisecond. "I would never lie to you, my sweet Orchid, and I know our Pedagogue is right about you. I can feel your strength, and the bones can see it, too."

Andromeda ever so slightly tightened her grip on Orchid's hands. "You don't take our Pedagogue or me as liars, do you, Orchid?"

Orchid looked a bit shocked. "No, ma'am, that's not what I meant at all. I was just excited to hear that—"

Andromeda interrupted the now clearly frazzled and nervous young woman. "Good, of course. I didn't think you would ever feel that way. Our Pedagogue speaks only the divine truth that flows through him through the strength he taps into, and through the channels of intertwining masculine and feminine energies that he, through his own mastery of self, has been able to harness. With time, you will know this to be a Devine truth."

Orchid nodded her head and looked at the floor. "Apologies, Andromeda, I didn't mean—"

Andromeda warmly embraced the young woman again. "It's okay, my love. You're family; you're home. This is where you're supposed to be. It's only natural. It takes time to see the light after being blind and in darkness your entire life. Soon you will feel so relaxed, you will find that you fit in and feel a belonging you have never felt before. You're going to be so good. You're already so good; you're already perfect!"

The door chimed as another customer walked into the little tea boutique.

Andromeda whispered to Orchid, "This one is all yours. I'm right here. I'll watch over you."

The young woman approached the customer, with her hands in front of her sternum as trained, and recited her greeting: "Salute! We welcome you to her Majesty's Tea House and Supply. How may I honor your strength and heal your body today?"

Andromeda beamed with pride from behind the register as she observed Orchid about her task, assisting the customer and honoring her Pedagogue.

Andromeda mused to herself while straightening up the already perfect countertop. *She's going to be fine. She's going to be just fine.*

Jesse walked Eastman to a table on the outdoor patio of Everest restaurant in La Crescenta. Everest was one of those little mom-and-pop burger places that served a little bit of everything.

Burgers and fries, of course, but also Mexican, Greek, salads, and breakfast.

It was one of the two places Jesse would go and eat.

As a matter of fact, he went there so often, the staff there got to recognize and know him well. It was like his version of "Cheers," but with burgers instead of beers.

"Wow . . . Nice place," Eastman said sarcastically as she took a seat at the little table that was partly shaded by the fiberglass parasol bolted to it.

Jesse looked at her and smiled. "Trust me," he said as he placed the little numbered placard on the edge of the table.

"You said you wanted pancakes? Well, these are the best in town."

"I'll believe it when I taste it," Eastman said with a pleasant, playful tone.

The glass door of the little restaurant opened and out walked a heavy-set older woman with two bright orange trays. "Order fourteen?" she called out, then started walking toward the table where Jesse and Melantha were sitting after Jesse waved her over.

"Good morning, darlin'. How are you today?" said the waitress as Jesse stood to help her with the heavy trays of food.

"I'm okay, Irma. How are you? How are the grandkids?"

"They're great. Thank you for asking." The woman gave Jesse a hug and nodded to Melantha.

"She's cute!" the waitress said to Jesse with a playful wink and nod.

"Yeah, she is. Thank you, Irma. Have a good day."

"Enjoy your breakfast, and if you need anything, just holler at me."

"Will do."

Irma gave Eastman another smile and went back inside.

"You come here pretty often, don't you, Jesse?" Eastman said as she eyed the heaping tray of food that was laid out in front of her.

"Yeah, I guess you could say that," Jesse said, flipping the top pancake with the giant pad of butter upside down and onto the other, so it all started melting together.

"This is a lot of food," Eastman said, wide-eyed. She picked up her plastic fork and knife and stabbed at the three giant pancakes, eggs, and hashbrowns that were divided onto two large plastic plates.

"Wait . . . no syrup?" she asked as she watched Jesse take the first bite of his pancakes.

"No, I don't like syrup on my pancakes," Jesse said clumsily while covering his mouth and chewing.

"Blasphemy," Eastman laughed, shaking her head in clear disapproval as she dumped her portion and Jesse's syrup on top of the now melty, buttery stack on her plate.

Jesse watched as she took her first bite and closed her eyes.

"Well?" Jesse said with an anticipative smile.

"Mmm, perfection," she said. Chewing happily with her mouth still full of her first bite of breakfast, she squeaked out, "Okay, you were right about this place."

Jesse just smiled. "Hate to say I told ya so, but . . ." He took another bite of his pancakes.

Eastman chewed as she reached into her oversized purse and pulled out a blue file folder. She placed it on the table next to her giant bag.

"How was your sleep last night, Jess?"

Jesse swallowed his bite of pancakes while he considered Eastman's question. "Actually, pretty good. The best I have slept in a long time. I liked having you there next to me."

"Good. Maybe we can make a habit of it," Eastman said with a smile as she glanced around the outside patio to make sure it was empty. She picked up the blue folder and handed it to Jesse.

Jesse placed the inch-thick folder on the little table beside him and opened it.

There was a printed screenshot of an attractive young woman's Instagram page.

"@GoddessAndromeda? Is this another victim?" Jesse asked as he took a sip of his orange juice.

"Keep turning, sugar," Eastman said, shoveling another heaping fork-load of pancakes into her mouth.

Jesse thumbed through the printed pages and pages of direct message conversations between the young woman and Katia.

@GoddessAndromeda: *"You're going to fit in so perfectly here, as soon as we help you escape from that prison you're living in with that brutal man. You're going to ascend and reach your full potential; you may be the beacon."*

@oneofmymanymasks: *"yes, I cannot wait to get out of this hell!"*

Jesse nearly spat out his orange juice.

"Brutal man? This hell?" He looked up to Eastman from the blue folder. "Brutal? Who is this girl talking about? She can't be referring to me. Why would Katia say that?" Jesse looked to Eastman with eyes full of shock and disbelief.

She shrugged her shoulders while taking another bite of her breakfast. "Keep reading. I'll explain how it all works with them after you're done. I'll tell you what we are going to do about it."

Jesse reached the end of the transcriptions with @ GoddessAndromeda and came to another screenshot of another

Instagram profile of a young man, maybe in his mid-twenties. Handsome, in great shape, and apparently some sort of male model: @7hePer7ectGen7leman

The communication between him and Katia was limited, but it was there, and it was enough to raise an eyebrow.

Mostly, it was this guy telling Katia how fabulous her life was going to be once she joined this so-called "family."

"Who's this pretty-boy clown?" Jesse asked as he thumbed through the conversations between his wife and this . . . this boy . . . and got to the next Instagram profile.

"He's 'The Hero,'" replied Eastman. She broke the yolk on her eggs over medium with a piece of wheat toast and took a bite of it, taking care not to ruin her lipstick.

Jesse looked up at her and paused. "The hero?"

"Almost done, sweetie," Eastman said. She was either completely focused on her food or deep in thought.

The next printed screenshot was of a burly looking man. Most of his pictures were of him lifting weights and engaging in martial arts training. "@IzzyIzBad - Grateful initiate of @ThePedagogue."

Jesse flipped back to @7hePer7ectGen7leman's print out and read the description aloud, "Grateful initiate of @ThePedagogue . . . I think I'm starting to get the picture."

Melantha took another bite of her toast. "You have no idea, love. Keep going."

Jesse skipped the minimal text between Katia and the tough guy and found the next profile.

"@GoddessSerena - Devoted to self-mastery, love, and light. Grateful initiate of @ThePedagogue."

Another young woman, somewhere in her mid-twenties, and the most hippie-like of the bunch. A typical Instagram witchy girl.

Jesse flipped through the transcripts of the direct messages exchanged between her and Katia. It was a bunch of nonsense and babble about reaching the highest elevation of self through the teachings of the Pedagogue.

"Okay, so, it's like . . . a church or something?" Jesse asked, tossing the book on the table in disgust.

"A church? No, sweetie, this is what we refer to as a *cult*." Eastman paused and pulled the crumpled, tear-stained red folder out of her bag. She opened it up to the photo of the older man with the shaved head and tattoos peeking out from his crisp white shirt.

The stark black and white photo was creepy enough, but the fact that you couldn't see any sort of expression on his face, and his eyes were entirely blacked out by shadows, made the image that much more disturbing.

His darkened eyes almost seemed to vacuum up the light like a black hole

"The leader goes by the name 'The Pedagogue.' His real name is Robert Fischer."

Jesse stared at the picture, letting the image of the man's face burn into his corneas.

"I have been trying to track him down for . . . a long time. He's a real piece of shit. He's sixty-five years old, and he fancies himself the next Jesus Christ, Allister Crowley, Charlie Manson, and David Koresh all rolled into one . . . Well, depending on his mood that day. His methods are simple. He is a predator, and he does what predators do."

"How do you mean?" Jesse asked while dumping a ton of tabasco and ketchup on his hash browns.

"Well, Jess, he finds the weak, the sick, the very young, the lost . . . and he goes after them." She took another bite of her toast.

"About twenty years ago, he came up with this 'Pedagogue' persona. This is back before the MySpace days, mind you. Think more like . . . AOL. That's when he started luring in young women to his 'religion' with his bullshit poetry and philosophy that he has cobbled together from several different ideologies."

Eastman started counting on her fingers and talking with her hands. "Satanism, Gnosticism, Wicca, the Occult, and anything else he could twist and form into a weapon—a weapon that he could use on young women just looking for some sort of relief from the very real demons they were facing."

Eastman shook her head.

"He started out as, well, maybe that's a story for another day. Anyway, years ago, he started luring young women . . . young women with problems, promising that he could 'heal them.' The women that suffer from mental disorders, depression, bipolar, OCD, bulimia, anorexia, body dysmorphia—you name it."

"How does he find them?"

Eastman pointed to her iPhone sitting next to her tray of food.

"Hashtags."

Jesse looked confused.

"Hashtags?"

"This is the most fucked up part of it all: the internet is a great resource for people with these issues to support one another, to call out for help, and to find strength in a community and in each other.

"You have heard the adage, 'None of us are as strong as all of us,' right? Well, the problem is when a wounded, exhausted baby seal is marooned on a buoy, crying for its family, the sharks hear it too. I have a copy of his search history here." Eastman flipped to the back of the blue folder to a string of what looked to be sixty or maybe seventy hashtags and combinations of them all.

Jesse scanned the hashtags as she continued. "Well, sweetie, he would use them and abuse them. From what I can tell, he's looking for someone specific. Someone he calls his 'beacon.' So, he brings them in, and if, for whatever reason, they don't line up with what he is looking for, he still finds a use for them. After he has them broken down entirely and programmed, he sells them as ready-made slaves to the very lucrative sex trafficking trade." Eastman paused and took another bite of her yolk-slathered toast.

"He's not stupid—not in the slightest. As a matter of fact, he's quite brilliant and meticulous. I don't expect him to make any mistakes that would be enough for me to build a solid case against him. He thinks he's untouchable, but he's wrong. We can reach out and touch him. But he has his core people, the archetypes in the group that he doesn't rotate in and out. The ones he has trained to help him find his beacon. He's been looking for her for as long as I can remember."

Jesse shook his head while rubbing his temples. "Earlier you mentioned 'the hero.' What was that about?"

"I thought you would never ask." Eastman stole Jesse's last bite of pancake off his plate, dipped it into her syrup, and stuffed it into her mouth. "The goddess, the hero, the muse, and the warrior."

"Our little friend, Robert—excuse me." She did dramatic air quotes, accompanied by her famous eyeroll. "'The Pedagogue' is obsessed with archetypes."

"Archetypes?" Jesse replied, an inquisitive expression on his face.

"Yes, a recurrent symbol or motif in literature, art, or mythology, like Persephone, Demeter, Hecate, Gorgon, Medusa. More contemporary examples would be Harry Potter, Luke Skywalker, and Gandalf. It's all Jungian psychology. Jung used the archetype as a primitive mental image inherited from the earliest ancestors. Present and reoccurring in the collective unconscious.

"Our boy here is obsessed with the idea that everything is connected to everything, so he has built his 'family' around this idea. Or should I say, he is trying to rebuild his family to what it used to be."

"Huh?" Jesse looked to her. She just shrugged.

"I'll tell you about that part soon, it doesn't matter right now."

Eastman flipped through the blue folder and stopped at the photos of the man in the boxing ring.

"@izzyizbad. Izzy, the MMA guy, is the warrior. He's the intimidation strongman of the group. If someone in the family steps out of line, he handles them. Brutally. He also sells quite a lot of drugs on the side to fund the family. And, let's just say he has some . . . vile sexual appetites." Eastman flipped to the young hippie woman.

"@GoddessSerena. Serena, twenty-six years old. She's the flower child of the group, just your typical happy-go-lucky girly girl, with a dark side. She's the muse. She is our boy's personal Aphrodite. Let's just say it's her job to keep his creative juices flowing and help groom the new recruits."

Eastman moved to the handsome young man in the suit and tie.

"@7hePerfec7Gen7leman. Jason Lewis. This poor kid . . . The Pedagogue found him tricking himself out in West Hollywood when he was fourteen. Had a nasty drug habit, and it has all gone downhill from there. He does some legit modeling work, and he helps Izzy with the drug business. Selling to the models on shoots, getting them hooked, and trying to rope them into the family. Most of the drugs are sold out of their 'tea business.' He's the hero archetype. Because, well . . . look at the kid. He looks like a Greek God."

"Tea business?"

"Yes, The Pedagogue fancies himself to be a 'master' of all things, including holistic herbal medicine. He owns and operates a small boutique tea business on the West Side."

Jesse's eyes grew wide.

"Katia was obsessed with tea for, like, the last eight months." Jesse's thought trailed off into the ether as all the puzzle pieces connected in his mind. "Maybe I should go pay the tea shop a visit."

Eastman smiled and put her hand on Jesse's tense arm.

"Honey, that would be a terrible idea. Plus, I have something better planned for them," she said with a wink, then continued going over the pages in the blue folder. "We almost forgot the most important, and the most dangerous one of all: @GoddessAndromeda."

Jesse picked up the blue folder and stared at the image of the attractive raven-haired woman.

"I—I know her! Katia would FaceTime with her all the time! She would put me on to say hello. She . . . she said she was an old friend of hers from Florida. Katia said they grew up together. I spoke to her several times and would invite her to come out to LA so she and

Katia could spend time together!"

Eastman glanced over to Jesse and sighed. "Wow, that's . . . fucked up. I'm so sorry, Jesse."

"She acted like she was my friend and thanked me for being so kind to Katia. What the fuck is wrong with these people?"

Eastman took a sip of her orange juice. "I'm sorry to tell you this, but I'm not surprised at all. She's very, very dangerous, a master of manipulation, and very loyal to her master. She is the Pedagogue's right hand. She is the second in command, and indeed, the 'Judas Goat' of the operation."

"Judas Goat?"

"The Judas goat is trained to associate with the other goats and sheep, only to lead them to a specific destination. A Judas goat will lead sheep to the slaughter while its own life is spared."

She paused. "She is the one that really reeled Katia into his arms, Jesse, and into his bed. She's as guilty as he is."

Jesse sat there, staring at the text conversations.

"It's her fault also. She lied to Katia and lied to you. She is the one that poisoned Katia's mind."

Jesse stared at the blue folder. A vein in his temple was visibly throbbing along in time with his quickening pulse.

"So then, what do we do?"

Eastman looked over her shoulder once again at the happy families walking hand in hand with their kids into the best pancake place in the foothills. She smiled and turned back to Jesse.

"When you're aggressively going after cancer, you have to dig out every little bit, every tiny cell, or else it comes back . . ." She raised an eyebrow and hissed a deadly whisper across the tiny table, "You are going to destroy his family, his life—the way he destroyed yours. That's what you want. Isn't it, Jesse?"

Jesse didn't even look up from the folder he was staring at. He just answered, "Yes."

Eastman nodded. "You are going to take out the circle from the outside in. You want vengeance for Katia? You want blood? You got it, but you're going to have to do exactly as I say. You only get one chance at this. We just get one shot to avenge Katia and what they did to you."

Eastman leaned in and grinned. "How does that make you feel, Jesse?"

Jesse smiled and squeezed her hand. "Fan-Fucking-Tastic."

She brought the straw of her orange juice up to her lips and smiled as she took a sip.

"Perfection . . . I'm here for you, Jesse. I'm never going to leave you or steer you wrong, do you understand?"

Jesse squeezed her hand again, and with a smile, a real smile on his face, answered, "Yes! Thank you for this! Thank you!"

Eastman glanced back at the families, and then back to Jesse.

"We have work to do, sweetie. They destroyed your life, the life you fought so hard for. They left you broken in pieces. And now, Jesse, now is the time to pick up those pieces, and sharpen them into knives."

HAPPINESS IN SLAVERY

I write about the power of trying, because I want to be okay with failing. I write about generosity because I battle selfishness. I write about joy because I know sorrow. I write about faith because I almost lost mine, and I know what it is to be broken and in need of redemption. I write about gratitude because I am thankful – for all of it.

—Kristin Armstrong

Jesse and Katia held hands as they rode the elevator up to the fourth floor of the professional office building on Walnut Ave. Jesse gave Katia's hand a squeeze as the elevator door slowly stuttered open.

"Ready, my love?"

Katia gave Jesse's hand a squeeze back, leaned over, and gave her man a peck on the cheek.

"You make me so happy. Thank you for everything you do for me—for us," Katia whispered softly to Jesse as they started down the hallway, passing by all the doors until they reached suite 413.

The door was slightly ajar, and Jesse gave it a gentle nudge. It slowly swung open.

Lynn was sitting in her chair at her desk when the door opened. She turned and stood up to greet the couple as they entered the room.

"Thank you so much, Lynn, for taking the time to see us on such short notice. I really appreciate it." Katia went in for a hug and greeted Lynn. She knew Lynn much better than Jesse, as she had been going to see her twice a week for the last eight months. Katia had seemed to be making significant progress, but in the previous few months, something had shifted. Something had changed, and Katia hadn't quite been her mostly happy-go-lucky self.

To get to the bottom of what had been bothering Katia, Jesse had booked an appointment for them both—just to get some dialogue going in a controlled, mediated environment.

Not that there was any lack of communication at home. After all, Jesse and Katia's relationship was built off of a six-year friendship, and Jesse felt safe talking to Katia about anything. He always felt that was a two-way street.

But. just to be sure, he wanted to go see Lynn and make sure all the Ts were crossed and all the Is were dotted.

Lynn motioned for the two to have a seat on the big black couch that was against the wall in her little office. The room was small—maybe ten by ten—but cozy, and tastefully decorated.

Lynn's specialty was EMDR and CPTSD, a great combination to help Katia tackle some of the issues she had from her childhood. Although Lynn was not cheap, Jesse didn't mind going the extra mile and spending the equivalent to a mortgage payment every month to have Katia see the kind-eyed, heavy-set brunette woman that she felt comfortable sharing her feelings and demons with.

And for a while there, it felt like it was helping—like Lynn was making a difference.

"So, how are you guys doing today?" Lynn said with a big inviting smile.

Jesse looked over at Katia, who had her giant "Katia smile" plastered across her face.

"Things are, like, really going well!"

Lynn nodded and looked at Jesse.

Jesse smiled and put his hand on Katia's knee, and Katia interlaced their fingers, resting their hands on her lap.

"I'm very proud of her. She's amazing," said Jesse.

Katia turned and smiled at him.

"Any issues between you guys that you want to discuss here in therapy?"

Jesse was slightly shocked when Katia started a line of dialogue with Lynn.

"Lynn, do you remember how a couple weeks ago, we talked about my privacy, and how important that is to me?"

"Yes, of course I do, Katia. Why?"

Katia's brow furrowed as she pulled her hand away from Jesse's and moved his hand out of her lap.

"I wanted to talk here, in front of Jesse about it, so he understands how important it is to me."

Lynn looked over at Jesse.

"Do you know what Katia is referring to, Jesse?"

Jesse sat there a bit dumbstruck, wondering what Katia was talking about. But, that's what he was there for.

"Katia, tell Jesse how you feel." Lynn sat back in her leather chair and readied her pen and notepad.

Katia turned and looked at Jesse, her eyes already glazing over, her hand reaching for the Kleenex box positioned conveniently by the sofa. Before Katia started to speak, she pulled two of the tissues out of the box. She stared at them and started worrying them in her hands.

Katia looked again to Jesse, who sat in confused silence.

"Lover, I know we talk about everything, but I really need you to hear me on this."

Jesse looked over to Lynn, and she nodded and started writing on her yellow legal pad. Jesse took that as a cue to look back to Katia, determined to understand.

"It's just that, I . . . I want you to know. You remember how I told you about how when I was growing up, I had, like, zero privacy?"

Jesse nodded empathically and smiled. "Of course."

"Well . . . I just like want you to know, like, it's vital to me that you respect that and never look at my stuff."

Jesse sat and listened intently.

Katia started crying and brought the well-worried tissue up to her face to dab the newly formed perspiration from each of her eyes before her makeup got smeared. "It's just essential to me that you know that. I need to know that my privacy is safe—my email, my social media, my journal, everything."

Katia put her hand on Jesse's knee, and Jesse took Katia's delicate hand in both of his.

"Of course, my love. Is that all you wanted to say?"

Katia smiled and nodded.

"Oh, my sweet baby, that's it?" Jesse was now smiling. "I wouldn't ever, ever go into your personal stuff. I remember very well the conversation we had about that, and I know how important your privacy and your personal space is to you. I appreciate you caring enough to tell me again how you feel, and letting me know exactly what you need."

Katia threw her arms around Jesse and kissed him.

Lynn leaned back in her chair and smiled. "Katia, do you feel that Jesse heard you?"

"Yes, very much so. He's always been a good listener and very attentive to everything I need. I always feel respected."

"Jesse, do you feel that what Katia has voiced here today is valid and that are you okay with it?"

"Completely. I just want her to feel safe and respected in every aspect of our relationship."

Katia gave Jesse another peck on the cheek.

The couple talked for the remaining forty-five minutes of the session about immediate family and communication.

Most of the dialogue that day was whether or not Katia was going to continue having a relationship with her parents, and what role Jesse could have to help facilitate in that. Jesse was of the mind that he would ultimately support Katia in whatever decision she made, but also, he hoped to help mend the relationship if he could.

"Times up, guys." Lynn got up from her big chair and gave the couple each a big hug.

"Usual card fine, Jesse?"

"Of course."

"Katia, would you mind if I had a quick word with Jesse alone?"

"Not at all. See you downstairs, lover. Bye, Lynn!" Katia gave Lynn another big hug before she turned and walked down the hallway. Lynn waited a couple of seconds to make sure Katia was out of earshot and turned to Jesse.

The look on her face had gone from jovial to serious.

"How do you feel our girl is doing—really?"

Jesse shrugged his shoulders. "She's doing okay . . . The binging and purging is becoming troubling and seems to be happening more and more often. She is having issues sleeping, and her mood is all over the place."

Lynn reached to Jesse and gave his arm a quick reassuring squeeze.

"I know, we talk about that . . . a lot. Is there anything else that you're noticing, any other changes in behavior?"

"Other than her now being totally obsessed with tea?"

Jesse and Lynn both chuckled.

"No, just the usual . . . any tips, doc?"

"Just keep a close eye on her. My Spidey-sense is tingling a little. I'm sure it's nothing, but better to be safe than sorry. Let's make a deal: I'll work with her in here, and you work with her at home, deal?"

"Deal," Jesse said with a smile. He was grateful that Lynn cared so much about Katia, and he didn't have to feel alone in dealing with some of her issues.

"I know how much you love that woman, Jesse; I know what she means to you. She's fortunate."

"That's funny, doc, because all this time, I thought I was the lucky one."

Lynn gave Jesse another big hug. "Have a great week. Text me if you need anything."

"Will do."

Jesse walked down the hall to the elevator, and back into his picture-perfect life.

Jesse knocked on the big red door with stained glass and antique hardware.

He tried to ignore the heavy perfume of the lavender that was in full bloom and shrouded the porch of the once-house now-office. The sun dipped in the horizon and the first chill of September air flowed down from the canyons and into the streets and alleyways.

A couple seconds after his initial knock, the hardware on the door *clicked, clacked,* and groaned as the door swung on its hinges.

Eastman stood at the threshold, her blue eyes looking up at him, her crimson lips parted and opened to reveal her perfect smile.

"Right on time as always, Jesse." She let out a satisfied sigh as she embraced him.

A quick push onto her tippy toes, and her lips met his. She lingered slightly longer than was needed for just a simple hello kiss, to rub her face briefly against his scruffy beard.

Back down on her heels, she took Jesse by the hand and led him into the room behind her regular counseling session area that was her private office.

As soon as Jesse walked into the room, she closed the door behind him.

Jesse turned and analyzed the private back office.

He inspected Melantha's private desk, her belongings, everything neat, tidy, and exactly where you would expect it to be. His eyes landed on a worn short sword that was mounted on the wall.

Jesse smiled turning to Eastman.

"Cool sword, you like movies about gladiators?"

"It was my dad's," Eastman whispered as she motioned to Jesse with her head, directing his view to the wall behind him.

Jesse turned and froze, staring at the wall of images and printed direct message exchanges of three woman, one of whom was Katia.

Eastman stood beside Jesse and silently stared at the wall with him.

After what seemed to be several minutes, the silence was finally broken when Eastman spoke.

"It's a lot to take in, isn't it, Jesse?"

"Yes . . ."

Jesse stared at the wall of photos and texts as if it were a thousand miles away. He scanned and analyzed all the data in front him, looking for any sign of recognition of the other women there, and any sort of pattern or rhyme or reason to put together any frame of reference to his otherwise shattered life.

"So, let's plan. I'll let you know who the first target is, and how we are going to do this." Eastman went and sat on the big brown leather love seat in the corner of her private office and gave the cushion next to her a couple 'come sit with me' taps.

Jesse came and sat down next to her without looking at her; he was still focused on the wall.

"Okay, sweetie, so here is what's going to happen . . . Sweetie? Jesse?"

Jesse turned and looked at her, and then down to the floor.

"I'm . . . I'm not sure I can do this."

"Do what, sweetie?"

"I . . . I just don't feel good about this. You have all this information, all these messages . . . This isn't enough to put these people in prison?"

Eastman stared at Jesse.

Jesse looked down at his shoes. "None of this will bring Katia back."

The look on Eastman's face shifted.

"You're right, Jesse. None of this will bring Katia back. You're absolutely right."

She paused, and in an icy, clinical tone, she stated, "Maybe we shouldn't see each other anymore. Personally or otherwise. Here, I'll show you out."

"Wait, what?" Jesse looked up at her as she got up from where she was sitting next to him.

She walked over to the door of her private office and opened it, standing at the threshold and staring at him with an expressionless look on her face.

"Thank you for your time, Jesse, but I think you need to leave now."

Jesse sat frozen in the chair, a look of fear and confusion had washed over his face.

"But I thought—" Jesse stammered, but was sharply cut short by Eastman.

"Goodbye!" she said coldly as she motioned to the door with her hand.

Jesse didn't budge from the love seat. He was paralyzed.

She tore into him, "Maybe you're not ready for this, or for us. And that's fine, Jesse, that's totally fine. But I'm not going to waste my time with you if you're not ready for and dedicated to what needs to be done. I understand, but I wanted this for us—I wanted this for you . . . But if you think you can use me, my resources, my body, and then say to me, 'This won't bring Katia back,' after I have invested my time, energy, and love into you—? Not to mention my putting my ass on the line for you with all of this illegally obtained information . . . Really, Jesse, that's totally fine!"

Eastman looked down at Jesse. Her eyes were razor blades.

"I thought we were on the same page, Jesse. I really did, I thought we had a future together, but I guess you were just playing games with me . . . Using me."

She was clearly on the verge of tears. "Leave. I don't want you here!"

Jesse was still frozen on the brown leather love seat.

"Get out! Get out! Get out!" She briskly walked over to Jesse and grabbed him by his arm and started pulling him out of the love seat.

"I said get out!"

Jesse, now being pulled off the sofa and onto his feet, started begging, "I don't understand. I don't understand!"

"No, Jesse, you do understand! You knew what you were doing this whole time!" Eastman sobbed as she pushed Jesse to the door of her private office.

Jesse turned, stopping the sobbing woman in her tracks.

"I'm sorry, Melantha, please—"

Eastman stood in front him, looking up at him, her eyes still burning with the angry salt of her tears.

"'This won't bring Katia back.' Are you serious? You're just going to let this slide like everything else in your life? 'I'm sorry, Melantha'? Really, Jesse? That's all you can say to me, really?"

She poked Jesse hard in his chest with her index finger. "It's fine, Jesse. It's outstanding! . . . Just go . . . but before you do . . ." She walked over to her filing cabinet and flung it open.

She reached in, seized a folder, and threw it full force across the room at Jesse. Printed documents and photographs exploded into the air and floated to the ground in a lazy seesaw motion.

Brightly colored, glossy images of flesh and crimson.

Jesse looked at the floor, a patchwork of documents and large photographs.

The images were of Katia chopped up in pieces, and they made their way into his senses. More images he hadn't seen from the coroner of her body cleaned up and laid neatly on the slab.

Images of her almost looking whole again.

Eastman fumed and hissed at him, "Was she ready for that, Jesse? Did she have a choice?"

Eastman picked up two of the photographs by her feet and shoved them into Jesse's chest.

He looked down at the first: it was a photo from Katia's Instagram of when Jesse proposed to her on the Eiffel Tower.

The other photo was of her severed head in a pool of her blood on the hardwood floor of their house.

"Do you even care what she went through while she begged and pleaded for her life? Tell me, Jesse, do you think she was calling out your name and begging for her life while the beast sawed her head off? Because I can tell you right now, she fucking *begged*!

"She was supposed to be the love of your life. You were supposed to protect her and keep her safe. Now that I think about it, Jesse, I really don't want you in my life. You let Katia down, and she was supposed to be your *soulmate*, so I'm sure you would let me down too!"

Jesse looked up from the floor to Eastman's bloodshot, tear-filled blue eyes.

"Get the fuck out, now!"

Jesse broke and crumbled onto the Persian rug beneath his feet.

The voice slithered out from its rusty cage and started its rasping from a dark corner of Jesse's mind.

You fucked this one up too? She was into you, and you blew it? You're entirely fucking worthless, you're nothing!

Jesse sobbed.

"No, Mel. Please!" was all Jesse could scream as he coiled into the fetal position, sinking into the sea of photographs of Katia.

Eastman went to her drawer and flung it open. She grabbed her service weapon and threw it at Jesse.

"You let this happen to Katia, and you're going to let this happen to other innocent women? Why don't you just kill yourself?" Eastman walked over to Jesse and stood over him as he sobbed uncontrollably at her feet.

She kicked the still holstered automatic pistol at Jesse, and it bounced off his chest.

"Do it!" she whispered coldly as Jesse eyed the pistol laying in front of him.

DO IT, PUSSY! Hahahhahahhaha!

The little voice inside Jesse's head squealed with glee as Jesse reached for the weapon.

Eastman watched and raised an eyebrow as Jesse fumbled with the pistol, only to throw it to the corner of the small private office.

"You fucking loser. I knew you couldn't handle this. I knew you didn't have what it takes to finish this cycle. Pathetic!"

Eastman turned and sat in the brown leather love seat, then put her face into her hands and started sobbing.

Jesse crawled through the ocean of pictures and documents and rested his head at her feet and babbled, "I-I have work to do."

Eastman looked up from her hands. Her perfect eyeliner now fashionably streaming down her face, giving the appearance that she wept crude oil.

"What? What did you just say, Jesse?"

Sniffling and slobbering on her shoes, Jesse once again sputtered out, "I'll do it. I'll do anything. Please, please let me prove myself to you!"

Eastman slid off the couch and straddled Jesse. She leaned down and was face to face, eye to eye, mouth to mouth with him.

"What did you say, Jesse?"

"I'll do it, Melantha . . . I'll do it . . ."

Eastman leaned in and kissed Jesse on his forehead.

"Are you sure? You're sure you are going to do this for us?"

Jesse was still clutching at her feet, pleading for her forgiveness. "Yes, I'll do anything. I'll do anything."

"Are you going to follow the white rabbit?" She started kissing Jesse as she cradled him in her arms. "You're going to do it, my love?"

"Yes, yes, yes, yes." Jesse crumbled. "I'll do anything for you. I'll do anything for you. I'll do anything for you . . ."

The little brass bells hanging from the doorknob of Her Majesty's Tea House and Supply jingled as the large glass door swung open.

A huge man filled the doorway and stepped into the little shop, casting a shadow that flooded into the store.

The man was about six-foot-five, all muscle and covered in tattoos—ugly black and gray tattoos, the kind that looked like they were done in a garage during a meth deal, or maybe in prison, just to help the time pass.

He was wearing sweat-stained gym clothes and cross trainers. As he entered the store, he took off his sunglasses and hung them off the neck of his sweaty tank top. He looked around the room like a predator sizing up his environment.

His small sports backpack, slung over one shoulder, looked even smaller compared to the mass he carried on his thick frame. He stood still as he was approached by a tiny woman beaming with a big, overly happy smile.

"Salute! We welcome you to her Majesty's Tea House and Supply! How may I honor your strength and heal your body today?"

The big man looked down and through the young woman in disgust. Without even acknowledging the girl in front of him, he looked up and over her and called out into the back of the store.

"Andromeda!"

He started walking forward, wholly ignoring the woman and nearly knocking her out of his way as he passed her.

"Andromeda!" the big man called out again as he got up to the perfectly organized countertop of the little boutique tea house. He removed the bag on his shoulder and dropped it carelessly on the counter.

Ding! He rang the little bell on the counter and called out once again, "Andromeda!"

The young woman approached the big man once again, doing her best to stand up straight with her shoulders thrown back.

"Sir, if I can be of any assistance, I-I can assure you that I am here to service and nourish your body and spirit with our lovely assortment of organic herbal teas and accessories."

The big man didn't even look down. Orchid saw his eyes roll as he pounded on the bell once again.

The beaded curtain that separated the back room to the storefront parted like a waterfall as Andromeda flowed through it and into the storefront.

"I heard you the first time you called for me, Izzy," Andromeda said, smiling at the big man who was now unzipping the small backpack atop the counter.

"Then you should have come out faster," Izzy growled. He stopped unzipping the bag when he noticed Orchid was still standing beside him.

He glowered at her.

"I'm sorry, Izzy, I was on the phone with our Pedagogue. He was telling me his plans to relay to you and the rest of the family for tonight. Should I call him back and tell him that you have an issue with me receiving his orders to transmit to the family?"

"No. I'm sorry, Andromeda. I didn't realize you were talking to our Pedagogue." Izzy looked back to Andromeda and motioned with his eyes to Orchid, who was standing silently beside him. Orchid was now also looking at Andromeda.

"Oh, excuse me, how rude of me!" Andromeda exclaimed as she made her way around the counter to where Izzy and Orchid were standing.

"Izzy, this is Orchid. Orchid, this is Izzy. He's a big part of the family, and helps to ensure that . . . we are all safe and follow the protocols set forth by our Pedagogue."

"You're the Orchid that my Pedagogue told me about?" Izzy asked, his eyes going back to the girl beside him. "I'm so sorry. What an honor it is to meet you, Orchid! I've heard great things about you already, and I could sense your strength as soon as I walked into the door."

Orchid blushed and smiled. "Our Pedagogue told you about me?"

"Oh yes, we spoke this morning, and he told me how proud he is to have found you."

Andromeda placed her hands on Orchids shoulders and smiled to her. "Like I told you, Orchid, you're all everyone in the family is talking about. That's why I was confused about why you wanted to call and talk to your friend back home so soon. After all, you just got here."

Izzy's face went back to being severe and expressionless. "What do you mean she wanted to call home to a friend? She is home."

"We will let her call home and let her friend know she's safe after the party tonight, Izzy. Our Pedagogue already said he's happy about that."

Izzy's now cold gaze never left Orchid's as hers broke from his and moved to the floor.

"Okay then, if that's what Pedagogue says."

"Did you come here to spoil the surprise of Orchid's introduction to the family tonight, Izzy? Or are you here on business for our Pedagogue?"

"Right!" Izzy huffed as he went back to the little backpack on the counter and proceeded to finish unzipping it. He pulled out two large stacks of cash, bound together by doubled up rubber bands.

"Here's ten from the first . . . and here is the other ten from the second."

Andromeda smiled as she saw Orchid's eyes go wide at the sight of more money than she had ever seen before in her life.

"Stay right here. I'll be right back, Izzy." Andromeda took the cash and walked around the corner and into the back room.

Izzy turned his attention back to Orchid and took half a step toward her, so he was now towering over the petite young woman. "So, you want to call home, huh?"

"I-I just thought it would be nice to let my friend know that . . ."

Izzy stepped a bit closer. Orchid could smell the sweaty oil of his skin.

"I'm sure you will change your mind about that after tonight. As a matter of fact, I'm willing to bet on it."

Orchid stood frozen. Her little heart was beating as fast as it was last night.

The tension was broken when Andromeda came back into the room.

"You did well, Izzy. Our Pedagogue will be pleased. We will see you tonight then?"

Izzy turned to face Andromeda and grabbed his small backpack. "Always a pleasure to serve our Pedagogue!"

Izzy turned back to the girl who was still frozen like a petrified bunny rabbit. "See you tonight, Orchid. It was a pleasure meeting you, and I'm sure you will think about what I said."

Andromeda laughed and started shooing Izzy off. "Izzy, no need to frighten the girl. We will see you tonight."

Izzy gave Andromeda a wink and a nod and made his way back to the door of the shop.

Orchid didn't lift her head until she heard the little bell chime, signaling that the door had been opened. She stayed still and listened until she heard the door shut once again.

Orchid turned to Andromeda.

"He scares me."

Andromeda chuckled. "Who? Izzy? Don't worry about him. He's a big teddy bear once you get to know him."

"He sells our Pedagogue's homemade medicines for the family. I bet you didn't know this, but our Pedagogue is a master of herbalism, and Izzy takes his healing love to the masses. Once people try it, they feel so good and empowered, they can't stop. So, Izzy drops off the medicine to others so they may get it to even more and more people. Before you know it, our Pedagogue is going to change the entire planet!"

Orchid smiled proudly.

"The money that is made here at our shop, the work that our Pedagogue gets for Jason, the medicine, and other business dealings our Pedagogue handles is what supports all of us. He really is such a kind and selfless man. He takes care of all of us and makes sure we are all safe and empowered."

Andromeda nodded her head, and Orchid mirrored her actions.

"Isn't that wonderful of him?"

Orchid kept nodding and smiling. "Our Pedagogue is a great man . . . I was thinking, maybe I don't need to call home later."

Andromeda laughed and embraced the young woman.

"We will talk about it later. Our Pedagogue wants you to feel safe and at home, but ultimately you stand in your power in your choice, and it will be honored."

"Thank you, Andromeda, but my mind is made up. I am standing in my power, and my power is here. I'm home."

Orchid threw her arms around Andromeda's neck and hugged her tight. "Thank you for everything. Thank you for this!"

"Of course, we are family. I knew you were special from the first time we talked on Instagram all those months ago. We are your family now, and you're a huge part of this. You're Orchid, who the

Pedagogue has foreseen coming to help us all ascend to our power. He has been looking for you for a very, very long time. He even thinks you might be the beacon!"

Orchid released her grip on Andromeda and looked at her with wide eyes. "He really said that?"

Andromeda looked down to the young girl and caressed her cheek.

"I've said too much. Let's get back to work; you have a big night ahead of you."

The bell on the door chimed again as a customer wandered into the store.

"I got this!" Orchid said with a smile as Andromeda winked at her and made her way behind the register.

The following several hours at Her Majesty's Tea House and Supply were filled with light-hearted conversations, laughter, and excitement for the dinner party that was happening that evening.

It was a significant night indeed for Orchid. To be formally introduced to the entire family, and to take her place among them under the loving care and guidance of her Pedagogue, was the biggest thing she could possibly imagine.

Tonight was her night.

She could hardly stand the excitement.

Around 6:00 p.m. Andromeda told Orchid to start the nightly closing rituals at the store. Orchid had memorized with perfection all her daily duties and protocols.

Close out the till, wipe down the counters, dust and straighten the shelves, and sweep what little debris had accumulated on the shining wood floors. Her very last duties was to flip the sign on the big glass door from open to closed and lock the door.

On the ride home, Orchid asked Andromeda questions about what was going to happen tonight, and who was going to be there. What should she do and how she should act, and—oh my, how she should address people? A dozen other "what ifs" and "maybes" came to her mind.

Andromeda just smiled in silence as she drove through the traffic-filled streets of the west side of Los Angeles. She parked in her reserved space in the parking garage of the monolithic concrete tower they called home. She turned the ignition key and the Jaguar sedan went silent. She turned to the young woman in the passenger seat and put her hand on her knee.

"Orchid, today is the most important day of your life so far. I don't want you to worry. You're going to be perfect. Just do as instructed, and I'll be there to keep an eye on you. I won't let you fall. Do you understand?"

Orchid nodded and smiled.

"Thank you. You're, like, the best person I have ever met!"

"That's what family is for," Andromeda replied, spreading a broad smile.

"Let's go upstairs. We have work to do before the rest of our family arrives."

The two walked hand in hand through the underground parking structure, their heels *click-clacking* through the cavernous dark corners of the space. The waiting elevator open for them, a brightly shining light in the otherwise dimly lit garage.

STICKY SWEET

My life closed twice before its close;

It yet remains to see If Immortality unveil

A third event to me,

So huge, so hopeless to conceive,

As these that twice befell.

Parting is all we know of heaven,

And all we need of hell.

—Emily Dickinson

"Where is my God damned journal?"

Jesse looked up from his iPhone to see Katia standing in front of him, her arms stiff by her side, her fists clenched tight. Her eyes were fixed on him with disgust.

"Your journal, babe?" Jesse asked while glancing back at his iPhone and clicking the sleep button.

Shortly after Katia had moved in, Jesse had gifted to her a leather-bound journal for her to pour her thoughts and feelings into. It was her private space, and Jesse had never once thought of looking in it, and even avoided touching it when helping with cleaning and the chores around the house.

For hours while he was painting, Katia would be posted up in a chair next to him and would lose herself in her words while he lost himself in his art. It was the perfect example of "being alone, together."

THE BEAST IN THE FIELD

"Don't play stupid with me! I had it this morning. Where the fuck did you put it!?"

Jesse gave Katia his trademark smirk and softly tried to defuse the situation.

"I can assure you I haven't seen your journal, Kat. Did you look all over for it?"

Katia's eyes started misting over.

"We talked about this with Lynn. You promised me I could have my privacy. You promised me that you would respect me!"

Jesse stood up from his reclining chair and tried to embrace his wife.

"Don't you dare fucking touch me!" Katia maneuvered herself around Jesse and fled into the bedroom with Jesse following closely behind.

"It was here, it was right here!" Katia was pointing frantically at the nightstand by her side of the bed.

Jesse used a calm, slow tone of voice. "Kat, if it was there this morning. I am sure it hasn't gotten far. Let me help you look for it."

Katia spun on her heel to confront Jesse, her face was bright red, her hands still balled into fists by her sides. "What the fuck did you do with my fucking journal?"

Before Jesse knew what happened, there was a shock of blinding red. It took a second to register that Katia had just hit him in the side of his head.

It had been years since Jesse had been in any sort of physical altercation, but the all too familiar bell ringing shock and confusion of being hit in the head isn't something you forget, no matter how much time passes.

He was in shock, not so much from the pain, but from the fact that Katia—the woman that he had known for years, the woman that he adored and worshipped—had just struck him.

Jesse looked into Katia's eyes, behind the tears that were now streaming down her face, Katia was no longer there.

He was looking into the eyes of a stranger.

"You . . .You just hit me, Kat," was all Jesse could muster to say.

Katia turned back to the bed and walked over to the nightstand.

"I put it right here—right where I always put it—and now it's gone. Tell me where it is!" Katia started pulling out all her other books that she kept on the bottom shelf of the little nightstand and flinging them across the room.

Jesse watched in horror as this . . . this stranger that had taken over the delicate form of his wife laid waste to the neatly organized nightstand in the corner of the bedroom, next to the bed where they laughed and talked about their goals and dreams. The sacred space where he held her close every night and whispered to her how grateful he was she was there.

A second later, Katia froze.

She pulled the journal from behind the nightstand, where it had fallen. It had been there the entire time.

Jesse, still staring in bewilderment as the stranger in the corner stood and turned to face him, asked, "You, you found it?"

"Yes," Katia hissed coldly as she again walked by Jesse and into the kitchen.

Jesse followed her and stood there as she went to the cupboard and got out her favorite mug. He watched as Katia calmly went to the baker's rack and selected one of her many boxes of teas she had perfectly lined up on the shelf.

"What are you doing?" Jesse asked, still holding the side of his head.

"What does it look like? I'm making tea," Katia said robotically, as she put the kettle on and stared at the blue flames that sprang from the burner on the cooktop.

"Babe, do you have anything you want to say to me?" Jesse asked in disbelief at the scene that was now unfolding in front of him.

"No. What would I have to say to you?" Katia replied, pouring the dried leaves carefully from the small container into the waiting tea strainer.

Jesse's tone changed from shocked to a blend of confusion and anger. "Well, first off, 'I'm so sorry for accusing you of taking my journal, Jesse.' And, I don't know, maybe, 'I'm sorry for hitting you.'"

Katia slowly and precisely closed the tea strainer and placed it into her favorite mug. She stood motionless, watching the kettle.

What seemed like an hour passed before she spoke, and when she did finally speak, the words were hollow.

"I am sorry if you feel like what I did was wrong."

Jesse stood there, expecting more. The kettle came to a boil. Katia took it off the burner and poured the boiling water over the waiting tea strainer. She took in a deep breath of the aroma and watched the rich brown hues of the tea intermingle in the boiling water.

Jesse took a deep breath, too, and pictured the face of their therapist Lynn.

He spoke slowly and chose his words carefully. "Babe, that wasn't much of an apology. What you did right now really scared me. You hit me . . . I don't understand why you would do that, and why you would think that's okay. That's not okay. That's not who we are."

Katia turned to Jesse and took a sip from her tea.

"I thought that my privacy was disrespected. You know that's a big deal to me. Don't ever touch my things." Katia walked out of the kitchen and back into the bedroom, closing the door behind her.

The intercom of the penthouse chimed a scratchy burlap tone that echoed through the 2,200 sparsely decorated square feet of living area.

The sound reverberated off the gleaming wood floors and pitched off the stark white and contrasting gray walls, dissipating into the dark corners of the rooms.

The pattering sounds of *click-clacking* of high heels approached the intercom. A well-manicured finger reached and pressed the button, subduing and silencing the 1980's wall unit.

"Salutations, this is Orchid. Who am I addressing, and how may I honor you?'

An overtly pleasant, feminine voice melted through the old paper speaker hidden behind the clean, polished grill of the intercom.

"Greetings and salute, Orchid. This is Serena. I am here with Izzy and Jason. We request permission from our Pedagogue to enter his domain and honor him as he honors us."

"Greetings, Serena. I will make your request known to our Pedagogue. Please be patient while he considers your request."

The manicured finger released the button. Slowly and mindfully, Orchid turned to relay the question to her Pedagogue, who was getting dressed and prepared in his bedchamber. Orchid nearly bumped into Andromeda.

"Oh, I am so sorry, Andromeda. I didn't know that you were right behind me."

Andromeda smiled. "It's perfectly okay, Orchid. I was coming to let you know that our Pedagogue is expecting our guests and he grants their request for entry."

Orchid gave a slight bow to Andromeda and turned again to the intercom.

"Greetings. Serena?"

The intercom once again was filled with the singsong feminine tone of Serena's voice.

"Salute, Orchid. Has our Pedagogue heard our request?"

"Salute, Serena. He has, and he grants you, Izzy, and Jason admission."

Andromeda reached over Orchid's shoulder and hit the button to open the door to the building and allow the group entry.

"You did very well, Orchid. Just as we rehearsed. Your attention to detail and your devotion to mindful perfection has brought pride to our Pedagogue. You should be pleased."

"Oh, that makes me very happy to hear. I am honored that he has taken the time and energy to train me in the ways of his will and protocols."

Andromeda smiled. "As I told you, our Pedagogue sees great things in you, Orchid. However, how you perform tonight will determine your place in our family."

Orchid nodded and cast her eyes to the floor.

"I will not let you down. I have come so far. I will not let you or our Pedagogue down."

There were three gentle knocks at the door.

Orchid looked back to Andromeda, who gave her a gentle smile and nod. With that, Orchid spun gracefully on her high heels and walked through the living area to provide entry to the guests arriving for the big night. Orchid's big night.

The door opened, and the silhouette of Izzy's massive frame nearly blocked the light from the hallway of the top floor of the complex and completely blocked the view of the petite young woman and man standing behind him.

Orchid performed a perfectly rehearsed deep bow and, while still holding the position, spoke in a quiet monotone and clearly memorized tone, "Our Pedagogue welcomes you with open arms, and an open heart. You are here to be brought from the darkness of the world we live into the light that he brings, for he is the light."

Orchid paused. "And he is the way."

The group standing at the threshold echoed back to her in a perfect tempo to match her own. Orchid stood from her deep bow, slid out of the way of the trio, and gestured the group admission.

There was a silence as Orchid closed the door, locked the multiple deadbolts, fastened the chain, and turned to see Izzy once again looming over her.

With a gruff, sandpaper-like growl, like that of a predator at the zoo expecting feeding time, a tangle of words spilled from Izzy's lips. "We will see how you do tonight, little one. I don't have very high expectations. No matter what anyone else says."

Orchid shuttered.

"Izzy, stop razzing the poor girl. She's been through quite enough from you lately, you big ole softy." The tension was shattered by Andromeda's light and natural tone.

Orchid looked up to Izzy to see something she had thought the man was incapable of: a big toothy smile.

Izzy roared with laughter and picked Orchid up in an unexpected hug, enveloping her in his massive arms.

"I'm just giving you a hard time, little one. No need to worry about old Izzy, eh?!"

Orchid's high heels dangled a foot from the floor as she let out a squeal of delight. Everyone started clapping and laughing along at what must have been an inside joke among the four of them.

"Okay, Izzy, put the poor girl down before you break her. Let's properly introduce everyone."

Izzy gently placed Orchid on the floor and shot her another big smile, paired with a wink. "You're all right, little one. You're all right."

"Out of the way, you monster!" Andromeda gave Izzy a playful, friendly elbow as she nudged by his hulking body and took Orchid by the hand to properly introduce her to the other two guests, who were still eclipsed by Izzy's bulk.

Andromeda, with her sweet tone and almost with a chuckle, lovingly exclaimed, "Okay, Orchid, you know Izzy. Oh, is your back, okay? He didn't break any of your ribs, did he?"

Andromeda shot Orchid a quick, playful wink. The group laughed again as the mood continued to lighten.

"These two gorgeous creatures before you, you will know from chatting on IG. But since this is the first time you have laid eyes on them in person, please let me have the honor of introducing you."

Andromeda motioned to the gorgeous young woman with blonde hair and stunning blue eyes.

"This is Serena. She is our Pedagogue's muse and helps inspire him to write the words that captivate, motivate, and save so many tortured souls, who sadly are still in the ignorance and darkness of this world like we all used to be."

Orchid bowed and smiled.

"Salute, Serena. It is an honor and a pleasure to make your acquaintance. Our Pedagogue speaks very highly of you, and it is a privilege to finally meet you after talking to you online for the last few months."

Serena spread a smile that was oh-so-wide, it couldn't have been faked, even by the most skilled of actors.

Serena darted forward and threw her arms around Orchid to embrace her tightly. "We have talked so much. I feel like I already know you."

Serena's ultra-soft and feminine tone echoed through the room and was sweet music to Orchid's ears. "I can sense your eagerness and excitement! My empathic abilities never steer me wrong. I can tell that you and I are going to grow very close—after all, we are now sisters."

The joy that was filling Orchid's heart was immeasurable. This is what she has been looking for her entire life.

A family, a real family. A place where she fit in and had a purpose. A place where she was loved, truly loved.

The torrent of ecstatic bliss and gratitude that filled Orchid's heart for the first time spilled over and manifested as tears that rolled down her cheeks. The tears created fractured jigsaw-like streaks on her porcelain skin.

The young man stepped forward. He was tall, nearly six-foot-two. His modern black tailored suit clung to his athletic swimmer's frame. His dress shoes were shined to a mirror-like finish, and his dark hair was cut angular and sharp to match his chiseled jawline.

269

He was gorgeous. The perfect blend of masculine and feminine features.

Andromeda stepped forward and took the young man's hand and placed it into Orchid's.

"Orchid, this is Jason. I'm sure you remember chatting with him online, and certain insecurities you both used to share?"

Orchid, embarrassed, cast her eyes downward again. "Yes, of course. I remember you, Jason. I very well remember our talks. It's just hard to believe that you once thought that you were unattractive and unworthy."

The handsome man smiled.

"I was a drug addict, living on the streets. but thanks to our Pedagogue, I'm now clean and have a wonderful career." Jason paused and glanced to Andromeda. "If it wasn't for his strength, patience, and guidance, I don't know where I would be. I owe the life I have today to our Pedagogue."

Jason, still holding Orchid's hand, gave it a squeeze and turned back to her. "I'm glad you're here . . . You made it, and you deserve the life our Pedagogue will also give to you."

Orchid threw her arms around the young man and squeezed him tight.

She let Jason go and stepped back to address the four people standing before her.

"I am so happy right now. I'm finally home where I belong. I'm home."

"Salute!"

The four spun around to see the tall older man smiling from the hallway to his bedchamber.

His crisp white shirt was left casually unbuttoned at the collar and his sleeves were rolled sharply up his forearms, exposing his tattoos.

"My ears were burning. You must have been talking about me," the man said with a warm smile on his face.

"Only the truth, our wonderful Pedagogue." Andromeda beamed as she and the other four went and greeted the man standing in the hallway.

This wasn't at all what Orchid had expected. Up until this point, everything had been so formal and rigid. But this was different. This was welcoming. This was . . . love.

"So good to see you all here. I am so glad you could make it for Orchid's big night," the tall man said as he exchanged handshakes with Jason and Izzy and a warm embrace with Serena.

"We wouldn't have missed it for the world," Serena cooed as she gave her Pedagogue a kiss on his freshly shorn cheek. His well-manicured goatee picked up the slightest pigment of her ruby red lipstick.

Serena licked one of her delicate fingers and wiped the smudge off the smiling man's silver scruff.

"Andromeda and Orchid have prepared a wonderful feast for us all. Please, let us make haste. We have a long night ahead of us. I'll put on some music. Please find your way to the dining room so we can start the festivities."

The family made their way to the dining room where the table was already prepared. Throughout the next three hours, the laughter and stories flowed like wine, and the wine fueled the stories and laughter while the man at the head of the table held court over his loving family.

Orchid's head was swimming as she was regaled with tales of hope and redemption from each of the guests. Their lives had been transformed by the man sitting quietly at the head of the table.

She had never been so proud of herself in her entire life. She had taken a leap of faith, threw caution to the wind, and landed in the safest place she could have imagined.

This indeed was her family now. This truly was her home.

The man at the end of the table rose and tapped his wine glass with his large signet ring.

Immediately, the group of reveling partygoers went silent and gave the man their full undivided respect and attention. He smiled at the faces adoring him, and in a quiet and calculated tone, spoke, "Tonight is an extraordinary night for us all. Tonight, we welcome a new member of our family. She has come a long way since she arrived a few short weeks ago, but thanks to my strength and my light, she has made great leaps and bounds in learning our ways and customs."

The man smiled warmly, his eyes going to each of theirs.

"As many of you know, Orchid came to us from a most unfortunate situation. She grew up knowing nothing but hatred, abuse, neglect, and self-imprisonment. She was abused, and when the abuse stopped, she started abusing herself through eating disorders, drugs, and weak moral hygiene. But tonight, she will once and for all break the shackles of her old life. Tonight, she will close the door on all that once was and walk into the illumination of the Self. And I have foreseen, soon, we will all be together at our Sanctuary."

The other members of the family exchanged glances and smiles across the table. Going to Sanctuary meant something very special was happening.

The man locked eyes with Orchid. "My dear sweet girl, are you ready to know true strength? Are you ready to stand in your power?"

"With your strength and guidance, my Pedagogue, I can do anything."

The man smiled and turned his eyes to Andromeda.

"Andromeda, it is time."

Andromeda rose and folded her napkin, placed it on her chair, and mindfully pushed the chair back into place.

"Thy will be done, my Pedagogue."

Andromeda excused herself and walked gracefully out of the room.

The man turned his gaze back to Orchid, who was still fixed on him.

"I know you are ready, Orchid. Now the time has come for you to show me."

All eyes turned back to Andromeda as she re-entered the room, only now, she was holding a large box.

Izzy stood from his place at the table and walked over to Orchid's seat. He cleared the plate and half full wine glass that was in front of her to make space for Andromeda to set the box down in front of her.

Izzy and Andromeda then returned to their places, but didn't sit. They both remained standing. The man walked over and stood directly behind Orchid. He placed his strong hands on her shoulders and gave her a gentle squeeze.

"Jason, Serena, rise."

The air in the room became thick with silence and anticipation.

Orchid looked at all the faces that were, moments ago, smiling and laughing. Now, they were as still and expressionless as broken mirrors.

The silent, still room was broken by the man's voice.

"Andromeda has done you the favor of contacting your friend, your old roommate, via text using your phone and arranging a gift to be sent to you. Of course, you understand she had to pretend to be you, but this was only to ease your old friend's fears and to make them feel at ease knowing that you're safe."

Orchid looked over to Andromeda, and Andromeda gave her a smile and a nod. The slight bit of warmth from Andromeda put Orchid back at ease. The man could feel the muscles on Orchid's back and shoulders soften as he began to speak.

"Everyone here has had to do what is in front of you, yet everyone's door manifests differently."

The group of four all exchanged glances and nodded.

"Like the great serpent, we must shed the skin of the past to be reborn anew—stronger and more beautiful than before. Are you ready to shed that old skin, Orchid?"

The young woman craned her neck to make eye contact with

the man standing behind her, and with a smile, replied, "Yes, my Pedagogue."

The man smiled down to her in return.

"Then my child. You may open the box."

Orchid lifted the top of the box off and peered inside.

"RYUK!" Orchid squealed with delight as she reached in the box and pulled out a large black and white cat.

"Oh my—I never thought I would see you again, Ryuk! I missed you so much!"

Orchid pulled the fat cat out of the box and in close to her in a tight embrace. She held him to her chest, stroking its long black and white coat.

Ryuk's purring was a testimony to its shared happiness as Orchid's giggles, nuzzles, and "I missed yous." Orchid had found Ryuk as a kitten when she was a little girl. It had been nearly frozen and starving in a Taco Bell parking lot. She'd bottle-fed and nursed it back to health.

"Thank you, my Pedagogue. Thank you, Andromeda. Thank you, Thank you, Thank you!"

Orchid looked around the room to see the faces of her family still blankly staring at her. She paused and looked to Andromeda, whose kind smile was now gone, replaced by a dry ice stare.

Andromeda reached over and removed the box from in front of Orchid, placing it on the floor.

"I'm so happy you all surprised me with Ryuk. This is the most beautiful night ever!" said Orchid gleefully to the group, looking, hoping, wishing for some sort of warmth to return to the room.

There was none.

Orchid's smile and laughter quickly faded as the Pedagogue placed a large knife on the table in front of her.

"It is time for you to destroy what's left of your old life, Orchid, so that you may be born again. You will pick up the athame."

Orchid stared at the long, ornate blade on the table.

The Pedagogue's gaze turned from Orchid to the large man standing next to her.

"Izzy . . ."

Without hesitation, the large man grabbed the feline from Orchid's cradling arms and slammed it on its back onto the table.

The confused and frightened animal let out a yowl and dug its teeth and claws into the big man's forearm. Streaks of crimson appeared on the man's arm, but his grip was unwavering, and his arm held fast.

"Orchid, pick up the athame. It is time for you to stand in your power."

Orchid looked up to the man, hoping for some glimmer of mercy in his eyes, but she was left wanting. She looked down at her hand, and somehow, she was holding the athame. She looked at her knuckles straining a corpse-white grip on the hilt.

The man's voice over her shoulder whispered in her ear, "Orchid, do what must be done."

Orchid's eyes went back to Ryuk, pinned on the table, scared and defenseless.

He was the one thing that had been a constant in her life since she was a little girl. He was the one part of her old life that felt like home. She had been traded by so many foster families when growing up, but he had been with her through each of them, always by her side, always there to curl up on her chest and console her. He was the reason she made it so far in life. He was the reason she was alive.

Her eyes were fixed on Ryuk. The old cat's expression was one of horror, and a desperation to be saved by the one who had always taken care of him. Somewhere in his eyes, Orchid could hear her baby begging her, "Help me, Mom. HELP ME!"

The next sensation Orchid had was that of the blade in her hand plunging, pounding, hammering into the large granite table— through the body of her best friend.

Ryuk's screams were over before they could even be registered by Orchid's ears. Ryuk's blood bloomed on the marble of the table, and it flowed down and spilled onto Orchid's lap.

Izzy stepped back so the man behind Orchid could reach over her and pry open the cat's rib cage.

With surgical precision, the man reached into the cavity and produced a small fig-sized organ.

It was Ryuk's heart.

The man then placed his hand under Orchid's chin and guided her gaze to his.

"You have done well, Orchid. You have shed your skin, and now it is time for you to stand in your power once again as you bravely cross the threshold into this family, and a much bigger world."

The man parted Orchid's lips and slid the still warm organ between her teeth.

"Now complete the cycle, my Orchid. Take the first step to into your new skin, your new life."

Orchid never broke her gaze with the man, and she bit down and chewed and chewed on the tough, rubbery, copper-flavored plum that he had presented to her.

She was now in her power.

Her old skin was now shed and cast off.

And there was nothing left of that little girl from the end of a dirt road in the small town in the Midwest . . .

OF WOLF AND MEN

There is no hunting like the hunting of man, and those who have hunted armed men long enough and liked it, never care for anything else thereafter.

—Ernest Hemingway

Jesse pulled up the driveway and parked behind Katia's little white SUV.

As he put his Prius into park, he noticed that Katia was sitting in her car, oblivious to the fact that Jesse had just pulled in the driveway.

Jesse got out of his Prius, quietly approached her car, and noticed that she was wholly immersed in her phone. The cold blue glimmer of her iPhone illuminated the cockpit.

Jesse rapped on the window, and Katia jumped up in a fright.

"Hi, love." Jesse beamed as he opened the door of Katia's SUV for her.

"Jesse? You scared the shit out of me!" Katia said while giving Jesse a playful punch in the arm.

"I'm freaking out!" Katia said while biting her lip and looking up to Jesse with her big green eyes.

Jesse took her by the hand and helped Katia out of the car. "What's wrong, my love?"

Katia let out her cute little groan that Jesse had heard many times before—it was her purr of anxiety and frustration.

"Tell you what, Kat, how about we go out to our Indian place? And you can tell me all about it over some yummy noms?"

"Yay! You read my mind. Just let me put my bag in the house!"

Katia skipped up the three steps that led to the threshold of the house, unlocked the door, and put her purse inside.

Jesse had gotten home quite a bit earlier than usual from work. He wanted to surprise Katia with a night out at her favorite local restaurant, and it was even better if she needed some cheering up. Sometimes, it's the little things that you can do for your partner to let them know they're special.

The restaurant was a little hole-in-the-wall Indian place with wallpaper that looked like bricks. The tiny eatery had only six tables and was owned and operated by a husband-and-wife team that made some of the best naan in town, and well, the only naan in town.

Katia came outside, and Jesse walked her around to the passenger side of his car.

Katia slipped into the seat and shot Jesse a toothy grin, and he closed the door for her, making sure that her feet were clear, and her dress wouldn't be caught.

The restaurant was just a short drive down Honolulu Avenue to Ocean View Blvd, nestled in a little strip mall, wedged tightly between a karate studio and a car broker.

Jesse and Katia found the place on accident one night when they were out on an adventure looking for good ramen, as they drove by, Jesse made a hard right into the driveway and parked.

"Why not Indian?"

That was the start of the newlywed's love affair with the little eatery.

Jesse and Katia had made it a staple for date nights ever since.

Katia would always order the same thing: coconut masala with chili garlic naan.

Jesse would usually get anything that could be prepared extra,

extra spicy.

The couple would joke and laugh with the owner, Pari, as she and her husband made small talk and exchanged pleasantries before, during, and after ordering. As they parked in the little strip mall, Jesse turned to Katia and took her hand in his.

"I know the last couple weeks have been hard for you, my love. I want you to tell me all about what's bothering you. I'm here for you, and Lynn is here for you, and I'll do anything in my power to make sure that you're as happy as you can possibly be."

"I know. It's just, um . . ." Katia's brow wrinkled—her brow only wrinkled when she was under distress.

Jesse waited, then chimed in, "Let's get inside and order, and we can walk our way through this together. Deal?"

Katia took a deep breath and nodded.

"Deal." Katia smiled and gave Jesse a kiss on the cheek.

The couple were greeted by the owners and took their usual table. It was a small table with only two chairs on the right side of the entrance.

That was their table.

The glow of the green Christmas lights that adorned the inside of the restaurant was a bit strange at first, but added to the intimate and charming décor of the small establishment.

The owner greeted their familiar faces with a smile and predicted their orders perfectly.

That's the nice thing about going to small places: people get to know you, and you get to know them.

The Garlic naan was, of course, the first item ordered, then glasses of water were filled, and the entree was selected.

Jesse looked across the tiny table to Katia and took her hand.

"Okay, love, please share with me what's going on."

Katia looked down at Jesse's hand that was holding hers and caressed it gently with her free hand.

"Well, it's just that . . . I got a text from my dad today. He said he is coming out for a visit." Katia let out a big sigh of relief after saying what was bothering her.

Jesse was secretly relieved that it wasn't something that he had done to upset her. Although, as he went through the catalog in his mind of fuckups he had made recently, nothing stood out that would warrant such an upset to Katia.

In the last couple of months, Jesse had become accustomed to playing hopscotch on eggshells with Katia's constant mood swings and upsets.

She seemed displaced and paranoid, not at all herself.

She would have bouts of rage out of the blue and her eating disorders had come back with a roaring vengeance. All signs that his sweet Katia was fighting a battle that Jesse wished he could shelter her from. If he could have used his body as a shield and taken the arrows of her anxiety, the rusty spears of her depression, and the guillotine of her self-doubt, he would have in a heartbeat.

Jesse would have absorbed every ounce of pain she felt to give her a moment of relief.

"Okay, so your dad is coming out for a visit. When?"

Katia gave Jesse's hand a squeeze.

"In just a couple days. Dad said he has business out here, and he wants to see me, wants to see us."

Katia had minimal contact with her father since moving out to be with Jesse—and that was just fine with her.

Jesse could see that all she wanted was approval from the man that, according to her, was hardly there when she was growing up. At the same time, she had a fierce fire of independence burning inside her to say, "Look what I did, Dad. I did it all without any help from you!"

Her relationship with her father was a tightrope ballet to be sure. Jesse was gentle and mindful of that fact.

Jesse repeated himself, "How do you feel about that, Kat?"

Kat hesitated and bit her lip. Her brow furled once again, and the pace of her stroking Jesse's hand became almost manic.

"I don't . . . Like, I don't want to see him. I'm going to tell him I don't want to see him."

Katia pulled her hands away from Jesse, picked up her iPhone, and opened the texting app.

Jesse gently put his hands over hers. "It is your choice, my Kat. However, you haven't seen your dad in nearly a year. . . I know you're not super comfortable with seeing him, but consider this . . ."

Katia paused and looked up to Jesse, her expression still somewhat stressed.

"He's on our turf. We don't want or need anything from him."

Katia's face went to genuine optimism, but she didn't quite get it. She leaned closer to Jesse and asked, "But, like, how do you mean?"

"Well, the way I see it, babes, is that you're damned if you do and damned if you don't. In other words, if you don't see him, he will just be bitter, and it won't further your relationship at all. However, if you choose to see him, and we go out there and meet him, I'll be in total control of the situation. If he gets weird at all, we can just get up and leave. Then you can say that you showed up and did the best you could. No matter what, I have your back with whatever you choose, but I want you to be comfortable. That's my number one for you, always."

Katia's tongue darted back and forth quickly, and Jesse could tell that she was considering her options.

"Okay, yes! We will go see him! He can see how good we are doing, and I can lowkey, like, rub it in his face!"

Jesse smiled and retook Katia's hand. "In a nice way, right, my sweet baby?"

Katia laughed and smiled. "In the nicest way possible," she said, conjuring up the most plastic smile she could muster and looking lovingly across the table to her husband.

"Thank you, my love. You always know what to do."

"Well, I never assumed you married me for my looks," Jesse said with a wink and a smile.

"You're my handsome husband, and you know it!" Katia laughed and gave Jesse's hand a squeeze. Jesse was relieved to notice that the tension had melted away from her touch and not a wrinkle in Katia's brow was to be seen.

"Okay, guys, food's here!"

The couple looked up to see Pari approaching their tiny table, bringing over two large plates of food with a big smile on her face.

"Let me know if this is spicy enough for you this time!" she said with a smile.

"I'll let you know, thank you, Pari. Oh, can we please get some more naan?"

"Of course, my dear. I'll be right back."

Jesse looked back to Katia. She was already digging into her food, which was a good sign since Katia would never eat when she was stressed.

"Hey, Kat."

Katia looked up to Jesse to see him smirking.

"Yes, lover?"

"Did you hear about the time they ran out of bread here? It was a naan issue."

"Oh. My. God. Maybe I married you for your looks after all," Katia replied with a chuckle.

The soft glow of the green Christmas lights illuminated the couple and cast fractured shadows on the wall as they laughed throughout their meal. They talked boldly about their future and their dreams, and forgot all about the great big world outside of their own favorite teeny-tiny hole-in-the-wall.

At 3:34 a.m. the doors to the elevator opened, and the three passengers got inside.

The big man pressed the button for the lobby, and the elevator doors slowly, lazily started to close. With a shutter, the elevator in the building started making its descent to the earth below.

After what seemed like an enduring silence, the female passenger spoke: "Orchid did well tonight. She made our Pedagogue proud."

Jason could hear the smile on Serena's lips and looked over to her with a sideways glance. "Do you think I was too hard on her tonight?"

Serena laughed and blushed, brushing her long hair away from her face.

"Jason, it seemed to me that she enjoyed you thoroughly. The energy exchange you two had was intense. And the eye contact you made with her was simply spellbinding. Izzy, on the other hand . . ." Serena gave the big man standing in front of her and Jason a playful push between his shoulder blades. "It seemed like you were trying to fuck a hole through her back. This is supposed to be a loving, divine family bonding experience, not some sort of snuff porn scene."

Izzy chuckled and hissed between his teeth as the doors opened, "That's funny, I thought I was 'loving.' And besides, I had to get some payback from her for what that fucking cat of hers did to my arm! I did enjoy pulling it to pieces after she was done with it. That felt pretty good."

Serena rolled her eyes in disgust only the way a woman can when a man says something that is unbelievably dull and senseless.

The elevator came to a sudden jolting stop, and the doors opened to the lobby of the old building.

Izzy stepped out first and motioned for Jason and Serena to pass.

"Always the gentleman," Serena said in a breath so monotone that the sarcasm went right over Izzy's head.

"Why thank you, m'lady, I'll walk you two to your car."

Serena didn't even look over her shoulder as she pushed the big bronze and glass doors open from the building leading onto the sidewalk.

"We're fine, Izzy. Goodnight!" With that, Serena and Jason made a left and started walking up the street to their car, leaving Izzy in front of the building.

"Fucking cunt," Izzy mumbled to himself as he turned and started down the dark street on the west side of Los Angeles. As he walked, his mind wandered. He replayed the events of the evening and the sadistic pleasure he got out of holding down that cat and feeling its body go limp. Izzy stopped when he reached the corner and looked at the wounds on his arm under the pale yellow-green glow of the lonely streetlight that was overhead.

"Dirty little fucker," he said to himself as he flexed his hand into a fist and felt the sharp cutting pain that the cat left on him as it fought for his life.

Izzy continued down the blackened street. The only sound was the echo of his footsteps as he rounded the corner to the street where he had parked.

"Got a light?"

Izzy spun around to see a man in a suit standing about ten feet behind him.

"What? No. Fuck off."

The man just stared at Izzy silently.

"Didn't you hear me? I said, fuck off!"

Izzy took a warning step toward the man standing before him.

The man took a couple of steps toward Izzy. And in a calm, conversational tone, said, "You're right, I'm sorry. I forgot. I totally have my own."

The man raised his hand and pulled the trigger of his Taser X26P. Two darts exploded from the device. Izzy didn't have time to react as one dart penetrated his chest, imbedding itself deep in his pectoral muscle. The second dart flew true and lodged deep into his thigh. As soon as the darts found their purchase, fifty thousand volts of electricity radiated and surged through his body, short-circuiting his nervous system, and dropping the big man instantly to the ground without so much as a whimper.

The stranger walked up, dropped the spent Taser from his fist, and pulled an auto baton from his back pocket.

With a flip of his wrist, the black metal cylinder expanded into a heavy-tipped bat. The man raised that bat over his head, and with all his force, he brought it down several times onto the back of the stunned man's head.

He only stopped when he was certain that the big man was indeed well and truly unconscious. It was a bit of a struggle to drag the man from the sidewalk to the back of the waiting SUV, but the man managed to get him into the open trunk. With some effort, he got the man handcuffed behind his back and got his legs bound at the thighs and feet with Gorilla Tape.

The man then took a rag out his pocket and soaked it with liquid from a waiting bottle in the back of the truck.

He covered Izzy's mouth and nose with the rag and taped it, wrapping loops of Gorilla Tape around his head.

The man checked the handcuffs, then checked the binds on the man's feet and thighs. He checked to make sure the rag was still covering the man's nose and mouth, and with a gentle pull, he drew the privacy cover over the unconscious man.

The man then calmly, slowly closed the trunk of the little white SUV, walked around to the driver's side, let himself into the car, and closed the door.

The man sat in silence for nearly a minute while he watched the neighborhood.

Not a single house light went on. No police cars pulled up. There was nothing.

The man heard a gentle muffled moan emanating from the cargo area for the SUV, and he smiled.

"Sleep well, you big bastard. Sleep well."

He then started the car. "Helena," the first song from the album *Three Cheers for Sweet Revenge*, automatically started playing.

"Here we go."

Jesse put the car into gear and started off down the darkened street.

THE TASTE OF COPPER

Stronger than lover's love is lover's hate. Incurable, in each, the wounds they make.

—Euripides, Medea

Pitch vantablack darkness . . .

The color of soot. The abyss . . .

The nothing . . .

The Pit.

That was all that Izzy could see as he jolted back to consciousness.

The big man took a mighty inhale into his lungs and coughed, then heaved from all the chloroform that he had breathed for the last thirty minutes as he lay unconscious in the cargo area of the white SUV.

As Izzy became more lucid and his faculties returned, he slowly came to realize that he was strapped down to a chair, naked, and unable to move at all.

He tried in vain to move his feet, his legs, his hands, his arms.

He tried to lean forward. He attempted to rock, to shift, to get any leverage.

There was none.

There was no quarter for him. There was no opportunity for him to use his strength.

He tried to call out, but he found his tongue unable to move. It was pushed deep into the back of his throat. He tried to push and prod with his tongue but soon discovered that something was filling his mouth.

His mouth was stretched so wide that he couldn't even bite down on the alien object that was gaping his jaw.

There was nothing he could do.

For the first time, Izzy felt something that he hadn't felt in a long time.

Fear.

The only sense that he had at his disposal, the single umbilical cord that let him know that he was indeed still alive, was his hearing, and the only sound he could hear were heavy footsteps.

Immediately, Izzy froze his attempts to move, and his heartbeat quickened.

The footsteps were coming from behind.

They echoed off the walls of the room.

He could tell it was a large room, a cold room, an empty room from the way the sound danced and bounced around him.

The footsteps drew closer; they were in a perfect rhythm. They were calculated, precise, cold.

And then they stopped.

All at once, there was silence.

Now, the only sounds Izzy could hear were his panicked heart pumping cold blood through his veins and his own frantic breathing. He tried to slow himself down. He tried to *get a fucking grip.*

Slow it down. Listen, slow it down, Izzy said to himself as he cocked his head from side to side, hoping to pick up another echo—or even the sound of breathing. The sound of *anything.*

Yet, the silence persisted.

Then at once, the silence was shattered.

"I see we are awake. Did we have a nice rest?"

It was a man's voice—a voice Izzy didn't know. The voice was smooth and sounded well-rehearsed, as if this was something the man had said to himself in the shower as he fantasized about this moment for an eternity.

The footsteps started once again, and from what Izzy could tell, the man walked from directly behind him to be in front of him.

Izzy could feel the energy—the man's presence drawing closer.

Izzy had a flashback to being a young child at sleepovers, when he and the other little boys would play games in the darkened rooms. Where usually after a night of watching "Ripley's Believe it or Not!" and other 1980's trash TV, they would take turns sitting perfectly still and see if they could 'sense' when the other kids were getting close to them. Then, they would all take turns trying to do one-arm handstands and use "the force."

The only thing Izzy could do now was keep perfectly still and try to guess where this man was—and to figure out what the fuck he wanted.

"I'm glad you got your rest. You're going to need it."

Izzy sensed that the man was now inches away from his face.

Izzy jumped when he felt the man's hands touch either side of his head. and then there was a blinding, shooting pain as the Gorilla Tape, which had by now bonded entirely with Izzy's skin, eyebrows, and eyelashes, was suddenly ripped off, taking most of the bonded hair with it.

While Izzy's eyes struggled to adjust to the overhead light and his brain raced to deal with the shock, fear, and pain of the situation, the man's voice quietly whispered in his ear, "Deep into that darkness peering, long it stood there, wondering, fearing, doubting, dreaming, dreams no mortal ever dared to dream before."

There was a pause. Then the smooth voice continued, "Do you know who that quote is from, Izzy?"

Izzy's eyes came into focus and the form of a man came into view.

Not an overly big man, not an excessively tough looking man, just a man with average height. A man with a shaved head and a well-trimmed beard. A man in a black suit with a white shirt and a black tie. The kind of man you would pass on the street or at a farmers market and not even give a second glance to.

Izzy's eyes left the man and darted around the room.

He was in some sort of warehouse or garage. It was dark and dingy, and trash was strewn around the room. Empty, broken storage racks lined the windowless walls. The peeling paint was flaking off those same walls like skin after a bad sunburn. The putrid, musty smell of mold wafted from the drains in the floor.

It looked abandoned, neglected, forgotten.

"I asked you a question, Izzy," the man whispered while he placed a bag on the small table next to Izzy.

"Mmmph! Mmmph!"

"That's right, Izzy. It was Edgar Allen Poe. Good for you. I didn't fancy you much of a reader, but I guess you never can judge a book by its cover . . . Get it?" The man chuckled to himself while he unzipped the bag and pulled out a red binder.

"That was a *punny* joke, wasn't it?"

"Mmmph! Mmmph!"

"Calm down, Izzy. I'm going to let you out of the chair soon, don't worry."

Izzy tried to rock back and forth in the chair, but it was secured to the floor.

"MMMPH!"

"I know you're curious, Izzy. I'm getting to it. Don't worry, you will know why you're here in just a moment."

Izzy watched the man go grab a small folding chair and place it in front of him. The man sat in the chair and set the red binder on his lap, opened it, and slowly started thumbing through the pages until he reached a dog-eared page. He slowly looked up at Izzy and into his eyes. With a sideways smirk, he whispered, "Okay, Izzy. I'm ready now. Do you know who I am?"

"Mmmph!"

"Oh, I forgot, you're not really much for conversation at the moment. Don't worry, I'll enlighten you."

The man looked down at the red binder in his lap, then back up at Izzy, and smiled.

"Just nod for yes and shake your head for no. Okay, Izzy?"

Izzy nodded his head.

"Do you want out of that chair?"

Izzy nodded yes.

"See, this is simple, isn't it? Oh . . . excuse me. How rude of me." The man extended his hand, as if to shake Izzy's, and left it hanging there.

"Hello, Izzy. My name is Jesse—Jesse Silver. Pleased to meet you."

Jesse watched as Izzy's pupils widened and his eyes went big like saucers.

"Oh, so you have heard of me? Good, good," The man—Jesse—smiled and lowered his hand back to the binder. "I'm quite sure you know why I'm here, then, yes??"

Izzy slowly nodded.

"Great, but just in case. please allow me to refresh your memory."

The man mumbled as he read the lines of direct message exchanges on the sheets of paper in the red binder. "Drugs . . . tea . . . drugs. Pedagogue, Pedagogue, Pedagogue . . . Ah, here we are."

The man pointed his index finger on one of the many lines of text on the dog-eared page.

"'Don't worry, Katia, our Pedagogue and I will take care of that monster for you.'" Jesse looked up at Izzy, a slight smirk on his face.

"Monster? Really?" he scoffed, but soon continued reading. "'Once you are here with our Pedagogue, I'll take care of him personally.'"

Jesse looked up at the man again and smiled. "That's interesting stuff, isn't it, Izzy?"

"Mmmph! Mmmph!"

"But you know what I find even more interesting?"

Izzy went silent.

"I find it interesting that you sell drugs to children. I find it interesting that you lure and predate sick young women, use them up, then sell them off to the highest bidder. You leave them and their families destroyed, wondering for the rest of their lives what happened to their loved ones."

Izzy shook his head.

"No?" The man sounded amused, and he let out a chuckle, shaking his head. "Well, allow me to continue. I find it interesting that you and your fucked up 'family' think you can operate like this without any reaction from the real families you left broken . . . Is that really what you thought? That you could all go around playing your fucked up version of house—that you could kidnap, torture, and kill people's loved ones—and just get away with it?"

Jesse pulled his lips into a tight grin, and his eyes shone with an excitement he couldn't mask.

"You really thought that someone, somewhere, sometime . . . wouldn't come for some payback?"

Jesse paused expectantly. ". . .Well, Izzy? Is that what you thought?"

Izzy just stared at the man, his eyes burning with hatred and fury. His teeth biting and grinding at the billiard ball lodged deep in his taped mouth.

Jesse shook his head and laughed. "I bet you would love to get out of that chair and tear me apart, wouldn't you?"

Izzy nodded slowly yes.

"Well, I'm going to give you that opportunity. Does that sound fair?"

Izzy paused and locked eyes with the man, then slowly nodded yes again.

"Great, well, let us get this party started."

The man got up from his chair and started emptying the contents of the bag onto the table. He chuckled to himself while he unpacked it.

"But first, I want to level the playing field a bit. After all, you have at least one hundred pounds on me. I mean, look at you! You look like someone shaved a gorilla."

Jesse glanced over his shoulder at the man who was craning his neck to see what he was taking out of the bag. "No, wait. That's not fair to gorillas," Jesse said, laughing at his own joke.

"Do they have weight classes in the kind of fighting you do, Izzy?"

Izzy watched as the man took off his black jacket and laid it neatly on the table. He pulled out a heavy black leather butcher's apron; it was long and hung just below his knees.

"I love this suit, you know that?" Jesse said as he placed his hand on the black jacket on the table. "This is the suit I wore on the day of my wedding. What a nice time that was . . . great memories." Jesse let out a sigh as he slipped on the heavy black rubber gloves and smiled as the visions of that day raced through his mind.

"Where was I . . . ?" Jesse asked, seemingly to himself, before pivoting on his heel to look back at Izzy. "Oh, right! Weight classes. Do you have weight classes, or is it just a free-for-all fuck-fest?"

Izzy just stared at the man.

"What are you—280? 290?"

Izzy was silent.

"Well, I don't think that would be a very fair fight at all. As a matter of fact, I don't think I would stand a chance. So . . . let's even things up a bit, then I'll let you out of that chair. Sound good?"

Izzy was still silent. His eyes were darting back and forth from the man in front of him to the bag on the table and back to the man.

Jessie turned back to the bag and produced a large Ka-Bar blade.

The smooth black blade shimmered in the pale fluorescent glow of the battery-operated work lights that were placed on the table and around Izzy.

Jesse turned and walked up to Izzy, sliding the folding chair off to the side. He got down on one knee and looked up to the hulking man, who was now struggling more than ever to get out of his bondage.

Jesse grinned.

"Want to know what I did for work when I was younger, Izzy?"

"Mmmph!"

"I worked as a butcher. It was a shitty job, but hey, it gave me some good experience. I remember every Tuesday morning we had to get to work by 5:00 a.m. and take in the deliveries of the big sides of beef. We had to debone them and trim all the cartilage, fat, and tendons to get to the actual steak . . . Do you like steak, Izzy?"

Jesse ran his thumb against the blade of the knife, testing how sharp it was.

"It's funny how little effort it takes to cleave flesh from the bone once you get used to it. You see, Izzy, it's almost an art form to make a good steak. To have it look clean . . . to do it right."

Jesse paused and slowly waved the large military-issue knife around like a paintbrush. From his position on the ground, Jesse could see the wavering of Izzy's pupils, the shift in his head and the tensing of his body. He was in the perfect place.

"Do you like art, Izzy? Steak . . . Art . . . I like it all." Jesse sunk the blade right behind Izzy's knee. The seven-inch knife easily penetrated through the opposite side of his upper calf.

"MMMMMMMAPPPPPPPPPPH!"

Jesse released the blade and let it sit, lodged in Izzy's flesh. He looked up to the big man that was attempting to scream around the billiard ball gag in his mouth. Jesse watched the perspiration start to form as the cold sweat of shock started overtaking the man's body.

"It's funny how in movies and on TV, there is so much blood. I know you can't really see this, Izzy, but there is only a tiny trickle coming out of the wound. Only a couple drops. If this were a movie, there would be a river of blood. I think that's funny," Jesse said, his eyes never leaving Izzy's face. The big man had his eyes screwed shut, though, and Jesse sighed. "Oh well . . . Let's keep it going, shall we?"

With a smooth, sawing motion, like that of a concert cellist, Jesse sawed and cleaved the flesh of Izzy's calf muscle away from the bone all the way down to his ankle, and finished the move by severing his Achilles' tendon.

Jesse removed the portion in one clean piece and held it up for Izzy to see.

"In my days as a butcher, I learned to weigh meat with my hands. I would say this . . ." Jesse teetered his head from side to side in contemplation. ". . . is about eight pounds."

Jesse looked back to the man with a wicked grin. "I've lost forty pounds in the last five months, Izzy. We have a long way to go before this fight is even."

Jesse threw the massive chunk of fleshy meat over his shoulder and looked down at the bone. Strings and scraps of muscle, tendons, and veins were hanging from Izzy's mutilated leg. He tapped on the bone with the edge of the heavy black blade, sending waves of blinding pain stampeding up Izzy's nervous system and crashing into his brain.

"Oh, Izzy, see! Here comes the blood now—Here, I've got you."

Jesse quickly walked over to the bag and brought back some heavy rubber tubing. Out of it, he made a tight tourniquet above Izzy's knee, stopping the blood flow to his popliteal artery. Jesse wiped the wound clean to make sure that no new plasma was pouring out of the open gash.

"Good job, Izzy, the bleeding's all stopped" Jesse praised, taking the Ka-Bar and giving Izzy's fibula another playful tab. He let out a chuckle as Izzy's throat strained out a cry. "Shall we continue?"

Jesse repeated the motion on Izzy's left leg. The muffled vowels of Izzy's screaming echoed through the room. Jesse laughed as he looked down at Izzy's leg, his Ka-Bar leaving nothing but bone exposed. Jesse quickly applied another tourniquet to stop the bleeding.

"About sixteen pounds lighter, Izzy! You're slimming down real quick," Jesse joked, throwing this slab of calf to the floor beside him.

"Now, I said I was going to untie you, so let's start with your feet. I am a man of my word after all."

Jesse reached down with his knife and cut the Gorilla tape holding down Izzy's feet.

"I know you can't move them, but I said I would set you free, didn't I?"

Jesse suddenly stood up, and without hesitation, he sunk his blade into the connective tissue right above Izzy's bicep and sawed until he hit bone. Then, with one fluid motion, he ripped the muscle out of Izzy's arm to the joint of his elbow, then with a flick of his blade, separated the hunk of meat from Izzy's body.

Izzy screamed over the billiard ball as Jesse grabbed the massive, bloody slab and presented it to Izzy, then dropped it into his lap.

"Oh, Iz, buddy . . . Let's get this bleeding stopped."

Jesse tied off the wound with the heavy rubber tubing and kept going, a jovial echo in his words as he said, "It's almost fighting time, Izzy!"

Jesse sawed off Izzy's left bicep and threw it behind him, over his shoulder. The chunk of flesh made a sickening slippery thud as it impacted with the filthy concrete floor of the warehouse.

"Okay," Jesse breathed out coldly, his friendly tone dissipating for just a few second as he tied off the last wound. When he straightened his back and stood up straight, his smile returned.

"Wow, Iz! You must have worked very hard for these muscles; they're quite impressive. I mean, look at them!" With his blade, Jesse motioned to the heap of meat on the floor in front of Izzy.

Izzy's head began to slump and roll on his shoulders, Izzy was starting to pass out.

"Oh, no you don't," Jesse shot out, walking to his bag to grab a syringe. "I need you fighting fit and sitting pretty! So, let's get some amphetamine in you. I want you to enjoy this as much as I am, Izzy."

Jesse plunged the syringe into Izzy's leg and pushed the plunger down deep.

Within seconds, Izzy was back to the world of the—well, *somewhat* living.

"There you are, Iz! Bright-eyed and bushy-tailed!" Jesse grinned at him, patting Izzy's cheek with the side of his Ka-Bar. As the metal hit the man's skin, Jesse eyebrows raised. "Oh—I almost forgot!"

Immediately, and one at a time, Jesse, sawed through either one of Izzy's triceps until he hit bone, and ripped them from his body.

"That's about thirty-five pounds, Iz. We're getting closer! Now, let's get those arms free."

Jesse produced a key for the handcuffs that were shackling Izzy to the chair. He unlocked them, letting the metal fall onto the ground with a *clang*.

Izzy screamed in horror as each one of his arms, from his shoulders down to his elbows, were now nothing but ragged, bloody bone. They were completely useless, flopping to his sides like a ragdoll. The visual of what was once the muscles he had packed onto his body now laying bloody and flaccid on the floor in front of him made him want to vomit.

"MMMMMMMPPPPH!"

"We're pretty much there, Iz. Are you ready to fight?"

"MMMMPHHHPH!"

"Oh, one last thing, just to make it fair and square."

Jesse took his blade, and with a sawing motion, cut into Izzy's chest just below his clavicle. He inserted the knife horizontally under the flesh and found the connective tissue for Izzy's right pectoral muscle.

Jesse looked Izzy in his eyes, the eyes where the pupils were fully dilated from the pain, terror, and amphetamines.

"Do you like BBQ, Izzy? You must—everyone loves a good BBQ. When I was a butcher, the most popular cut in the summertime . . . was ribs."

And with that, Jesse sawed the thick, heavy muscle off of Izzy's chest and ripped it from his body. exposing his ribcage to the cold, moldy air of the warehouse.

Jesse cocked his head and examined his masterpiece, clicking his tongue at the sight. "That won't do . . . We really need to do the other side, for symmetry."

Jesse looked away from Izzy's half-shorn chest and to his eyes.

"Did you know that symmetry is how humans perceive beauty, Izzy?"

He slid the blade under the flesh and muscle of Izzy's chest, then paused.

"But, well, they say beauty is in the eye of the beholder."

Jesse sawed off the remaining flesh and muscle of Izzy's chest and threw it on the floor with the rest of the bloodied meat, nodding his head in appreciation as he did. He stepped back to once again admire his handiwork.

The once strong "Warrior" archetype of the group, the bully, the enforcer, the muscle of the cult—was now only a heap of blood, sweat, tears, and exposed bone.

"You look like you took a swim with some piranhas buddy; you're all sorts of fucked up. But, now we can fight!"

Jesse walked over to Izzy and cut the remaining bonds that held him upright in the chair.

The massive man's form crumbled and collapsed onto the floor in front of Jesse like a marionette that just had its strings cut.

Jesse walked in front of Izzy and rolled him over with his boot.

Jesse started bobbing and weaving on his feet like a boxer, throwing shadow punches while Izzy watched in paralyzed horror.

"Okay, Iz, I'm ready! Bring it on!"

Jesse kept up the Mohammed Ali style dance while Izzy lay helpless in front of him, trying to move, but only making disgusting flopping motions as Jesse stood looking down at him, throwing shadow punches with a smile.

"Don't have any fight left in you? That's a shame, Iz, I was looking forward to it." Jesse stopped to caught his breath, smiling and panting. "Oh well," he shrugged, "looks like I'm done here."

Jesse walked over to the bag and pulled out a black trash bag. Izzy watched as he took off the gloves, placed them in the bag, removed the apron, folded it, and placed it in the bag as well.

Jesse then picked up the neatly laid coat and slid it back on, buttoning it as he put the trash bag into the duffle he brought with him, along with the red binder and the now wiped-clean, Ka-Bar.

Once he finished tidying up, Jesse looked at his watch and smiled at Izzy.

"Nearly 7:00 a.m., Iz. Time to go and join the rat race." And with that, Jesse walked to the door, opened it, and walked out.

Izzy lay there in silence, staring at the heap of his flesh in front of him, the tattooed skin—his tattoos. The door reopened, and Jesse returned to the room carrying only a gas can and a photograph.

He walked up to Izzy, who started floundering again.

Jesse squatted next to the broken man and placed his hand on his cheek.

Jesse placed the picture of Katia on Izzy's exposed ribcage.

"You didn't think I'd leave without saying goodbye, did you, Iz?"

Jesse stood up and started dumping the clear liquid from the large red container on Izzy's flopping form. The gasoline cascaded and washed over the spasmodic crippled mess of a man that was writhing in agony before him.

The liquid found its way between the sinew and cartilage of the man's rib cage, flooding his hulking husk.

"Can you believe the price of gas these days, Iz? Outrageous. That's why I drive a Prius."

Izzy rolled and splayed and drowned in a puddle of the pungent petrol.

"I cannot imagine how that gasoline must feel on your wounds, inside your body, Iz. I really can't. But hey, I guess like your

299

'Pedagogue' always says: Only growth comes from pain."

Jesse made a trail with the clear liquid from Izzy's body to the table, from the table to the floor, and from the floor to the exit of the warehouse.

"This has been real, Izzy, but I've got to get going," Jesse said, placing the gas can down beside him. Something had shifted in the man, and his playful tone from before had turned to ice.

"Before I leave, Izzy, I really need you to know something," he said, and Izzy, on the floor and in agony, watched with burning eyes as Jesse's expression shifted into severity.

"Her name was Katia . . . She was my world." Jesse paused, then continued. "Her name was Katia, and this is for her, and for all the other women and families you have destroyed.

"You have put too many people through hell here on earth, Izzy, and because of all the pain and suffering that you have caused, it's time for you to find out if hell is real . . ."

Izzy's eyes widened as Jesse produced a matchbook from his jacket pocket.

"Don't worry, Izzy, your—" Jesse did air quotes after procuring a match from the box—"'Pedagogue' will be joining you there shortly. I promise you that, and like I said earlier . . ."

Jesse struck the match and placed it in the pool of gasoline.

"I'm a man who always keeps his word."

With an audible *whoosh,* the liquid sprang to life in a dazzling dance of gold, blue, and crimson.

The last thing Izzy saw was the lake of fire racing toward him.

LIGHTS OUT

Revenge is an act of passion; Vengeance of justice. Injuries are revenged; crimes are avenged.

—Samuel Johnson

Jesse pulled the little white SUV up the steep driveway of the little house on Piedmont Avenue.

Jesse sat in the white Ford Escape and thought about the events of the previous night—of what happened within the last few hours.

The silence of the morning was broken by Katia's puppy Loki barking from the backyard, where he had spent the long night all alone.

"Oh, buddy, you must be starving!" Jesse said to the husky puppy that was bounding and doing cartwheels in the backyard behind the iron gate.

"I'll be right there, my sweet boy!" Jesse walked up to the front door, slipped the key into the deadbolt lock, walked inside, and closed and bolted the door behind him. He dropped the black duffle bag on the floor next to the door.

"Loki? Where's Daddy's big boy?" Jesse called out again, and the wailing song-like howl of the husky pup could be heard clear as day in the living room from the backyard.

Jesse reached the back door, unlocked the deadbolt, and turned the handle.

A streak of white and gray flew in from the backyard and rushed through the house at a breakneck speed. After a couple laps around the house, he finally returned to Jesse in the kitchen, where the husky-wolf hybrid jumped up and was nearly face to face with Jesse.

"Who's my big boy?'"

The puppy groaned and moaned his happiness as he showered Jesse with kisses.

"Okay, let's get you fed, buddy!"

Jesse walked over to the freezer, took out a pack of instant brown rice, and popped it into the microwave. The microwave came to life, heating and steaming the brown rice. Jesse then reached above the refrigerator and pulled down a large bag of high-quality dog food.

Jesse then grabbed Loki's stainless-steel bowl from the floor and gave it a quick rinse and wipe dry before adding some meal-prepped meat and chicken.

The monster pup sat patiently and watched Jesse preparing his breakfast.

"Is Daddy's boy hungry?"

Loki let out a mighty *WOOF!* followed by the typical husky groan.

"Okay, my sweet boy, here it comes."

Jesse put the food on the ground, and Loki remained still.

"Go get it!"

Loki pounced on the waiting bowl of food.

"Okay, Loki, Daddy needs to take a shower. You be a good boy."

The white wolfdog followed Jesse to the little pink tiled bathroom where Jesse turned the old backward knobs and started the water flowing for the shower.

Loki watched as Jesse got undressed, pulled the *Doctor Who* shower curtain to the side, and stepped into the cascading warm water.

Jesse stood there as he let the warm water hit the top of his head. The water flowed down his chest and over his shoulders to the small of his back.

While the water washed away the film of the events of that early morning, Jesse replayed the scene with Izzy over and over in his mind.

The look in Izzy's eyes . . . the muffled screams . . . the sweat dripping from his body. The blood . . . the shock and horror of it all.

Jesse savored it, going over the memories repeatedly like how one would when waking up from a vivid sex dream.

The little bathroom was now filled with heavy steam. The condensation was dripping from the mirror, the faucet on the sink, and the obscured glass of the closed window that faced west.

Jesse grabbed the shower loofah and filled it with the peppermint soap that Katia had turned him onto. He scrubbed himself down from the top of his head to the tips of his toes with the rich lather. And again, he stood in hot water, letting it cleanse him, redeem him, revive him.

Jesse turned the nobs of the shower and watched all the remanence of the water and soap slowly spiral down the drain.

He reached out of the shower and grabbed the fresh, clean towel that was waiting for him, partly dried himself off in the shower, then stepped out onto the waiting bathmat.

Loki, who was waiting for Jesse to get out of the tub, trotted over and started licking the water off Jesse's calves and knees.

"Okay, boy, enough of that," said Jesse with a smile to the wolf who looked up to him with his pale blue eyes and wagging tail.

Jesse walked into the room with the bed and opened the antique dresser. He pulled out a clean pair of boxer briefs, a warm pair of socks, a black V-neck shirt, and some sweatpants. He took his time putting on the clothes, only now realizing how exhausted he was.

"Don't worry, my sweet boy, we can cuddle soon. Just let me finish getting ready."

Jesse was eternally grateful for that wolfdog. He was convinced Loki was one of the reasons that kept him from taking his own life over the last couple of months.

Not only did Loki provide endless comic relief, but it was the companionship: someone to talk to, something to fill the void that was left since Katia was no longer there.

Jesse would still instinctively call out for her when he would wake in a throbbing, cramping sweat from his reoccurring night terrors.

"KAT!" Jesse would scream into the darkness, hoping to hear her trotting in from the kitchen or the living room, her book and highlighter in hand. She'd crack open the bedroom door and say, "I'm right here, my love. I'll be back to bed soon."

A couple of times, while Jesse was still in the netherworld between being asleep and awake, he could have sworn that he even heard footsteps—Katia's footsteps—walking to the door. His heart stopped, and he froze, waiting for the door to open, praying for a turn of the knob, wishing for her voice to break the inky black silence.

But morning never came, and only the mourning remained.

Jesse pulled down the heavy blackout curtains to the one window that was in the room with the bed, and the room went from morning light to nearly midnight.

He went over to his side of the king-sized bed that had a well-worn groove in the center of, where he and Katia held each other. But now that was vacant real estate, only to be filled by the occasional wolfdog. Jesse reached behind the nightstand and flipped the switch that turned on the sizeable Himalayan salt lamp and instantly, the room was illuminated with a soft, warm amber glow.

The wolfdog, who was at the foot of the bed on Katia's side, looked over to Jesse with his famous Loki "side eye," got up, and flopped down right against Jesse's leg. Jesse caressed Loki's coarse white and gray fur and cooed to the giant pup.

"Who's Daddy's good boy? You are! You're Daddy's good boy."

Loki's tongue rolled out of his mouth as he stared at Jesse with the sort of love that is rarely found in humans, but dogs give so freely.

Real, unconditional love.

The petting slowly stopped as Jesse's eyes grew heavy. Loki's breathing slowed, and concurrently, they drifted off to a deep, wondrous, dreamless sleep.

Somewhere near the Oregon border, a young married couple on an adventure in a black Prius stabbed northward.

The 5 freeway was open, the lights of the highway cast moving shadows on the dashboard and made the silhouette of the couple in the car seem to be much more animated than they actually were.

Jesse looked over to Katia, who was reading a book he had got her before they embarked on yet another of their epic road trips.

She had her reading glasses on. They were resting low on the bridge of her nose, and as usual, she had a pen in her mouth, clenched gently between her teeth, at the ready for underlining any passages that she found impactful, and, of course, writing notes in the corners of the pages that she could later ponder.

The book was one that she had picked out and begged Jesse to get for her. Of course, Jesse was happy to oblige. After all, their relationship started with their mutual love of reading, and Jesse would do anything to fan Katia's flames and her pursuit of knowledge.

The book was *Man and His Symbols* by Carl Jung.

When they stopped at the Vroman's Bookstore in Pasadena on the way out of Los Angeles, Katia brought it to Jesse while he browsed the art section, thumbing through a book on the life of Matisse.

Jesse was curious as to her interest in the book, as it wasn't something that she typically would have picked up for pleasure reading.

"This looks interesting, Kat. Jung, huh? Cool stuff!"

"Yeah, 'cause, like, everything we do in life is about symbols and archetypes. To find our deeper meaning and to find our power. We must master the use of this ancient knowledge, and . . . like, it's important to me."

Jesse pulled Katia in close and gave her a kiss on the top of her head.

"Well, let's get it for you then, babe, but please, share with me any deep enlightenment you find in there. It sounds fascinating!"

"I'm going to go over to the coffee bar. Will you meet me over there?"

"Sure, Kat. I'll go pay for this, and I'll meet you there."

And with that, Katia turned and skipped over to the coffee shop inside the large two-story bookstore in Pasadena.

Jesse went to the register and paid for the book, then made his way over to Katia, who was now at the head of the line at the coffee bar.

"White lightning, Kat?" Jesse smiled as he handed Katia her new book.

"No, just hot water. I brought my own tea from home."

Katia produced a small tin from her purse, opened it, and took out a small bag of cheesecloth contacting an atomic blend of what looked like herbs and leaves.

"Ooh, fancy, Kat! Where do you find the time to come up with this stuff?"

"This was sent to me by my friend Andromeda, she wants me to be as powerful, spiritually and physically, as possible."

"Oh right, An . . . Andromeda. I remember her saying hi over FaceTime that once, right?"

"Yes! That's her. She's wonderful and amazing. She's like a sister to me."

"I'm happy to see that you're making friends, my Kat. Let her know she's welcome to come over anytime. I'd be happy to cook a lovely meal for y'all while you guys hang out."

"I would, but she's actually in Florida, so I don't think dinner would work out very well."

"Oh, well, let her know that if she wants to visit LA, we can certainly host her!"

Jesse smiled. He was happy that Katia was making friends, even if they were across the world. He tried to introduce Katia to several female friends of his when she moved in, but they didn't seem to click for whatever reason. Katia didn't like any of the women Jesse knew and would isolate herself from them. Even when she was invited to several "girls night outs." However, if Katia was fond of this Andromeda, so be it. Even Lynn was behind Katia becoming more social. So, Jesse was pleased as punch to see her making friends—especially if Andromeda was interested in Katia's health and wellbeing. That made it even better.

"Hi, guys, may I take your order please?"

"Yes, hi. May I please get two shots of espresso plunged into your deepest, darkest iced coffee—to go, please?" Jesse looked over to Katia. "And for you, my love?"

"Just a large cup of hot water for me. I have my own tea, thank you."

The clerk put in the order and took Jesse's money, and moments later returned with their drinks. The two walked hand in hand out of Vromans and started on another epic adventure.

"How's the book, Kat?" Jesse asked Katia as he turned down the haunting sounds of her Chopin nocturne piano music.

"It's, like, really good. I am learning a lot from it. I feel powerful just holding it."

"Powerful?"

"Yes, like, we as humans, as soon as we, like . . . recognize the archetypes that we have used to govern our lives, and the symbols that surround those archetypes, we . . . like, gain power from it. Then we can use that to stand in our power."

"Stand in our power?" Jesse said with a chuckle. "Sounds intense, like camping . . . Kat, get it? In-tents?" Jesse looked over at Katia. She was less than amused.

"It's not, like, something to joke about! When are you going to take things seriously and have the desire to master your life?"

"Master my life? How do you mean?"

"Like, nothing you do has any purpose. You don't do anything—it's like you sleepwalk through your days. All you care about is your job. You don't spend any time mastering yourself, or mastering your life, and it's, like, really sad."

Jesse was silent for a moment, then he started humming a droning 'ohm' like hum.

"What are you doing?"

"Hold on, Kat, I'm 'standing in my power.' Does it still count even though I'm driving?" Jesse let out a quick laugh and looked over to Katia, whose expression had turned to one of outright disgust.

"This is what I'm talking about—everything is a big joke to you! And, like, you don't even care about transforming yourself and mastering yourself, or like, anything."

"I feel like I do a pretty good job at life, Kat. I take care of us, and we do cool shit all the time, don't we?"

Katia rolled her eyes and scoffed. "Ugh! There is so much more to the world that you will never understand. I'm going to become more powerful than you, than anyone . . . Just watch me!"

Jesse grinned. "Okay . . . I really hope you do, Kat. I think that would be nice."

"Ugh! I, like, seriously can't stand you sometimes!"

Katia went back to reading her book.

After a couple minutes of silence, Jesse spoke up. "Mind if I play DJ for a while, babe?"

"Whatever," Katia said, obviously still annoyed. Jesse disconnected Katia's phone from the car's Bluetooth and connected his own, opened the music app on his iPhone, and hit shuffle.

The first \ song up was "Battery" by Metallica.

"Fuck yes!" Jesse smiled as the Spanish guitar intro filled the car. He held up the devil horns as the Prius kept shooting north into the darkness of the Oregon-California border.

"Are you fucking ready for this shit, Kat?"

The Spanish guitar melody turned into face-melting frantic metal guitar riffs of James and Kirk, accompanied by the bone-crushing drums of Lars Ulrich.

Needless to say, Katia and Jesse now had very different tastes in music.

In fact, they didn't see eye to eye musically at all, although Jesse shared her obsession of the early 2000's emo that she used to rock out to. But lately, everything she used to love, even My Chem, had faded away, replaced with nothing but solemn dark piano music, which was fine at times, but unnerved Jesse after a while.

Jesse never complained about it, though.

"Kat, I forgot to tell you, Metallica is playing in a couple months. We have to go!"

"Not interested," Katia sighed. She closed her book and looked out the window at the billboards and lights that littered the side of the highway.

Jesse tried to carry on the enthusiasm and sell her on seeing the greatest metal band of all time. "C'mon, babe, it'll be fun! They're amazing in concert. You don't know a lot of their music, but they put on a hell of a show. I think we would have a blast!"

Jesse gave Katia a gentle nudge with his elbow, as if to conjure up a smile from his now utterly morose partner who was still staring out the window of the vehicle on its way to Portland.

Katia's neck snapped, and she glared at Jesse and hissed, "Why don't you take one of your *metal girls* to the show. I'm sure they would enjoy it."

Jesse turned off the music, immediately put off by her comments.

"My . . . 'metal girls,' babe?"

"Yes, all those girls that you know, who all they care about is tattoos and heavy metal. Take one of them; I'm sure they would love it."

Jesse was confused, and quite frankly getting upset. This was meant to be a fun, epic road trip, like they always did, and now his wife was implying that he had interest in other women.

"Where is this coming from, Kat?"

"Whatever. If what you want to do is, like, listen to gross music and not care about learning to master yourself—and not even care about the things I care about—then just take one of those fucking bitches."

Jesse stared at Katia is disbelief. She was now back to starting out the window.

"Kat?"

"I'm going to go to sleep. Please put on something else—this music makes me angry. I'm upset that you think I would want to lower my energy by going to one of those gross shows."

"Kat, I just thought that—"

Katia cut Jesse off, "No, you didn't think. You never think about me or my health. All you care about is bullshit!"

Katia grabbed her "thunder blanket" from the back seat, wrapped herself up, and turned her back to him. Jesse placed his hand on Katia's back, but immediately she seethed, "I don't want to be touched right now."

Jesse pulled his hand away, grabbed his phone, and put on a Sasquatch Chronicles Podcast.

"Wake me up whenever we get to where you're taking us. Goodnight," Katia said with a venomous hiss, and almost immediately fell asleep—or, at least pretended to.

Jesse pushed down on the accelerator and watched the mile markers, trees, and the billboards fly by. So much for their epic road trip.

Jesse was woken up by Loki barking and whining.

He laid there, still wrapped up in the comforters, in the same position he fell asleep in however long ago. As his senses came back to him, over the barking and the whining, Jesse could hear a knocking at the front door.

He immediately sprang out of bed and grabbed his phone that was charging on his nightstand.

1:34 p.m.

Another knock at the door.

A rush of fear and paranoia came over Jesse.

He had a brief vision of opening the door and there being several sheriffs waiting for him. They'd be ready with handcuffs and a one-way ticket to prison for the kidnap, torture, and murder of Izzy—someone who, by all accounts, had it coming, but nonetheless, the kidnapping, torture, and murder of shit-bags is still illegal.

"Coming!" Jesse called out from the bedroom, and the knocking immediately ceased. "Fuck," Jesse said under his breath as he looked at his outfit.

He wasn't going to go to jail in sweatpants and fluffy socks. He had been through that before—and he was *not* going through that again.

Jesse grabbed a pair of jeans and threw them on. He didn't bother with a belt because that would be taken. He put on a pair of Chuck Taylor's and threw a hoodie over his black V-neck t-shirt, that was a bit moist from being slept in, but that didn't matter.

"One second!" Jesse called out again, as he ran to the bathroom to put on some deodorant in case he was in the cell for more than twenty-four hours, which of course, he would be if they knew what he had done.

Jesse walked from the bathroom and to the heavy wooden front door of the little house one Piedmont.

Jesse took a deep breath and unlocked the deadbolt, then opened the front door.

"Good afternoon, sir. Special Agent Eastman with the FBI. Care to tell me where you were between the hours of 3:00 a.m. and 7:00 a.m. this morning?"

Jesse stared at Eastman as she put down her badge and cracked a big smile.

"Jesus, Melantha, do you have to scare me like that? Don't you think I've had enough trauma in my life?"

Eastman laughed and put her badge into her Louis Vuitton bag. "I'll let you know when you've had enough, sugar," she said with a wink.

"Please, come in, Mel. I just woke up." Jesse showed her in, and he motioned for her to have a seat on the couch while he took a seat and sunk into the comfy leather chair in the living room.

Loki was doing cartwheels of excitement as Eastman grabbed two handfuls of his coat and gave him vigorous scratches on his back. She squealed with delight as the giant wolfdog's tongue nearly took off her makeup from the barrage of kisses he covered her face with.

"Okay, Loki, that's more than enough," Jesse said, taking the puppy by the collar. "I'm going to put him outside; I'll be right back." Jesse walked Loki to the back door and let him out. The big dog bounded outside and did his usual patrol of the small backyard.

Jesse closed the back door and turned to see Eastman standing there, holding the big duffel bag from last night's nocturnal activities. She dropped it onto the linoleum floor of the kitchen at Jesse's feet, then produced a pair of latex gloves from her back pocket and slid them on while looking at Jesse.

"Is it done?" she asked in a nonchalant, almost happy tone.

"Yes . . ."

"Well, let us take a look then, shall we?" Eastman laid out the contents of the bag neatly on the wood floor.

"One Ka-Bar Bayonet, check. One red binder, check. One pair of heavy elbow-high rubber gloves, check. One leather apron, check.

"I saw the lights and gas can in the back of the Escape in the driveway when I walked up. So that's good . . ."

Jesse watched as Eastman inspected the gloves and the apron.

"There's hardly any blood on these, Jess. Good job. And I see your head is freshly shaved. Did you do that last night before you went, like I instructed?"

"Yes," Jesse said while he watched Eastman continue to inspect the apron and gloves.

"Where is your suit?"

"It's hanging up on the bedroom door, like you instructed." Eastman immediately went over to the room with the bed and grabbed the jacket, pants, and shirt that were neatly hanging on two hangers.

"Follow me, Jess." She grabbed her bag and the suit and walked with Jesse to the bathroom.

"Cover the window for me, will you please, Jess?"

Jesse grabbed the used black towel and covered up the obscured window in the bathroom as Eastman hung the suit up from the shower curtain rack. She dug through her purse and produced a small aerosol spray bottle and a battery operated mini black light.

"What's that?" asked Jesse as he watched her spray the suit down with clear, odorless mist from the aerosol can.

"It's called Luminol. It reacts with the iron in hemoglobin." Eastman looked at Jesse, who was standing there, staring at her blankly. "It makes trace amounts of blood glow under black light." She reached over and turned off the bathroom light, and they were both now in a darkened room until the click of her portable black light illuminated the small space with a pale ultraviolet glow.

She scanned the coat and shirt with the black light.

"You've got to be shitting me, Jess. I don't see a drop here. Let's take a look at the pants."

Eastman scanned the pants and the right leg illuminated with a bright blue glow.

"Here we go, Jess."

Jesse leaned in close to see the blue-green glow emanating from the tailored black slacks he wore at his wedding.

"That's blood?" asked Jesse while turning back to Eastman.

"That glow, Jess? That's enough to send you to jail for the rest of your life." Eastman looked at Jess and smiled. "Got any hydrogen peroxide?"

"Um, yes."

Jesse reached under the sink of the bathroom, produced a brown bottle, and handed it to Melantha.

"This will destroy the iron and leave it pretty much undetectable, not that there would be any reason to connect you to the body anyway."

The peroxide bubbled and fizzed on the black material. After a couple moments, Melantha dabbed it dry with a bit of tissue that she immediately flushed down the toilet.

"Okay, let's have another look, shall we?"

She sprayed more Luminol onto the pants and swept it once again with the black light. This time nothing glowed.

"Okay, this is good, Jess . . . This is good. Get me a black trash bag from the kitchen, please."

Jesse went to the kitchen and brought back a large black garbage bag.

"Your suit is clean, Jess. Put it where you always keep it."

Jesse took the black suit and put it in the closet, next to the bag where Katia's wedding dress hung.

Jesse stared at the bag that contained Katia's gown and slowly closed the closet door.

"Jesse, come in here. I need you."

He followed her voice, and found her in the kitchen, placing the rubber gloves, apron, and the gloves she was wearing into the big black trash bag.

"Bleach, please." She said while looking up to Jesse with a smile.

Jesse went to the laundry room and came back with a container of household bleach.

"Thank you, Jess." Eastman took the bottle from him. She reached into her bag and produced a plastic bottle filled with crimson liquid.

"What's that?" Jesse asked as Eastman unscrewed the bottle and dumped the thick red liquid into the trash bag.

"Pig blood."

"Pig blood?" Jesse asked curiously as he watched her swish the congealed red goo all over the contents of the black trash bag.

"Yep, good old pigs' blood from the butcher. This way, if someone opens this up and tests it for blood, they'll find it—but it will only be pigs' blood. Comes in handy for covering your tracks . . . Or ruining high school proms."

Jesse caught the reference but wasn't exactly in the mood for humor. "Interesting," Jesse said as he watched Melantha dump a couple capfuls of bleach into the bag.

"What's with the bleach then?"

"Well, if they do happen to test this, the results will be so bad and inconclusive that nobody will ever be able to use it, ever. But we won't have to worry about, since it won't be out of place if it's found."

"How do you mean?" asked Jesse. Eastman spun the bag and tied it off tightly in a knot.

"Well, Jess, you know that butcher shop up the street?"

"Harmony Farms?" Jesse replied curiously.

"That's the one. You're going to go up there after they close, and you're going to put this black bag into their trash, with all the other black bags filled with pigs' blood and gloves, aprons, and bleach. You feel me?"

Jesse nodded simply.

Eastman stood up from the floor and placed her hands on her hips.

"He was found about an hour ago. A homeless person called the fire department hours after you left, Jess. I have been listening to the scanner all day."

"Fuck . . . What does that mean?"

Eastman laughed. "For you? Nothing. Just another drug addict found dead and burned up. Izzy didn't have any friends or family outside of the cult—that's one of the first things they do. They isolate you from everyone. And, due to the nature of what they do, I doubt that they will be calling the police to file a missing person report anytime soon."

"Have they identified him?"

"Nope. He was under the radar and off the grid in life, and he will remain that way in death. The radio said that there was nothing left at the scene but char and bones. Apparently, the fire burned for about an hour before it put itself out. I just saw the images from the crime scene on my way here. It looked like nothing more than a puddle of burned flesh and charcoal. The fire burned so hot, in fact, they say that the teeth shattered, making identification by dental records pretty much useless, and as far as DNA goes . . . good luck on that."

Jesse smiled. "Good."

"Damn right it's good. That fucker had it coming. Now he's just another John Doe in a pile of other John Does on the already overwhelmed city coroner's desk. His body is just another body in a bin bag in the fridge, waiting for someone to claim it. But nobody will because he won't be missed by anyone. As far as you're concerned, you should feel good; you just exterminated a blight from this city that was praying on sick women and wounded girls. Plus, the man that owns the building made sure that there were no security cameras or evidence left to find . . . He also made sure there was a quick cleanup done before even the fire department arrived at the scene. Made it look like a homeless person broke into the building and accidently set himself on fire smoking meth . . ."

Eastman paused and looked up to Jesse. "How do you feel about this, Jesse?" Her eyes met his, and she scanned the dark pools of his pupils.

"I feel goddamn good about it," Jesse said coldly.

"Ready for more?" Eastman asked with a grin.

Jesse stared down at the black trash bag filled with pig blood. His head tossed to the side as he deliberated how to explain it.

"When they took Katia from me, they awakened something inside me that had been asleep for a long time—and while it dreamed, it dreamed darkly. Now that it's awake, it's starving, and it needs to be fed. It wants more, and I am ready for more."

Eastman smiled again and took Jesse by the hand.

"And you will have it. You'll have it all. With every family member you take from him, with every drop of blood you spill, you even the score. They started this; you will finish it. I will be there with you every step of the way. Every inch, Jess. I have you—you're mine. I won't let anything stop you from settling the debt they owe you and making this right. You just have to follow the white rabbit, Jess."

Eastman walked up to Jesse and placed her hand on his chest, then looked up into his hazel eyes.

Jesse reached up and grabbed a fistful of her hair from the nape of her neck and pulled her into him.

"Not so fast, tiger." Eastman turned and walked out of the kitchen and into the room with the bed, making a 'come hither' motion with her fingers to Jesse.

Jesse, curious, followed her.

Melantha opened the big wooden sliding closet doors, pulled the heavy suitcase out, and put it onto the bed.

She caressed the suitcase as she started unzipping the large bag.

Jesse watched as she slowly opened the suitcase and leaned her head down into it, inhaling a deep breath of the rich scents of long-neglected leather and heavy rubber toys inside of it.

Jesse watched as she pulled out his matched set of black and green floggers.

"Tell me about these, Jesse, what are they made out of? What are they for?"

"They are buffalo hide and suede, the black falls buffalo, the green falls, suede. Custom made and perfectly balanced for me and my height and reach."

Eastman whispered, on her knees, offering the floggers to the man standing before her, "Show me."

Jesse's eyes scanned Eastman from her knees that were spread nicely apart to the curve of her round hips that tapered into her thin waist and up to her ribcage that supported her perfectly round breasts.

Jesse's eyes lingered on her nipples, now erect, and traveled up to her clavicle, to the delicate curve of her neck and up to her chin, to her lips—the bottom one she was biting in anticipation. Her eager, hungry eyes gazed up at him.

Their eyes locked for more than a couple seconds.

And in those couple seconds, Jesse let go.

He lunged forward and grabbed the set of floggers with one hand and a fist of her hair in the other, pulling her to the closest wall. With his boot, Jesse kicked the door closed. His hand was still full of her mane of long blonde hair. He pulled the tiny woman up to her feet and kissed her deeply, passionately—not at all gently.

He reached down and grabbed the bottom of her tank and pulled it over her head.

Eastman stood frozen for a moment; her perky breasts exposed to the man for the first time. Melantha reached for Jesse's face and pulled him back to hers for another long embrace.

The primal, animalistic, savage sounds of their moans were muffled as they kissed.

Eastman's hands explored Jesse's body. He gently controlled her, moved her with the fistful of her hair.

Jesse pulled Eastman away, and for a moment, she stared at him.

Panting.

Primitive, savage breaths.

The look in her eyes was that of a predatory cat.

Jesse spun the petite blonde woman around and noticed something: her mid-back to her waist was covered in a patchwork of heavy scars.

Jesse brushed them with his fingertips, and when he did, she shivered.

Jesse kept moving her. She let out a faint snarl as Jesse firmly directed her against the closed door of the room with the bed.

"You want to see what these floggers are for?" Jesse whispered in Eastman's ear as she arched her back, jutting her ass towards his pelvis.

Jesse threw the floggers onto the bed beside where the two were standing.

Jesse's right hand instinctively raised, and his palm impacted on her round, firm ass in a loud *slap!*

"Is this what you had in mind?" Jesse aggressively whispered in Eastman's ear as he pulled her hair, arching her neck back.

The impact and sting of the unexpected spank left her with her knees weak. She pulled them together and squeezed to put pressure on her already throbbing clit.

Jesse's hand raised above his head again and impacted swift and heavy on Eastman's other ass cheek. Her knees buckled, and Jesse pulled her back to her feet.

Jesse reached down and picked up his floggers from off the bed. He threw the falls of his floggers over his left shoulder, and they balanced there on his body.

He reached his hands around Eastman and caressed her from her breasts down to her tummy, to the button of her jeans, which he quickly unfastened. He pulled them down, showing her bare ass, with a freshly-made, bright red handprint on each cheek.

Jesse looked down and grinned devilishly.

"No panties? You're a dirty little slut, aren't you?"

Eastman kicked off her heels, and they flew into the corner of the room with a bed.

She lifted each leg as Jesse slid her jeans off.

"I asked you a question, Melantha," Jesse said as he reached again around her waist between her thighs. "No panties and already soaking wet for me?"

"Yes," she whispered as she bucked and ground her pelvis against Jesse's fingers, that were now knuckle deep inside her.

His thumb stayed on her clit, letting her gyrations determine the pressure and rhythm.

"Deep, deep down, you're nothing but a little slut, isn't that right?" Jesse whispered in her ear, his fingers sliding easily inside her deeper still.

"I'm—I'm your little slut," she cooed back.

Jesse pulled his fingers out from between her legs and shoved them into Melantha's open mouth.

"I want you to taste what a little slut you are."

Eastman sucked and licked Jesse's fingers clean as he sank his teeth into her shoulder. She cried out in a silent scream as the pressure of Jesse's jaws sent her into a masochistic bliss of pleasure and pain.

Jesse ended his bite with a gentle stream of kisses that went from her neck to her ear.

"You're going to lean against the wall." Jesse gently directed Eastman's face close to the wall. "You're going to take your hands and cover the back of your neck."

Jesse placed her hands, fingers interlaced, on the back of her neck.

"I want you to flare your shoulders and give me as much of a target as possible, pretend you have wings, and you're spreading them."

Melantha complied and flared her back.

"This is where I am going to be striking you." Jesse touched Melantha in two places on her back. About three inches down from her shoulders, and about three inches outside of her spine.

"I'm going to warm you up first, then I am going to start flogging. I'm going to start off very light. and it's not going to be painful, it's going to be rhythmic, and relaxing. Is that okay with you?"

"Yes," Eastman whispered back to Jesse.

Jesse kept his hand on her shoulder, as he leaned in and whispered into her ear, "Here are my rules. If you're uncomfortable in a position, or need to slow down, or take a break, you say: Yellow. Do you understand?"

Jesse traced his fingers over Eastman's back, never breaking physical contact with her.

"Yes . . ."

"Good girl. Now, if you want everything to stop, and I mean *stop*, you say: Red. And everything stops, no questions asked. You have control. Do you understand?"

"Yes."

"Do you feel safe?" Jesse asked while kissing Eastman on her back, just below her interlaced fingers.

"Yes, very."

"Do you trust me?"

"Yes, yes, very much."

"Okay, then let's begin."

Jesse grabbed his phone and opened his Apple Music.

He selected his "playtime" playlist. The rhythmic sounds of Combichrist started pounding out of the big jam box on his nightstand.

Jesse began by lightly slapping Eastman on the targets that he had predetermined with her on her back.

The light thuds of Jesse's hands in time with the music were almost soothing and relaxing as he eased Melantha into this new experience.

In short order, her back had turned from porcelain white with a patchwork of scars to a pastel pink as the blood flowed up and under her skin from the constant stimulation. Jesse could feel the heat emanating off her back with his hands, and he slowed his rhythm.

Without ever breaking physical contact with her, he leaned forward and whispered in her ear, "Here we go."

"Drag me," Eastman replied in a sultry snarl as Jesse stepped about two and a half feet back.

The music continued to pulse in the background, but now Melantha could hear another sound: the sound of air being moved in time with the music.

When her skin got the first taste of the soft, heavy leather, she was hooked.

The falls brushing against her skin felt, to her, like warm running water.

Jesse gradually started increasing the amount of the tails of the floggers connecting with her body—his Florentine flogging style was in perfect throbbing rhythm with the tempo of the music.

The gentle laps of soft, buttery leather had now graduated to soft dull thuds. Each strike slightly moved her body in time to the sexy, gritty industrial music.

It was soothing.

It was hypnotic.

It was wickedly sexy.

Jesse deviated from his pattern to strike Eastman on her ass with one of the floggers. The sting on her skin was delectable as the sensation flowed up her spine and through her nervous system.

After several more minutes of the sultry rhythmic splendor,

Jesse paused and approached her, putting his hand on her now bright red back.

Jesse inspected his strike marks. They crisscrossed with her patchwork of scar tissue.

Jesse whispered in Eastman's ear, "How are you doing? Ready for a heavy hit?"

She pushed her ass against Jesse again, and cooed, "Give it to me."

Jesse stepped back and put both floggers in one hand.

He stood like a baseball player going to the plate, and swung away, the entire weight and heft of the leather impacted on her flesh and flowed deep into her musculoskeletal system.

"Yessssss!" Eastman moaned as she reset for another hit.

"Ready?" Jesse asked.

"Do it!" she replied, bracing herself for the impact.

The second strike Jesse laid on her reverberated through her entire body; she could feel it in her toes, in her hands, and deep inside her.

Jesse put the floggers down and went to his bag. He pulled out his vampire gloves. Jesse slipped on the black leather gloves, that looked like nice dress gloves, with one wicked exception.

On the palms and fingers, there were tiny sharp spikes that came out, like those on a thumbtack.

"Close your eyes," Jesse said to Eastman, but her eyes were already closed as she was lost in the explosion of sensations and the drone of the music.

"Smell," requested Jesse as he held his hand, encased in the rich leather, under her nose.

She breathed in the toned earthy aroma and smiled.

"Now just feel . . . really feel," Jesse instructed as he lightly grazed Eastman's flesh with the gloves.

The sensation was not at all unpleasant as she tried to figure out what Jesse was using on her.

All at once, Jesse wrapped both his hands around her arms and squeezed.

A yummy jolt of sharp pain filled Eastman's senses as she gasped in pleasure.

"Hold still for me, okay?"

She nodded her head in recognition of the request.

Jesse removed the gloves and Eastman could hear a box being taken out of the suitcase, the flipping and clicking of spring-loaded metal locks, the rustle and click of electronics being plugged into a socket.

"Eyes closed," reminded Jesse gently.

"Turn around and put your hands behind your head. Spread your legs wide for me."

Eastman happily complied, and with Jesse's hand on her shoulder, she felt safe doing so. She heard a dial click and a low humming sound.

Her nose picked up on the indistinguishable scent of ozone.

"Open your eyes."

She opened her eyes to see the room was now dark.

Jesse was illuminated by the glow of what looked to be a purple neon tube attached to a thin cylinder that was plugged into the wall.

"This is called a violet wand. I know you are going to love this. It isn't really painful; however, it is a wonderful new sensation I want to share with you."

Jesse stood there with a wicked grin.

Eastman cracked a smile, and with a wink, she said, "Use the force, Luke."

Jesse laughed and dragged the illuminated glass from her collarbone to her nipple.

Eastman jerked as every molecule in her body felt alive, new, and invigorated. She let out a moan of ecstasy as he dragged it from her nipple and made a circle around her breast and then over to her other nipple.

Jesse maneuvered the glowing, smooth glass, that every time he broke contact with her skin would arch a tiny lightning bolt of electricity off the nearly opaque glowing violet glass to reconnect with her body.

As if it was reaching out to her itself—as if the volts wanted to connect with her.

Jesse got onto his knees and put one of Eastman's legs over his shoulder.

He traced and drew a masterpiece on her thigh with the wand, and up he went. The electricity caressed Eastman's outer labia and her already wet pussy got even wetter.

Jesse brushed from her labia to her pubic area, taking his time to stimulate all the nerves that connected that skin to her pubic bone.

The violet glow was a stark contrast to her dark brown landing strip as he danced around her body with the electricity.

Eastman was writhing in lust and passion as Jesse rose back to his feet.

He leaned in and started kissing her on her neck, and he gently whispered in her ear, "How are you doing?"

"Mmmore."

Eastman kissed Jesse hard, then dropped to her knees in front of the man and unbuckled his thick leather belt. She hurriedly unbuttoned Jesse's jeans and in one motion pulled his jeans and his boxer briefs down to his knees.

Jesse's heavy, thick cock, bounced back and up at her as the boxers tugged it down. Melantha took a moment to admire it.

"Perfection," she whispered as she wrapped both of her hands around the engorged shaft—and was pleasantly surprised to see that there was still about an inch and a half protruding from her gentle grasp.

She released her grip and placed her perfectly manicured hands on his waist. She turned her eyes up to look at Jesse, and without breaking eye contact, she licked from the base of his balls all the way up to the head of his cock.

She opened her lips and slid the length of Jesse's cock into her mouth.

The girth made it more than a little bit of a challenge for her to take it all the way in, but it was worth choking back her gag reflex to feel him fill her throat.

She felt Jesse gently place his hands on her head as he slowly started to pump his hips.

Eastman pulled his cock out of her mouth, looked him again in the eye, and whispered, "Use me. I want you to use me."

Jesse obliged and started thrusting his cock down her throat as she choked, gagged, and drooled all over his balls and down his legs.

Eastman reached between her legs and started rubbing her throbbing clit.

She was lost in the whirlwind of imagination, dreaming of how that cock that was filling her throat was going to feel as it stretched her open, and he slid it in deep.

Jesse pulled Eastman off his cock and to her feet.

He wrapped his hand around her delicate throat and gave her a squeeze. Her mouth instinctively opened, and he kissed her deeply.

He spun the petite blonde around and shoved her onto the bed. She instantly raised to her knees, her ass in the air waiting for him. Eastman looked over her shoulder to see Jesse taking off his jeans and pulling off his undershirt.

And even in the dim room, the sight of his shirt off, with all of his colorful tattoos, excited her more than she expected.

She put her head down and took two fists full of the comforter on the bed in anticipation of his touch.

She felt the bed shift as Jesse put his weight on it.

But she was surprised when he reached for a pillow, grabbed it, and slid it underneath where her tummy was.

She was even more shocked when Jesse pushed her flat onto her belly—the pillow under her pushing her ass nearly straight in the air.

He's a dirty fucking freak—I love it! Eastman thought as Jesse slid his tongue inside of her. His hands squeezed and slapped her ass as he probed and explored her with his mouth.

Even with the flogging, the vampire gloves, the spanking, the electricity, even with all the excitement and stimulation going on, Eastman sensed a shift of energy—a feminine presence entered the room.

Must be Katia checking in to watch her man take care of me. Eastman mused as Jesse's tongue teased her. She arched her back, putting her ass higher in the air as she looked in the corner where the feminine energy was now center and focused.

Eastman smiled at the energy; she could feel the outpouring of emotions flowing to her from the corner.

Don't worry sweetie. He'll always be yours, but you won't mind if I borrow him for a little while, do you?

Eastman winked at the energy as she felt it dissipate and vanish like the wisps of smoke from a burning stick of incense. She felt Jesse's weight shift as he rose to his knees.

He climbed atop her and grabbed a fist full of her brassy gold locks, pulling her head back. Eastman felt the head of Jesse's cock easily slip inside her. She pushed against him, trying to get a bit more, but he didn't allow it.

"Are you ready, slut?" he whispered in her ear.

"Give it to me!"

Jesse snarled in her ear. "When I'm ready. Tell me, how bad do you want this cock?"

Eastman tried again to push back on it—to force him inside her. And again, Jesse pulled back, keeping just the head of his cock inside her.

"Tell me how bad you want it."

"I want it so bad. Please—please give it to me!"

Jesse pulled her head back with even more force.

"Beg. Beg for it, bitch."

Eastman was losing her mind. Nobody had ever put her, Doctor Melantha Eastman, in that sort of position before—and she loved every second of it. Every second of her not having to be the one in control, the one in charge. This new feeling was intoxicating to her.

To be able to *let go.*

This was huge for her.

She whimpered, ever so softly, "Please . . . Please, I need your cock inside me. Please give it to me."

With that, Jesse thrust the entire length of his cock deep inside her.

His girth felt like it nearly split her in two, the head of his cock smashing deep against her insides. She cried out in a symphony of pain and pleasure as she felt all of her stretch around him.

Jesse forced himself inside her as deep as he could.

"Fucking fuck me!" she screamed as she gyrated her ass on Jesse's pelvis, his cock stirring up her insides.

That friction finally scratched the itch that had been tickling inside Eastman since the moment she laid eyes on this man, and now, he was hers.

Jesse pounded away at her tiny body, using his body weight as leverage to drill deep into her.

Without letting his cock slide out of her, Jesse pulled Eastman to her knees. With a fist full of her hair, he started slamming into her. This time, he was angling up, as opposed to when Eastman was flat on her tummy.

"Fuck, I'm going to cum already!" she cried out. Her pussy was squeezing and clamping down on him as he thrust inside her.

She spasmed as she came all over his cock. Her pelvis muscles aching and contracting as wave after wave of pleasure from her nervous system cocooned her body in a web of pure bliss and satisfaction.

As soon as she was done cumming, she pulled away from Jesse and pushed him from his knees, knocking him off the bed to the floor, onto his back.

She pounced and squatted over him and took his rock-hard phallus into her hand. She put the head of his cock inside her and smiled down at the man.

"It's your turn now . . ."

She slammed down on Jesse's pelvis, taking all of him inside her.

Jesse's hands reached up and cupped her breasts, his fingers came together to tug on her nipples as her hips gyrated and pulled his cock back and forth inside her.

She licked her fingers and reached between her legs and started feverishly playing with her clit as she rode the big man. Her left hand was planted firmly on Jesse's chest, her nails like talons from a sort of winged raptor, clawing into the flesh pectoral muscle.

After a couple minutes of riding, her pussy began to get wetter and contract. She looked him in the eye.

"I'm getting close again, Jesse. I want you to cum with me."

She purred, now more animal than human. It was Jesse who was now being savaged.

"You better be close. I want your cum, and I want it inside me. Do you understand?" she said, her hand moving from Jesse's chest and grabbing his face by his cheeks.

Jesse didn't even realize it, but her command brought him to the edge.

He had never experienced anything like that before.

"Cum for me, Jesse. Cum inside me now!" Eastman screamed as her pussy squeezed and quivered on Jesse's cock.

It was all Jesse could take.

Eastman felt Jesse's cock explode inside her, filling her up to the point where she started overflowing onto his pelvis.

She collapsed on top of Jesse, and the two embraced and passionately kissed.

They laid down on the bed—covered in a sweaty, salty, delicious afterglow.

A wash of relaxation flowed over them.

Eastman got up, left the room, and returned with a large glass of ice water. Jesse tapped Katia's side of the bed and whispered, "Come here."

She slid next to him, nuzzled up close, wedging her head into the nook of his armpit, and lazily played with his chest hair. After a couple minutes of blissful silence, they both collapsed into the deep ether of dreamless sleep.

THE MISSING

Vengeance is mine;

I will repay.

—Leo Tolstoy

Andromeda typed out another text to Izzy while the Pedagogue watched. Her fingers were moving skillfully and effortlessly over the glass surface of her iPhone.

"Izzy, where are you? You were supposed to be here over two hours ago."

Andromeda hit send on her phone, and the text bubble went through green, again.

Andromeda looked up to the man sitting silently across the table from her. "Undelivered again, my Pedagogue."

The man sat back in his chair, tented his fingers, and took a slow, deep breath in. He let the air escape his lips what seemed like a minute later.

"Has Jason or Serena heard from him?"

"No. The last time they saw Izzy was after Orchid's initiation. They said that Izzy offered to walk them to their car, and Serena declined. She said he headed south from our building to where he was parked. I walked around the neighborhood, and his car is still here, with several tickets on it, my Pedagogue. Do you think Izzy has been arrested again, my Pedagogue?"

"No, my child, even our simple Izzy would have the common sense to call us to bail him out of jail. I suspect there is something more sinister at work here—I sense . . ."

The man paused and took another deep breath in, as if he was listening to an internal voice. After a long moment, he spoke. "Andromeda, bring me the bones, please."

Andromeda nodded, silently got up from the table where she was seated, and went into the Pedagogue's office, returning with a small ornately carved wooden box. She placed it gently before the man seated at the table.

His crisp white shirt and silver cufflinks were a stark contrast to the dark, almost watery looking depths of the massive marble table.

The man slowly opened the box and retrieved a small velvet bag, and a little fiber mat weaved in a circular pattern. The man then pulled out a colorfully designed scarf and placed it on top of the mat.

The mat had a circle in the center of it that was split into quarters.

The quarters were each a different solid color: black, yellow, white, and red. Around the circle, there were ancient looking designs. Jagged, ugly, unholy looking shapes and forms, much like the ones the man had tattooed all over his lean muscular body.

From the box, the man then produced three shells and placed them on the top right corner of the scarf. He then looked up at Andromeda.

"Water, please."

Andromeda walked over to the kitchen and filled a wine glass with purified water, then returned it to the man. He placed it at the top right of the colorful scarf.

Without having to ask, Andromeda went and fetched a white candle and presented it to the man, along with a book of matches.

The man lit the candle and took another slow, deep breath in.

The flame on the candle sparked and crackled as if even the wick itself was excited with the anticipation of what was about to come.

The man opened the small velvet bag and gently dumped a pile of small bones in the center of the multicolored circle. With his left hand, he started making a clockwise loop, stirring the bones as he recited a chant in a language that was unintelligible.

"Ah lapapleba, ah papalesenso, ah lapapleba, ah paplesenso."

At once, the man stopped the chant and the circling, as if he was given permission to proceed with the ritual.

He reached into the ornately carved box for the last time and produced a jicara—a dried half of a coconut. He scooped the bones off the colorful scarf with the jicara, then started shaking the bones in the jicara and chanting once again.

Andromeda watched as the man's eyes closed tightly and his chanting became more fevered, more intense. His voice started to rise. His tone became almost that of an angry scream. It was almost like the man wasn't there anymore, but some monster—some *beast* was channeling through him, speaking through his words and his movements.

A primal surge of energy filled the room, and the flame on the candle cracked and crackled, producing a sound like that of dead leaves being stepped underfoot on a brisk fall day.

In a deafening *crack,* the man slammed the jicara down on the scarf, letting the bones scatter and fall.

Then, there was only silence . . .

The man gently placed the jicara beside the brightly colored scarf and opened his eyes.

Andromeda watched as the man's eyes darted back and forth over the jagged heap of bones. She could see the man's pupils expand and dilate as though he were looking through them, off to another realm and back again.

She watched as he nodded and shook his head as if he was involved in a deep conversation that only he could hear.

After a couple moments, the man looked up to Andromeda and whispered, "Izzy is most surely dead."

Andromeda covered her mouth, but her gasp still escaped her lips like an errant poltergeist.

"My Pedagogue, what do you mean . . . Izzy is dead?"

The man, without blinking, drew a long slow breath in and quietly spoke.

"The spirits have spoken, Andromeda. Izzy is no longer in the realm of the living."

"What happened?" Andromeda begged while casting her eyes down at the pile of bleached bones. The man sat in silence.

"There is no way. There is no way Izzy was taken down by a man! I-I can't see how. I don't believe it! He—I mean, he was an animal. No man could have taken him down!"

The man looked down at the pile of bones again, studying and deciphering the ancient language in which they spoke.

After a long silence, he slowly, quietly said, "That night after Orchid's initiation . . . there was something, something out there waiting just for him. It wasn't a man, but a monster. A monster that took his strength and devoured him alive."

The man looked up at Andromeda. Her hand was still covering her mouth.

"My dear, it seems that our Izzy may have gotten himself into something even he couldn't fight his way out of. Alert the rest of the family. I want Jason and Serena over here as soon as possible."

The man locked eyes with Andromeda once again, and in a calm voice reassured her. "Do not worry, my child. You and I both know that our Izzy didn't exactly lead the life of temperance and mastery that I prescribed him. We both know that he had some very, shall we say, *dark appetites*. And those appetites caught up to him, as they always do.

"Feel safe that nobody will be able to make the connection to the rest of our family or us. He was a loner and an outcast when I found him, and I made sure that he completely severed all ties with anyone he knew in his former life. It has been over a decade since I allowed him any contact with anyone from his past. Nobody but us will miss him."

The Pedagogue kept his eyes trained on Andromeda as he continued to soothe her. "I can assure you that I have this under my control, and I will keep us all safe. I have foreseen it."

Andromeda lowered her eyes from the man's steely gaze and back to the pile of bones on the table.

The man licked his index finger and thumb and extinguished the candle.

"We will carry on business as usual. Do not inform Orchid of this yet; she needn't worry. Summon Jason and Serena immediately; we have much work to do."

Andromeda bowed her head.

"Yes, my Pedagogue."

And she went to the other room to start making calls.

The Bluetooth in Jason's Audi rang, interrupting the somber classical music that was softly playing in the background.

Jason took his eyes off the traffic on the 110 freeway briefly to see that the incoming call was from Andromeda.

He glanced over to Serena, who was in the passenger seat, and she leaned forward and accepted the call.

"Salutations, Andromeda. This is Serena. How may I honor you?"

"Serena, are you with Jason? I called his phone."

"Yes, we are together. Why?"

There was a brief pause on the line, as if Andromeda was contemplating giving Jason and Serena the news now or in person.

"Our Pedagogue requests that you come to the house as soon as possible. It is important."

Jason chimed in. He could sense that there was something wrong. "Greetings, Andromeda. Is everything okay?"

Another pause, and then Andromeda spoke.

"Yes, everything is fine. Where are you at the moment?"

"We are on our way to a shoot—well, live figure modeling. The artist is teaching a class and wanted a male and female. So, I suggested Serena join me. It is only for two hours, but the pay is great being that we just have to be statues for a half dozen students. Would it be acceptable to our Pedagogue if we came straight over after?"

"Jason, please give me a moment to pass your request onto our Pedagogue."

After a minute of silence, Andromeda returned to the phone.

"Yes, he says that's fine, but please call as soon as you're done and on your way here. Do you understand?"

"Yes, Andromeda, we understand," Serena replied in her sweetest, softest tone.

"Hold on." Andromeda cupped her hand over the phone, but Serena and Jason could hear the muffled voices of her and the Pedagogue in the background.

"Our Pedagogue wants to know if you have worked with this artist before."

"No. I was referred to him by Gerald, who I shoot with all the time. Is that acceptable to our Pedagogue, Andromeda?"

"Hold on . . ."

Once again, Serena and Jason could hear the muffled voices in the background, but this time Andromeda came back to the conversation almost immediately.

"That is fine. We will see you in a couple of hours."

"Thank you, Andromeda, and give our eternal love and devotion to our Pedagogue."

"Stand in your power, my loves. We will see you soon."

The call disconnected.

Jason looked over to Serena, who didn't seem at all worried about the conversation.

"What do you think that was all about? Do you think we are in some sort of trouble?"

Serena laughed and took Jason's hand.

"Not at all. If we were in trouble, Andromeda wouldn't have had any problems telling us."

Jason smirked and looked out the window as the buildings on the 110 flew by.

"We're almost there," Jason said as he flipped on his blinker and cut across four lanes of traffic, nearly causing a multiple car pile-up in his effort to get off at the Rosecrans exit.

Serena squealed with delight when the Audi A4 seamlessly cut across the pock-ridden asphalt of Los Angeles' crumbling gray infrastructure.

Jason made a sharp right at the off-ramp and hit the accelerator, and the German car sped effortlessly down the road.

A couple of minutes later, they arrived at their destination.

Jason put the car into park and pushed the button to kill the engine.

The only sound for a moment was the somber music that was playing in the background as they both stared at the run down and heavily graffiti-covered industrial space.

"Are you sure this is it?" Serena said in an apprehensive tone.

"This is it," said Jason as he double checked the GPS on his cell phone.

Jason opened his signal messaging app and read the note aloud. "Go to the back of building and knock on the gray door. I'll be setting up when you arrive."

"Is it often like this, these 'modeling jobs'?" Serena said, her apprehensive tone now even more nervous.

"More often than not. Just follow my lead," Jason replied as he got out of the car.

The two walked around to the back of the old industrial building, stepping over the spent spray paint cans, rubbish, and filth that covered the ground of Los Angeles' warehouse district. The two paused as they reached the heavy gray door. The sound of muffled music coming from the inside of the building set them both at ease, as well as the large brightly colored poster board taped up next to the door that read: "Figure Painting Course Today!"

Jason paused and looked at Serena, who was now visibly relieved. She gave Jason a big smile as if to say, 'Sorry for being paranoid.' Jason took Serena by the hand and pulled her in close for a quick kiss.

"Love you, sister."

Serena looked into Jason's eyes. "I love you, brother."

Jason gave her hand a squeeze.

With his free hand, he knocked three times on the heavy gray door.

HEADHUNTER

The old door barely moved due to its weight. The solid steel core absorbed most of the force from Jason's knuckles.

"Figure painting class. This should be interesting. Have you done one of these before?" Serena quietly asked as Jason reached again to the door, this time giving it another set of three harder knocks.

"Yes, several. You get put in a position, and you must hold it while people use you as a reference for their paintings. It is a wonderful chance to meditate and master oneself in the stillness."

"Oh, that sounds easy. Who is the artist?"

"Some freak who calls himself 'Mr. Nobody.' He is some weirdo modern street artist from what I can tell."

Jason paused and now pounded three times on the big steel door with the meaty part of his fist.

"He messaged me on Instagram a couple weeks ago. Said he saw my work with Gabriel, and I would be perfect for this class."

The two looked at each other, and Jason looked at his phone, checking the time and shrugging his shoulders.

The tall man brushed his hair out of his face and regained his composure, slid his phone into the back pocket of his jeans, turned, and looked at the massive industrial parking lot that was filled with fifty-five-gallon drums and shipping containers.

"Artists are always such flakes." Jason pounded again on the door, but after the third knock, the sound of a heavy lock being turned could be heard coming from the other side of the door.

The heavy door swung slowly inward, and the music that was muffled as they approached the building now came flooding out of the opened door.

A figure stood in the large, darkened room. It was difficult for Jason and Serena to make out the figure's features since the room was a stark contrast to the bright orange-yellow hue of the midday Los Angeles sun.

And then, the mysterious figure spoke.

"You must be my models! Please come in! Come in! We have much to do before the students arrive!"

Jason looked at Serena and gave her a quick wink as he took her hand. They crossed the threshold and stepped into the darkened space.

Jason found himself raising his voice to just under a shout as he extended his hand to greet the man in the darkness.

As Jason's eyes adjusted, he could see that the figure before him was wearing a mask. The mask was white and had the appearance of an Ancient Greek Chorus mask. The mysterious figure was dressed in a very nice black suit with a white shirt and skinny black tie.

"Hello, I'm Jason, and this is Serena. You must be . . ."

The man held up a finger in the *one-second* gesture and walked over to the Bluetooth speaker that was still booming music. The man lowered the music and turned back to Jason and Serena.

"Now, we can properly make introductions."

The man stepped forward and dramatically took Jason's hand.

"It is my divine pleasure to meet you two. I am Mr. Nobody."

The man in the mask turned to the petite blonde standing beside Jason and reached for her delicate hand. *"Bonjour mon tresor."*

Serena smiled and let out a giggle as the man bowed and pretended to kiss her hand with the lips of his mask. With the tone and timber of a vaudevillian actor, the man spoke in a booming voice.

"It is my great honor to have you both here at this time and in this place. Today is a fundamental class. A wonderful opportunity for learning for all, I'm certain—as a matter of fact, I'd bet my life on it!"

The man walked over to a corner of the room and flipped a switch. Instantly the large industrial-like space was illuminated, revealing a room lined with rusty built-in steel shelving in one far corner, and a dozen or so fifty-five-gallon drums in the other.

Near the center of the room, two large heavy wooden chairs, almost like thrones, were placed side by side and close enough to almost be touching. Surrounding the thrones were six folding chairs in a semi-circle, and behind the chairs were easels holding large canvases. The images on the canvases were of women in head-to-toe latex catsuits.

There were also two other easels with what appeared to be paintings on them, but they were covered with stark white sheets.

Jason and Serena stared at the art.

"I like these!" Serena gasped as she approached one of the canvases to get a closer look.

The thick impasto paint, even though long dry, still looked wet on the canvas. She stood in front of the large four-foot by three-foot image and, wide-eyed, she drank it all in.

Each stroke, each swipe, and cut of the pigment that the palate knife's blade left on the canvas drew her in closer, more in-depth into the painting.

"You may touch it if you like . . ."

Serena turned to the man in the mask and smiled. "Really?"

"Of course, my dear. You see, I believe that art is for much more than the eyes. It is to be felt with multiple senses."

The man in the mask took Serena's hand and placed it ever so gently on the canvas.

Her delicate tapered fingers traced and explored the hills and valleys of the rough-dried paint on the taut stretched cotton.

Serena turned to the man in the mask. "Wow, thank you. I love it even more!"

The man in the mask gave Serena a nod. "You're most welcome, my dear."

The man turned to Jason, who was still looking at the dark, ravishing scenes of the latex-clad vixens.

"Before I forget, Jason, the fee for your and Serena's time."

The man in the mask reached into the inside pocket of his coat, pulled out an envelope, and handed it to Jason. "I trust cash is acceptable, my good sir?"

Jason opened the envelope and thumbed through the crisp one-hundred-dollar bills.

After a couple of moments, Jason looked up to the man in the mask and nodded.

"So, what do you want us to do?"

"Ah, yes, always the professional, Jason. I should have expected as much from all your work I have seen. I suppose we should get you two into position, as the students will be arriving shortly, and as soon as they walk in, we will get to work. Please . . ."

The man in the mask motioned to the large heavy wooden chairs in the center of the room.

"I will ask you both to kindly disrobe and take a seat on the big chairs. It doesn't matter which, as they are both identical."

Jason immediately took off his coat and started unbuttoning his form-fitting dress shirt.

The man in the mask approached Jason and took his garments.

"I'll relieve those from you, Jason. We don't want them anywhere near the paint; they do look like they were quite expensive."

Jason looked over to Serena, who was still admiring the canvases.

"Serena, it's your turn."

"I'm coming. I just can't get enough of your art, Mr. Nobody. It's so fascinating and masterful."

"Why, thank you. What we create here today, my dear, I hope to be an even more compelling masterpiece."

The man turned to see Jason, who was now fully nude, holding his jeans and shoes.

"Will you put these with my shirt and jacket, please?"

"Of course, I will be happy to. Oh! I must request you both turn off—not silence—your cell phones. I do not wish to be disturbed as soon as I start instructing the students."

"Sure, no problem." Jason reached into the pocket of his now folded jeans and turned off his cell phone.

"Serena, your cell?"

"No problem here, I left mine in the car."

"Ah, excellent. Shall we, my dear?" The masked man motioned Serena to the heavy wooden chair.

The young woman slid with ease and fluidity by him, giving him a slight smile as she passed and untied the waist tie on her sundress, letting it fall to the floor, exposing her completely nude body underneath.

The man in the mask stared at the two young people, admiring their forms.

"You're both quite impressive, quite impressive indeed."

Jason and Serena exchanged a quick glance while the man in the mask looked them both up and down.

The masked artist stepped toward the two, and slowly circled them both as if studying every inch of their bodies. Taking in every fold, crease, muscle, shape, and form.

"Yes, you're both perfect for this class. My students will be ever so pleased."

343

The man once again stood in front of the two and motioned to the chairs.

"Won't you please both have a seat? We must get you in position for the class, and I don't want the students to walk in while we are doing this; it would be bad form."

Jason and Serena both sat down in the heavy wooden chairs. The man in the mask walked over to the table, on top of which the Bluetooth speaker sat, and returned with a large black duffle bag. He placed it on the floor in front of them.

"Are we ready to make some art?"

The man in the mask unzipped the sizeable black duffle bag.

"If what we do today comes out anything like what I saw on your canvases, I'm all in!" Serena said with a smile that stretched from ear to ear.

The man in the mask tilted his head and looked at Serena. She could tell he was smiling at her.

"My dear, if I could capture only one-tenth of your beauty. It will be one of the greatest works of all time in memorial."

The man stared at the two, and after a moment, pulled two large rolls of Gorilla Tape.

"Kinky!" Serena squealed as her eyes fell on the glossy, black, three-inch-wide rolls of industrial strength duct tape.

The man in the mask paused and locked eyes with the young girl.

His hazel eyes pierced into her black pupils afloat in the light blue cornea, the color of a late autumn morning.

"You have no idea, little one."

Serena squirmed in her chair a little in anticipation of the moment, and the man looked over to Jason, whose eyes were fixed on the rolls of glossy black tape.

"So, the idea—rather, the *concept* is that you are bonded together. Forever."

The man with the mask came up to Jason with a roll of the tape and pulled Serena and the chair she was seated in as close as he could to him, lining them both up perfectly.

"Jason, would you please take Serena's hand?"

Jason reached out and took Serena's hand. The man in the mask immediately rolled out two feet of the tape. That looked more like black patent leather, and wrapped it around their wrists, and halfway up their forearms. The masked man stopped just below their elbows as Serena's arms were a couple inches shorter than Jason's.

"Symmetry is the key to beauty. We have to make this perfect. I will accept nothing less than perfection for my art."

Jason chuckled and looked up to Mr. Nobody.

"You sound like me; I can respect that."

"Thank you, Jason. I hope you enjoy this process as much as I do."

The man then slowly wrapped the heavy tape up Jason and Serena's legs, and then around and around the legs of the chair, and up to their knees.

The man paused.

"Now, please understand. this won't be the most pleasant to remove after we are done, but I hope you're okay with suffering for my art. Lord knows I have."

Jason and Serena exchanged a smile and a laugh with each other and nodded to the man.

"Now, the other hand. if you please."

The man wrapped Jason's left hand to the chair in tight spirals with the tape, up his arm and measuring with eyes, and stopping at the same point as on Jason's right arm that was bonded with Serena's.

The man walked over to Serena. She smiled up at him as he started wrapping her.

"You're a man of perfection and mastery. You're obviously very good at what you do. Perhaps you would like to take your mastery to the next level?"

Jason laughed out loud and complimented Serena. "I was just thinking the same thing. You're obviously in control of your art. However, how would you like to learn to truly channel and control your power and destiny?"

"I'm intrigued. Tell me more, please. Oh, and Jason, lean back as far as you can for me, won't you, my good sir?"

Jason leaned back as the masked man requested, and Mr. Nobody stepped behind the two. Carefully, precisely, he ran the tape around Jason's torso and arms, and then, around the heavy wooden chair.

As Mr. Nobody was slowly wrapping the tape, Jason looked up to the man.

"Serena and I are grateful initiates of the Pedagogue."

"The what?" the man casually asked as he inspected the rows and layers of tape that anchored Jason to the back of the chair.

Serena chimed in, "The Pedagogue isn't a 'what,' silly. He's a who. He is truly a great and powerful man—well, more than a man, really. He taught us to both first master ourselves and truly stand in our power. Through his divine guidance, we will ascend and become one with all that is and will ever be."

"Why, that sounds very interesting to me indeed, this is going to be a terrible crime, but I may have to cover up your breasts with the tape if you don't mind, Serena. Is that okay with you?"

Serena looked up to the paper-mache face and smiled.

"You're the master artist. Use me as your muse."

"A most humble honor it is indeed, my dear. Please, do me the kind favor of leaning back in the chair as Jason did for me?"

Serena leaned back in the chair, and the man coiled the tape around her, bonding her petite frame to the chair. Layering and layering the tape in dense, strong rolls, taking care to make sure that it was linear and even.

"There, now we are almost ready. It is almost time."

The man said as he stepped back to inspect and admire his handy work.

"Do me a grand favor, you two, and try to wriggle for me, please."

The two squirmed in the big chairs but couldn't really move more than a couple of centimeters in any direction.

"Good. Now we know the poses will be maintained for the students."

"So, would you be interested in becoming the best version of yourself and learning what it is to stand in your power?" Jason asked as he watched the man walk over to one of the covered easels, pick it up, and start carrying it over to where he and Serena were seated—where they were *bonded,* to the chairs.

"But of course! I am very interested in meeting the Pedagogue, actually. But, alas, I still have a lot of work to do before I can, I'm afraid."

The easel he was carrying came down with a heavy thud as it rebalanced itself on its three legs.

"Well, I am sure he would find you fascinating, and he could take you and your art to the next level!"

The man in the mask chuckled then sighed. "I'll be seeing your Pedagogue soon. I'm quite sure of it. Now, are you two ready to see something truly beautiful?"

Serena nodded her head in excitement as she gazed up at the expressionless face of the mask.

"Voila!"

The man tore the sheet off the easel, Jason and Serena found themselves staring at their own reflections in a large old mirror that was placed in the landscape orientation on the easel.

"I don't understand. How will the students see us, be able to paint us, if the mirror is in front of us?"

"Leave that to me. Tell me, my dear, what do you see?"

Serena gazed into the beautiful mirror with the lovely, thick, gold antique frame.

"I see myself and Jason."

The man walked behind the seated pair and gazed upon the mirror with them. "Look closer, and tell me, what do you really see?"

Serena giggled. "Now I see myself and Jason, and *you*."

The man took out two little plastic bottles from the inside pocket of his coat and unscrewed the caps.

Serena and Jason watched the man behind them as he carefully placed the caps back into his coat pocket.

"Is that food coloring?" Jason asked as the man leaned down, so the expressionless mask was just beside Jason's face.

"More interesting than that, I would think," he replied with an audible grin.

The man grabbed Jason's head and snapped it back, forcing his mouth open. In the same motion, he squeezed the entire contents of the first little plastic bottle into Jason's mouth and clasped his hand tight over it, keeping the liquid in, holding fast until he felt Jason swallow.

"What are you doing?" cried Serena as the man released Jason and sprang on her, grabbing a fistful of her long blonde hair and pulling her head back, then filling her mouth with the colorless, flavorless liquid. He held her mouth closed until he was sure she had swallowed every drop.

Jason started screaming as the man in the mask caressed Serena's now tear-stained cheek.

"Let us the fuck out of this shit. This is over! Do you hear me!? Over! Now! Cut this shit off us! We are out of here!"

The man calmly walked to the little table and grabbed a stool. He then walked back over to the couple, who were now both screaming at him in unison.

"You fucking asshole! You're going to pay for this! You don't know who we know, and when he hears about this, he's going to tear you apart!"

The man placed the stool in front of the screaming duo in the chair.

Jason started laughing. "Your little art project just cost you your life, my friend. When our Pedagogue hears about this, you will wish you were dead when who he sends after you catches up with your ass!"

The masked man, seated quietly on the stool, tilted his head and asked, "Who? Do you mean Izzy?"

Jason and Serena instantly went silent.

No more screams, no more laughter, no more threats.

The man stared at them, expression hidden behind the mask, but his tone spoke lengths. "Oh?" he mused, drawing out the syllable in a monotonous drawl. "You haven't heard?"

He shook his head as he continued in a somber, dramatic tone, "I'm afraid I have already taken care of Izzy . . . Tell me, when was the last time either of you heard from him?"

The two looked at each other and back to the man sitting perfectly still on the stool.

"Who are you?" Jason screamed again, the tones of fear starting to manifest in his voice.

The man tilted his masked head to the side, almost the way a dog would if it was confused. Then, he slowly pulled off the expressionless mask.

"Damn, it feels good to take that stupid thing off." The man sitting on the stool started fanning his face with the mask and making a comical expression of being overheated.

"Oh, do you mind if I ditch the fancy artist talk? I felt like a real asshole for the last thirty minutes, talking like that."

"Who . . . who the fuck are you?" Serena sheepishly asked.

"Really? No idea? How about you, Jason. You know this face, right?" Jesse made a big cheesy smile and pointed to himself.

"Never seen you before in my life."

Jesse scoffed. "Shit! Are you really telling me I didn't have to wear that stupid mask in the first place? Now I really do feel like an asshole!"

Jason and Serena looked at each other with equally confused expressions.

"Well, shit, here we are, I guess . . ." Jesse rolled his eyes to himself, before looking back at the who in the chairs. "As I said, I took care of Izzy a couple days ago, and yes, I am very interested in meeting your—" Jesse made his overly dramatic air quotes— "'Pedagogue.' But I have a hot date with Andromeda first. Excellent recruitment speech, though; you almost had me ready to sign up!"

After his hollow praise, Jesse furrowed his brows in genuine confusion. "You don't really *believe* in that, do you?" He again made air quotes and, with a dopey expression on his face, said, "'Stand in your power! Blah blah blah!' The fuck does that even mean? It's like some Dungeons and Dragons shit, like, to the max!"

Jesse started laughing as the two looked at each other and back at him in disgust.

"Wh-What do you mean 'took care of Izzy?'" Serena said in a venomous hiss, but her hesitation made her fear evident.

"Well, you've met the guy, so I'm sure you understand when I say that I really had to . . . *disarm* him that night!" Jesse laughed at his own joke, but it didn't seem to appeal to the audience. He sighed, his comedic talents wasted here. "I cut the meat off of his arms— among other parts of his body, too."

Jesse smiled, his eyes going off to somewhere beyond where they all were now, remembering that night. "I had him tied him to a chair—I'm sure you could've guess that—and I made him stay awake and watch while I let him nearly bleed out . . ."

The two looked at each other in horror. Serena looked in Jason's eyes for a glimmer of hope, for a sign that he knew a way out of this . . . but didn't find one.

"Oh, well, actually!" Jesse piped up again, his eyes finally back to the pair, "I guess, technically, I burned Izzy to death, because I set him on fire afterwards. But you should have been there for the cutting part—it was mega-dramatic."

Jesse let out a sighing laugh. "But if I were you, I wouldn't be worried about Izzy right now."

Jesse pulled one of the little plastic vials from his pocket and held it up so the two could clearly see it. "If I were y'all, I'd be more worried about the fifty hits of high-quality liquid LSD you both swallowed."

Jesse pulled up his sleeve and looked at his non-existent watch. "Hmm, I would say you both have about twenty-five, maybe twenty minutes left before it starts to kick in—and shit starts getting weird. And when shit starts getting weird, we start making art. So, I would suggest you both . . ." Jesse made overly obnoxious air quotes again and yelled at the top of his lungs, "'STAND IN YOUR POWER!'"

With that, Jesse got up, went over to the little Bluetooth speaker, and cranked up the music that had been playing from his phone this entire time.

"Hey! Alkaline Trio? I love this band!"

Jason and Serena screamed for help as Jesse turned the music up even louder and walked over again to them with the portable speaker. He held it as he danced to the dark music of the three-piece punk band from Chicago.

Jason and Serena screamed from the top of their lungs, "Help us! Somebody! Help us!"

"Okay!" Jesse back yelled in return. "I've got that song, hold on."

Jesse pulled his iPhone out of his pocket and opened the music app.

He made the *one second* gesture with his finger as he scrolled through all his songs.

"Ah, here we go!"

Jesse hit play on his iPhone, and the song "Help me" by Alkaline Trio started blaring from the Bluetooth speaker.

"It's funny, Alkaline Trio is my favorite band. My wife, she loved

My Chem. Well, I love them, too, but she was a superfan. I've been listening to them a lot more over the last six months or so."

Jesse started dancing again in front of the two screaming, and now sobbing people bound firmly to the chairs.

"Oh, here is the chorus!" Jesse said as he turned the volume of the speaker to its maximum setting, and he sang along as loud as he could into the faces of Jason and Serena as they cried and struggled in vain to break out of their bondage.

"Help me, help me, won't you? Sing me, sing me one last song, Help me, help me! Somebody help me, save me from myself! Take me from this hell . . . Isn't Matt Skiba awesome? His lyrics—*wow*—they just hit right here."

Jesse placed his finger on Jason's left breast, under which his heart was beating like the piston of a steam engine pulling a load of lumber up the Sierra Nevada pass.

Jesse lowered the volume on the speaker.

"Okay, so you don't know who I am, like, really? There is no need to be shy at this point, is there? I mean, like, fifteen minutes ago you wanted me to join your creepy cult!"

Jason, now seeming to realize that there was no escape, and that he couldn't get out of his ties, had now resorted to begging.

"Listen, man, please just let us go. We won't say anything to anyone, will we, Serena?"

Jesse looked over to Serena, who was now just sobbing and babbling uncontrollably, and looked back at Jason.

"Is this what your Pedagogue would call, 'standing in your power?' Because I'll tell you what. You have about ten, maybe fifteen minutes of lucid thought left before that acid starts kicking in. Once it does, I don't think I have to worry about you saying anything to anyone ever again, actually. So, you don't have very much equity with me, buddy. Let's make these last few minutes where you can actually speak count, shall we?"

Jesse walked over to one of the easels with the covered canvases, carried it over, and placed it beside the mirror so Jason and Serena could see it.

Jesse ripped the sheet off the easel, this time revealing a three-by-four-foot portrait that he had painted of Katia.

The look of horror in Jason's and Serena's eyes told Jesse that they had put all the pieces of the puzzle together.

"It's . . . it's you . . ." Serena sputtered out as her eyes scanned the painting.

"That's right!" Jesse exclaimed. "It's me."

He cleared his throat to begin speaking in his best dramatic reading voice. "'And I looked and behold a pale horse, and he who sat on it had the name death, and hell was following him,'" Jesse recited as he reached into the duffle bag and pulled out a red binder. "I learned from my time with Izzy to put a bookmark in here, so I can get right to the offending pages. I don't want to waste any time—which reminds me." Jesse looked again mockingly to the imaginary watch on his wrist. "You guys feeling okay still? Or are things starting to feel kinda—off?"

Jesse waved his hands in Jason's face, and Jason's eyes easily tracked his movements. Jesse stepped back, shrugged, and let out a muffled humph.

"I honestly have no idea what's going to happen to you two when that LSD kicks in, guys. But wow, it's going to be fun to watch. I mean, Jesus, fifty hits of high-grade liquid LSD 25! That's something that would make even Hunter S. Thompson blush. The anticipation is killing me, I hope it doesn't end." Jesse grinned. "That last bit I just said was from the movie *Charlie and the Chocolate Factory*."

Jason and Serena just stared at Jesse blankly.

"Gene Wilder?"

The two young people looked at each other and back to Jesse, their expressions still blank.

"Don't you mean Johnny Depp?" Serena said sheepishly.

Jesse shook his head in disgust. "Fucking Millennials! Anyway, where was I?"

Jesse looked down at the red binder and thumbed through the pages until he got to the page he had bookmarked.

"Tell me, Serena, does this sound familiar?"

Jesse put on a mocking 'hippie girl' voice as he read from the red folder,

"When you get here, and you're free of that awful man, you and I and our Pedagogue will all be together. He will take care of you, as he takes care of us, and finally, you will know true peace, love, and serenity."

Serena nodded her head slowly up and down.

"Jason, on March fourth, did you type the following?" Jesse put on a 'surfer dude' voice for Jason. "You will be safe, you will be with family. You will be the Pedagogue's main girl. He sees greatness and strength in you, and he knows that you will be able to be healed, and his light will be the lantern that leads you to your greatness and away from that monster."

Jesse looked up from the binder and smiled. "Monster?"

Jesse pointed at himself.

"*Moi*? Really, Jason? That kind of hurts me right in my feels."

Jason's head started to roll on his shoulders, and his pupils began to dilate. Jesse got up in Jason's face with the red binder and showed him the printout of the Instagram direct messages.

"Did. You. Type. This?"

Jason looked at the page. His eyes were starting to cross. Jesse slapped him, sending his head to his right to face Serena—who cried out in horror as she looked into his eyes and saw that the drugs were starting to take effect. She screamed because she knew that she didn't have much time left either.

Jason just nodded his head.

"Excellent!" Jesse exclaimed as he put the red binder back into the duffle bag. Jesse then walked behind the two and placed his hands on the tops of their heads.

"Mirror, mirror, on the wall, who's the fairest of them all? I don't know about you guys, but whenever I did hallucinogenic drugs, the last thing I wanted to see was my own reflection in the mirror.

"As a matter of fact, when we were kids and we would party, we used to cover all the mirrors in the house with towels when we would eat mushrooms or whatever. Thus, we wouldn't be subjected to seeing our 'meat suits' while we were in that state. However, that was only a couple grams of mushrooms or two or three hits of acid—tops.

"So, I was thinking to myself: these two are so beautiful. As a matter of fact, they make their living, earn their keep, with their looks . . . So I wondered, what would happen if all of a sudden, you two weren't beautiful? What if, for once, you two looked in the mirror and didn't like what you saw? Like, you know, the rest of us."

Jesse patted the tops of their heads as he monitored their condition in the reflection of the mirror.

"How you guys feeling?"

Serena's eyes were now solid black, the pale blue of her eyes eclipsed entirely by her pupils. Jesse looked over at Jason, and his condition was the same.

"Music! We need music! Let's put on something a bit more appropriate to this current predicament, shall we?"

Jesse scrolled through the albums on his Apple Music app.

"Ah, perfect!"

Jesse hit play on his iPhone. "The End" by The Doors started playing.

Jesse grabbed them both by the back of their necks and held them steady, making sure they were staring straight on into the mirror.

Jesse put his lips up to Serena's ear and whispered, "Please tell me what you see, Serena. Tell me everything you see."

Serena's eyes rolled around the room. Her teeth were chattering like she was standing naked in a blizzard.

"Tell me what you see. Tell me now . . ."

Serena's lips parted, her breathing was shallow and rapid.

What started as barely a whisper turned into a scream as wave after wave of the drug flooded her mind, overriding all of her senses. Her whole body felt as if it was being electrocuted. Her thoughts were uncontrollable, random, and horrifying.

"Tell me."

"I can see . . . I can see my face . . . my face is . . . it's not my face! It's not my face! I don't know what it is! It's not me! It's not me! IT'S NOT ME!"

Jesse whispered in her ear, "Tell me, Serena. What is it?"

"It's a monster! I see a monster! I see the devil!"

Suddenly, Jason came to life and screamed out, "THE DEVIL! I SEE IT, TOO. I SEE IT!"

Jason and Serena started screaming in unison as their once beautiful reflections twisted and mutated into the forms of featureless creatures, and back again, and back again.

Jesse started laughing like a maniac.

"The devil, you say? Well, let me introduce you two properly!"

Jesse walked over to the easel with the mirror and slid it closer to them. It was now about fifteen inches from Jason's and Serena's faces.

The two screamed in horror as their reflections came at them in slow motion—morphing and twisting into hellish, hairless bat creatures.

Their teeth felt like wax. Their skin felt like a membrane of hypersensitive glass. Each hair that moved on their heads sent a shockwave of communicative impulses up their spine that exploded in an overload of cognitive information in their brains.

Everything that made them, "them" had now been stripped away by the drug. All that was left was the base animal instincts—the lizard brain. The ego was dead. All they could do was try to perceive the torrent of information pouring into their system.

Jesse reached into the duffle bag, pulled out a black binder, and held it in front of Jason and Serena as they spiraled into the drug.

Jesse whispered, "Want to know why I'm here? Want to see why I'm here?"

Jesse opened the black folder and held the glossy printed photographs of the dismembered body of his wife on the living room floor of their home.

Jason's and Serena's screams became animalistic and primal. They echoed around the room, and the cries found their way back to their own ears, creating a signal loop of feedback that wouldn't stop.

"Take a long, long, look at what you did to her. Was this your work, Jason? Was it your work, Serena?

"No. I'm pretty sure your master did this, because from what I can tell, you're both nothing but his slaves. But don't you worry, I have something extraordinary planned for him."

Jesse sat down on the stool and snapped his fingers until the two were focused in on him, well, as much as they could be in their ever-deteriorating mental states.

"Do you have any idea what it was like? What it was like walking through the front door of my house—our house—and finding my wife . . ." Jesse started to tremble. All the emotions, the anger, the pain—it all came rushing back to him in waves as he looked down at the glossy black and white photos of the crime scene.

"Do you know how it feels to walk into your house, and out of a life you had worked for, longed for, hoped for, dreamed for, prayed for? DO YOU!?" Jesse screamed in the faces of the two horrified, and now thoroughly gone young people who were off in "never-never land."

Jesse got up from the stool, walked over to the table, and put on a pair of black heavy rubber gloves. He picked up two sealed mason jars, both filled with a clear liquid, and returned slowly to the stool and sat down.

Jesse collected his thoughts and composed himself.

"Of course, you can't. You can't imagine what that was like. I mean sure, you can try to put yourself in that situation. You can try to comprehend what it was like to be there. To see that, to smell it, to feel it. But how could you *know* it? How could anyone?"

Jesse placed the two mason jars on the drop cloth that was laid underneath the heavy wooden chairs.

"The way I see it, you two are beautiful, and you have been beautiful all your lives. Most people haven't. I haven't, and that makes me very, very angry."

Jesse pulled out a spray bottle from the black duffle bag, stood up, and sprayed a fine mist on Jason's and Serena's faces. The two reeled at the sensation of cold water misting their skin, and they looked up to Jesse with their swollen engorged pupils.

"Some of us haven't had the luxury. Wait . . . what is it you kids say these days? Oh right, the 'privilege' of being attractive with perfect bodies. You see, Jason, some of us had to rely on being witty, charming, and caring—more than just eye candy poured into a tailored suit. See, the way I see it is that you have been pimped out and used. Used for your looks to help fund 'the Pedagogue's' stalking, manipulating, and luring of some very, very sick girls.

"Girls that turned to the internet for help with their mental and emotional issues. He abused that, and, by proxy, you abused that, Jason.

"Serena, you used your looks and charm to lure the girls in also. To be an icon for them, to show them that, 'Hey, I'm a pretty girl, who is strong and independent, and safe here with this *family*.' So, the way I see it, you leveraged your looks to help him reel them in also . . . And that's not okay, I can't abide that at all.

"So now, I am going to take that weapon from you."

Jesse picked up one of the mason jars, carefully unscrewed the lid, and stepped behind Jason.

Jesse placed a gloved hand over Jason's eyes and gently tilted his head back. Jesse then carefully poured half of the contents of the mason jar on Jason's face, taking care to not let the liquid go into his eyes.

Immediately, Jesse released Jason, tilted Serena's head back, and repeated the same procedure.

"I know that right now the sensation you feel is warm, and it's going to keep getting warmer . . . As a matter of fact, you may soon realize that it's burning."

Jesse tapped on the reflective glass.

"Watch the mirror, guys. Watch the mirror. This is going to be fun."

Jesse carefully put the lid back onto the mason jar and sat back down on the stool.

"In case you were wondering why you feel that burning—and believe me, guys, it's going to get worse and worse—it's because I just poured sulfuric acid on your beautiful faces."

Jesse watched as Serena's and Jason's faces started to turn bright red and blister. The water he had misted them with acted as a catalyst, helping to speed the acid's work.

The two started screaming in pain, their bodies buckling and writhing in the centimeters of wiggle room they had in their binds.

"No, no! You don't get to look away. You have to watch!"

Jesse got up from the stool and circled behind Jason and Serena. He held their heads in his gloved hands and forced them to watch as their faces continued to bubble and froth.

"Even though I covered your eyes, you may notice that your eyelids are starting to melt off, Jason. Do you see that? Do you know what's happening? You will also see that all your soft cartilage in your nose and ears—wow, especially yours, Serena—that it's starting to melt away, isn't it?

"Oh, your lips, too . . . See that, Serena? Your perfect full lips and cupid's bow, they're totally being destroyed—right before your very eyes! I told you this would be fun to watch, especially tripping balls on acid. This indeed is an adventure, isn't it, guys?"

The two couldn't stop staring at their reflections, and throughout that hour, they slowly burned. Their once flawless skin now nothing more than festering, frothing, bubbling ooze of red, white, and the sickening oily beige of their decaying flesh.

"Okay, lets clean this and see what's under this bubbly mess, shall we?"

Jesse unscrewed the cap from the other bottle and splashed Jason's and Serena's faces with water. They screamed in agony as the force of the liquid pulled away chunks of their flesh that was just hanging on by threads of skin, muscle, and tendons.

"Wow, you guys look fucked up. Just look at yourselves, look!"

Jason and Serena stared at the mess of skin, blood, flesh, and exposed skull where their perfect faces had been.

Their minds, under all the LSD, all the horror and pain, were still trying to piece together what was going on, trying to analyze and interpret the images flowing into their damaged, dissolving, blood-soaked eyes.

Jesse reached into the bag once again, pulling out a large black leather apron, and slid it on.

Jesse then pulled out a hideous werewolf mask. He slipped the mask over his head, and the two recoiled in horror at the image of the snarling muzzle and long latex canine teeth.

Jesse removed the heavy rubber gloves he had used while handling the acid and put on a pair of yellow gloves. They looked like the kind you would use to do the dishes in the kitchen after a family dinner.

At last, Jesse reached into the bag and pulled out a pair of metal barbecue claws. They looked almost like metal bear claws: black, shiny, and razor sharp.

Jesse slipped one over each fist. They fit like brass knuckles and were typically used for scraping flesh from the bone after a nice, long slow cook in a meat smoker.

But today, Jesse had found a new, more 'artistic' use for them.

"Look at me, Jason. Look at me."

Jason's eyes turned up to the man standing before him—to the werewolf, to the monster.

"In your messages to my wife, you called me a 'monster,'" he recalled. "Well, I wasn't then; I was just a man . . . A man who got up every day and worked so his wife could be taken care of and happy. A man that held her when she cried and loved her the best I knew how through her pain.

"I did the very best I could to calm her demons. But sadly, I was just a man back then. But now, Jason . . . Now I am so much more."

The werewolf looked down at his shiny black claws.

"You see, you manifested this. You and Izzy, Serena, Andromeda . . . and the fucking 'Pedagogue' created this—this monster. You know what they say, Jason? 'Everyone wants to be a beast until it's time to do what beasts do!' Now, let me show you . . ."

Jesse stood over Serena and started taking long, hard, thick, brutal swipes at her face with the claws.

With every stroke, muscle, flesh, tendons, and chunks of bone were ripped off the girl's face.

Jason sat in silence and watched through his LSD-addled perception as the wolf tore apart his best friend.

Mists and splatters of Serena's blood covered Jason's face as he sat and watched his "sister" be deconstructed, swipe by swipe.

The acid had withered and weakened the bones of Serena's face and skull, and they snapped and crumbled like Styrofoam under the unending mauling of those claws.

Jesse didn't stop until there was nothing left of her head other than the hollowed-out skull cap.

Her brain and nerve stem had scooped clean out, laid dead on the floor beside the chair. What was left of her naked skull was like the hollowed-out insides of a watermelon at a Fourth of July party.

In a moment of clarity, Jason let out a slight sound. Just above a whisper, two words escaped his lips:

"Help me."

The werewolf paused from looking over his kill and slowly turned its head to look at the deformed skull that was somehow managing to speak. To utter anything other than a monosyllabic vocalization was a miracle in itself.

The werewolf took a step to its right and straddled Jason. The wolf tilted its head and surveyed what was left of the once handsome man. Then, without saying a word, the wolf lunged with both hands in an uppercut motion. The monster plunged both of his claws under Jason's jaw, and with a single, brutal ripping motion, tore his entire lower mandible from his head.

The sound of what used to be Jason's face was quite unique—a deep guttural gurgling, like that of an old claw foot bathtub in a Victorian house draining the last two inches of water—as Jason, tried to aspirate through his esophagus.

The werewolf walked behind Jason, held his head to the now blood splattered mirror, and whispered in his ear, "I want the last thing you see before you die to be what you have become. You made me into this monster, so I, in turn, made you into one as well. Look at yourself, Jason. Look at what you really are . . . Finally, your outside matches your insides."

An hour later, the empty space was clean.

As instructed, Jesse sealed the bodies of Jason and Serena into airtight fifty-five-gallon drums and placed them in a shipping container in the back lot of the building with the hundreds of other shipping containers full of fifty-five-gallon drums.

Everything was cleaned, bleached, wiped, and bagged.

The lights were turned off. The building was locked up and secured.

The art, easels, and chairs were loaded into the back of the little SUV.

As instructed, Jason's Audi was parked down the street with the keys left in it and the windows down.

Less than two hours later, the Audi was on its way to a chop shop, to be quickly painted with new plates and a new VIN, and then on its way to its new home in Mexico.

As Jesse drove away in the little white SUV, he saw a full moon peeking over the mountains in the far, far away.

Jesse let out a long drawn-out howl. He turned up the stereo and the sounds of "Ohio is for Lovers" by Hawthorne Heights drowned out his thoughts and helped take him deep into his memories of road trips and romances, good times and slow dances, and everything that happened in between him and that moon.

K THX BAI

The little white Ford Escape merged onto the on-ramp for the 105 freeway heading toward Los Angeles International Airport.

"So, Kat, how are you feeling?"

"I'm okay, I guess. Like . . . Yes, I'm fine."

"Are you sure? You haven't seen your dad in nearly two years. Are you sure you want to see him? I'm happy to turn this car around right now and text him. You can tell him that I'm sick. Put it on me, it's totally cool."

Katia reached over and took Jesse's hand in hers. "I want to do this. I want him to see how good we are, and like you said, if he isn't nice, we just leave, right?"

"That's right, my love. If he starts up, I'll excuse us, and we just leave."

"Yay! I feel so safe around you. Thank you for always being here to take care of me. Like, really."

Katia leaned over and put her head on Jesse's shoulder.

"Always, my Kat, always."

Twenty minutes later, the little white SUV was parked at the hotel a couple of miles from the airport, where Katia's dad was staying.

The two sat in the parked car, and Katia took out her phone.

"I'll text him and let him know that we're here," she said, but after unlocking it, she just stared at her screen.

Jesse could feel her anxiety rising.

Slowly, Katia opened the app and scrolled until she got to the conversation she had with her father, and quickly texted to him: *"We're here."*

Katia put the phone down immediately and stared at it.

"Maybe . . . maybe he won't text back."

Jesse smiled and took a long drag off his vape, taking care to blow it out the cracked window of the SUV. He exhaled and looked over to Katia with a smile.

"It will be what it is, sweet baby. We will have a good day no matter what."

Katia smiled, leaned over to Jesse, and gave him a big kiss before looking longingly into his eyes. "Grateful for you, lover."

Jesse brushed a scarlet lock of hair from Katia's face and smiled back at her.

"Grateful for you, my love."

Ding!

Katia's phone illuminated and she looked down at it, the messages banner filled the screen of her iPhone.

Dad: *I'm at the pool, come on in.*

"Okay, here we go, Kat. This is going to be fine."

Jesse got out of the vehicle and walked over to Katia's side.

He opened her door, and she took a quick look at herself in the vanity mirror on her sun visor before she got out and slid beside Jesse so he could close her door for her.

"Shall we, babes?" asked Jesse, motioning to the double glass entry doors of the hotel.

Katia went through the doors and Jesse walked beside her, his hand gently guiding her on the small of her back.

The automatic doors opened, and in the lobby, there was a large reception desk on the right-hand side with a couple of people working efficiently behind computers. Straight ahead was a large glass wall that opened to the patio and pool area.

Jesse took Katia's hand and walked her through the doors and past the rows and rows of deck chairs.

Reclining on the last chair in the row was Katia's father, and as soon as she saw him, Katia let go of Jesse's hand and ran up to him.

"Hi, Dad!"

"Hi, pumpkin!" Gary stood as he responded, giving her a big, tight hug. "I've missed you so much!"

His artificially-tanned skin was slathered with suntan lotion, and although it was chilly in Los Angeles on that March morning, for Gary, who got off a plane from the still frozen over Midwest, the mid-sixty-degree temperature was like summer to the workaholic businessman.

"Dad, what happened to your chest?" Katia said after Gary finally let her loose from his loving bear hug.

Katia pointed at the long vertical scar that ran down the center of her father's chest.

"Oh, that? I had open heart surgery six months ago. Had a pretty bad heart attack. It's fine now."

"What? Why didn't you tell me?"

"I didn't want to worry you. I know how you get, Katia."

Jesse watched the interaction between the two.

Katia always made her father out to be some sort of cruel monster. Jesse had seen glimpses of the man's temper but never found him to be all that bad at all.

Of course, he would never say that to Katia. Who knows what people are really like behind closed doors, when nobody else is looking? Jesse always took Katia seriously when she would share the horror stories of her childhood with him.

Jesse's approximation of the man was simple:

He was the owner of a multimillion-dollar business with a Type A personality.

He was a boss—Indina's very own Donald Trump.

He fired people when he felt like it and enjoyed every minute of it.

He employed hundreds of people and micromanaged every single one of them.

He ruled his company with an iron fist and demanded 110% from everyone, every single day.

He worked seven days a week, three hundred and sixty days a year.

When he had to take days off, he hated it, and Jesse could understand that.

Momentum was a real thing; you had to keep that boulder rolling up that hill.

Some days, Gary even slept at the office, especially if the Indiana weather was being a pain in the ass, which it usually was between November through April.

"Worry me? Like, oh my God, Dad! We would have totally come out and helped you!"

Gary smiled kindly at Katia and shook his head.

"It's fine, pumpkin. I was back in the office three days after surgery. Can you believe that they wanted me to not work for a month? I told them to go fuck themselves."

Gary reached down and opened a fresh Red Bull. There were two empties on the little table next to his lounge chair.

Katia stared at her father in disbelief and bit her quivering lower lip.

Jesse could tell Katia was about to pop. Her eyes were starting to mist, and he could feel the tension welling up within her.

"I can't believe you almost died and didn't tell me! I don't know what I would do if something happened to you!"

Gary pulled Katia in for another big hug and held her close.

"I'm not going anywhere for a very long time, pumpkin. Don't you worry about that." Gary gently patted Katia on her back as she embraced him.

As Jesse watched the exchange, he was trying the best he could to analyze the dynamic. Jesse, never having had a *normal* family himself, didn't really have any sort of basis for comparison. As a matter of fact, he always felt awkward when he was young and went over to friends' houses for sleepovers or dinner, and everyone was there together like a *real* family.

It was always jarring to Jesse to walk into a big, beautiful, clean house, and see professionally done, framed family photos on the walls—or better yet, on the grand piano in the living room.

Everyone dressed in the same color scheme, sometimes even in matching outfits.

The big white smiles . . .

The perfect hair . . .

Even the golden retriever looking perfectly into the camera. The dog also smiling, of course.

To Jesse, those things never seemed like they could be real.

It always seemed like the set of a 1980's family sitcom. Fucking *Silver Spoons* or *Mr. Belvedere* and all the other shows that Jesse was raised on, or rather, that had raised Jesse.

All those shows, all his friends with their families, Jesse's friends that had moms and dads that openly and often showed affection to each other. Friends with their siblings that all got along, ate dinner together at an actual table, had family reunions, and went on vacations every summer together. Families that came back with more than just keychains from the gift shop at the airport, but instead, returned home with rolls of unprocessed film filled with photos of pleasant memories of sunshine and laughter. All those things reinforced to Jesse, at some untouched level of consciousness, that in some way, he wasn't worthy of those things.

No, those weren't for him at all.

"Hi, Jess. How you doing?" Gary reached out and gave Jesse a firmer-than-needed handshake.

"I'm good, sir. Glad you came out for a visit. It's nice to have you here."

"Knock off the 'sir' shit. Just call me Gary."

For a good three seconds, Gary held Jesse's eyes in his. It was a classic salesman's dominance game, and Jesse knew it well.

The old he-who-talks-first-loses and all that old-school sales shit.

Jesse squeezed back, matching Gary's grip without breaking eye contact.

As a matter of fact, Jesse even cracked a little smirk.

After seven or eight seconds of the staring showdown, Jesse had enough. After all, he was here for Katia. If this had been in the realm of his work, heaven help the poor schmuck on the other side of the table.

"How are those scripts working out for you, Gary?"

Gary scoffed and shook his head. "I haven't seen you in nearly two years. and the first thing you ask me is about the sales scripts you wrote for me?" Gary said, now with a big smile and a chuckle.

"I know you track how everything performs. How did they do for you?"

"Really good. Damn good as a matter of fact!"

When Jesse was courting Katia, he wrote some scripts for the salespeople at Gary's business to use. He jumped through hoops trying to win Gary over. Eventually, he decided he wasn't sure if there was such a thing as "winning Gary over," so Jesse just settled on a strategy of consistency.

"Good, let me know when I get my stake in the profit sharing," Jesse said with a wink as he released his grip to Gary's hand, letting him win the little victory.

Gary roared with laughter. "Kiss my ass!"

The tension was officially broken.

Gary smiled as he grabbed his towel and put on his sunglasses. "Let me go back up to my room and get changed. Let's go get some lunch."

"Great! I already have a plan. I'll drive," Jesse said as he slid his arm around Katia's waist. She looked up to him and smiled.

"We will meet you in the front of the hotel in ten minutes, fair?"

"Sounds good. I'll be right down."

Jesse walked Katia back out through the lobby and out the big glass doors to the parking lot.

"I think that went okay. How do you feel, babe?"

"You think that went well? He had major surgery and didn't even tell me! I hate it. He always does things like this, I hate it!"

"Well, he said he didn't want to worry you. Let's focus on being the best we can be today, and not let that sour it. Does that sound good, Kat?"

Katia sighed. "You're right. It is, like, nice to see him, I guess."

Jesse gave Katia a big hug and kiss. "I'm proud of you. You're doing great, you know that?"

"I love you, lover. You always take care of everything."

"Love you too, my Kat."

After ten minutes, Gary emerged from the hotel. "You love birds ready to go?" he called out from across the parking lot, waving at the couple and sliding his phone into his pocket.

"Yep, we are ready!" Katia replied as she smiled.

Jesse clicked the button on the little white SUV's key, and the doors unlocked.

Jesse opened Katia's door for her, and she got in. She shot Jesse a smile of gratitude as he closed her door, and opened the rear passenger door for Gary to get in.

"Thanks, Jess."

Jesse got into the car and dialed in his GPS to the Queen Mary.

"Oh, fun! You're taking us to the Queen Mary for lunch?" Katia squealed with delight.

"The Queen Mary?" Gary asked from the back seat.

Jesse looked in the rearview to see Katia's dad scrolling on his phone, most likely looking at work emails as Jesse backed out of the parking space.

"Yeah, Gary, it's really cool. The Queen Mary is an old steam liner from the 1930s. Bigger than the Titanic. It served in World War II, carrying service members to Europe. Now, it's a hotel and tourist attraction, but there are good restaurants on board, and we can take a fun tour, I thought you would like it."

Katia turned to Jesse and gave him a huge smile.

She knew that when she told Jesse a couple years ago that her dad was a big fan of WWII and history, he was listening. He always listened to everything she said.

"Hey, that does sound cool!" Gary said from the back seat, now putting his phone down.

Jesse could tell that he was actually excited about the day trip. Jesse smiled to himself as he mentally checked off another point in his head.

An hour later, they arrived at the thousand-foot-long steam liner.

Jesse let Katia out of the car and was happy to see her and Gary chatting and being physically close.

"I'll get the tickets, guys. I'll be right back."

Jesse approached the ticket booth, purchased three tickets, grabbed a couple of glossy tourist guides, turned, and paused.

Jesse watched Katia and her dad laughing and being playful with one another. He saw the little girl in her come alive at that moment. Jesse could read her joy, and it was real. It made him very happy. He knew how much Katia longed for her father's attention, love, and approval.

Jesse understood that all the torture Katia had put herself

through in high school, to get straight A's and to excel in sports and dance, were just cries for attention from her dad.

It was paramount to Jesse to do his best to gently facilitate the beginning stages of healing their relationship, in any way he could.

Ultimately, Jesse really did care if Gary liked him.

It mattered to Jesse.

Because Katia mattered to Jesse, and he wanted to be a part of her family.

"I got our tickets," Jesse called out as he put his wallet in the back pocket of his jeans.

"Great. Let's go in!"

They got into the elevator that had replaced the old loading ramp onto the giant antique steam liner.

"I'm starving. I can't wait to eat!" Katia said as she gave Jesse a kiss on his cheek.

"The reviews of the restaurant on here are good. It's called the Chelsea Chowder house and bar. It overlooks the water and is supposed to have a great lunch menu."

Upon entering the restaurant, one could have sworn that they stepped into a time machine. The gleaming tile floors with deco prints were reflected in the ornate sparkling white tile ceiling. The little wooden chairs with salmon pink cushions pushed into the crisp white tablecloths indeed invoked visions of the days when the old luxury liner would steam the rich and famous across the Atlantic Ocean from Europe to America and back again.

During the war effort, the grand ship was repurposed and repainted drab gray to take US servicemen to fight the Nazi war machine.

During that time, the ship was called "The Gray Ghost" after its new paint job.

They say that until this very day, the old ship is still host to all manner of ghosts and hauntings. That the spirits of the dead walk the halls at night. By the late 1960s, the age of steam liners was over—replaced by the speed and efficiency of the jet plane.

And the grand old ship found a permanent home in the port of Long Beach, where now it played as a hotel and tourist attraction.

But, in those empty halls and corridors, they say if you listen carefully, you can still hear the banter of the GIs on their way to the European theater. On some nights, the big band music still plays in the grand ballroom where lovers danced those long nights away at sea.

The three chatted away at lunch. There were no upsets and no heavy talk.

Jesse kept an eagle eye on Katia the entire time, reading her body language and monitoring her mood.

After lunch, they took the tour of the enormous ship.

Gary loved the engine rooms down in the bowels of the ship. It was dark, damp, and extremely claustrophobic.

After the engine room, they wandered the halls while Gary told Jesse stories of Katia when she was little, the kind of stories that were embarrassing, and at the same time, endearing.

On the top deck, Jesse took photos of Katia and her dad together.

Gary even asked a passerby to take a photo of the three of them with his phone. That was a big deal to Jesse, and it was a big deal to Katia, too. The two looked at each other as Gary handed the stranger his phone to take the pic.

Katia squeezed Jesse's hand and shot him a huge smile.

It was happening.

It was really happening.

Sometimes, the little things aren't so little.

The pleasantries continued on the car ride back up north. Jesse pulled into the parking lot of the hotel and parked the little white SUV. He sat as Katia and Gary got out and talked for a couple minutes. Jesse didn't eavesdrop, but he kept an eye on Katia, just to make sure.

He watched the two talk as he played on his phone. After several minutes, they embraced and approached the SUV.

Jesse got out and walked around to meet them.

"You know, Jesse, when you told me that you wanted to be with Katia and have her move back out here, I . . . I gotta say, I was a bit nervous. But after seeing her and you, and how you guys are doing, I want you to know I'm very happy for you both. I wanted to say thank you for taking such great care of her."

Gary gave Jesse a big hug. Jesse looked at Katia while her dad hugged him, and he could see that she was doing the happy dance internally.

"Wow, thank you, Gary. That really means a lot to me."

"Ah, it's all right. You're a good guy. Just keep taking care of my little girl the way you have been, and we'll be good."

"Deal."

"I have another day here tomorrow. You guys wanna do dinner?"

Before Jesse could respond, Katia let out a huge, "Yes!" She squeezed between the two men and gave her dad a big hug and kiss on his cheek.

"Okay, I'll see you guys tomorrow for dinner then!"

Gary watched as Jesse opened the door for Katia, and she got into the car. They waved goodbye and pulled out of the parking lot of the hotel and onto Sepulveda Blvd.

Katia turned up her favorite Panic! At the Disco song and made their way back home, singing every word to every song along the way.

"Push, Victoria, push!"

Victoria bared down and pushed with the contraction that

cramped and contorted her midsection so much that she felt as though she may, in fact, snap in half.

They had already been at the hospital for twelve hours while Victoria was in the latent phase of labor.

Amador and Eastman held onto Vic's hands, told stories, and made jokes as she pushed and pushed.

When they had arrived at the hospital, Victoria was already dilated at two centimeters. Eleven hours later, she was fully dilated at ten centimeters. Her uterus had fully effaced, and the contractions that had started off as mild cramps, not unlike what she was used to during a bad period, now had become body twisting, back-breaking earthquakes.

"I can't do this! I can't do this!" Victoria cried to her husband as she dug her nails into his arm, leaving deep white impressions in his skin.

"You got this, babe. You're doing great. Just remember to breathe!"

"Thanks, hun. I'll try to remember to *breathe*! Got any more motivation for me, Tony Robbins?!"

Eastman stroked Vic's head and brushed a wisp of her long brunette hair off her face as she breathed and tried to recover from the last wave of contractions.

"You're okay, Vic. We're here for you. It won't be long. You're almost done."

Victoria smiled at Eastman, but that smile quickly turned to a grimace as another contraction pulsed through her body.

"FUCK! It feels like there is a rusty chainsaw going crazy inside of me, trying to rip itself out!"

"Breathe and push. Breathe and push!" Amador's voice had the tone and timber of a drill sergeant as he barked out commands to his wife. She sat up on her elbows and pushed as hard as she could, trying to visualize forcing the now watermelon-sized lump in her belly down to her feet.

Victoria cried out, took in a deep inhale, and pushed again.

The obstetrician looked up to Victoria, gave her a nod, and said, "The baby is crowning! We are almost there! Come here, Dad, you're going to want to see this."

The doctor's cool and collected tone reassured Victoria as she felt another significant contraction coming on.

"Another is coming!" Victoria cried out as Amador maneuvered himself next to the doctor.

Eastman got close to Victoria's face and held eye contact with her. She kept her attention and whispered to Victoria, "Are you ready to become a mom?"

"Yes!"

The doctor chimed in one last time as she readied to take delivery, "One last big push and we will be there. Okay, Mom, are you ready?"

Victoria's gaze was still looked on Eastman's.

"Push, Vic! Push!"

Victoria took a deep breath and squeezed Eastman's hand as she channeled the last of her strength and will and pushed with all her might.

Eastman squeezed her hand back and never broke her gaze.

"The baby is out! The baby is out!"

For a moment in the delivery room, everyone froze as after all the exertion and expectation, there was nothing, nothing but pin-drop silence.

Nothing moved. It was as if time had stopped.

Victoria and Eastman looked over at the same instant to see the doctor frantically, and almost roughly, rubbing off the blood and excess fluids from the tiny, still form in her arms.

A moment later, the silence that seemed to last for eternity was shattered as the high-pitched squeal of tiny lungs taking their first breath of air pierced the room.

The doctor placed the baby on Victoria's bosom, and the

exhausted woman broke down into the purest tears that Eastman had ever seen. A tiny hand reached up blindly and touched Victoria's face.

Amador was sobbing tears of joy, as if this moment washed away all the sins he had to commit while deployed, and his slate was finally, thoroughly, and forever perfectly clean.

"Dad, would you like to cut the cord?"

The doctor handed Amador a pair of medical scissors and directed him where to cut. He was a bit shocked when he found cutting through the umbilical cord felt more like cutting through a garden hose than soft tissue.

Eastman excused herself for a moment to step outside. She looked down at her iPhone and tapped the screen, bringing it to life.

She scanned the notifications:

Emails, emails, emails, and several text messages.

She had trained pretty much everyone that she interacted with to never call her, unless it was an absolute, bona fide, 911, house-on-fire emergency, and even then, "text me first."

The 'phone' on the iPhone was her least liked, and least used, feature. She often wondered when Apple was going to release the 'i,' and just get rid of the phone altogether.

She swept right on Jesse's notification from 8:28 p.m.

"Are you busy later?"

Eastman smiled. That was the pre-communicated signal that all had gone well, and Jesse's work was done.

"Perfection," she whispered under her breath as she slid her phone back into her purse and walked back into the delivery room.

THE LAST SUPPER

If the path is beautiful,

Let us not ask where it leads.

—Anatole France.

Jesse was nearly home when he received the call from Dr. Melantha Eastman

"Hello?" he said, answering the call that was put through his car's speakers. There was a brief silence on the other end of the line before the doctor's voice rang through.

"Hey, Jess. Are you busy?"

"No, almost home. What's up?"

The shrill sound of a baby's cries could be heard in the background as she spoke up a bit louder into her phone.

"I'm at Verdugo Hills Hospital with Victoria and Amador. They just had their baby, and we need a favor. Will you please help?"

The crying of the baby continued as Jesse considered the question.

"Hello? Jess?"

"Oh, hey, sure. I need to stop at the house and unload the car first." Jesse glanced in the rear-view mirror of the white SUV at the easels, mirror, stacks of canvases, and of course, his large black duffle bag from his long day's work.

"Great. They are going to transport Vic to a room soon. I need you to come to meet me in the ER parking lot, and I'll give you instructions from there. Please text me when you're on your way, okay?"

"Yeah, sure . . . Give me, like, thirty minutes, and I'll be right over."

"Thank you, hun. See you soon."

The music instantly started playing again as the call disconnected, and Jesse turned it down.

They must really be desperate if they are willing to stoop so low as to ask me for help, Jesse thought as he merged onto the off-ramp to La Crescenta Blvd. Two minutes later, he pulled into the driveway of the little house on Piedmont.

Jesse pulled the SUV all the way up the driveway and parked right against the door of the garage. He got out and smiled as he saw a streak of gray and white come bounding up to the gate off the detached garage.

Loki was ecstatic to see his master and proceeded to break into a chorus of howls, as Jesse acknowledged the husky.

"Hey, buddy. I'm home!"

"Rowwww rooowr rooooowwww," Loki sang back to Jesse as he spun in circles and danced his happy husky dance around the confines of the backyard.

"I'll be right there, buddy!"

Jesse walked around to the front of the little house and walked up the three steps leading to the front door.

Loki continued to dance and sing even though Jesse was out of his line of sight. As Jesse put the pink key up to the lock, he stopped and stared at it, and was teleported back in time to years ago.

Jesse turned to Katia and handed her a small brown paper bag.

"What's this?"

"Open it, Kat."

Katia opened it and emptied the contents into her hand.

A bright pink house key with a little black cat enameled on it landed in her palm.

"That's the key to our house—your house."

Katia looked up to Jesse with a mix of delight and exhaustion.

Having just completed over twenty-five hundred miles of their vagabonding road trip adventure, they were both weary and looking forward to nothing more than crawling into bed.

Katia threw her arms around Jesse's neck and stood up on her tippy toes to kiss him.

"Thank you. Thank you for showing me what it's like to really feel appreciated and enough."

Jesse closed Katia's hand around the key as she lowered herself down from the kiss.

"I promise I will always do the best I can for you."

Katia looked deep in Jesse's eyes, her own misting over with gratitude.

Jesse looked back into Katia's eyes, swept a wisp of her hair off her face, and gently kissed her on her forehead. "Always," he promised.

Jesse shook off the memory as he slipped the key into the lock and turned it ninety degrees.

All his friends, Hunter, Andy, and the rest, had urged Jesse to get the locks to the house changed after what happened, but Jesse refused.

"What's the point?" Jesse would laugh as he looked at the door. "Let him come back. I wish he would."

Plus, somewhere deep down inside of him, he wanted to hold onto anything that Katia had touched, used, and kept close to her.

That's why he kept her SUV going, kept making the payments on the lease; he didn't have to.

Jesse had no use for two cars until now.

And still, even now, the center console of the little white SUV was filled with Katia's lip gloss, receipts from a year ago, those little purple licorice-flavored candies that she adored—the same ones that Jesse always thought tasted like soap—and, of course, emergency tampons.

That's why the storage shed in the backyard was overflowing with big black trash bags filled with her clothes.

He couldn't find it in him to let them—let her—go.

Jesse opened the door to the little house on Piedmont and walked inside.

The howling and yowling from the backyard were still going as Loki sang the song of his people, up until Jesse opened the back door and let him run inside. He did two laps around through the living room and kitchen before returning to his master to jump and cover Jesse's face with those heavy wet wolf kisses.

"Hey, big boy! I'm home! Daddy's home!"

Jesse went into the bathroom and turned the knobs on the old plumbing in the shower, and the hot water started to pour from the spigot, instantly steaming up the bathroom.

Loki watched as Jesse turned the central knob, forcing water out of the shower head as he climbed inside of the tub, for a quick rinse off.

Jesse stood there in the shower for a good ten minutes as the streams of water pounded the top of his head and flowed down his body in a torrent of mini tsunamis, which convened in a whirlpool that floated down the drain.

His thoughts, his memories, his being, would never be clean again.

Jesse grabbed Katia's pink luffa and filled it with his favorite soap—the one that she got him addicted to right after she moved in. He scrubbed himself down from head to toe, and let the water carry away the dried sweat and tension from the day and its events.

Jesse sat in the tub and put his hands on his head . . . Just like he had done after Izzy, Jesse searched his feelings thoroughly and deeply for any remorse, regret, or anything for what he had done that day.

The images of the claws filleting and deboning the flesh from Jason and Serena.

The smell of melting flesh.

The echoes of their screams that were still ringing in his ears.

Jesse searched. He found nothing.

He didn't feel anything: no regret, no remorse, no joy, no sense of conquest.

There was nothing.

Jesse was jolted back to the present moment by Loki's tongue licking the water flowing off his shoulder.

"Hey buddy, okay. I'm getting out."

Jesse turned off the shower and wrapped a towel around his waist as Loki pranced after him into the room with a bed in it.

Jesse hung up his suit and threw his white shirt onto the bed.

He opened up the drawer of Katia's heavy wooden dresser that he had taken over since he took her clothes out of it.

Jesse slid on a clean pair of boxer briefs, a mismatched pair of black socks, dark blue jeans, and a V-neck black t-shirt. He grabbed his black zip-up hoodie and threw on a beanie.

Jesse sat on the corner of his side of the bed and laced up his ratty New Balance sneakers.

Loki watched with a a confused expression on his face. He didn't understand why Daddy, who had just gotten home, was putting on his shoes again.

"I'll be back soon, buddy. Then we can both have a much-needed nap. You stay inside and be a good boy. Do you understand?"

Loki tilted his head in the typical husky fashion as if to say, "I hear what you're saying. but I'm going to be a bad boy anyway."

Jesse got up, grabbed the keys to the Prius, clipped the key hook onto the belt loop on his jeans, and started out to the door and on his way to the Verdugo Hills Hospital.

"You have reached the voice mailbox for 310-215—"

The phone was hung up.

Andromeda looked to the man who was sitting at his desk, fingers tented against his lips.

"Still no answer on Jason's or Serena's phones. Straight to voicemail on both. What . . . What should we do?"

"Where's Orchid?"

"She's still asleep. Should I wake her?"

"No, not yet, and you're not to let her out of your sight. Do you understand?"

"Yes, my Pedagogue. What should we do?"

Andromeda looked to the man who she felt always had total control of himself, his house, and the world around him, and for the first time ever, she saw him unsure, not contemplating, not pondering, but uncertain, and almost scared—and it frightened her immensely.

"All of this had to happen. I have foreseen that our family will go through great trials before the beacon brings us to our former power and glory."

Andromeda started trembling. Her grip on her cell phone was now causing her knuckles to turn white. She opened the phone app and hit redial for Serena's phone.

"You have reached the voice mailbox for 626-720—"

She hung up the phone and glared at the man still sitting at his desk staring off into space.

"But what about Jason and Serena? Should—Should we call the police? What are you going to do about this? What if they're in trouble?

"All will be revealed in time, my child."

"But . . . But what about Serena and Jason?"

Andromeda was now visibly upset, but still trying to maintain her composure and protocols. The man looked from the skyline of Los Angeles, and up to her, and furrowed his brow in anger.

"We are in but a spiral. It must go down before it can turn again and ascend. I have foreseen all of this. Do not worry, my child. Do not worry."

Andromeda cast her eyes to the floor and nodded her head. She turned and walked out of the room and into the bathroom in the hallway.

She ran the shower and watched the water caress the drain in the delicate dance of the Coriolis effect, and the steam of the near scorching hot water filled her lungs and beaded condensation on her naked skin.

She undressed and got in, stood perfectly still, and sobbed.

Sobbed alone, secretly, quietly, and was careful to muffle her cries.

This was the first time in years that she had cast off the yoke of 'self-mastery' to feel human again—and she hated herself for it.

She hated every cell in her body for feeling this way.

As the hot water mixed and commingled with her tears, she covered her mouth with her hand and bit down as hard as she could.

Stand in your power . . . Stand in your power . . . Stand in your power! Andromeda said over and over in her head. The words bounced off the corners of her mind, looking for the same meaning and purchase as they once had.

But there was no soil for the seeds of the words to take root, and there was not a single blade of grass for her to mentally cling to.

The words had lost their meaning in this moment and fell into the dark, lonely corner of her soul as she rocked in place, and bit down harder until she broke the skin on the meaty part of her hand.

She sat in the corner of the tub, where the water was still be hitting her, and continued to sob and pray for Jason, for Serena, for

Izzy, and for herself.

Jesse sat in the parking lot of the Verdugo Hills Hospital, having just texted Eastman to let her know he arrived. He took a couple long draws off his vape as he scrolled through the feed on his Instagram and liked some of his friends' photos.

As he exhaled, the dense cloud of pancake-scented vape billowed from the open window of his Prius.

Scrolling and liking, scrolling and linking.

He didn't even notice Eastman was standing outside the window of his car, watching him with a huge grin.

"Wow, a forty-year-old white guy that drives a Prius and vapes? Swoon!"

Jesse looked up to see her smiling, and she gave him a sly wink as their eyes met.

"Yeah, I know. I'm a real catch." Jesse winked right back as he got out of the car.

"So, what's the plan?"

Eastman reached into her purse and pulled out a folded piece of paper.

"Here is Amador's address. You're going to go to their house. You're going to feed the dog—put out enough food for a couple meals. Her name is 'Leah Dog.' It's written down on the paper so you won't forget."

Eastman paused and gave Jesse a quick, playful poke in his ribs.

"You're going to put her outside and then clean up any mess she may have made. Then you're going to grab the big suitcase by the front door—that's all of Victoria's stuff that they pre-packed for the hospital stay. Then you're going to lock the front door on your way out, and you're going to come back. Do you understand?"

Jesse looked down at the note in his hand with Eastman's practically perfect script outlining exactly what she just told him, word-for-word.

"Yeah, I think I can manage that."

"Good boy. And on your way there, I want you to stop by Ralph's and pick up some stargazer lilies. Make sure that most of them are unopened. She will be here for a day or two, and I want them to be blooming when she gets home. You're going to get a card and fill it out from both of us, and leave that on the kitchen counter with the flowers. Got it?"

"Roses, got it!"

Melantha laughed out loud and punched Jesse in the arm.

"Go! And when you get back, we will talk about how things went, okay?"

"Can't wait," Jesse said as he turned to open the door to his car.

"Hey."

Jesse turned, and Eastman jumped into his arms and kissed him deeply.

"I can't wait to spend some time with you later, if you know what I mean."

"Oh, really?" Jesse said with a smirk. She embraced the big man again and gave his ass a firm squeeze.

"Yes really. Now get going, they're waiting."

"Yes, ma'am!"

Jesse gave her a military solute and got into his Prius.

"Hey! So . . . you want me to feed the suitcase and bring the dog, right?"

Eastman laughed and presented Jesse both of her perfectly manicured middle fingers.

"I'll see you when you get back. Oh, and Jess, thank you for doing this."

Jesse pulled out of the Verdugo Hills Hospital parking lot and made his way up to Foothill Blvd.

As he passed from La Cañada into the neighboring town of La Crescenta, his mind wandered.

He thought back to the screams of Jason and Serena and smiled.

His memories of the scene were like black and white movies, except for the blood. The blood was as vivid and crimson as could be.

He chuckled to himself as he tried to comprehend and imagine the horror that must have been going through the minds of the two people bound to the chairs as the LSD kicked in hard, and their grip with reality was thrown into the abyss of boundless non-perception.

Sometimes when the chickens come home to roost, their beaks and talons are razor sharp.

And sometimes, just sometimes, karma gets that much needed little push.

Once in a great while, people get what they have coming.

Only few will bear witness to the revenge of the roosters.

After stopping by the floral department of a supermarket and grabbing a congratulatory card, Jesse was greeting a golden retriever inside a modest post-war era home on Greeley Street in Tujunga.

The big floppy dog bounded up to him and started giving him kisses.

"Hey, buddy! Some guard dog you are!" Jesse laughed as he stroked the dog's large floppy head and ran his fingers through her golden bronze hair.

"Wanna go outside?"

The giant dog cocked her head to the side and bounded to the back door and scratched on it with eager anticipation.

"Okay, Leah Dog, go outside!"

Jesse opened the back door, and the dog made a beeline to the green grass, where she promptly went potty.

Jesse looked around the living room of the house.

It was clean and cute.

Pictures of Amador and Victoria adorned the mantle of the small fireplace, along with an American flag and the Purple Heart Amador received after being wounded while he was in the service overseas.

Jesse did a quick walkthrough of the house to make sure that Leah Dog didn't leave any "special presents" on the floor while she was trapped inside all night.

Good dog, Jesse thought. He could imagine the destruction that Loki would have dealt out if he was cooped up in the house all night. He opened the pantry, made Leah Dog a big bowl of food, and placed it outside. The golden chowed down on it as soon as it hit the ground. Jesse smiled.

Jesse made his way into the kitchen, found a vase, and filled it with water, and as instructed, left the lilies next to the coffee maker.

He made his way back to the front door and picked up the large navy blue suitcase that Victoria had packed for herself in the last couple of weeks of her pregnancy.

"Okay, here we go."

Jesse locked the door behind him and started making his way back to the hospital.

DOUBLE DOWN

*The desperate usually succeed because they have nothing to
lose.*

—Jodi Picoult

The little bell of the door of Her Majesty's Tea House and Supply jingled when Andromeda turned the key to unlock the door and open up shop.

Orchid stood silently behind her, holding her hands at her pelvis, her eyes cast downward.

The short car ride to the shop had been an awkward one.

Orchid, unaware of the unfolding events in the family, could sense the tension in Andromeda as she drove silently, robotically, impatiently through the busy morning bumper-to-bumper traffic of the west side of Los Angeles.

And when Andromeda yelled out the window at a minivan full of children and a Starbucks sipping mommy, mashed the gas pedal of the early 2000's era Jaguar to speed in front of her, and cut off the woman in a fit road rage, Orchid knew something was happening that she wasn't being let in on.

Andromeda pushed open the door to the small boutique. She walked briskly into the back room while Orchid followed her closely.

"Turn on everything and get the store open. I'll be in the back."

Andromeda's bitter tone reaffirmed with Orchid that something was very wrong today.

"Yes, Andromeda."

Orchid went through the routine of turning on the computer and booting up the point-of-sale software.

She went around the store, turning on the lights, lighting the candles and incense, and switching on the little bubbling Zen fountains.

Orchid froze as she heard Andromeda's cell phone ring.

She made her way back behind the counter and pretended to be busy as she tried to eavesdrop on the hushed tones of the conversation going on in the back office of the little tea shop.

All Orchid could make out of the conversation was, "No, I haven't mentioned anything to her about it." And, "Yes, my Pedagogue, I understand. Yes, I agree. We need to bring more sheep into the fold. Have . . . Have you heard from Jason or Serena yet? Okay, let me know if you hear anything, please."

Orchid stood there silently as she watched the computer finish booting up and the point-of-sale software automatically launch.

The little shop was quiet as a church except for the rhythmic bubbling of water flowing over the river stones of the fountain in the corner of the room.

Orchid searched her feelings as she stood there.

What could be going on that she wasn't allowed to know about?

Why wasn't she included in everything that went on in the house?

Wasn't she part of the family too?

"Is everything ready?"

Orchid nearly jumped out of her skin as she spun around to see Andromeda standing right behind her.

"Yes! Yes, everything is ready," Orchid said as she put on her best fake smile and tried to act as nonchalant as possible.

"Good, then we are open for business."

Orchid looked into Andromeda's eyes. She could tell that the woman was reading her. She could tell that Andromeda knew that she knew that something was wrong.

"Go put some music on, dear." Andromeda stared coldly into Orchid's eyes.

Orchid turned to the computer, opened the browser, and went to Pandora. The Bluetooth speakers around the store instantly came alive with the sounds of the French café station.

Orchid stared at the screen, and before her mind could even process what her lips were doing, the words fell out of her mouth and onto the floor.

"Is something wrong with Jason and Serena?"

Andromeda froze.

"What . . . What makes you say that, Orchid?"

"It's just that I haven't heard from either of them in the last day or so. Usually, they always reply to my messages."

Andromeda walked around the counter and to the door, where she turned the sign on the glass door from closed to open. She paused, stared out the window, and smiled.

She turned and held Orchid's gaze and walked toward her with the same smile.

"They're fine, my love. They had to go on a last-minute essential journey for our Pedagogue. They were given strict orders to not use any electronic devices while on this mission . . . as not to interfere with their pineal glands. They will need to be as focused and tuned in as possible to make sure that the mission is executed flawlessly and in line with our Pedagogue's expectations."

"Oh, how exciting for them! When will they be back? I miss them very much."

"They will be back soon. Hopefully. This journey could take days or months to accomplish. It is vital to our Pedagogue, but it all will be what it is, my sister. It will be what it is."

Andromeda stared at Orchid.

They both were wearing masks, and both their masks were

slipping.

The stare was broken as the door chime jingled when the brass knob turned. Three men walked through the door and closed it behind them, turned the sign from open to closed, and locked the door.

They were heavily tattooed, tall, bearded, biker looking types.

The denim vests they wore were emblazoned with dozens of sewn-on patches denoting gang affiliation, demons, and skulls.

The patches scared Orchid, but not as much as the men, whose tattooed arms and faces told the same story of long prison terms, hate, and violence.

This was not exactly the type of clientele that Orchid was used to seeing walk through the door of Her Majesty's Tea House and Supply.

Andromeda spun around and froze when she laid eyes on the three men standing in her store.

"Hello, Hello, Jonas. Welcome. To what . . . do we owe this pleasure?"

The big man in front of the other two smiled and gave Andromeda a nod.

His wicked smile was framed by his salt and pepper beard.

He slowly walked toward the two women, followed closely by the two other men that had expressionless faces. Their hungry eyes were fixed on Andromeda.

"Oh, I'm sure you can guess why I'm here, Andromeda. But let's make a game out of it, shall we?"

Andromeda turned to Orchid. "Honey, go in the back and put on a kettle. I'm sure our friends could do with a brew."

Orchid started to turn toward the door leading to the back room as the man with the salt and pepper beard spoke again.

"Young lady, that's far enough. Stay where I can see you. You don't want to make my friends here nervous, do you? Because when my friends get nervous, they get scared, and when they get scared, they get angry, and when they get angry, terrible things can happen to young ladies like yourself.

"So I would ask you very nicely, for your well-being, do not to make my friends nervous."

Orchid froze and looked to Andromeda, who was looking back at her but no longer smiling. Her eyes were filled with an emotion that Orchid wasn't aware that Andromeda was capable of. Fear.

"That's a clever girl. Just stay . . . right . . . there," the man hissed through his teeth as he took two more steps toward the woman in front of the counter.

"So, since you're in the mood to play games with me, Andromeda, I'm going to give you three guesses to figure out why I'm here today. Ready?" He snapped his fingers in the air to get Andromeda's attention. Her eyes were still fixed on Orchid's, and her bottom lip was quivering.

Andromeda slowly turned her head and faced the man who, now, was less than two feet in front of her. A bit too close for comfort as far as western personal space would dictate.

Andromeda's voice was trembling as she stammered out her reply, just over a whisper, "I-I can't imagine why, bu-but if you want, I am happy to arrange a meeting with my Pedagogue with you, Jonas."

Jonas dragged his tongue over his lips. He smiled and turned to one of the nicely made-up tables in the middle of the little boutique.

With one quick and violent thrust of his boot, he kicked the table, chairs, and all the fine China across the room, and it slammed against the wall, sending countless boxes of tea, trinkets, crystals, and tiny treasures flying everywhere.

Orchid gasped and covered her mouth with her hand as she stood frozen. She looked down to see Andromeda's hand grip tightly on the countertop.

"I'm sorry, Andromeda. I didn't hear you. Did you say that your first guess was that your boy Izzy has thousands of dollars of my product? And about fifty thousand dollars of money from last month's sales. Product he and your—whatever you call him—oh, right, 'Pedagogue' said that he could move for me in less than a week?

"I'll tell you what. I have been calling Izzy, and I have been texting him. You wanna hear something funny, Andromeda?" The man motioned around the store, as if he was expecting someone to speak up and tell him the answer he was hoping to hear.

"I haven't heard back from him. So, I thought I would come here and entertain you by playing a game. Tell me, do you like the game so far? Are you ready for your second guess?"

Andromeda was still frozen in the same place she had been when Jonas started talking, her hands on either side of her on the counter as if she was trying to meld into it, become part of the background.

"Izzy . . . Izzy is missing," she said as tears started streaming down her face.

The words sliding over her tongue like sandpaper on a chalkboard. Jonas stared at Andromeda. The smile disappeared from his face. His eyes darted from Andromeda to Orchid, who was still staring at the floor, and back to Andromeda.

The man raised his right hand and snapped his well-calloused fingers.

Immediately, the men standing behind him started destroying everything in the store. They toppled over tables and kicked in shelves. The shattering glass and splintering wood thundered and ricocheted off the walls, and debris filled the air.

The two women screamed out in fright as the two men started toward the register.

Jonas raised one finger, and the men stopped dead in their tracks. Their hulking frames heaving like some sort of relic hominids.

Jonas moved his finger to his lips and made a quiet shooshing sound.

"Shhhh, calm down, Andromeda. I couldn't make out your second guess over all the noise and screaming. Did you just say that Izzy is missing? Well, I guess that would mean that my product and my money is missing too, then, doesn't it?"

Jonas pulled a cheap cigar out from the front pocket of his denim vest and lit it. He took a couple deep puffs and blew the smoke in Andromeda's face.

"Not to mention that the word on the street is that your boy has been very naughty. Very naughty indeed. The people that run this city, well, the underground at least, we don't take kindly to people that deal in the trafficking of children."

Jonas watched as Andromeda held his gaze, a look of horror stretching across her face.

"Oh, you didn't know that everyone knows about that? I guess that means we have a card on you now too. Might have to pull it soon. You never know."

Jonas took another puff from his cigar and flicked it into the corner of the room, where it exploded into a flurry of ashes and sparks, falling and smoldering in a lonely corner of the shop.

He took another step closer to Andromeda and was now towering over her. Her nose was nearly buried into his chest.

"Now you listen to me, little girl, and you listen good. You tell that sick fuck of a cult leader of yours that he is cut off—forever. And you tell him, I don't care how he does it, how many ghosts he needs to talk to, or how many spells he needs to cast, but he had better conjure up Izzy with my product and my money—all sixty thousand dollars of it—in the next three days, or else . . ."

Jonas glanced at Orchid, who still had her hand clasped over her face and tears streaming down her pale porcelain cheeks, then back down to Andromeda, still frozen at the level of his sternum.

The man hissed, "Or else, it's game over for all of you. Are we clear, Andromeda?"

Andromeda just sniffled and nodded her head slowly.

"Good! Always good doing business with you. And remember: you have three days. Say it with me now, Andromeda."

Jonas put his hand under her chin and jerked her head up

violently, so his eyes pierced into hers.

"Say it."

"Three . . . Three days."

"Good. Clear like crystal, then?"

Jonas looked over his shoulder to the men standing behind him. "Let's get some breakfast, boys. All these games this morning have really worked up an appetite."

Jonas turned back to the two women standing before him and smiled warmly before holding up three dirty fingers.

"Three days."

With that, Jonas led the two men out of the store, the little bell jingled as the door closed behind them, leaving two women still frozen in place, breathing in a mix of lingering incense and the smell of cheap cigar smoke.

"You really came through for us today. Thank you, Jesse."

Amador reached out his hand in a token of friendship as Eastman and Victoria looked on.

Jesse smiled and took Amador's hand. His grip was firm, but not to the extent of trying to be dominant.

Victoria chimed in as she looked down to her newborn son, who was firmly attached to her breast and enjoying a feed.

"Thank you, Jesse. I really do appreciate you getting my stuff from the house and taking care of Leah Dog."

"It's really no big deal. I'm happy to help."

Eastman got up from the orange chair in the corner of the hospital room and grabbed her bag from off the handle of the door where it had been hanging.

"Okay, Jess. Let's let these two—excuse me, *three* have their time alone."

She smiled at Vic, Amador, and baby Londyn.

"Get some rest you, guys. You've earned it. We will talk in a couple days."

As Eastman leaned in to give Victoria a peck on her cheek, her phone and Amador's phone both started vibrating and alerting at the same time.

For a moment, time stopped as Eastman and Amador looked at each other and both pulled out their phones.

"Shit," Amador said under his breath as he read the message.

"Shit indeed," Eastman replied as she looked up from the screen of her iPhone and up to Jesse.

"What? What is it? What's wrong?" Victoria said as her eyes went from her husband and back to Eastman. Eastman threw her bag over her shoulder and started toward the door of the hospital room.

"There has been another murder. Amador, text Durazo and tell him I'm on my way. I'll keep you updated."

"Yes, ma'am," Amador said as he looked back to Victoria and took her hand. He gently rose it to his lips and kissed it every so softly.

Eastman smiled and turned to Jesse.

"Go home and get some rest. I'll come by later."

Jesse nodded.

"Hey, Jesse, Eastman," Amador called out as the two started toward the door.

"Thank you both again, for everything."

Eastman spun on her heel and looked at the two exhausted adults and smiled.

"You earned this, Amador. You and Victoria both earned this." She turned and walked out the door, Jesse following closely behind her.

Victoria held sleeping baby Londyn close and gently kissed the infant on his soft bald head.

Victoria looked up to Amador and smiled an exhausted smile.

"See, babe, I told you he wasn't a bad guy at all. Are you still going to keep following Jesse around now?"

THE COLLAPSING TANGLE

Love cannot save you from your own fate.

—Jim Morrison

Eastman pulled out of the parking lot of the Verdugo Hills Hospital.

She mashed down on the accelerator, and the engine of her big black SUV roared to life.

As she came to the first light on Verdugo Blvd, she reached into her purse, and with her right hand grabbed her iPhone and swiped the screen opening the text messaging app.

Eastman selected the most recent message, hit the info button, and tapped the phone icon. She did all this without so much as a second glance at her phone.

After a couple of rings, the call was answered.

"Durazo here. Thank you for calling me back so fast, doctor."

"Talk to me, sergeant. What do we have?"

"You're not going to like this one, Eastman."

She could hear the hesitation and churlishness in Durazo's voice.

It was a tone and timber that she recognized all too well, and she hesitated. After a brief silence, the silence was broken again by Durazo.

"Where are you now?"

"I'm just leaving the hospital. I was visiting with Amador and Victoria. Where am I meeting you?"

"You remember the Ackles' residence on the Journeys End Drive?"

Melantha swallowed hard. "Is it Judy?"

"Meet me here as soon as you can. I have kept everyone out of the scene. I want you to be the first eyes on."

"I'm on my way, sergeant."

A few minutes later, Jesse pulled up to the little Spanish style house on Piedmont. He was so exhausted, he nearly fell asleep on the three-mile drive home from the hospital.

It was the kind of tired that you can't even reason or negotiate with. The kind of tired that takes you prisoner, latches onto your neck and nearly bleeds you dry of every drop of consciousness and sanity you have left.

As the Prius silently pulled into the steep driveway, he breathed in a deep sigh of relief. He got out of the little black car and closed the door behind him.

Jesse climbed the three concrete steps that led to the front door. It seemed to take the same amount of effort and focus as it would to hike up one of the mountainsides he loved to frequent in Pasadena.

His feet felt like concrete as he lifted them up the steps to the big wooden door. The toe of his sneaker clipped the last step on his way up, and he nearly stumbled and fell, if not for being saved by the wooden railing that adjoined the steps.

Jesse slid his key into the door and pushed it open with his index finger.

The door swung open freely, letting loose a tired sigh and an almost cliché creak as the old brass hinges took on the weight of the ancient oak plank.

He instinctively and robotically turned and hung his keys on the line of key hooks by the door.

Katia's keys dangled next to his and swung ever so gently from the disturbance caused by the added weight of the keys of the Prius. A ray of sun penetrated the curtains and cast a beam of golden amber morning light that hit Katia's hanging keys. The glimmer reached out and captivated Jesse. The reflection off the keys casting a beam across his face, calling him in, seducing him.

Jesse reached out and gently touched the keys. He was lost in a moment, a memory of his old life, something that seemed so misty and far away.

Like a lazy, hazy flashback memory on a TV show. The kind you used to love when you were a kid. The kind you would get up extra early on Saturday morning for, snuggled in front of the big old tube TV, with a heaping bowl of sugary cereal in your lap.

But now, all these moments, days, weeks, months, and years later, you can barely remember the characters' names or why you even were so enamored with the show in the first place.

But it was the past. It was barely even a single grain in the ever-flowing river of the sands of time, but it was still there . . .

The energy was still there—right beneath the surface.

And occasionally, that old life, that old dead thing would scratch and knock at the windows of Jesse's subconscious.

No matter how much he tried to push it back those, old clattering memories would sometimes rattle and shift and leak, leaving a puddle of memories that he adored and feared, loathed and cherished. They were precious to him even still.

The hypnotic spell was broken by a yowl coming from the living room. Loki was standing only several feet in front of Jesse, staring at him expectantly after his dances and cartwheels went unacknowledged by his master.

"Hey, buddy," Jesse finally greeted, which was all Loki needed to run up to him and jump.

Jesse held him close and gave him scratches on his cheeks and down his back.

"Whoosa good boy?" Jesse laughed. The puppy's excitement gave him a momentary reprieve from his own exhaustion.

"Youza good boy, isn't you?"

The puppy jumped and licked Jesse's beard.

After letting Loki out, the two filed back into the house to finally get some rest.

"Let's go to bed, big boy."

Loki immediately ran into the room with a bed and jumped on the king-sized mattress. Jesse followed close behind. He slipped off his shoes, collapsed onto the covers, and threw an arm over the still panting wolfdog pup.

Jesse ran his fingers through the huge dog's coarse fur, and as Loki's breathing slowed, and his eyes started to slowly relax and close, so did Jesse's.

Within seconds, they were both fast asleep.

Durazo stood at the oversized arch-top front door at the house on Journeys End Drive, watching his deputies milling about, looking for any evidence outside the home and putting up the thick yellow police line crime scene tape. That morning, the only sounds in the quiet, upper-class neighborhood were the sporadic songs of birds announcing the start of the day and confirming their territory—along with the distant sound of leaf blowers being swung like metronomes by the gardeners that played the endless game of pushing leaves from one property to another.

A smile came across Durazo's face as the rumbling report of a big

V8 started to echo up the winding suburban street, accompanied by the muffled subsonic thud of the bass from the SUV's always blasting stereo.

Moments later the Black SUV pulled up and parked in front of the house.

Durazo could see his reflection in the blacked-out windows. The music was still thudding.

A few seconds later, the engine stopped rumbling, and with it, the music stopped.

The street went back to the sounds of leaf blowers and birds.

Durazo could barely see through the limo tint of the truck. All he could make out was the silhouette of the woman behind the driver's seat, sitting perfectly still. He could see her taking several deep breaths, as if she was gathering up her courage and readying herself to jump off a high dive into a deep, dark pool of frigid water.

A moment later, the driver's side door of the black SUV opened, and in a single fluid motion, Eastman swung her heel shod feet out of the door, and in unison, they hit the cobblestone drive.

Durazo watched as Eastman almost robotically, mechanically, closed the door of her truck and walked around to the back of her SUV.

As she opened the liftgate, she looked over and made eye contact with the sergeant, who was now making his way up to meet her.

"Good morning, Special Agent Eastman. Thank you for getting here so fast."

"That's my job, sergeant."

Eastman paused and looked into Durazo's dark brown eyes, and just over a whisper, let out the words, "Please, don't tell me it's Judy."

Durazo broke eye contact with her and let out a long sigh as he glanced back at the stunning *Better Homes and Gardens* picturesque house on Journeys End Drive.

"It is Judy?" Her voice was fighting back a quiver.

Eastman was done hesitating. She put on her FBI windbreaker, gathered up her long, flowing, curly blonde mane and twisted it into a bun, which she secured with a black hair tie that was waiting to be utilized on her tapered wrist. She grabbed the lanyard that held her badge and credentials and flung it over her head and around her neck.

"How long, sergeant?" she asked as she pulled out a small green velvet pouch from the large duffel bag and dumped out several stones and crystals onto the carpeted trunk of the SUV.

"A couple days at most. We responded to a wellness check a couple hours ago, when her sister called us to check up on her. Apparently, Judy hadn't answered any of her calls and texts for a few days, and so, like people would do, she got worried and sent us over.

"But because of the recent history here, I authorized the deputies to go into the backyard and look around. That's when they saw the scene through the kitchen bay window."

"They . . . They haven't gone inside?"

"No. Nobody has gone inside yet."

"Perfection," she whispered as she picked up a large, smooth, rounded black stone from the pile and slid it into the tiny and nearly useless front pockets of her skinny black jeans.

Eastman reached into her bag and pulled her holstered weapon out, checked if it was loaded, and slid the holster onto her belt, securing it with an audible *click*.

"Why that specific rock?" Durazo asked as Eastman slapped the automatic lift gate control in the truck of the SUV, and the big liftgate slowly came cascading down and locked into place.

Eastman looked down the rounded cobblestone driveway and observed the outside of the house.

"It's Apache tear, sergeant." She started down the driveway with Durazo walking beside her.

"Apach-Apache tear?"

"Yes, sergeant. Apache tear is used for healing grief, sorrow, and trauma. It can help transfer those lower energy vibrations and experiences into those of healing and love."

As they got to the landing of the big arch-top front door in unison, Eastman and Durazo drew their weapons. Durazo motioned to his deputies to cover them. They prepared to breach the door. Durazo thumped his Motorola walkie-talkie, signaling the deputies in the backyard that they were going in and to cover all the exits.

"I didn't think this kind of stuff affected you, Eastman. You seem to handle these situations better than most seasoned combat veterans I know. I didn't think you would have needed a rock to help ward off bad energy and to heal you."

Eastman looked up to the big man that towered over her and gave him a grave matter of fact answer. "It's not for me, sergeant. It's for Judy." She looked back at the door, glanced at the deputy waiting behind Durazo with the battering ram, and gave him a nod.

"On three, gentlemen."

The deputy stepped out from behind Durazo, hefted the heavy steel battering ram, and lined it up with the deadbolt on the oversized dark wood front door.

The deputy looked back at Eastman once again as if to say, "Ready."

Eastman steadied herself and gave the verbal.

"One . . ."

"Going in," Durazo whispered into his transmitter.

"Two . . ."

The deputy swung back the battering ram into the ready position, and Eastman flipped the safety off her weapon.

"Three!"

With a thundering, momentous *kwathuck!* the heavy steel collided with the antiqued heritage hardware that, truth be told, was more for aesthetic than it was for security. The screws and deadbolt gave way and surrendered to the dominating kinetic force from the battering ram.

"GO! GO! GO! GO!" Eastman called out as she was the first one through the door, followed in lockstep by Durazo, and another deputy carrying an AR-15.

Eastman's view was that of the sights of her .40 caliber weapon as she swept it over the living room and dining room.

"Clear!" she called out as the deputy with the AR flanked her and went into the office to the right of her and Durazo.

"Clear!" the deputy in the office called out, and the trio continued forward from the living room into the dining room that connected to the open floor plan kitchen. A sweeping green laser bounced from the corners and into blind spots in front of them from the deputy's AR-15 and gave Eastman a strange sense of comfort and security.

Two other deputies rushed upstairs, clearing and calling out that all was well, and made Eastman breathe a sigh of relief.

Eastman kicked in the door to the downstairs guest bedroom and swung her weapon from the blind corner to the closed bathroom door that connected to the small guest room.

She slowly reached out her hand and turned the knob. The door swung open, and she burst into the room.

It was dark and silent except for the *drip drop* of the showerhead leaking behind the closed, opaque curtain.

Eastman stepped silently up to the curtain and pulled it open.

There was nothing.

"Clear!" she shouted out and walked back into the guest bedroom.

Durazo was waiting there for her.

"We all clear, sergeant?"

"Yes, ma'am."

"Excellent work from your team."

"Thank you, ma'am."

It was then that the stench hit Eastman.

She wasn't sure if it had been there the whole time, or if she had so much adrenaline pumping through her veins during the sweep, that her mind shut off one of her senses to make her vision and hearing more acute.

The mind does do that, she thought. Eastman thumbed the safety on her weapon and slid its sleek black form into the waiting holster on her belt.

"Okay . . ." She walked past Durazo and out of the guest bedroom, through the dining room, to see two deputies frozen at the entrance of the open kitchen.

"Holy Mary, mother of God," one of the deputies whispered as he crossed himself. The two men both turned to face Eastman. The first's face was pasty pale white—the color of Elmer's glue. His eyes were staring blankly, as if looking a thousand yards away. The other froze, then turned his eyes down to the floor.

Eastman looked at the men and gave them a nod toward the front door. The deputies nodded solemnly, lowered their heads, and walked by her.

Heavy boots creaked with every step on the perfectly polished hundred-year-old wooden floors.

Eastman walked forward and stepped into the kitchen.

"Get the broom."

Those were the first words spoken in the once impeccably perfect but now utterly destroyed tea shop.

Orchid stood frozen in place like a statue as the little bells that dangled on the knob of the door to her Majesty's Tea House and Supply dwindled down from a ringing jingle to an inaudible hum.

"Get the broom, Orchid."

As if waking from a bad dream, Orchid shuttered and went to the back room to collect the broom and dustpan.

Even in the back room, the muddy yellow fragrance of the cheap cigar the man was smoking still lingered and permeated the air, like a stain.

As Orchid grabbed the broom, she paused, and noticed Andromeda's purse on the desk. In that purse, atop of all of Andromeda's belongings, was her cell phone.

Orchid stared at it.

She could feel her heart beating inside her chest as she looked at the device that usually never left her hand, and at furthest was in her pocket.

She even slept with it placed carefully next to her pillow, as it softly serenaded her with her 'nature sounds' sleep app, as it charged throughout the night.

"Orchid!"

The scream from the storefront immediately threw Orchid's eyes to the floor, and she walked robotically through the beaded curtain.

"Start sweeping everything into separate piles. We have to clean this up as fast as we can. Do you understand?"

Andromeda was already in the process of picking the broken shelves off the floor and putting them back in to place.

"Yes, Andromeda." Orchid started sweeping the shattered, jagged pieces of teacups, ceramic spoons, incense urns, and other little treasures that had been thrown against the walls and on the floor of the tiny shop.

Andromeda went to the back room and returned with some large black trash bags.

"Put everything into these bags. I don't want you to stop moving until this mess is cleaned up."

Orchid started sweeping the piles that she had collected into the dustpan and dumping the debris into the large trash bag that Andromeda was holding. After a couple of heaping piles were dumped in silence, Orchid got up the courage to speak. In a mousy, squeaky tone, just over a whisper, she managed to let out, "Andromeda, what is going on?"

Orchid paused and met eyes with her friend, her mentor, her sister, and in those eyes, she saw nothing. There was no emotion, just empty black pools.

"This is a test of our faith. This is our opportunity to show our Pedagogue our devotion and love—and a chance for us to truly stand in our power."

"Who were those men?"

"Those were the Profane. The Unclean. They have been sent by the universe to prove to us our Pedagogue's strength, power, and wisdom. When he hears of this, this . . . *violence*, they will regret their foolish choices."

Orchid silently nodded and scooped up another pile of debris while Andromeda watched her coldly.

"You do not doubt my words of truth, do you, Orchid?"

Orchid raised her eyes from her task to meet Andromeda's, and this time, her eyes were met with a gaze of hot blue fire emanating from her sister.

"No, of course not. I was just . . ."

Andromeda dropped the now heavy bag, and before Orchid even realized what was going on, Andromeda had a fist full of her hair. With one big yank, she pulled Orchid off balance, slamming her face-first onto the floor. Tiny splinters of broken glass embedded themselves into Orchid's right cheek. Orchid let out a shrill cry of shock and pain as Andromeda ground her face into the floor.

"Don't you ever again question our Pedagogue!"

"Yes, Andromeda. I'm sorry."

"He has foreseen all of this. He is in control, do you understand?"

Orchid wasn't even struggling as Andromeda continued to apply pressure and friction to her head. She twisted the knotted fist full of hair and clung to it like a pit bull.

Orchid took a deep breath, and as she let it go, she went limp, lifeless, empty. Her physical body mirrored how she felt inside at that very moment.

Andromeda kept grinding Orchid's cheek into the shattered glass and hardwood.

As calm as a morning breeze, Orchid replied, "Yes, Andromeda. I understand."

Andromeda pulled Orchid up to her feet and wiped the tears and blood from her bright red and already bruising cheek.

"I can now feel the power returning to you, Orchid. Let it flow into you. Let the truth that your soul knows be awakened inside of you."

Orchid smiled and nodded. Andromeda pulled her close and held her in a warm embrace and gently rocked her side to side while cooing, "You are family, you are home. You are family, you are home. You are family, you are home."

What Andromeda couldn't see while she was embracing and rocking Orchid was the still dead, empty look in Orchid's eyes as she repeated her mantra back to her.

"I am family, I am home."

But even with those dead eyes, Orchid's gaze focused on one thing. Through the wisps of Andromeda's hair that clung and stuck to her bruised, cut, and bloodied face, over the counter, past the beaded curtain to the desk in the back room, and on that desk Andromeda's purse, and in that purse—her phone.

"I am family, I am home. I am family, I am home . . ."

6IX FEET DEEP

You care so much you feel as though you will bleed to death with the pain of it.

—J.K. Rowling, Harry Potter and the Order of the Phoenix

Jesse's feet felt thick and heavy as he climbed the stairs to the podium inside the little church nestled in the quiet suburb of Los Angeles. He looked out into the crowd of the couple dozen attendees that were mostly made up of his friends, a couple family members, and coworkers. Jesse gave a nod to Lance, Hunter, and Yvette, then looked over to his left, where Katia's casket was draped with fresh cut lilies.

The sickly-sweet smell of them permeated the small church.

Jesse reached into the breast pocket of his suit, produced his notes, and took a deep breath.

"I'd like to thank you all for coming here today. It really means a lot to us, to me." Jesse paused and winced as if he just bit into something extremely bitter.

"When I first laid eyes on Katia all those years ago, I knew that instant, that second, that she was going to be the woman I'd marry. But I never imagined she was also going to be the woman I was going to bury."

There was a quiet murmur in the small crowd, and people nodded their heads and dabbed their eyes with tissues.

With his voice almost cracking, Jesse managed to stutter out his words.

"That woman, that perfect woman, gave my life a whole new meaning. She inspired me to work harder than I had ever worked before. She inspired me to dream bigger than I ever thought possible. She showed me just how deeply I could love another human being. She inspired me to be a better man."

Jesse started trembling and was now nearly relying on the podium to support him.

"But I can't help but feel like I failed her."

Jesse looked over to the glossy white casket.

"I failed you, sweet baby. I failed you."

Jesse broke down and started sobbing. His words were nearly an incoherent babble.

"This wasn't supposed to happen. This isn't the way it was supposed to be!" Jesse collapsed onto the podium and started weeping uncontrollably. Most of the onlookers in the audience couldn't take the outpouring of grief emanating from the churches PA system, as it amplified every wail and tear from the man crumbling in front of them. Most of them averted their eyes and looked down at their shoes. A couple of Jesse's close friends started to get out of the pews to help him but stopped as a tall man approached Jesse from behind and placed a hand on his shoulder.

Jesse turned to see his old friend Andy, who was directing the funeral, and without a word, the man embraced Jesse and held him as he wept.

Andy helped walk Jesse to a seat, helped him down, and handed him a box of tissues.

Andy approached the podium and looked out into the audience, and after a moment, the tall man took a deep breath and spoke.

"Hello, my friends. I am sure that some people, many people, maybe some of you here today, would find solace and relief in the thought that God has a plan for everything that happens in our lives. That somehow, someway, everything happens for a reason, and that there is always a silver lining to be found in the work of God. Even if sometimes it is challenging to see that silver lining when you're in the middle of it."

People in the audience nodded their heads and turned to each other in agreement as muffled murmurs echoed through the little church.

Andy leaned in close to the microphone.

"But I disagree."

The room went silent, and all eyes were on the man who turned and looked back at Jesse. Jesse looked up from his tattered, ragged Kleenex and stared with puffy, bloodshot eyes at Andy.

Andy motioned to Jesse and continued, "I have known that man for over twenty years. I am sorry to say, I only got to be around Katia a couple of times, the first being at their wedding."

Andy smiled and shook his head.

"That was a perfect day, and after that, we got together for dinner a couple of times. But you know how it goes: people are busy. You put off plans, and life goes by very fast. The problem is, you think you will always have time. It's always, I'll see you tomorrow, next week. or maybe next month. But those days never come, do they? Life isn't supposed to go by this fast."

People in the crowd nodded. Andy could see the couples in the audience take each other's hands as they exchanged loving glances.

"For those of you who know Jesse, who knew Katia, who knew them both, you know what I'm talking about. If you knew them, you knew how he looked at her. You know how she looked at him. You knew how truly, how deeply, he loved that woman. You know how they met because he was sure to tell you the story of the first time he laid eyes on her at the car dealership where they both worked.

"You heard the story of how he proposed to her on the Eiffel Tower on her birthday. You, of course, know all about the time they swear they saw bigfoot in Oregon."

Andy smiled and rolled his eyes, and friends and family in the little church smiled and laughed for the first time that day, as the energy in the room shifted slightly.

But Andy shattered the relief as quickly as he inspired it.

"But that's why I disagree with God on this one . . ."

You could hear a pin drop in the room as Andy scanned the audience. His smile was now gone; his face was most serious.

"Jesse is right. This wasn't supposed to happen. This isn't the way it was supposed to go."

Some of the crowd nodded, but most just stared.

"I have buried many people over my fifteen-year career. Some were young, this is true. However, most of the people that I have the honor to bury are elderly. They got to live a good, long, full life. Many of them served in World War II, members of what we all happily refer to as the 'greatest generation.'

"Most of the people I have buried were lucky enough to be married. They had a partner—a husband or wife they were lucky enough to share their lives with. Sometimes, the surviving spouse would come up here on this very podium and speak about their forty, fifty, sixty plus years together. Years filled with children and grandchildren, sometimes even great-grandchildren. Memories of celebrating birthdays, anniversaries, and fireworks on the Fourth of July. Memories of Christmas mornings with their grandkids and funny stories collected over a lifetime.

"You know what's funny? It is never the business promotions or the cars they bought that are talked about at this podium. No, friends, it's the little things people talk about up here. It's those tiny moments in between. Those are the things they remember the most. Those are the treasured memories that they hold onto the tightest."

Andy looked back to Jesse again and turned back to the mic.

"My wife was taken from me also. It was chance, it was an accident, it was bad luck, and it still destroyed me. But, when the priest talked to me alone after her funeral, he told me that 'God always has a plan.' That gave me some soft comfort. It gave me something to grasp onto. It helped me in some strange way that I cannot explain because what happened to my wife wasn't on purpose. It, it happened, but it wasn't done on purpose. It wasn't planned, plotted, and executed."

Andy paused and took another deep breath in.

"But that accident robbed me of my wife. Just like how that man behind me was deprived of his. Death is seldom ever fair, they say. No, my friends, it doesn't discriminate between the rich or poor, young and old. Death is seldom ever fair.

"But the difference is, most of the time it is expected. Sometimes death is even welcomed, especially after a long fight with some terrible disease. But not today.

"Today, we are not welcoming death. Today we are not celebrating a life fully lived. Today we are not here for the happy memories. No, my friends, not at all. Today, we are here to mourn. We are not only mourning Katia and trying to comfort Jesse in his moment of loss, what we are genuinely mourning here today is the grand theft of potential.

"Today, we are mourning all the possibilities and experiences that they still had out in front of them. Today, we are mourning the future they had together, the memories that they had yet to make, the children they had yet to raise, and the birthdays, anniversaries, Christmases, and New Years they were supposed to share—together. No, my friends, death is not welcome here today . . ."

The crowd was still, all eyes locked on Andy as he slammed his fist onto the podium.

"God had nothing to do with this."

"He said you have three days to come up with the money and product or else." Andromeda's voice quivered as she spoke just above a whisper to the man staring out the window of the penthouse apartment. His hands were clasped behind his back, his posture rigid like a stone. His body immediately became visibly tense. His hands, still clasped, were squeezing so tightly together that the color left them, and they now were a pale white.

The man spoke softly and deliberately in a monotonous tone. "Those are all lies, Andromeda. He is trying to turn you against me, against our family. He is trying to weaken the very foundation of your faith that makes you powerful."

The man turned from the cityscape to face Andromeda.

"Our latest offering of that old woman to Moloch will help start to turn the tide. I can assure you, I can feel the shift coming—even now . . . We will overcome this trial and be stronger because of it. This is merely a test for us, Andromeda. A test for our family before we bloom and ascend into our full power. Izzy, although physically powerful, was weak minded and expendable. We both know that."

"What—what about Jason and Serena?"

"Time will tell its story when it is ready, my dear. As for now, we must focus on Orchid. She is the one who will bring balance to the family. She is the one who will break the chains that are holding us back from unlimited power."

Andromeda nodded.

"Summon her."

Andromeda kept her eyes fixed on the man and called out for Orchid.

The soft patter of bare feet on hardwood came down the hallway, and a moment later, the young girl materialized in the doorway.

"Yes, Andromeda?"

"Our Pedagogue seeks an audience with you now, my dear."

Orchid immediately dropped to her knees, rested her hand's palms up on her legs, and cast her eyes to the floor.

"What is it you wish of me, my Pedagogue?"

"I understand that there was an upset at our shop today, Orchid. Andromeda told me that some bad men came into the store and destroyed it. She also told me that they had many lies to tell about me and about our family. How do you feel about that?"

"I am family. I am home."

The man walked up and brushed the side of Orchid's long black hair behind her right ear, exposing her bruised and cut up face. The man knelt before the young woman and ever so softly gave her a kiss on her porcelain forehead. He stood and placed his hand under her chin. Gently, he raised her head until she was looking him in the eyes. To Orchid's surprise, the look on the man's face was soft, kind.

"I believe your role in the family has been foretold, little one. I have been looking for you for over thirty years. There have been many who I thought may be the beacon. There have been many who have tried and many who have failed. Many have come, and many have gone. This coven—this *family* started from nothing, little one, it's pure alchemy. You see, Andromeda and her sister were the first to join the family you have known. Soon after, we found Izzy, and after him, Jason and Serena joined and became more than they ever dreamed possible.

"But there have been many others who have petitioned to take our ancient rites of passage, but sadly, they were not evolved enough and couldn't handle the wisdom I had to give. They didn't have the strength to stand in their power.

"But I can feel the strength within you, Orchid. I can sense your power growing. I believe in my heart that you will be the one that was said to bring us to power. You will be the beacon."

The man looked over to Andromeda, who smiled and nodded to the young woman.

"Everything that happened today had been long planned by us to test you. We had to test your power and devotion to our family. We had to be sure that you were who we were foretold would restore our family to power. But now, all doubts have been extinguished, now we know it to be true. You are the one who will break the chains. You are the light bringer. You are the beacon."

The man reached down and gently took Orchid's hands and brought her to her feet. He turned her around and untied the string of her sundress and slid the delicate garment off of her shoulders, letting it fall to the floor.

Orchid stood there nude, robotically still, awaiting direction.

"Andromeda, the mark and the flame please."

Andromeda walked over to the large, chunky dark wood armoire in the corner of the room, opened the ornate doors, and retrieved a butane torch and an eleven-inch long piece of iron. On the end of the metal rod was an elaborate design about four inches across.

"Now you start the journey to become so much more, little one. Now you step into the mark for the first time."

Andromeda turned on the gas and clicked the button on the self-igniting torch. She held the hot blue flame to the sigil on the end of the iron rod and bathed the design in the fire. In seconds, the design began to glow a hot yellow crimson, the color of a summer moon fire.

Orchid was still and focused, eyes fixed on the cityscape in the distance. The floor-to-ceiling windows of the penthouse displayed the majesty and ugly beauty of the sunset dipping over west Los Angeles.

The man took the glowing iron from Andromeda and placed his left hand on Orchid's spine. Andromeda walked around the two and faced Orchid. She smiled and put both her hands on the naked girl's sleek, contoured shoulders.

Orchid quivered as she felt the man's hand brush up her spine and interlace his fingers with Andromeda's on her left shoulder.

"We have been waiting a long while, little one. We have been waiting for you. Now you will be honored with the mark." With that, the man plunged the foundry hot iron deep into Orchid's left shoulder blade. The searing metal instantly burned her skin.

The sickening smell of burning flesh filled the room as he pushed the design deeper into her back. Orchid took a deep breath and transmuted the pain, her mind a million miles away, and her body perfectly still. The man pulled the metal from her flesh, and what was left was the perfect transference of the design from the iron rod onto her back.

Marked, branded, and forever scarred.

Eastman gathered herself and waited until she heard the massive front door swing closed before she stepped into the kitchen in the house on Journeys End Drive.

As her blue eyes scanned the scene in the room, she unconsciously, automatically reached into her pocket and pulled out the Apache tear stone.

She started rubbing it, as if by instinct, between her thumb and index finger. The smooth polished black stone felt sleek and creamy to the touch.

Her eyes darted from the circular kitchen table, large enough to seat six people comfortably, to the monolithic soapstone island in the center of the kitchen, to the cooktop, and back to the kitchen table.

The only thing Eastman heard was the pounding of her heart in her chest and the swarming buzz of the small carnivorous insects that were circling in a dirty cloud around the room.

Her eyes kept scanning the scene, trying to make sense of the macabre macramé strewn around the once-warm and inviting kitchen, which now took on the appearance of a Bosch painting.

"Have you ever . . . ?" Durazo's voice trembled as he stood behind Eastman, joining her in the kitchen. Her eyes locked onto the hollowed-out husk that was once Judy's body, propped up and posed in a chair at the kitchen table.

"Never . . ." was all Eastman could mutter back to the seasoned veteran sheriff standing behind her.

She kept rubbing the glossy black stone between her fingers.

With her left hand, she pulled out her phone from the back pocket of her jeans and opened the voice memo app.

"Female, deceased, age fifty-two. Name: Judy Ackles."

Eastman walked up to the body and inspected it closer. Peering deeply into the empty vessel that was once, not that long ago, warm and breathing.

"Judy appears to have been slit open with what looks to be a surgical Y incision, starting just below the clavicle and traveling all the way down to her pubis. It appears that the large and small intestines, kidneys, liver, lungs, stomach, and heart . . ."

She took a step away from the body and turned to Durazo.

"Jesus, it's like they completely scooped her insides out, Durazo."

The Sheriff just stared at the body, still trying to make sense of what he was looking at.

"But why? Why did they do this to you, Judy?"

Eastman then looked down at the table. On it, five place settings, all meticulous and perfect. The fine China heaped high with decaying rotting flesh. Flesh that almost looked alive and moving due to the number of maggots swarming and feeding on the necrotic tissue. At each plate, a wine glass filled with a putrid dark black goo, what Eastman could only determine was Judy's blood.

What used to be the attractive woman's hands were placed neatly on the table. Long red cables extended from her wrists and wound around the table like rusty, dry red roots.

Durazo eyed the dry, jerky-like tangle.

"What are those, agent?"

"Her veins, sergeant. Those are her veins."

Eastman could hear Durazo swallow hard. She took a deep breath and continued.

"Rate of decomposition has been exasperated by the infestation of insects. I am noting a considerable amount of what appears to be blowfly larvae overwhelming the corpse and plates surrounding her—it. The larvae appear to be somewhat mature and looks as though they have already gone through their first molting stage."

Eastman grimaced as she stepped back and looked over the

scene, trying to see the whole thing as one image. Looking for a pattern, her eyes scanned the room.

"This isn't like the others. This isn't just a butchering. This means something. This is important."

Durazo glanced over to Eastman. She was rubbing the stone. and whispering a chant just below a whisper. making it nearly inaudible.

"What are you thinking, agent? What do you think it means?"

"This . . . This is a ritual. They performed a ritual here."

Eastman glanced at the double-hung windows that flanked the sides of the large bay window. The windows were wide open, screens removed from the inside and placed neatly on top of the seat of the bay.

"He wanted to put on this show for us, Durazo. He wanted us to see Judy like this—devoured. This is symbolic. Look, he opened the windows and took off the screens on purpose so that the flies would get to her, and we would walk into this mess."

"Maybe that's how he got in, agent, through one of the open windows."

Eastman walked over to the open bay windows and looked outside. "There is a water feature below these windows, Durazo. He could see inside, but I don't think this is how he got in, look."

Eastman pointed to the cream-colored pillows that made the bay window into a little seating area, or better yet, a reading nook.

"These are spotless. For him to get access to the windows, he would have had to go into that little pond out there, and these would be thrashed."

"Good observation, agent."

Eastman went back over to Judy and studied her face.

"He took her eyes . . ."

"Agent?"

Eastman looked up and motioned him to come closer.

Durazo hesitantly stepped and leaned into the nightmare that was laid out before him.

Eastman pointed to the sunken orbital cavities on Judy's face.

"He took her eyes. This isn't from the larvae; it's too clean. He scooped out her eyes."

"Christ. I've seen a lot of things in my day. Brutal, hellish things, agent. Some of the things that the Vietcong did to our boys that were captured." Durazo paused and shook his head, as if he were trying to develop a Polaroid picture, or perhaps dissolve a memory that just flashed into his mind.

"Some of the things I saw those people do to our boys, I didn't think I'd ever see anything even close to it. I . . . I just chalked it up to the savagery of war, ya know? But this? This is beyond anything I imagined a human could do to another human . . ."

"Call your team in here, Durazo. There is nothing left for us to do for her."

"We haven't been able to find anything at any of these nightmares yet, agent. Not a fiber. Not a latent print. We have nothing."

"I know, sergeant, I know. But we do have something."

"What's that, agent?"

Eastman motioned to the ceiling. Durazo craned his neck to look up and see a sigil scrawled on the ceiling, but this one was different than the others at the other horrific scenes.

"His symbols will be his downfall, Durazo. Now, call your team in here and make sure they double check everything."

Durazo nodded and thumbed the Motorola walkie-talkie on his vest, relaying Eastman's message to the waiting forensics team outside.

Eastman looked at the husk of Judy, raised the small black stone to her lips, and gently kissed it.

"Find your peace, Mom. Your work is done here." She turned and started making her way to the front door, Durazo trailing closely behind her.

"Agent, this is the third murder in my town this year. So far, we have come up with nothing. Please give me some ray of hope that you have a lead you're working on."

"Right now, sergeant, all we can do is follow procedure and hope for the best. He will make a mistake at some point, and when he does, we will be waiting for him. Remember, *you're always most hungry just before you eat,* and I for one am starving. We will either put this animal in a cage for a very long time or into the morgue. And to be honest with you, either one works just fine with me."

Eastman turned and pointed again at the sigil on the ceiling.

"His symbols will be his downfall."

HELLO AMBROSIA

Sandra's seen a leprechaun,

Eddie touched a troll,

Laurie danced with witches once,

Charlie found some goblins gold.

Donald heard a mermaid sing,

Susy spied an elf,

But all the magic I have known

I've had to make myself.

—Shel Silverstein

Jesse woke up in the middle of the night to the warm, soft legs of a woman's caressing his.

He laid there silent in the pitch-black room, his mind processing whether or not this was a dream or in fact, waking reality. He reached over his right hip and grazed his fingers over the smooth skin of the mystery guest lying next to him.

He could hear Loki get up from his spot on the foot of the California king-sized mattress, hop onto the floor, do three circles, and lay down in an audible *huff*, only to let out a big wolfdog sigh.

Jesse's faculties returned to him, and he whispered softly into the darkness.

"Kat?"

Still, in the fog of dreams, he wasn't sure where, or when, he was.

"I'm here, Jess. It's okay. I didn't wake you, did I?"

Jesse's body relaxed fully when he heard Eastman's voice behind him. Her breath tickled his ear.

"What . . . What time is it?"

Jesse reached for the glass of water next to the bed. It wasn't there when he collapsed on the mattress several hours ago.

"It's just past midnight, sweetie. I just got done at the station on Briggs, so I thought I would come by and check on you."

"I'm not upset in the slightest, Mel." Jesse paused after he took a big sip of the ice-cold water. "How did you get in?"

Melantha let out a quiet and innocent little chuckle and gave Jesse some light back scratches.

"The back door. I hope you don't mind that I let myself in."

"No, no, it's fine, Mel. I've missed your face. You didn't have any problems with Loki, did you?"

"That big pussy? If by 'problem' you mean smothering me with kisses as I came in? No, he's a good boy."

Jesse laughed and spoke out to the darkness where he heard Loki lay down, "Some watchdog you are."

"Who needs a watchdog when you got me?"

Jesse winced as Eastman laughed and gave him a playful bite on his shoulder. He twisted around, and in one smooth motion was on top of the petite woman, kissing her deeply. After returning the kiss, she gently pushed Jesse off her and rolled onto her side, facing him, and in a light-playful-easy way said, "None of that tonight, Romeo. You need your rest. I have a big day planned for you tomorrow."

"A big day? Are we going to Disneyland?" Jesse laughed as he again reached for the glass of water, finishing its contents and getting up from the bed. He walked out of the room and into the bathroom.

As Jesse stood there peeing in the dark, Eastman popped her

head into the doorway.

"Hey, Jess, how much do you like boats?"

Jesse, not even looking up from the dim outline of the toilet only illuminated from the moonlight streaming through the window, laughed.

"Boats? Like, Boat-Boats? Like boats in water boats?"

"Yes, silly man! Like boats on the water!"

"I like them just fine. Why do you ask?"

"Have you ever piloted a boat before, babe?"

"Yes, plenty when I was a kid. My mom's boyfriend had a boat down in Marina Del Rey. We would take it out every weekend. Why do you ask, love?"

"Perfection." Eastman laughed as she skipped back into the room with the bed. Jesse heard her slide onto the mattress and wrap herself in the heavy blankets.

As he walked back in, Jesse paused, closed the door behind him, and locked it.

"What's all this boat talk about, babe?" Jesse yawned as he crawled in next to her and pulled her close.

Eastman leaned over her side of the bed and reached into her purse. A moment later, she returned to Jesse and handed him what felt like a spongey-smooth item with a key dangling from it.

"What's this?"

"Oh, a couple of years ago I helped bring to justice the murderer of a wealthy businessman's daughter. During the investigation, I found out that he was one of the biggest importers of cocaine in the country. But, since I don't work in narcotics, I let that slide. Let's just say he was grateful for that."

"I would imagine so, Mel."

She smiled and curled up next to Jesse. "Of course, he was even more grateful when I delivered the shit-bag that murdered his daughter to him, so he could take care of him personally. Sometimes the legal system isn't as satisfying as proper, old-fashioned, biblical justice."

She gave Jesse a playful nudge in his ribs and smiled. "You know the feeling, don't you, babe?"

Jesse smirked as he examined the yellow sponge with the key attached.

"We remained close friends ever since. I guess you could say he helps me with information from time to time, and I make sure that his import-export business goes—how should I put it? *Unnoticed*. He treats me like family. It's sort of . . . nice."

Eastman paused and smiled. "Who do you think owns the warehouses where you have been doing your work lately? Do you think I just pick random addresses out of the phone book and send you there with my fingers crossed?"

"Cool story, Mel, but what's this key for?"

"His boat, silly!"

"Are we going on a three-hour tour? 'Cause that worked out kinda shitty for Gilligan."

Eastman ignored Jesse's stupid dad joke. "No, but I have some instructions for you for tomorrow, and I want you to carry them out exactly as I say, do you understand?"

"But why a boat?"

Eastman put her hands on Jesse's face and pulled him in for a kiss.

"You will find out tomorrow. This one is going to be easy, and dare I say, fun?"

Jesse handed her back the key with the floaty on it, put his hands behind his head, and let out another big yawn.

Eastman nuzzled up to Jesse and took a big sniff of his neck while she gently played with the salt and pepper hair on his chest.

"Mmm, you stink good, babe."

Another yawn overtook Jesse as he replied, "Thanks, babe," but while in mid-yawn, it sounded more like, "Nantes habe."

"Always. Now close those eyes. You have a big day tomorrow."

Eastman buried her head into Jesse's chest and threw her arm and leg over his body.

In unison, they both sighed a sigh of deep contentment, and in a few minutes Jesse's body relaxed, and his breathing started to slow as he began to drift off to sleep . . .

Eastman kept her hand over Jesse's heart. She counted the rhythmic beating of his pulse.

She took her hand off his chest and waited a few minutes while still listening to his breathing in the dark. When his breathing slowed and became more regular, deeper, and less labored, she gently placed her hand again on his chest.

His body temperature was noticeably cooler than it was just a few minutes ago.

NREM 2, she thought and continued to monitor Jesse's breathing patterns. For another ten minutes, she waited, still and silent in the dark inky-black room.

Again, she reached out and placed her hand on Jesse's chest.

His heart rate had slowed dramatically from where it was the last time she checked.

She smiled in the dark as she felt confident that the man was now in the NREM 3 stage of sleep.

Eastman slipped away. She slid out of bed, so smooth and slow that Loki didn't even stir at the movement in the room.

She slipped her purse from the floor over her shoulder and stood naked and silent in a darkened room, watching over Jesse. She mirrored his breathing; she felt his energy. Her body so stationary that she felt as though her bare feet became one with the carpet beneath them.

Eastman walked over to the large chest of drawers that sat catty-corner in the room and above that, a floating bookshelf filled with trinkets and treasures that Jesse had collected over the years.

She reached blindly in the darkness, and her fingertips probed the shelf until she found one of the many LED candles that she noticed before and memorized the placement of the last time she was over.

She flipped the switch on the bottom of the electric candle, and the tiny torch ignited in a faint amber hue.

Not bright enough to cast a shadow in the pitch-black room, but, when you're in darkness, even the smallest spark can light your way.

Eastman carefully took a tray down from the floating bookcase.

On it was all that remained of Katia's "alter of things." After Jesse ransacked the room, he had put most of the surviving things into the storage shed in the backyard and sent the family heirlooms back to her beloved grandmother.

Eastman used the tiny LED candle to illuminate the tray. She analyzed the curios on it, and slowly waved her hand over the items, as if she was 'feeling' for something to speak to her. Instantly and silently, she homed in on one specific relic and picked up the small velvet sack in the center of the tray.

It pulled to her. It sang to her. The energy radiating from it to Eastman felt like the air being pushed by a speaker with the volume turned all the way up.

The small sack wasn't heavy, but what was in it felt hard, smooth, and powerful. She placed the bag on the dresser, and carefully put the tray back into place.

She froze in place as Loki got up from his spot in the corner of the room and approached her from behind. She slowly turned, and with the light from the little LED candle, she could see the form of the big wolfdog standing there in the darkness, his tail wagging lazily, his eyes reflecting the light of the candle.

She stood frozen, her eyes darted over to Jesse, and then back to the overgrown puppy. His tail was now wagging quickly as if he was saying to her, "Play time?"

Eastman put her hand out as if making the sign for 'stop,' and Loki sat down and stared at her in attention.

His eyes were still glowing amber-red from the LED giving him
the appearance of Cerberus, his tail yet wagging.

She knew that at any moment he was either going to A. Bark for
play, or B. Jump on her and most likely cause a huge commotion
doing so. Either one would wake up Jesse, and she needed him well
rested for tomorrow. In a bold move, she took her hand from the
stop position and pointed to the bed.

The huge wolfdog leaped effortlessly onto 'his' corner of the bed,
did a slow circle, and laid down. Eastman stayed frozen, her eyes
fixed on Jesse to see if he was disturbed at all by the one hundred
and ten pounds of fur that just levitated onto the bed.

Jesse's breathing didn't change.

NREM 3. Eastman smiled to herself in the dark as she reached
out and gently stroked Loki's massive head. The big dog put his
head down on the bed and let out another big sigh.

Like a ghost, Eastman walked over to the door, and slowly
unlocked the deadbolt that Jesse had installed months before. The
audible *click* sounded thunderous in the silent room, and she paused
and looked to Jesse again, and while still looking at the sleeping
man, opened the door and slipped out of the room.

She closed the door behind her and breathed a deep sigh of
relief.

She walked into the bathroom and turned on the light. Eastman
examined the everyday little velvet bag that was tied closed with a
green string. She pulled the small knot and dumped the contents
into her hand.

A single quartz crystal rested in her palm.

She smiled to herself as she felt the energy that Katia infused
in the small translucent stone radiate through her body, sending
chills from her through the tips of her fingers down to her toes. The
essence and vitality left goosebumps on her naked skin.

"I couldn't have asked for a better gift, Katia. Thank you . . ."
Eastman slipped the piece of quartz back into the little black velvet
sack and put it into her purse. She pulled her phone out and sent

out a single text: *"Now."*

Seconds later, the text went from 'delivered' to 'read,' and she slipped her phone back into her purse. She stared at herself in the little bathroom mirror and smiled.

The Ouroboros is turning, all is one, one is all. Everything is everything, and everything is connected.

Eastman flipped off the light switch, went back into the room with a bed, gave Loki a scratch behind his ear, curled up next to Jesse, and fell fast asleep.

"It seems as though the universe has smiled upon us, Andromeda. Not only do we now have a new supplier for our product, but our new friend is willing to help us solve our little problem—or shall I say, *Izzy's problem* with Jonas."

Andromeda looked up from the altar where she was kneeling in meditation in the light of the rising sun and smiled at the man standing before her.

"I knew you would take care of this, my Pedagogue. You are the way and the light."

The man extended his hand and brought Andromeda to her feet.

"Moloch is pleased with his offering and gifted us this. I have been talking all night with Mr. Perez. I contacted him several months ago, and as the universe serves those that serve it, Mr. Perez got back to me last night. We had a wonderful conversation and made a mutually beneficial arrangement that not only gets us back on track, but also will ensure that we have all the abundance needed to truly ascend and evolve as a family."

Andromeda's eyes lit up, and she threw her arms around the man, embracing him tightly.

"This is wonderful news! Thank you for all you do for us, my

Pedagogue!"

"You will be meeting with him this afternoon to pick up our first order and the money to pay off Jonas. Do you understand?"

Andromeda gave the man another big squeeze, released him, and took the printed out Google map page from his hand.

"San Pedro?"

"Yes. He owns several commercial fishing boats that are docked there. He explained to me that he always does first meetings this way. You will be meeting with one of his representatives on a boat called *The Orca* to do the pickup. I trust that you will follow the instructions exactly."

Andromeda nodded her head and bowed.

"I will not fail you, or our family, my Pedagogue."

The man smiled warmly at Andromeda and placed his hand on her shoulder.

"I know you won't, my dear. The meeting is at 2:00 p.m., so you have plenty of time to prepare yourself."

"I'll let Orchid know what the plan is, my Pedagogue."

"No. They requested you come alone."

"I understand." Andromeda smiled, spun around, and started making her way to the kitchen.

"Now, how about we make a big breakfast to celebrate?!"

"You read my mind, Andromeda, you read my mind."

***

As the juicing machine whirred and churned out fresh juice.

As the eggs sizzled and fried.

As the smell of food cooking and upbeat music filled the air in the apartment on the West Side of Los Angeles.

Orchid sat.

Orchid sat naked on the edge of her bed.

Her arms were crossed, with a hand on each of her shoulders.

Her elbows resting on her knees.

Her right hand gently caressed the scabs that were starting to form on the day's old brand on her left shoulder.

She didn't notice the sound from the juicer, and she didn't smell the food cooking. Orchid just stared at her feet and played with her wound.

The wound on the outside, and the wounds within.

And she wondered . . .

Is this family?

Is this power?

Is this me?

SINK OR SWIM

What would an ocean be without a monster lurking in the dark? It would be like sleep without dreams.

−Werner Herzog

Jesse watched from the deck of the forty-one-foot yacht as a Jaguar pulled into the Cabrillo Marina parking lot.

He checked the time on his phone, and it was precisely 2:00 p.m. Jesse smiled as he pulled the bill down on his cap, put the hood of his hoodie up, and slipped on his sunglasses while chuckling to himself, "Right on time. Now that's what I call mastery."

A raven-haired woman got out of the vehicle and started walking towards the dock. Jesse waved to her, getting her attention. The woman waved back and smiled as she made her way to the steps that brought her up to the entrance of the boat.

"Come aboard, we're expecting you," Jesse replied as she stepped onto the deck.

"Thank you very much for meeting with me today, Mr. Perez, and it is an honor to meet you."

"Oh, I'm not Mr. Perez, but we are going to meet him right now. We never conduct business in the harbor," Jesse said as he untied the bow, stern, and spring lines that attached The Orca to the dock.

The woman stood watching the man letting loose the last bit of the thick 5/8" rope, and he quickly climbed back up the stairs and back onto The Orca.

"We—we are going somewhere?" Andromeda apprehensively asked as Jesse passed her and ascended the ladder to The Orca's flybridge.

With the touch of a button, the boat's twin C-8.7 Caterpillar engines roared to life. Jesse eased on the throttle and slowly steered the luxury fishing vessel into the marina, leading it out to sea.

Andromeda climbed the ladder to join Jesse on the flybridge.

"Yes, Mr. Perez always insists the first meeting is out at sea. He feels less exposed that way. I was instructed to tell you, if that's an issue, I can turn us around right now, and you can go somewhere else." He entered the open zone and pushed forward on the throttle, and the powerful boat lunged like a torpedo, cutting through the water at 35 miles per hour.

"No, this is fine. I look forward to meeting Mr. Perez, and I am happy to follow his wishes."

Jesse looked over to Andromeda and smiled.

"It's funny, that's what everyone says. The ride is going to be about an hour, so if you want to go down to the deck and relax, please feel free. I bet we will see some dolphins or whales while we're out here!"

Andromeda smiled and nodded her head, turned, and made her way carefully down the ladder and relaxed on the deck of the boat as it now entered the open water with nothing but blue on the horizon.

The Orca sliced through the waves and chop of the open sea for another forty-five minutes when Jesse yelled down to Andromeda to look off the starboard side of the boat to see a pod of dolphins leaping out of the water and playing in the wake of the ship's powerful engines.

"This is fantastic!" Andromeda yelled back as she raised her arms in the air to greet the jumping dolphins. She smiled as the sea mist hit her face and the sun caressed her skin. The coastline of California was no longer visible. There was nothing but an endless expanse of blue.

Jesse brought the throttle down and killed the engines. The Orca drifted silently to a rolling stop. The only sounds heard were the small swells lapping against her hull. Jesse climbed down from the flybridge and joined Andromeda on the deck.

She smiled at him and looked out onto the horizon. "So . . . what happens now?"

"Here he comes," Jesse said as he pointed over Andromeda's shoulder. She turned to look, and when she did, Jesse pulled the Taser out from the pocket of his hoodie and fired two darts right between Andromeda's shoulder blades, immediately sending fifty thousand volts of electricity into her body, short-circuiting her nervous system. Andromeda's body hit the deck of The Orca, seizing and flailing as Jesse kept the trigger of the Taser engaged, ensuring the flow of current coursing through her tiny body.

Jesse knelt next to the still convulsing woman, drew back his fist, and brought it down on her forehead, bouncing her skull off the deck of the ship immediately knocking her unconscious. Jesse stood and looked at the now motionless woman on the floor of The Orca. He rolled her body over with his boot and pulled the two Taser darts out of her flesh.

Jesse easily picked up the woman and threw her petite frame over his shoulder. He started singing as he walked her body over to one of the heavy chairs on the deck.

"Love, exciting and new, come aboard, we're expecting you, Love, life's sweetest reward, let it flow; it floats back to you."

Andromeda started to regain consciousness as he dropped her onto the chair. Jesse started singing loudly in her face.

"Love Boat soon will be making another run, The Love Boat promises something for everyone."

Jesse went into the cabin, grabbed the duffle bag, and threw it onto the deck. He unzipped it and pulled out a roll of Gorilla Tape.

Andromeda's eyes rolled open and tried to focus on Jesse, but all she could see was his dark silhouette and the blurry forms of the seagulls that circled about the boat. She murmured to Jesse, who was still singing while wrapping layer upon layer of tape around her body, fixing her snugly to the chair.

Jesse then wound the two-inch shiny black tape around the legs of the chair and her ankles. She was so petite, her feet could barely reach the deck while in the chair. Jesse figured it was better to be thorough. Plus, it was not like the tape was that expensive anyway.

Andromeda's head fell forward as she started to lose consciousness again. The rhythmic rolling of the sea coupled with the bright light of the late afternoon sun lulled her already straining nervous system to close her eyes and pretend like none of this was actually happening.

"Oh, no you don't, you don't get to tune this out. I need you here with me now!" Jesse went back into the cabin of the ship and grabbed a small pot from the galley. He marched with purpose back over to the stern of *The Orca*, threw a bucket attached to a rope over the side, and scooped up some of the briny water into it and threw it into Andromeda's face.

Andromeda gasped for air, and her body lunged forward, pulling against her restraints. Her eyes, now wide open and alert, focused on Jesse.

"There we go, much better." Jesse laughed as he placed the pot on the deck of the boat.

Andromeda's eyes were like daggers as she seethed, "You're going to pay—"

Jesse cut her off mid-sentence, and he conjured up the most obnoxious voice he could while doing a little dance around her chair and yelling at the top of his lungs, "You're going to pay for this once 'the Pedogauge' finds out!"

Jesse plopped down, sat in front of Andromeda, and looked up at her. He pulled off the hoodie he was wearing, his sunglasses, and baseball cap, and smiled up at her.

"Yeah, I heard that from Izzy, and Jason, and Serena. It's getting kind of boring."

Andromeda's mouth hung slightly open as she scanned Jesse's face, knowing now who he was and why she was there. Jesse smiled and sat there silently, waiting as all the puzzle pieces started to come together for Andromeda, letting her play out the movies in her mind of what happened to her missing "family members."

"You—you are the one who killed Izzy, Jason, and Serena!"

"Ding! Ding! Ding! You won the first round, Andromeda!"

Jesse got up, walked into the cabin, and emerged a moment later with a large ice chest. He rolled the 120-quart ice chest to the stern of The Orca, right beside the duffle bag.

Jesse unzipped the bag and pulled out a red file folder, opened it, and started flipping through the pages until he landed on a dog-eared section. He pulled out several pieces of paper, closed the red binder, and put it back into the duffle bag.

Jesse walked up to Andromeda and placed the printed pages of Instagram direct messages on Andromeda's lap.

Andromeda's usually full red pouty lips tightened into a thin white slit.

"I have to tell you, Andromeda, this is starting to feel a bit like a broken record to me. See, I lure one of you sick little cult freaks to meet me—well, I didn't exactly 'lure' Izzy. I found him on the sidewalk down the street from your house like the piece of dog shit that he is—err . . . *was*. Jason and Serena were easy. I just appealed to their narcissism and, to a slightly lesser extent, their greed.

"And as for you, well, I know you would do anything for your beloved 'Pedagogue.' Even, getting on a boat with a complete stranger and going out into the middle of the ocean . . . I mean, who in their right mind would do that?" Jesse shrugged his shoulders and looked around, as if motioning to an imaginary crowd of people.

"Nobody in their right mind would do that, Andromeda! Didn't anyone ever warn you about 'stranger danger' in school?"

Andromeda sat there silently, her eyes fixed on the pages on her lap, the ocean breeze slightly fluttering them with its soft caress.

"Well, I guess I'm not really a 'stranger' to you, I mean, we have FaceTimed a couple times, NBD. And I must admit, I've been in sales a long time, and I didn't even get a bleep on my bullshit meter from you . . . Good show, Andromeda. Good show.

"So, I guess what I am trying to say is, I hoped I wouldn't be a stranger after how intimately our lives have become intertwined. Nobody has impacted my life in the way you have. It's almost like we are connected, bonded in a strange way. So, I would say that I'm not a stranger. But, you are in fact, in danger.

"I have a surprise for you, and I'm sure that this will come as a shock, but I'm a nice man—a fair man. So, what I am going to give you is the opportunity that you never gave to any of the women . . ." Jesse paused, shook his head, and smiled. "And girls, that you have predated upon and lured over the last several years."

Jesse walked over to the large ice chest and opened it. Immediately, a putrid greasy stench filled the air. Jesse stood there for a moment, examining the dark red slop inside. He then turned and walked back over to Andromeda, who slowly turned her eyes up from the pages on her lap to the man standing in front of her.

The seagulls that were circling above *The Orca* flew down a bit lower, entranced by action on the deck and enticed by the contents of the ice chest. Their squawks and caws becoming almost frantic.

"Have all the puzzle pieces fallen into place?"

Andromeda's lips parted as she stared into Jesse's cold hazel eyes. Other than the soft cries from the gulls above and the sound of the gentle lapping of the rhythmic swells of the ocean against the hull of The Orca, there was an endless, empty silence.

"Nothing to say? That's fine, I'm happy to do the talking."

Andromeda turned her eyes up to Jesse again, only now, something that Jesse couldn't have anticipated happened—she smiled.

"Do as you will, for all actions that you conduct at this time and in this place are at the will and pleasure of my Pedagogue."

Jesse sighed and turned, then picked the pot off the deck. He walked over to the ice chest and scooped a pan full of the oily slop and tossed it overboard.

"So, you're telling me that this is all part of your 'Pedagogue's' plan? Wow, he sounds like an awesome guy."

An oily rainbow glinted and shimmered across the water as the pulped-up bits of fish meandered in the current.

"Oh, but he is!" Andromeda exclaimed, her energy becoming yet more calm and stoic.

She looked back to Jesse and smiled. "He knows all and sees all. Did you really think for one fleeting moment that he isn't aware of how all of this is going to play out?"

A couple of the seabirds broke their circling formation and dove beak-first into the water to take advantage of the larger fatty chunks of flesh that loitered on the surface.

"I belong to my Pedagogue. Mind, body, and soul. He sent me here because he willed it that I had to be here, and that this had to happen. So you are only doing his bidding."

Jesse smiled as the birds took flight from the sea and went back to their circling duties above the boat. He walked over to Andromeda and grabbed the pile of paper off her lap.

Jesse looked down at the stack in his hand. He stared at it, through it. He whispered to Andromeda, a whisper just above the wind that blew across the bow, "Well, since he knows who I am, and why I'm here, I'm sure you're just fine with me doing what I have to do?"

Andromeda's smile never broke as she stared back at Jesse. "Do what must be done."

Jesse grimaced, walked up to the small woman taped down to the chair, grabbed a fistful of her hair, and pulled her head back with a sharp jolt, exposing her delicate throat.

Jesse leaned in close and hissed, "You know what you did to my wife!"

He released her, turned, and walked back to the ice chest. He looked down to the stack of papers in his hand and ripped the paper into shreds.

Jesse then took the pot and stirred the bits and pieces of paper into the concoction of sludge.

"I know you like stories, Andromeda. I know you do because you tell them to yourself every day. Stories of how 'powerful' and 'wise' your 'Pedagogue' is. How this is all his will at work, and that's fine with me. You can tell yourself those stories all day long, I don't care. Because that's your life, your business. But on those pages, I saw you tell Katia a story. A story of how she was 'weak,' a story of how she was being 'held down' and 'oppressed,' a story of how she was being 'taken advantage of.'

"But it was your words, your stories, that burrowed into her mind like termites infesting a piece of wood. Manipulating and undermining her thoughts and emotions. Taking someone that was—was perfect, delicate, and flawless, like a diamond, and polishing her to believe that everything in her world was wrong, upside down, the opposite of her actual reality."

Jesse threw another two full pots of chum into the sea as he spoke. Andromeda watched, silently, still smiling.

"When I brought Katia home, I promised to always keep her safe, and that wasn't just a promise I made to her. It was a promise I made to her father, to her entire family . . . That first year, I watered her daily with love and kindness, and you know what happened? I watched her bloom, Andromeda, she bloomed. The seeds of patience and kindness that I had planted years before in her broke through the surface, and she became a beautiful garden."

Jesse scooped up another pot full of bloody slush from the ice chest and heaved it over the side. He looked out onto the endless horizon, as if getting lost in a faraway memory.

His grip on the pot tightened.

She just smiled.

"But then something changed, something shifted. Something changed inside her . . ."

Jesse turned back to Andromeda, the look in his eyes had changed, from cold to dead.

"It started with little things, Andromeda. She started getting sick—physically sick, emotionally sick. It was like, like the demons that were lulled to sleep inside her, suddenly woke up, and they woke up hungry."

Jesse went back to the ice chest and threw another pot full of blood and oil into the sea.

"The current is taking it right out. I know you can't see it, but the slick looks to be like a mile long now."

Jesse shook his head and softly laughed . . .

"You know what it's like when you look into the eyes of the love of your life, and you don't even recognize them anymore? Do you know how that feels? Of course you don't . . . You have no idea what love is, do you? I am sure you have been witness to many sacrifices with that fucked up little family of yours, but you have no idea what true sacrifice is.

"Sacrifice isn't about spilling blood . . . Sacrifice is about putting the things you want, the things you desire away so that you can put that energy into someone else. Sacrifice is saying 'no' to your dreams and saying 'yes' to theirs. Sacrifice is about compromise."

Jesse threw another scoop of the slop into the ocean.

"Do you have any idea what it was like to hold her as she had her daily nervous breakdowns? Can you even fathom what it was like to lie on the floor of the living room next to the woman you adore, while she sobs, and kicks, and screams? And you're totally powerless to do anything?"

Jesse looked out into the gently rolling swells of the open water.

"Do you know what it was like to watch her crumble?"

Jesse turned back to Andromeda.

"You know I had the tea you gave her analyzed?"

Jesse walked up and stood in front of Andromeda, who instinctively cowered in the chair.

"Katia always kept things in order. It was almost like a compulsion for her. She was great at organizing things—the best. So when you gave her all that tea, she labeled it. The first batch you gave her contained amphetamines and Ambien. Mixing a stimulant and a hypnotic? That must be helpful for making someone feel 'empowered' by the snake oil you were selling her. The Ambien must've been useful for keeping her open to your suggestions."

Andromeda smiled up to Jesse, and Jesse smiled back and winked at her before he turned back to the ice chest, throwing three more heaping scoops of chum over the side of *The Orca*.

While he was throwing the rotting bloody filth into the water, Jesse continued. "The second batch, a higher dose of amphetamines. No wonder she couldn't ever sleep at night, and Alpha PVP, which the kids on the street call 'Flakka,' that can induce an 'excited delirium' and make people angry, violent, and cause them to overeat."

Jesse paused and threw another scoop into the water.

"No wonder her eating and mental health issues came roaring back. The spark was always there, but you and your cult threw fucking gasoline on it . . ."

Jesse looked back to Andromeda as he dunked the pot back into the ice chest, filling it with the putrid smelling mix, and threw the sludge over the side.

"But you know what the worst part is, Andromeda? The worst part is that—" Jesse was interrupted by a loud splash right off the side of the boat.

He looked over the side to see a dark gray dorsal fin slicing through the water.

"Right on cue," Jesse laughed as he walked over to Andromeda, grabbed her chair, and dragged her over to the edge of the stern.

"I want you to meet my friends, Andromeda."

The water was churning with fins and tails, long, sleek, slender gray shadows right below the surface.

Andromeda watched, a serene smile on her face as Jesse threw another pot full of the greasy muck into the sea. The sharks instantly honed in on the sound and scent of the fresh blood cloud in the water. One of their tales kicked, splashing Jesse and Andromeda with a chill haze of rain and mist.

Andromeda spoke in a soft, fluid, slow tone. "I have experienced the omnipresent love of my Pedagogue. His love always penetrates and surrounds me. Your school-boy crush on your wife is inconsequential compared to the depth of joy and bliss she felt with us."

Jesse turned and pointed at the sharks circling around the boat. "You see them? They're just the opening act. Blue sharks prefer deep open water. We are waiting for the landlord . . ."

Andromeda smiled in the chair and glanced over her shoulder at the churning water.

Jesse eyed the woman coldly, and while maintaining his stare, threw three more scoops over the side of The Orca.

Over the next several minutes, Andromeda watched Jesse throw gallons of the festering sludge over the stern of the boat. The cold, deep green water was stained red with the blood and oil of the mulched-up bait fish. The pod of blue sharks slowly circled, but then, all at once, they were gone.

"I guess they got as bored of you as I am," Andromeda said cooly as Jesse looked over the side of the boat, his hands on his hips.

"No, Andromeda, they're not bored. They're scared."

A massive gray dorsal fin broke the water, at least fifteen inches tall, leaving its own wake behind it.

Andromeda smiled. The fin that stabbed out of the water was attached to a nineteen-foot shadow that lurked just below the surface. A shadow as black as cinder and as wide as a Volkswagen. The shadow of a living monster.

"Andromeda, meet the landlord."

Jesse walked up to her and smiled, throwing out a quote from one of his favorite movies.

"It's all psychological. You yell, 'Barracuda,' everybody says, 'Huh? What?' You yell, 'Shark,' we've got a panic on our hands on the Fourth of July."

Jesse pulled a box cutter out from the back pocket of his jeans and held it in front of Andromeda's face so she could see.

With a slow and deliberate *click-click-click*, Jesse extended the razor out of its sheath, the late day sun glinting off its fine deadly sharp edge.

Jesse walked around behind Andromeda and gathered her long black locks into his left hand, holding it close against the back of her scalp.

She sat calmly in place, watching the circling of the massive predator in the water, while Jesse, in a smooth sawing motion with the box-cutter, sliced off her hair, walked around to the ice chest, and dumped the twenty-four inches of blue-black hair into the pulp, and stirred it in with the pot.

Jesse withdrew a now stringy, bloody mess from the chest, and hurled it atop the monster's dorsal fin, that was now mere feet from the boat.

As soon as the clutter of hair, blood, fish, and paper hit the dorsal fin, a monstrous head emerged from the water. The devil's mouth, two feet wide, open, showing off row after row of serrated ivory triangles.

Jesse waved at the monster and blew it a kiss as Andromeda let out a slight giggle.

Jesse turned and walked to Andromeda, took the blade, and while taking care not to cut too deep, started slicing in long vertical strokes from the crown of her head, down her face.

A crown of crimson started to emerge, first in tiny beads, then in gushing torrent of red, painting the woman's face as Jesse slapped the open wounds to help aid with the flow.

The woman just looked up to him and smiled. "This is all for him, Jesse. You're doing perfect."

Jesse seethed, his eyes turned to the tape, and sliced it off, cutting Andromeda free.

Jesse reached down and pulled her up by her arms, standing Andromeda up like a department store display mannequin.

He cut the straps of her sundress, and it fell to her feet, exposing her nakedness to the now sinking sun in the western sky.

Jesse gripped her arms and positioned them straight out from her sides horizontally and started with more long shallow slices. He carved in long cuts across her sternum and breasts, her belly, and legs . . .

Jesse focused on slicing hundreds of tiny just-deeper-than-a-paper-cut cuts.

Every dozen or so, Jesse would stop cutting, and slap the area hard and repeatedly to get the blood flowing out.

He went down to her legs and kept slicing. Jesse stood and looked her in the face as he took each one of her arms and continued the messy pattern of slices from her deltoids to her wrists.

Andromeda smiled as he turned her to face the sea, and cut a jagged, random patchwork pattern of deep vertical slits into her back and down to her buttocks.

Andromeda just continued to smile. Her little giggles mixed with the blood in her mouth and flowing down her face.

Jesse stood behind the woman and whispered in her ear, "Do you see her circling? Do you see her calling to you? She desires you more than anything."

Jesse stepped to the ice chest and threw another pot full of rancid chum into the water. The Great White again breached the surface, eyeing Andromeda with its lifeless cold eyes.

Jesse reached into the pocket of his jeans and pulled out a thin silver chain. On the chain was a small silver medallion with a Masonic Square and Compass on it. He carefully put the necklace around Andromeda's neck and fastened it.

Jesse walked behind Andromeda and again whispered in her ear, "When I came home that night, to my wife in pieces, I walked into hell and met the devil. Now, for your crimes, for your sins . . . I will be happy to introduce you to her!"

Jesse crashed his fist into Andromeda's skull, knocking her to the deck. He went over to his bag and produced what looked like two large, oversized fishhooks, connected to each other with a rope about eight feet long. A carabiner hung heavy on the rope which he then clasped onto the arm of the deck crane.

He picked up the controls for the VX-Davit Yacht crane and extended the mechanical arm. The two hooks swung from the rope in rhythm to the sea.

He turned to Andromeda, who was now sitting, looking up at the hook,s smiling.

"Is this what your 'Pedagogue' wanted?"

He scooped the woman up off the deck, and grabbed Andromeda by the throat as he reached up and grabbed the first hook that was hanging off the crane.

Jesse roared as he plunged the hook into Andromeda's flesh, right where her neckline ends and her shoulders begin.

He worked the hook in deep, then turned it. In a brutal motion, he forced the handle of the hook skyward, forcing the bite of the hook to come out right below her clavicle bone.

Jesse torqued, severing flesh and muscle, until a good three inches of the pointed surgical steel emanated out of Andromedas chest, almost resembling a horn.

Jesses eyes flicked from the wound to the woman's face.

Her gaze was steady, her smile unbroken. Andromeda looked down at the hook protruding from her chest, up to the other hook, then back to Jesse.

"You have another one. Use it."

Jesse grabbed the second hook, and repeated the same grizzly task, only this time the plunge wasn't as clean, and he could feel the point of the hook scrape against and snap Andromeda's dainty clavicle. Bits of bone emerged with the hook as it penetrated though her chest.

Jesse, panting, looked to Andromeda.

She reached out a bloody hand and placed it on his shoulder.

"Good. Are you ready to finish this?"

Jesse stared at her silently as Andromeda took the hand off his shoulder, and gently took the crane controls from his hand.

"Allow me."

Andromeda pressed the button, and the crane came to life. As the motor whirred the woman's feet started getting light, and her toes lifted off the ground.

The cranes servomechanisms worked away and elevated her a whole two feet off the deck. Andromeda looked out to the beast of the sea doing lazy circles in the murky chummed-up water.

She looked down to Jesse and handed him the controls.

"Now do what must be done."

Jesse used the control to rotate Andromeda 180 degrees, so she was over the railing, then he extended the arm of the crane to its maximum length, a full twelve feet.

Andromeda swung there, arms outstretched to her sides, swaying lazily in the offshore breeze like an autumn leaf. She looked down to the massive shark in the water, back to Jesse, and then smiled.

With a click of the button, the motor of the crane once again came to life and started lowering Andromeda into the churning sea.

"This is only my beginning," Andromeda cooed and laughed as her toes hit the water.

The motor stopped.

There was a moment where time seemed to stand still, the only sounds were the lapping of the deep-water waves against the hull of The Orca, and the distant cry of a seagull.

Until the moment was broken by a huge, torpedo-shaped head breaking the water, breaching the surface in a violent uprising. The monster's mouth opened, jaws extended, teeth reached. The massive head enveloped Andromeda's legs and clamped down hard right below her pelvis. With one savage shake and rip, it took the whole of Andromeda's right leg, and most of her left, leaving tattered ropey bits of muscle and flesh dangling in the air. The creature sunk back into the water with a swish of its mighty tail dove.

Arteries dumped crimson into the sea.

Jesse howled with glee.

"That's what I'm talking about. I've been waiting for this!"

But he soon went silent when his eyes met hers. Andromeda's body was still swaying from the attack, but that smile hadn't left her face.

"This is what he has planned for me, Jesse. This is how it was supposed to be."

Jesse hit the button, and her ragged bits started descending into the cold water.

"Thank you. Thank you for serving my Pedagogue!"

As soon as the words escaped Andromeda's lips, the dorsal fin of the shark broke the surface about thirty feet from where she was, heading straight for her.

Andromeda smiled at Jesse as the shark once again broke the surface. Its entire head closed around her torso. The last sound to escape Andromeda's lips was the sound of the air being forced out of her lungs by the sudden compacting bite force of one of nature's top predators.

But the sound, in a strange way, was almost one of peace.

As the shark pulled its weight down, it snapped Andromeda's remaining clavicle, and the hooks slipped through the weak dermis.

All that remained of her was the lifeless upper torso, head, and arms.

Jesse watched as what was left of Andromeda bobbed up and down in the water like a cork.

Jesse threw the stinking empty ice chest overboard, and it gently collided with her remains.

He saw a couple of smaller fins break the surface. The school of blue sharks descended on the carcass in an absolute frenzy. In a few short seconds, there was nothing left of the matriarch of the cult.

The ocean was again calm, peaceful, and serene.

Jesse watched the sun dip below the horizon, projecting bright pinks, oranges, and ambers across the skyline that faded into a deep purple in the east where the first stars were just starting to kiss the sky.

Jesse cleaned up the mess then went up to the flydeck, and he sat quietly for many minutes before he punched in the navigation and powered The Orca back home.

~~COMMUNION~~

Beauty is mysterious as well as terrible. God and devil are fighting there, and the battlefield is the heart of man.

—Fyodor Dostoevsky

Eastman watched the sunset from atop the Mount Baden Powell Trail. The view from the 9,400-foot peak was breathtaking. Almost as breathtaking as the four and a half miles of steep hiking, 2,788-foot elevation gain, and over forty switchbacks. She reached out and placed her hand on the reticulated bark of a sugar pine, closed her eyes, took in a deep breath, and exhaled.

"This is the spot."

Eastman slipped off her backpack and carefully removed its contents. She laid everything out on the fertile soil and studied it.

Two black candles and one of white. Six teaspoons of mustard seed, basil, and black pepper.

In a small Ziplock bag, she had a chicken heart, liver, and guts. She also had a long piece of red string, a little cardboard box with a lid, a lighter, a small shovel, and a photo of the Pedagogue from his Instagram.

And last, but certainly not least, she pulled a small black velvet bag tied with a green string out of her backpack.

She looked to the west and watched as the sun slowly started to dip below the horizon line.

Eastman slipped off her shoes and socks, peeled off her jeans, hoodie, t-shirt, bra, and panties and stood there naked, at one and with the wild forest around her and within her.

The cool twilight breeze caressed her face as Eastman reached out with her feelings, flirting with the earth and nature. She smiled as a gust of wind blew up from the canyon and seemed to whisper in her ear, "It is done."

"So mote it be," she whispered in response to the earth as her feelings came rushing back to her, intertwining with the wind and the cold night air. Her toes dug into the soil. She knew deep down that Jesse had completed his mission for the day.

Eastman took another deep breath in and slowly let it go. It was as if the world was suddenly different to her now. In some strange way, it felt lighter, more vivid and peaceful with the knowledge that Andromeda was no longer in it.

Okay, let's get this party started.

She knelt on the ground and picked up the bag of warm chicken guts, unzipped it, reached in, and—while using care to leave the tough, rubbery heart alone—grabbed a handful off the liver and intestines.

The lustrous sodden innards seeped between her fingers, and she picked up the first black candle and anointed it with a coat of greasy film.

She placed the first black candle into the dirt, picked up the second, and repeated the measure, making sure it was fully coated and glinting in the moonlight that was just starting to rise behind her in the east. As soon as she was satisfied with her work, she placed the second black candle in the dirt about a foot away from the first.

Eastman picked up the white candle, coated it in blood and grease, and stuck it in the soil below the other two, forming what appeared to be an upside-down triangle. She picked up the lighter and lit all three, starting with the black in the top left corner, then the next black candle, and finally the white. The three flames spat and crackled as they were fueled by the wax and grease.

She then picked up the small box, removed the lid, and placed it in the center of the triangle.

She picked up the printed-out photo of the Pedagogue and focused on it. She dumped the mustard seed, black pepper, and basil onto the photo. Eastman then picked up the first black candle that she planted in the ground and held it over the picture.

She allowed exactly six drops of the hot black wax to drip onto the image, all the while focusing all her hatred, rage, and venom onto the man in the picture.

She repeated the action with the second black candle, and finally with the white.

By the time she was done, the photo was an unrecognizable mess of wax, blood, grease, and spice.

She then folded the image six times exactly, trapping the wax and contents inside, then carefully placed it inside the box. Eastman picked up the first black candle and again let six hot drips of wax fall onto the folded paper. She repeated that action again with the top left black candle, and then the white. Making sure that her hate for the man in the image burned as bright as the flickering orange flames burning in the now dark forest.

She reached into the bloody bag of chicken parts and collected the last of the guts, and finally the heart. She held the organs over the open box and squeezed. Whatever blood was still entrapped inside the organs now flowed and dripped onto the folded-up piece of paper. She kept pressing, digging her sharp nails into herself and lacerating the fleshy part of her palm, until her own blood started to flow, mixing and colluding with the blood of the long-dead foul.

A wave of energy rushed through her as a strong gust of wind billowed up the canyon, blowing her long blonde hair back and sending goosebumps cascading and spreading like a virus down her exposed naked flesh. Eastman let the energy guide her, and at the exact moment, when she knew it was time, she released, letting the heart and organs fall into the box.

Eastman reached down and snatched up the little black bag tied with a green string. She dumped the shard of quartz crystal into the palm of her greasy, still-bleeding hand.

Immediately, she felt Katia's energy seep into her hand like thick oily tar. She grinned and dumped Katia's crystal into the box with the folded-up picture of the Pedagogue.

"You two deserve each other," she hissed coldly, then put the lid on the small cardboard box and tied it shut with the long piece of red twine. She then sat and focused on the Pedagogue and seethed. A white-hot inferno of hate engulfed her. She mounted it, she harnessed it, she channeled it like a laser beam into that box while the candles burned and crackled. It was as if Eastman wasn't even there anymore. She was out of her body, riding a wave of karmic retribution into the cosmos.

Hours passed and the candles burned and dripped.

Dusk had turned to night, and the stars littered the sky above the Angeles National Forest.

At last, the candles had burned out, binding the spell completely.

Eastman grabbed the spade and got to her feet.

She picked up the box and took it to the sugar pine tree that had greeted her upon arriving at the plateau of the mountain.

She looked up at the big tree. Its mighty branches swayed peacefully with the wind that swept lazily up the mountain.

Eastman closed her eyes and swayed with the tree. Letting the wind, the earth, her guides, and her ancestors move her.

She then took the spade and stabbed into the earth below the tree. She scooped and dug with the ferocity of a wolf digging after a rabbit in the freshly fallen snow. Finally, when the hole was about two feet deep, she stopped and placed the box in the moist hallowed out earth. Then covered it, packing it down tight with the weight of her body.

As soon as her task was completed, Eastman let out a mighty howl that echoed through the hills and valley below. For the moon was out, and it pulled to her, and she pulled back to it in a delicate dance of nature and femininity. And there, in her nakedness painted orange with moon fire, she was more a wolf than a woman.

She stepped to the precipice, felt the warm winds blowing up the canyon and encircling her body with the perfumed musk of earth and air. She heard the soft flapping of wings, looked up, and saw a crow circle overhead.

She smiled up at the bird and whispered to herself, "She's here!" A rush of excitement consumed her. She pulled all the energy she could and screamed into the dark canyon below, "Macha, Goddess of the Woods, I summon thee!"

A soft breeze blew over her from the valley below.

And then . . .

Nothing.

Melantha waited in eager anticipation but was greeted with nothing more than the caw of the crow flying overhead. The bird cawed a couple times more, almost like laughing, and beat its blue-black wings that sounded like silk scratching against the wind.

The woods once again were silent.

The trees swayed gently in the breeze, saying nothing more than the hallowed sounds of the creaking of their old trunks.

Eastman watched as the crow lazily rode the stream of warm air rushing up from the valley and floating off into the distance.

She shook her head in disgust and looked down at her stained hands and sighed, just above a whisper, "Fuck you for never being there when I needed you. Why would I expect you to be there for me now? I have made it this far without you, and I can finish this without you."

Eastman shook her head and clenched her teeth.

"I will finish this."

Darkness was falling over the West Side of Los Angeles.

In the penthouse of an apartment building, a man was pacing . . .

Pacing on old, creaky wooden floors. The man's heavy, intentional steps were echoing through the apartment, keeping perfect time like a nervous metronome.

His pace quickened, his tall, lean muscular frame was heaving, his heart was pounding.

Tiny beads of sweat were forming. Every molecule in his body seemed to be buzzing, almost spasming and cramping as he once more paced from the door of his bedroom to the floor-to-ceiling windows that overlook the city.

And there he paused, staring out onto the town as the hue subtly shifted from a tangy orange to a soft pastel violet then a Prussian blue as the moon slowly climbed, making her ascent into the eastern sky over the San Gabriel Mountain Range.

"You have reached the voice mailbox of 310—"

The man hung up the phone and again tapped on the phone number for Andromeda.

Again, the phone went directly to voicemail.

His pulse quickened.

The man put the phone on his desk, went from his bedroom to his office, and opened the heavy wooden doors of his armoire. He retrieved his small, ornately carved wooden box, walked briskly back into his bedroom, and placed the box on the floor directly in front of the windows that look out over the city below.

He sat, opened the box, and pulled out the red velvet bag, the small fiber mat, the colorful scarf, seashells, a single white candle, and the little velvet bag of bones.

He got up and walked quickly into the kitchen to fill a glass with water and rushed back into the bedroom. He turned off the lights and closed the door behind him.

He sat back down and lit the white candle.

The candle immediately, violently, crackled and spattered with a bright red flame.

The man watched as the candle spat off red sparks that seemed to fly with intelligence, not unlike that of lightning bugs before wafting out into oblivion.

He sat and meditated on the question that he needed to have answered.

Is Orchid the beacon?

He grabbed the velvet bag, dumped the bones onto the colorful scarf, and started rolling his hand over them, stirring them like dominos on the mat.

"Ah lapapleba, ah papalesenso, ah lapapleba, ah paplesenso!"

The man reached into the carved box and pulled out the jicara. He then scooped the bones off of the colorful scarf and started shaking them violently inside the coconut shell.

The man closed his eyes and drew in a deep breath, yelling again into the air while the sound of the bones rattled and clattered loudly inside the jicara.

"Ah lapapleba, ah papalesenso, ah lapapleba, ah paplesenso!"

The man then slammed the coconut shell down atop the colorful scarf.

The room was silent.

As the man slowly lifted the jicara off the scarf, the candle that was still dancing and fluttering whiffed out.

The man paused . . . He watched as the trails of smoke floated from the candle and into the air in chaotic whirlpools of blue and gray.

The man looked down at the bones that he had just slammed down onto the floor. They were all laid out in a perfect circle, and one . . . one in the center was standing straight up, as if at attention, defying all logic, reason, and physics.

The answer the bones gave were not for the question that he had asked. But instead, he received a savage vision. In his mind's eye, he viewed Andromeda being torn apart and devoured by a monster.

"Andromeda . . . No," escaped the man's lips in a violent whisper as the single bone standing in the center fell—joining it's bleached white brethren in the circular formation.

The room was silent.

There the man sat, and somewhere, off in the far-off distance, the man heard a faint, lingering howl.

The white candle burst to life again.

Self-igniting out of nowhere and throwing off a bright amber flame that rises ten inches off the wick and was bright enough to cast shadows across the floor.

The brilliant luminosity of the candle illuminated the man so much that he now could see himself in the reflection of the floor-to-ceiling windows in front of him. He could make out the expression on his face and he watched as the form of a naked woman started to materialize behind him.

The man turned and looked over his shoulder. There was nothing but his own shadow dancing on the wall behind him.

His head swiveled back to his reflection, and to his horror, the apparition of the woman was now standing right behind him. They locked eyes for what seemed like an eternity, and in a quivering, gasping whimper, the man stuttered out, "Who . . . Who are you?"

The phantom in the reflection just cocked her head to the side and smiled. The apparition started to flicker and shutter. The translucent kelpie started morphing, changing. Her face was elongating. She dropped to her knees behind the man as he stared, frozen with terror at the beautiful feminine form crouching behind him—that transformed into a huge white wolf.

The man, paralyzed, screamed as the monster in the reflection reared up on its hind legs. Its hind legs made a sick popping sound, like cracking knuckles and breaking bones. Its hands were still almost human but tipped with black, razor-sharp claws. Its eyes burned like amber lanterns, its muzzle pulled back into a snarl, exposing gleaming white fangs.

The man kicked his legs out in an involuntary expression of

panic, knocking the candle over and extinguishing the brilliant flame. The room once again went dark.

At that moment, the sounds of the city returned. The honking of car horns, the passing of cars, and the jets flying over on their way to LAX.

The man curled on the floor, drenched in his own sweat.

His heart was pounding in his ears.

He opened his eyes, and the lights of the city and the full orange moon were all that he could see in the floor-to-ceiling windows of the penthouse apartment on the West Side of Los Angeles.

A gentle knock at the bedroom door startled the man. He got up, composed himself, wiped the sweat off his brow, and opened the bedroom door.

"Is everything okay, my Pedagogue? I thought I heard you call out for me."

"Yes, I did, my child. Please, come in and have a seat, I have much to tell you."

The man took Orchid by the hand and led her over to the bed, motioning for her to have a seat.

He smiled down at Orchid and spoke in a smooth, slow tone, "I have sent Andromeda to assist Jason and Serena. They will all be back in a couple of months. Until then, it is just you and me."

Orchid nodded her head slowly, keeping eye contact with the man.

"Now, I want you to get your things together. We are going on a spiritual journey up to our family's compound in the North."

Orchid nodded her head again, got up, and briskly walked out of the room.

The man closed the door behind her and once again sat in front of the floor-to-ceiling window in front of the bones. He reached for the candle and hesitated, as if it would have been hot to the touch still. The man grimaced, grabbed the candle, and lit it. The candle burned like any other candle would.

He picked up the jicara and scooped the bones up once again. He started shaking them violently in the half coconut shell.

"*Ah lapapleba, ah papalesenso, ah lapapleba, ah paplesenso.* Please give me the answer. I need to know."

He slammed the shell down onto the colorful mat and slowly lifted it to reveal the bleached ivory like bones. The man closed his eyes and took a deep breath in, feeling the energy, hearing the message.

The bones were speaking to them in their primitive, long forgotten language, and the message was clear.

The man opened his eyes and smiled down at the bones. He leaned forward, bowed, and kissed them.

He sat back up, looking at his smiling reflection in the window. He looked past his reflection to the moon that now hung fat in the sky and whispered back the message from the bones.

"Orchid is the one . . . She is the beacon . . ."

S33K AND D3STROY

*I hate to advocate drugs, alcohol, violence, or insanity to anyone,
but they've always worked for me.*

-Hunter S. Thompson

"How was the traffic on the way home from San Pedro, babe?" Eastman asked sweetly as Jesse walked into the front door of the little house on Piedmont.

"Took nearly three hours. Typical LA bullshit traffic." Jesse laughed as the petite blonde wrapped her arms around his neck and covered his face with multiple kisses. "How was your day?"

"It was good. Just went for a hike alone to clear my head." Eastman smiled as Loki jumped off the couch to greet Jesse also, his tail wagging furiously.

"Don't let him fool you; he's been fed and pampered all day, and who's been an exquisite boy today?"

The big wolfdog looked up Eastman with his silver-blue eyes and muttered out an exclamation, "Uff!"

They both laughed at the overgrown puppy as he sat there with his best "derp face" on.

Eastman walked into the kitchen, calling Loki as she went, "C'mon, Loki, let's go outside!"

Loki scattered on the linoleum floors as he fought for traction, clearly loving the idea of going outside.

Jesse heard the back door close and lock, and Eastman called out from the kitchen, "I'm going to grab my purse; let's go get some Mexican food. I'm dying for some chips and salsa!"

"Great, let me wash my hands. They still smell like fish guts."

"Don't tell me anything about your day until we get to dinner. I want to hear all about it!"

Jesse looked up from his lathered hands to see her smiling in the mirror behind him.

"Deal, Los Gringos Locos?" Jesse asked as he dried his hands with the towel hanging by the sink.

Eastman cocked her head and smiled. "Perfection."

Fifteen minutes later, the black SUV pulled into the parking lot of the family-owned Mexican restaurant in La Cañada.

They sat silently across from each other in a cozy red vinyl booth.

Eastman smiled at Jesse as she went over the menu, and under the table caressed his leg with her tiny foot, just letting him know she was there.

The back room of the restaurant was Jesse's favorite. Dimly lit, deep red walls filled with photographs and old newspaper clippings, the sunken ceiling a beautiful woven web of wicker, and the mood of the crimson room was topped off by the flickering of LED candles at each table.

The best part of it all: copious amounts of chips and salsa.

A couple minutes later, margarita in one hand, a tortilla chip heaped with salsa in the other, Eastman looked doe-eyed across the table at Jesse and gave him a long-satisfied sigh.

"Now you may tell me all about your day."

"Smooth sailing. But you really want to talk about this here?" Jesse asked while glancing over his shoulder at the family enjoying food in the booth directly behind them.

Eastman raised a single eyebrow and took a long sip from her margarita. She smirked and got up for their booth, drink in hand, and walked over to the table directly behind Jesse. The family looked up from their dinner and smiled at the pretty blonde who waved at them and put on a huge corny smile.

"Shit," Jesse whispered as Eastman started talking, putting on a thick southern accent just for fun.

"Hey, folks, sorry to bother y'all, but my husband and I are just tuckered out from a long day of hunting down satanic cult members and feeding them to sharks. I just had to ask you, what is that you ordered? It looks just fantastic."

The table erupted with laughter as the wife raised her own margarita and clinked it against Eastman's.

"This is the mole plate. I would highly recommend it."

"Thank you, and by the way, your kids are so well behaved— makes me almost want to have some." She gave the woman at the table a wink and once again, the couple laughed out loud and raised their drinks to Eastman.

"Have a good night now, ya hear?" she walked over to the table and slid into the booth across from Jesse.

"See? Nobody cares!"

"Touché," Jesse replied as he shoveled another salsa-heaped chip into his mouth. Eastman took another sip of her now nearly empty margarita and dripped out the honey-thick southern accent to Jesse, while flagging down a waitress and waving her now empty glass in the air in the universal sign of "refill, please."

She leaned toward Jesse, as if threatening to get up again.

"So, you wanna tell me about your day, sugar, or do I have to go and make a bigger fool out of myself to get you to talk?"

Jesse laughed and relaxed back into the big cushy booth. "No, babe, that won't be necessary. And not to worry, I followed your instructions exactly. I dumped the ice chest overboard. I hosed off the deck while still out at sea and wiped everything down before I got off the boat."

Jesse paused while he took a sip from his ice water. "But what worries me is, when I got back to the marina, I noticed that her

Jaguar was gone."

Eastman held up her index finger to Jesse in the "just a minute" gesture as a waitress came up to the table to put another double margarita down in front of her. She immediately took another big sip and smiled at the waitress.

The smiling waitress looked at the pair, her pad and pen ready. "Are you guys ready to order?"

Jesse spoke up while Eastman continued to work on her drink. "She will get the mole plate, and I'll get the veggie fajitas, no cheese, no sour cream, white rice, black beans, corn tortillas."

The waitress wrote down the order and read it back entirely to Jesse.

"Oh, could you please bring out some extra hot, hot sauce, please?"

The waitress nodded her head and made her way back to the kitchen to put in their order.

"Mr. Perez."

"Huh?" Jesse asked while grabbing another chip and dipping it into the not quite hot enough, but still flavorful, salsa.

"Mr. Perez had the Jaguar picked up and towed to a chop shop he has in Mexico. He did the same for Jason's Audi. I bet by now it's already in Tijuana being repainted."

Jesse reached for another chip, stirred it into the salsa, and shrugged his shoulders.

"So, what do you want to know, Mel?"

"You followed the instructions exactly, right?"

"To the letter."

"You went to the exact GPS location?"

"I did indeed."

"You cut off her hair and mixed it into the chum?"

"I didn't understand why you wanted me to do that, but yes."

Eastman smiled and reached to Jesse with her foot. Although it was quite a stretch for her petite frame, she managed to get her toes from Jesse's calf and up to his thigh.

"And the cutting?"

"All the cuts, just like you drew out for me. But what difference does it make, I'm curious to kn—?"

Eastman cut Jesse off in mid-sentence and grinned gleefully at him.

"You don't need to understand the why; you just need to do as you're told. That's what's important." She gave Jesse a wink as she broke a chip in half to resemble a shark's fin, and stirred it into the salsa while mimicking the theme from *Jaws*.

"Look, babe, a salsa shark!"

Jesse chuckled as he took another sip from his water.

"Did any of our finned friends show-up today?"

"Yes, several."

"Did Mr. White make an appearance?"

"He did indeed. He's the one that took her."

Eastman bounced in her booth in excitement, like a schoolgirl that got a pony on Christmas morning.

"Was she terrified? Was she screaming? Was there anything left?"

Jesse shuddered and shook his head while taking another salsa-filled chip.

"She was . . . calm, accepting, almost like she expected it. I couldn't think of a worse way to go, but she didn't even let out a whimper." Eastman looked at Jesse and shrugged. Jesse continued, "Anything left? Just bits and pieces. Some blue sharks took care of the leftovers. By the time they were done, there wasn't enough to fit in that bowl of salsa."

Eastman laughed a bit louder than was appropriate, even for the casual family restaurant atmosphere, causing several other patrons to turn their attention to their table. She leaned back in the booth as though a weight had been lifted from her shoulders and wiped a tear of laughter from her eye, being careful not to smudge her eyeliner.

"Good. She had it coming more than you know."

Eastman smirked impishly while she stirred and stared into her almost empty margarita, as if reviewing an old memory. "Revenge is a bitch, and her stripper name is karma."

Jesse looked over Eastman's shoulder to the waitress walking to their table, both arms full of sizzling plates of food.

"Speaking of ravenous animals . . ." Jesse smirked as he cleared space on the table for the waitress to put down the heavy hot plates.

"How's everything look, you guys?" The waitress looked down and smiled at the couple sitting in the booth.

Eastman held up her now empty, fishbowl-sized glass and exclaimed, "Looks great! 'Rita me again, doll!"

The waitress smiled, nodded her head, took the glass, and walked away from the table.

Eastman looked over at Jesse's look of "oh, you're ordering another?" as he grabbed a corn tortilla from the warmer, and she started to speak, but Jesse cut her off mid-sentence with a laugh.

"Yeah, yeah, I know, Mel. 'Drag me!' right?"

Eastman laughed and gave a playful kick to Jesse's shin under the table. "Smartass!"

"Better than being a dumbass!"

"Oh, touché for you this time, big boy!"

Eastman grabbed the "salsa shark" from the bowl where it had been sitting for the last minute, and smiled as she chomped into it, once again laughing.

"Om nom nom nom!"

Jesse rolled up and bit into his overstuffed tortilla as he watched Eastman amuse herself across the table.

"Ya know what's really funny though, Jess?" she said, a giggle still stuck in her mouth.

"What's 'really funny,' Mel?"

"It's funny that you're worried about the people around us overhearing our conversation," she motioned to the room full of families, happily enjoying their dinners, oblivious to the world.

"Do you really think any of these, these 'sheeple' have any idea of what is really going on in the world? And even if they were told, would, or could, do anything about it, or even care?"

Jesse dumped more of the dark picante sauce onto his taco and took another bite.

"How do you mean?"

"I just told the people behind us exactly what you did today, and did they care? Not one bit. It's easier for them to laugh it off and go about their day than to even try to wrap their heads around what I said."

"I'm pretty sure they thought you were kidding with—"

She cut Jesse off. "My point is, do you really think there is such a thing as 'privacy' anymore, Jesse?"

"What do you mean?"

"Do you really think that you can do anything, or go anywhere without someone, somewhere knowing about it? Do you think that your little 'fishing trip' today hasn't been logged and sent to some database somewhere? I can assure you it's already been analyzed, categorized, and cataloged by some AI bot . . . Oh, and our other little 'hunting trips'? Same thing."

Jesse laughed and started greedily filling another warm corn tortilla with rice, beans, veggies, and picante sauce. He rolled his eyes and sighed. "Okay, Mel."

The waitress came up with a third margarita and placed it on the table.

"How's everything here so far?"

Eastman looked up at the young brunette and smiled. "Hi, what's your name?"

"Erin."

"Hi, Erin, I'm Melantha and this is Jesse."

Jesse waved to the young girl, nervously anticipating where Eastman was going with this line of questioning.

"I just wanted to thank you for your service tonight, Erin. You are doing a great job, and I just wanted you to know that."

The waitress smiled politely.

"Thanks, Melantha, let me know if there is anything else you guys need, okay?"

"Sure thing, Erin."

The waitress walked away from the table, and Eastman pulled out her phone. She started texting away as Jesse finished his second hand-rolled taco.

"What was all that about, Mel?"

"Just going to prove my point, babe, that's all."

Eastman put her phone down on the table and took a couple bites of her mole.

"Damn, this is good, why is this the first time you have taken me here, Jess?"

"I wanted to make sure you were a keeper, I guess," Jesse said with a chuckle as he scooped another pile of beans into a tortilla.

Ding!

A text notification appeared on Eastman's phone. She glanced at it, looked up to Jesse, raised an eyebrow, and smiled while she opened the message.

"Our waitress is Erin Riley. Born in Mansfield, Ohio. 9-3-1998. Looks like she moved here straight after high school and is currently going to Pasadena Community College with a focus on acting. Decent GPA, although not perfect. She has 1,323 followers on Insta, and she had a Facebook but deleted the account last year. That's okay, I have a file here of everything she ever posted even though she 'thinks' she deleted it.

"Here is where she lives, here is where she goes often, her medical records, buying habits, political affiliation, oh, and here is where the AI predicts she will be tomorrow morning at 10:00 a.m., noon, and the evening based on her habits."

Eastman looked up at Jesse, who was frozen at the table, his face a lighter shade of pale.

"Are you serious? You got all that in, like, less than a minute."

She put her phone back into her purse, looked back to Jesse, raised an eyebrow, and smiled.

"Oh, honey, I didn't even mention the audio files of the last two weeks that her phone has recorded and sent to us. It's always listening and sending data, even when she's not using it or has it turned off. But that only becomes an issue if one of the bots that 'listen' to the recordings 'hears' a keyword or string of keywords that we deem to be 'no-no' words or phrases. Then it gets flagged and listened to by a human. Then that human decides if any action is needed."

"What does—What does this mean for us, Mel?" Jesse was now clearly nervous, his face showed not a hint of humor.

"You mean with your hunting trips? It means nothing. Nobody is going to miss any of them. If there are no calls made, there is no investigation. If there is no investigation, there is nothing to worry about."

Eastman smiled and took another triumphant sip from her margarita.

"I must admit, Melantha, this is a lot to take in. What about the Constitution and Bill of Rights? What about people's privacy?"

"Let me ask you a question, Jesse."

She took another bite of her dinner as her mood became a bit more somber.

"Have you ever wondered why we always seem to be at war? Have you wondered why everyone seems to be miserable, or why most people are up to their eyeballs in debt? Have you ever wondered why you were raised by a single mom with one job, but she was able to buy a house in a nice neighborhood, yet you make four times what she did and you have to rent? Have you ever wondered, Jesse, why all of a sudden, we have all these school shootings, riots, and crime? Are we just to assume that human beings—human nature—changed radically in the last twenty-five years, and that is what drives all this misery and suffering? Or is it something more? Is it more deliberate?"

She took a big swig of her drink and stared into it, gently sloshing the blended ice beverage, forming a tiny whirlpool.

"What if I told you, Jesse, that nothing happens by accident. That everything that goes on in the world has been planned by a tiny group of people that basically run everything. What if I told you that this small group of people run all nations. the international banking systems. the church, the news, and entertainment media. What if I told you they run the agricultural companies that make all the food we eat and all the pharmaceutical companies that are supposed to help us if we get sick? What if I told you that all of the social media was their idea?

"You're worried about privacy? We used to have to spy on people for years to get 1/100th of the information we have on people now. Do you know what the best part is, Jesse? They volunteer it! People put everything they do online. All we have to do is collect.

"What if I told you that they use their media outlets to sow division, to set black against white, woman against man, Muslim against Christian? What if I told you all that disgusting shit was manufactured and fed to the masses to keep them distracted from their real oppressors? One big giant sleight of hand trick . . .

"What if I told you that those people—those families that are in power—are the ones that have always been in power, and very few people have tried to fight back against them . . ."

Jesse stared at Eastman as she downed the last bit of her drink.

"One man tried to fight back. He became president in January 1961. He knew about them and wanted to expose them for what they are, and bring back freedom to America. We know how that ended up for him."

470

She makes her fingers into a gun and pretends to shoot at Jesse.

"I mean, look at the opioid epidemic in America now. You used to sell drugs in the '90s. Tell me, Jesse, did you know anyone that did heroin or popped prescription pills back then?"

Jesse shook his head. "No, nobody."

"Exactly! Don't you find it strange that since we invaded Afghanistan, who happens to be the largest producer of heroin in the world, that all of a sudden, our streets are flooded with that shit?"

She looked at Jesse, raised an eyebrow, and smirked. "Do you believe in coincidences?"

Jesse grabbed another corn tortilla and heaped some rice and beans into it. "This is a lot to take in, Mel. Sure, I've heard about the Illuminati, and the Bilderberg group. But I thought that was all 'tin foil hat' shit. People attack me online all the time for being a Freemason. I always laugh at them because they're convinced that we worship the devil and ride goats, but to be honest with you, we don't do shit except get together and have barbecues. But with all this shit you're telling me, if that's all real, then what else is real. Flat Earth? Lizard people? The staged moon landing? Chemtrails? 9/11?"

Eastman shrugged her shoulders and took another bite of her mole. "I don't know about all that, but I do know that MK Ultra is a very real thing."

"What's MK Ultra? Sounds like a goddammed laundry soap!" Jesse grabbed another handful of chips and started digging into the picante sauce.

"MK Ultra was one of a series of programs that came out of the CIA during the Cold War that were experiments in mind control to turn people into assassins. Think *Manchurian Candidate* and so on . . . They played around with drugs, electric shock, insulin shock, and other techniques. How do you think LSD became popular and available to the masses?"

Eastman grabbed a chip from Jesse and swirled it around in the thick red sauce on her plate.

"The CIA spent over twenty-five years and millions of dollars on mind control and psychic warfare experiments. Programming people to be spies, to remote view, even mass population control, you name it."

"Like *The Men that Stare at Goats*? Wait, you're telling me that people can travel anywhere with their minds or be brainwashed to be some sort of super ninja assassin? C'mon, babe!" Jesse sniggered as he rolled his eyes.

"Yes, Jesse, like *The Men that Stare at Goats*. The CIA was basically picking up where the Nazis left off. After WW2, there was 'Operation Paperclip,' which you have probably heard of. That's when we got a bunch of German scientists to assist us with our space program. But what most people don't know is, we also got our hands on some Nazi witches, too. Hitler was obsessed with the occult. He spent huge amounts of wartime resources tracking down 'magical' and religious artifacts and relics. He was consumed by it."

She paused and winked at Jesse. "Like in *Raiders of the Lost Arc*. Hitler was certain that his victory was foretold by omens and lore. He was, ironically, using the Kabbalah and planning his attacks with numerology. He was sure that he couldn't be defeated. But, thankfully for the allies and all of humanity, he was wrong.

"Anyway, the government used all the resources they had acquired from Hitler to try to get ahead, not only in the space race but also in the race of the occult and mind control. They called it the 'ODI,' or Occult Defense Initiative."

Eastman's tone got more serious as she looked down at her drink.

"The Russians lost the space race, everyone knows that, but what the public doesn't know is that they were dominating us in the black arts. I mean, what good is sending a man to the moon if, when your astronauts come home, they don't have a home to come back to? It never made the news, and you will never see this in a history book, but this secret battle—this 'Occult war'—was nearly lost. Thousands were killed. And it looked like this country, this experiment called 'America,' was going to be destroyed, not by a mushroom cloud, but by dark magik.

"Just when we thought we had no hope left to hold on to, and when all looked darkest, in the early 1970s, the CIA brought in a young man. His parents were both Nazis. His father, a brilliant rocket scientist, and his mother was basically Hitler's 'Queen witch.' He was brilliant, like, off the charts smart. He had a mastery of the occult that far surpassed anything the reds had. He was the Jack Parsons of our time. It's hard to believe that over the course of ten years, he almost single-handedly turned the tide of that war and saved every man, woman, and child in this country."

Eastman hesitated.

"After the dust settled and all was said and done, after spiritual peace had returned, he demanded that the Occult Defense Initiative be made public. He wanted his team of witches to come out of the shadows and have their moment of triumph. He wanted them to be recognized for the American heroes that they were. He wanted to change the country's, the world's, view of witches and religion forever. He wanted the dawning of a new age of the occult and science for the betterment of all humanity.

"But, after the war, there were no ticker-tape parades, there were no medals, no honors, nothing for him . . ."

Eastman shook her head and sighed.

"He was just a weapon, plain and simple. Just another relic from the Cold War, like an old B-52 bomber. Without an enemy to fight, he was just obsolete, an outcast and a freak . . . The Defense Department's dirty little secret. So, of course, the government did what the government does best. It got rid of its dirty little secrets.

"His team was hunted down one by one and slaughtered. And it wasn't just the men, but the women and children in the program too. They tracked him and his wife to a small farmhouse, broke down the door, and murdered his wife in front of him. He took a couple of bullets as he tried to shield her body, and just before the team could finish the job, he used the last of his power to 'influence' them to turn their guns on each other.

"He burned the farmhouse to the ground with the bodies inside, and with all the heat and flames, it was assumed that he burned up with it. He nearly did, and he has the scars to show for it. He vanished deep into the country—the very country that he fought to save, and that now wanted him dead.

"His blind hate and rage of having his wife and team killed drove him mad. He was turned from a shining beacon of hope and liberty, into something dark and perverse. He was seduced and consumed by the same evil that he took an oath to destroy. And ever since then, he has been trying to assemble a new team, a new 'family' of witches to wage his own war, to stand in his power . . ."

Eastman still had her eyes locked on Jesse.

"So, I suppose you could say that some fairytales you had heard when you were a child about witches, ghosts, and monsters are real, but most grownups choose not to believe in them anymore.

"Or, you could say that maybe these are all just old wives' tales that parents tell their kids to keep them out of the woods, and safe in their beds. But like you said earlier, Jess, 'if all this is real, then what else is real? And out there waiting for us in the dark.'"

Jesse sat there silent and mesmerized, trying to absorb everything that Eastman had just enlightened him to.

"Anything else I can get you guys?"

Jesse nearly jumped out of the booth with fright as Erin's melodic question broke the spell.

"No, just the check, please," Eastman said as the two girls giggled at the big man trying to play off nearly jumping out of his skin as smoothly as he could.

Jesse handed Erin his debit card, and she ran off to bring back the check.

"So, I might not be the smartest man in the world, Mel, but from what you just told me, that sounds like our friend we are going to go visit soon."

Melantha nodded. "That's him."

"Fuck," Jesse said under his breath as Erin returned to the table with his card and the receipt to be signed.

"You're not scared now, are you, Jess?"

Jesse signed the bill and gave Erin her well-deserved twenty percent.

"Who? Me?" Jesse laughed as he smiled at Erin and handed her the signed copy. He looked back to Eastman; her face wasn't showing a hint of levity . . .

"You should be, Jess. You should be . . ." She got up from the booth and reached for her phone. She glanced down at the screen; there were three missed calls from Geo.

"Shit, Jess, let's go. You drive." Eastman threw Jesse her keys, and he followed her out of the restaurant and into the parking lot where she was already hitting redial, calling back Geo.

The phone rang three times.

"C'mon, answer!" she said impatiently as she looked around the parking lot, walking briskly to the big black SUV.

"Hello, Mel?"

"Talk to me, Geo, what's up?"

Jesse unlocked the truck, and they both climbed in. As soon as Jesse started the vehicle, Geo's voice could be heard over the speakers.

"I put a thirty-mile location tag on your friend here. I felt I needed to after I saw what he has been up to."

"Good job, Geo. What's happening?"

"Well, he just broke the thirty-mile leash I have on him. Looks like he's on the move somewhere. He's heading north."

"Great, keep me posted. If anything changes, please let me know."

"You got it, Mel, will do."

The phone disconnected and Eastman looked over to Jesse and smiled.

"You ready to finish this?"

SANCTUARY

Orchid watched the countryside slowly pass by from the passenger side window of the vintage Mercedes as it made its way up the long lonely road leading to the compound.

She hadn't seen another set of headlights for the last forty-five minutes of the nearly four-hour drive.

She was grateful that for most of the trip, the conversation had been minimal. She even fell asleep somewhere between Castaic and Bakersfield.

Although she wasn't asleep for long, her time in the ether was filled with sweaty, vivid dreams of her early childhood. Misty dreams of running through sprinklers on hot sticky green afternoons. Visions of the summers she would spend her time catching pollywogs and fireflies at her grandparents' house in the country . . .

But the dream turned from joyful to rancid as young Orchid was transported from a vision of playful, childlike frolic, back to when her childhood officially ended too soon . . . She was teleported back to a lonely dark country road.

The farm worker that plowed head-on into her grandfather's Cadillac had walked away from the accident without so much as a scratch, which is typical for drunk drivers.

476

What wasn't so common, though, was the little girl who was trapped in the back seat of that same twisted, mangled wreck . . . A little girl, no more than three, who sat screaming and begging for an hour for her grandparents to wake up. She was still screaming as the first responders shattered glass and sheared through steel to free her from the contorted automobile.

"You can always come home."

"What?" Orchid said as she looked over from the dark country road, and there in the driver's seat was her grandfather.

"Pops?" Orchid squeaked out, staring in disbelief at her beloved grandfather, who was the only man in her life who ever treated her with love and kindness. Pops had a big smile on his face. He turned and looked at Orchid as he drove his big late '90's Cadillac.

"You can always come home."

Orchid woke up with a jolt and tears streaming down her face. First of joy, then because of the immediate realization that it was just a dream, and at that moment remembering where she was and the particulars of her situation. The tears, which made a path to her upper lip where her tongue subconsciously scooped them up, were saltier than any lake.

"We're here. Get your things."

Orchid looked over to the driver's seat, half expecting to see Pops still there. But in his place was just the dark silhouette of the Pedagogue.

"Yes, my Pedagogue."

Orchid wiped the remaining trails of tears off her porcelain cheeks. The side of her face was no longer black and blue from the thrashing that Andromeda had bestowed on her a couple days prior in Her Majesty's Tea and Supply. Now the bruises had faded into a sickly pale, eggnog yellow. She opened the heavy door of the Mercedes and stepped out.

There was nothing but an inky pitch-black abyss around her, and she could tell from the earth underfoot that she was standing on sandy, loose gravel.

But the stars . . .

The stars were beautiful . . .

"Follow me."

The cold blue beam of an LED flashlight illuminated the path that led up to the secluded, off-grid compound. Orchid followed as the man approached a small arched river rock and masonry bridge that seemed to go over a trickling stream.

They entered what felt like a large courtyard, and from there, Orchid could make out what appeared to be the outline of a church steeple.

The man swung the beam of light, slashing through the darkness, landing it on a pair of ornately carved wooden doors. He produced a key from his pocket, unlocked the doors, and walked into the old building. Orchid stood at the threshold as she heard the man's footsteps walk into the darkness and stop.

He flipped on the lights, and at once, the interior of the old building was illuminated.

Orchid's jaw dropped as she stepped into the vast, open room.

"What is this place, my Pedagogue?"

"Welcome to the sanctuary, my dear."

"Is this . . . a church?"

"It was indeed, my child. For three generations, the same family owned this church and the land it sits on. For over 150 years, people came and worshipped here. When the property came available, I acquired it for our family."

Orchid's eyes drank in the dramatic wood beam vaulted ceilings. The mix of dark stained and natural pine gave the huge room a rich rustic look. Rows and rows of dark wood pews accented with vibrant red velvet to match the red and gold patterned carpet floors led up to a pulpit, and behind it, a massive pine crucifix that had gorgeous inlay to match the pews. The five substantial wrought iron chandlers hung from the ceiling seemed to be swaying ever so slightly with the excitement that someone had entered the sanctum.

"We would come here for special rituals that would require more privacy. Follow me. I'll show you our living quarters."

The man flipped the light switch once again, and the room went dark. He clicked on his flashlight and led Orchid though a set of interior doors that led through a grand banquet room holding half a dozen rows of set up tables ready for a feast. As their footsteps echoed off the cold tiled floor, Orchid could almost hear the laughter and wine glasses clinking together as the ghosts of parishioners long dead celebrated forever in the dark hall.

They walked through a huge industrial kitchen, and from there into the living quarters. There was a huge common area with a TV, game tables, couches, and shelves among shelves filled with books and magazines.

A fine layer of dust covered the furniture and electronics in the room like skin.

The man flipped on the lights when they entered the hallway. He opened the doors, and in each room, there were five bunk beds, equaling ten beds total.

"These will be the living quarters for our family. Come, I'll show you the nursery."

Orchid nodded and followed the man as he opened the last door on the left.

There were five brand new cribs, two changing tables, stacks of diapers, and even a couple of toys.

"For the family who is yet to be born."

The man smiled and looked down to Orchid.

"You are the key to all of this. You are the missing piece to the puzzle. It is through you that I will be able to reclaim all that has been lost. It is through you, and from your womb, that my family will be reborn."

The man closed the door to the nursery and walked Orchid to the end of the hall to a black door with a symbol painted on it.

"This is our quarters."

The large bedroom had only a dresser, a mirror, a writing desk, and what appeared to be two king-sized beds pushed together to make one huge mattress.

The man motioned to the door beside the bed.

"The bathroom is there. Go bathe, then come to bed."

Orchid cast her eyes down and walked briskly into the bathroom. A moment later, the sounds of water running and filling the tub in the shower brought a smile to the man's face.

The man closed the door and locked it. He got undressed, turned off the lights, got into the bed, and waited there in the dark for Orchid to join him.

It was about 3:34 a.m. when Jesse sat up, screaming and covered in sweat. He desperately looked around the salt lamp-lit room with a bed for any sign of danger. The tapestry of his long reoccurring nightmare still interwove with the frayed fringes of reality. A large white and gray form rose up from the floor in front of the bed. Jesse rubbed his eyes, trying to clear the haze of disconnected, tangled night terror from his vision. He blinked hard. His eyes snapped into focus to view his big wolfdog staring at him. Loki's head was cocked inquisitively to the side in the classic "Are you okay?" look.

"Quick, tell me everything you remember about the dream."

Jesse snapped his head to the side and saw the silhouette of Eastman lying next to him. The salt lamp behind her on the nightstand almost gave the appearance that she was glowing—an angel bathed in the soft pink and amber hues of hand carved Himalayan salt.

Jesse reached over to his side of the bed and grabbed the glass of water that he always kept on the nightstand and took several gulps. After nearly finishing it, he paused and took a deep breath. Jesse placed the glass back on his nightstand and slowly laid back down on the bed. He put his hands on his chest and took several more deep breaths.

"Jesse?"

"It was the house dream again."

Eastman turned onto her side and placed her head on Jesse's shoulder. "Tell me everything you can. It's important."

"I don't really know what to say, Mel . . . It was the same goddammed dream I have been having for years."

Jesse hesitated.

"I'm sorry, I didn't mean to be a snapper gator, it's just that . . . That it really fucks me up. I have been having this dream since I was in high school, and every time, it's the same thing."

Jesse took another slow, deep breath to try to slow down the beating of his heart.

"I am in the house. I am going deeper and deeper into it, from room to room to room . . . and I get to the door, the very last door. I can't open it. It's like I'm paralyzed, like whatever is behind it is so bad, so wicked, that it just . . ."

"Just what, babe?"

"I don't know. I don't even know what it is, but what I do know is that whatever it is, I—I can't face it."

Jesse reached for his vape on the nightstand and took a significant drag. He held it in and closed his eyes, going over the dream again in his mind, trying to remember any detail that he may have left out. He slowly exhaled the thick sweet-smelling smoke.

"It's fucked, babe . . ."

Eastman just laid there, running her fingers gently through the hair on Jesse's chest. "Know what I think?"

"What's that?"

"I think that whatever is behind that door, Jess, is maybe something from your childhood. Or maybe it's something that you have stuffed away, locked up in a dark corner of your mind for a very long time that you didn't—or couldn't—look at. But, Jess, at some point, you're going to have to face it."

She reached over, took the vape out of Jesse's hand, and took a big hit off it.

She immediately started choking and coughing, which Jesse found entirely entertaining.

"How you can do this all day escapes me," she sputtered out between coughs as she threw the device back on Jesse's chest. He grabbed it and took another big hit, producing a massive cloud of smoke.

"What can I say? I'm a man of many talents!"

Eastman gave Jesse a playful nudge, grabbed the covers, and did a spin, wrapping herself up like a burrito and leaving Jesse basically blanketless and naked.

"Hey!" Jesse grabbed the covers back from her, and they both laughed and giggled in the dimly lit room with a bed. Eastman turned her back to Jesse, and he scooted up behind her, brushed her hair off the side of her face, kissed her gently on the nape of her neck, and whispered into her ear as he spooned her close, "This is almost over, isn't it?"

"Yeah, it's almost over." Eastman gave Jesse's hand a squeeze as she nuzzled back closer to him.

"What happens after this?"

"After this? Well, we can talk about our options then, babe. It depends a lot on you. Do you want to settle down, or keep following the white rabbit?"

". . . Sorry, Mel, I must have fallen asleep for a second there."

Eastman smiled, gave Jesse's hand another squeeze, and finished off the display of affection with a kiss.

"Let's get back to sleep, babe, and no more bad dreams."

Jesse whispered back as he yawned and let out a big sigh, "No more bad dreams."

4 THE L6VE 6F G6D

"Son, the greatest trick the Devil pulled was convincing the world there was only one of him."

—David Won

Orchid woke up to a sound that she hadn't woken up to since she could remember: the sound of birds singing.

She rolled over in the giant bed and peeled one eye open to see a large open glider window in the bedroom that she hadn't noticed last night.

As her vision came into focus, she saw beautiful, lush trees and gently sloping green mountains in the not so far off distance. Funnily, it kind of reminded her of home.

Orchid smiled as a bird landed on one of the branches of an ancient California oak that was closest to the house. The bird let out a couple cheerful chirps and fluttered off about its business as birds in the morning tend to do. Orchid gave a little wave to see the bird as she stretched out long and hard. The brand on her back, although still healing, was now fully scabbed over and was now itchier than it was painful.

Orchid rolled onto her belly, then went into 'child's pose.' She took several deep breaths in and out to get the energy in her body moving as the Pedagogue had instructed her to do every morning as soon as she awoke.

The routine had become a habit, a ritual. She didn't even have to think about it anymore, she just woke up and went into motion. At first, Orchid found all the daily rituals that the Pedagogue had her do to be a bit overwhelming, but with weeks of mindful practice, she realized that they were in a way, quite empowering.

Orchid heard a truck pulling up the long drive to the compound. Not one of those new, sweet, modern $60,000 pickup trucks, but a real truck, a farm truck, a work truck. The kind of truck she would hear pull up the old country roads back home where she grew up. The type of truck that, when you were riding in it on one of those old country roads, sounded like it was about to fall apart and felt like it too. The kind of truck with dings and dents all over it from long hours of work, the sort of pickup that never got washed, except for when it rained.

She got out of her 'child's pose' and walked over to the window. The sweet country breeze flowing through the screened window caressed her now goose-pimpled nude body.

Orchid pulled one of the heavy drapes and used it to cover herself as she watched the truck pull up and park. She smiled, for the truck was nearly identical to the one she had imagined in her mind's eye.

She then noticed that the truck was towing behind it an even more rickety trailer filled with what looked to be four goats. Stacked in the bed of the truck were several wire cages with about a dozen chickens. Orchid watched as a man, and what appeared to be his son, got out of the truck and greeted the tall man that approached them, shook hands, and looked over the living cargo.

Orchid turned and noticed that a dress was hanging by the door of the room.

Also on the hanger, there was a white apron. Orchid took the dress off the hook and placed the apron on the bed. She held the dress up and inspected it.

It was simple and rather dull. Not at all soft and flowy, but more utilitarian. She put it on and noticed it had a bit of a *Little House on the Prairie* look to it, especially when paired with the white apron, that when tied twice around her waist, showing off the gentle curves of her body.

Orchid snatched her hair up, wound it several times, and put it into a bun. She looked at herself in the mirror and giggled, feeling she would fit right in with the Amish people she would see selling homemade cheese on the side of the road when she was riding around on Sunday afternoons with her Pops when she was a kid.

Orchid's smile wiped from her face as she heard a man's voice call her name from outside. She slipped on her black shoes and walked briskly through the cavernous building, trying her best to retrace her path to the front door from the night before. Last night the building felt big, dark, and empty. In the daylight it felt lonely, but strangely, also warm and homey. Exactly how you would expect a large church in the country that had been tenderly loved and maintained by multiple generations of a family to feel like.

"Orchid!"

Her pace quickened as she heard the man's voice echo through the house.

As she stepped out of the ornately carved doors and into the bright morning sun, the man turned and smiled at her.

"I see you found your clothes. Very good. Please assist this young man with the animals and bags of feed. You will put them in the barn behind the building, and make sure that they have water, and also be sure that you give them some of the feed. Do you understand?"

Orchid smiled and nodded her head.

The man's son, who couldn't have been older than twelve, opened the door of the trailer and let the ramp swing down. He walked into the trailer and gathered the goats' leashes and handed two of the frayed bits of rope to Orchid and smiled.

Orchid gave the ropes a gentle tug, and then she and the boy started leading the goats around the back of the main building. As they approached the barn, Orchid looked to the small boy and chirped, "Is that your dad there with you?"

"Yes, we have a farm on the other side of town where we raise animals."

"I bet you're a great helper."

"I have been helping my dad since I was a kid, and someday I'll be in charge of the business."

Orchid smiled as they neared the barn that was about a hundred yards from the main house. It was old but well maintained, looking precisely like you would expect a barn to look: bright red with Navajo white trim and a shingle roof. Sure, it was true that some of the paint was worn and peeling, but it gave the barn a certain rustic charm. It was even topped off with a classic rooster weathervane.

"I like this place," the boy said as one of the goats that were trailing him let out a bleat.

"I went to Sunday school here, and after service, all the kids and I would play out here in the pasture while the grownups cooked lunch. We would spend every Christmas here too. My grandpa and grandma were friends with Father Riley and his family. They even went here when they were little, when Father Riley's grandfather preached here. It feels like this old place has been here forever. But when they sold the property and moved away, everyone in town has been wondering what was going to be done with it. Is this going to stay a church?"

Orchid looked at the boy, smiled, and shrugged her shoulders. "I'm not sure what's going to happen to it, but I'm sure it will be well taken care of."

The boy smiled up to Orchid. She could tell he had a bit of a crush on her. "Is your dad a preacher? He looks like a preacher."

"I guess you could say that." Orchid was going to elaborate on what her "dad" does, but quickly thought better of it. She unlatched the lock on the barn's big doors and swung them open. Inside the barn was just as picturesque as it was on the exterior: a row of animal pens on either side, various supplies, tools, and workbenches in the back, and a ladder that led up to the second-floor loft.

"Let's show these guys to their new home," Orchid said as she gave her ropes a little tug. They stepped into the barn, the goats following close behind.

"Where are all the other animals?" the boy asked, looking around the empty barn.

"We don't have any other animals, just the ones you brought here today."

The boy walked over to one of the empty pens, rested his hand on the gate, and turned to face Orchid.

"We were here a couple months ago dropping off goats and chickens, just like this morning. I remember it exactly. There was a man, a big man, that helped us unload. He didn't say much, and he had a lot of tattoos. There was another girl with black hair, like yours. She didn't say very much either. They weren't nice like you, though. They scared me a little."

"Oh, yeah, they can be kind of scary, I guess."

"What happened to the animals?"

Orchid decided it was best to change the subject. She didn't want to say anything out of turn, and on top of that, she knew full well how fast rumors could start to fly in a small town.

"Here, help me get these guys in the pen, then you can help me with the chickens."

Orchid led her two goats into the waiting pen, and the boy ushered his pair in behind them. As soon as they were all safely inside, Orchid closed the gate and started leading the boy out of the barn. The goats began bleating loudly as they started walking out of the barn.

"Aw, the poor things are scared," Orchid said as she turned and gave one of the goats, a tiny white goat that seemed to be the most upset, a pat on its coarse-haired head.

"Yes ma'am, I raise all the goats—well, *all our animals* from the time they're born. My dad says not to name them, but I always do. And I really care about them. They're important to me."

"That's very sweet of you," Orchid said as she tussled the black mop of the little boy's hair. The goats kept making a ruckus in their pen.

"That's why I'm curious about the goats and chickens that we delivered here before. There was a big, white goat, I called her

'Starla.' She was my favorite. She was a good goat as far as goats go. So please, I promise I won't say anything to my dad or yours, I just wanna know if she's okay."

The goats went silent, and all huddled in the corner of the pen.

"They ran away."

Orchid nearly jumped out of her skin as she turned to see her Pedagogue standing in the doorway of the barn, a sixty-pound bag of feed over each one of his shoulders.

The man walked into the barn and dumped the enormous bags of feed by a large, galvanized trash bucket. He pulled the aluminum lid off the can and placed it to the side. Orchid and the boy stood frozen as the man easily manhandled one of the sixty-pound bags of feed, and in one fluid motion, he pulled a knife from his pocket and sliced the bag open, spilling the animal feed into the can.

The man smiled at the boy but didn't take his eyes off him as he hefted the second bag into the air and stabbed it, pouring its contents into the can.

"What's your name, my boy?"

"Mi-Mi-Michael," the boy stammered out.

Although he was young, and not quite yet of the age to read subtle social cues, the man's message had landed loud and clear.

"Well, Michael, it's an absolute honor to meet you, again. I am sorry to say that my friend that helped you last time you were here, the big man, do you remember him?"

The boy slowly nodded his head.

"Good. Well, that big man—his name was Izzy. He was huge, and he was powerful, but I'm sad to say that poor Izzy just isn't that bright . . . Sort of like a big dumb bull."

The man smiled at the boy.

"Well, one day, we were leaving for the weekend to go fishing, and Izzy left the gate to the pens open. And, well, I'm sorry to say when we got back, all the goats had run off. It was an unfortunate day. When we got back home a couple days later, we looked all over for them, high and low . . ." The man paused and the smile drained from his face.

"Did . . . Did you find them?" the boy asked hesitantly.

"We did indeed. In a canyon about three miles from here, way up in the hills. And, I am sad to report that they were torn to bits and pieces. It looked like coyotes, or maybe even wolves, had gotten to them. There were scraps of them everywhere.

"Just dried up chunks of brown flesh by that point. Not much left at all, except for their empty, hollowed out carcasses. But of course, there were some clumps of filthy hair here and there, and the dirt was sadly still stained red with their blood. It looked like by the time we got to them—well, what was left of them, I should say, whatever the coyotes or wolves didn't finish off, the birds and insects plucked and scoured from their bones. There, they baked in the sun, bleached white like piano keys."

The man took a step forward and smiled.

"But I want you to know, Michael, that Izzy, the big man, just felt terrible about that. Now, if you don't mind, Michael, I would very much appreciate it if you would go around to the truck, get the chickens, and put them in the coop, please. Can you do that for me now, Michael?"

The man slammed the lid down hard on the galvanized trash can.

Both Michael and Orchid jumped at the loud clattering of metal on metal.

"Ye-Yes, sir!"

The man watched the boy as he ran past him and out of the barn just as fast as his feet could carry him, and turned back to face Orchid, who had her eyes cast down at the dirt floor of the barn.

"I want you to supervise getting all the animals away, and as soon as they're away, you will come back inside. Do you understand?"

Orchid nodded without looking up. Her hands were clasped tightly behind her back, sweaty palms squeezed together, nails digging in.

The man turned and started walking toward the big open doors of the barn, and paused. He looked over his shoulder at Orchid.

"You would do very well not to have any more conversations with Michael or his father . . . Do you understand?"

Orchid nodded once, her eyes never leaving the moist dirt beneath her feet.

As the man left the barn, the goats once again started bleating.

"Three Rivers! He's in Three Rivers!"

Eastman handed Jesse a cup of iced coffee from the Black Cow Café as he opened his eyes and sat up in the bed. She turned and opened the drapes, letting the morning sunshine flood into the room, filling it with warm yellow light and washing over Jesse. The man squinted and forced one eye open as he took his sacred first sip of the dark brown cold brew.

"Where the hell is Three Rivers? I've never heard of it," Jesse mumbled as the caffeine slowly made its way into his bloodstream.

"About three hundred miles north of us. He must have some sort of safe house up there. We have got him on the run!" she stepped onto the bed and started jumping up and down, sending Loki scrambling for the living room and forcing Jesse to get off the mattress or risk spilling his precious coffee. As Eastman jumped, she squealed with manic breathless delight.

"We are going to kill the beast! Kill the beast! Kill the beast!"

With one last jump, she landed on the floor of the room with a bed, and took a big sip from her coffee while she was still panting with excitement.

"Geo sent me his location while I was out getting coffee. He said he would have sent it sooner but wanted to make sure that our bad guy was stationary and parked somewhere for several hours . . . He didn't want to send us on a wild goose chase."

"Great, so what's the plan then, Mel?"

"I want you to get cleaned up, dressed, and ready, my love. I need to go over by my place and get some special tools for tonight . . . I'll be back here in a couple hours, sound fair?"

"Sounds fair to me, babe," Jesse said as he downed three greedy gulps of his iced coffee.

Eastman cocked her head and smiled at Jesse. She took the coffee from his hand and placed it on the dresser.

"Tonight is the night, Jess. Tonight is the night we end this waking nightmare. You will finally, once and for all, have your revenge. You won't have to follow the white rabbit anymore."

Jesse nodded and slowly looked around the room, as if he was still waking up, and took his coffee off the dresser and finished it off.

"I'm going to go and get another one of these. I still feel super out of it."

"You go do that, babe, then get back here and get ready. I'll be back to pick you up at eleven!"

Eastman leaned in and kissed Jesse passionately and ended the kiss with a playful bite to his lower lip.

"See you soon, my love!" And with that, she turned and walked out of the room with a bed, leaving Jesse standing there with his now only ice-filled plastic cup. Jesse looked down at Loki, who had returned to the room and was sitting there, tail wagging, and derping hard. Jesse grinned down at the giant puppy who let out a muffled "oof" under his breath.

Jesse smiled at Loki.

"Laugh it up, fuzzball!"

Jesse put on his jeans and threw on a t-shirt and shoes.

He walked into the living room, and grabbed the keys to his Prius from the key rack by the door and went for a refill of his coffee.

He had the feeling he was going to need it.

BURN THE VVITCHES

Orchid watched the sun dip over the gently rolling green mountains in the distance as they took on a dark purple hue and faded into black at their foothills. The sunset was a brilliant explosion of vibrant color. The wispy stratus clouds hung lazily on the horizon and seemed to glow in a silent dignity as they surrendered to the dying of the light.

As she sat on the corner of the oversized bed, staring at the sunset, Orchid's mind churned. Pondering if this life, this crooked path that she had stumbled on, was indeed hers to take. Somewhere deep in the well of her being, beneath the peaceful ripple-free surface, currents were pulling, tides were forming, and the water in her well had grown bitter and brackish.

"It is time for your spiritual bath."

Orchid looked up to the man who stood in the doorway holding two large one-gallon water jugs.

"Wait here for me until I summon you. I'm going to prepare your bath."

Orchid nodded, and a moment later she heard the sound of old shower knobs squeaking as they were turned on, and seconds after that, the cascading sound of water falling into the tub. The subtle poltergeist-like whispers of steam were already hanging on the ceiling, creeping out into the bedroom, sticking and beading on the old door jamb.

"Come to me, my child."

The man's voice echoed off the old subway tiled walls of the bathroom and followed the steam into the bedroom where Orchid stood waiting. She walked into the bathroom and stood in front of the large old claw foot tub. The water that was pouring out of the shower head was obviously hotter than what people would typically call "comfortable" for a shower. Even though Orchid loved her showers to be hot, she could tell from the rising steam and the heat emanating from the tub, that this water is what most people would consider scalding.

The man smiled down at Orchid and reached to his belt clip, from which he produced a large folding knife. He flipped the knife open, and Orchid's eyes locked onto the glistening blade then back up to the man holding it. He smiled kindly, then in one motion reached the edge up toward her neck. Orchid froze, her eyes still fixated on the man. He placed the knife inside the collar of her dress, and stabbed outward, cutting through the heavy black utilitarian material.

"Be still," he said as he sawed, ripped, and tore through her dress, bringing the knife down the entire length of her body.

The man then pulled the remains of the now tattered textile off of Orchid's shoulders, and let it fall dead on the bathroom floor.

"Get in."

Orchid stepped into the big tub, and immediately her feet were scorched by the water that had been collecting there.

"Arms up."

Orchid raised her arms above her head and clasped them together like she had been trained as the man reached for the removable showerhead, and in broad sweeping motions started soaking Orchid from the top of her head to the bottom of her feet. Her pale porcelain-like skin turned instantly into a bright blotchy red as her heart pumped blood to the surface of her skin, as if the precious fluids inside her were trying to escape her body and the scalding, burning pain. The temperature of the water wasn't the sort that one could become comfortable with, even if one started off at a lower degree, and slowly raised it. No, this was not a frog in a pot situation, this was more a frying pan to the fire.

"Turn."

Orchid turned and the man hosed the liquid fire from the top of Orchid's head down onto her back. He let the jet of water linger over the scabbed brand on her back, and Orchid watched as chunks of the dried blood mixed with fresh and started making tiny splashes in the searing water that was now up to her ankles in the tub below.

But Orchid didn't seem to care or even notice the red-orange-yellow-white flashes of boiling pain that were coursing and crashing through her nervous system, attacking her brain, and begging for a flight or fight response.

Since she was instructed to turn around, her eyes were fixed out the window. She was somewhere in the far outreaches of the horizon, somewhere in one of those dark mountainous valleys, somewhere in those woods, somewhere that was nowhere near the scalding water and bits of flaked off scab floating around her feet.

Somewhere else.

She was pulled back into her body by the squeal of the shower being shut off.

Orchid stood, looking down at her feet that were now the same color as the sunset she had witnessed only minutes ago. Even though she was back in the bathroom, standing naked in the tub, she noted, almost curiously, that there was no pain anymore, just a dull, blunt thudding tingle somewhere deep inside her.

But that moment of peaceful serenity suddenly deliquesced into a shocking stinging pain as the man standing behind her dumped the entirety of one of the gallons of ice-cold water onto her naked body. The extreme of going from Hades hot to Klondike cold glitched Orchid's nervous system, causing her to instinctively cover her breasts as she wrapped her arms around her body, trying to shield herself from the shock of it all.

A moment later, the smell and burning set in.

Orchid looked down to see that now in the nearly drained out tub, there were flower petals, and bits of leaves and organic matter in the pungent water that was swimming around her feet.

"I am sure this isn't pleasant for you, my child, but this is what needs to be done to prepare you for tonight."

Orchid's teeth clinched and chattered, and she hugged herself tighter, trying to extinguish the rattling that was quaking deep within her.

"Turn."

Orchid slowly turned to face him, taking tiny steps in the slippery tub. He stared down at Orchid, locking eyes with her. He broke the gaze and glanced to her arms until she lowered them by her sides. He picked up the second jug of water and unscrewed the cap. Orchid looked at the clear jug that looked like the kind of big water bottle you buy at a gas station while you're on a road trip. She could see flower pedals and other bits of organic items that she couldn't identify floating about in it.

"What is that, my Pedagogue?"

"This is called a 'spiritual bath,' little one. It is made to not only cleanse your body but also remove any—how shall I put this? *Unwanted* energy from you . . . It is quite simple, really. I took the water from the river that flows around the Sanctuary. Do you remember that little bridge we walked over when we pulled up here?"

Orchid turned her eyes from the bottle he was holding, looked up to the man, and nodded her head.

"I took water from there, that is why it is so cold, but it is important to the process. The flowers and herbs you see floating in the water, I gathered here locally also."

"It smells strong," Orchid whimpered as he started slowly pouring the second gallon of water over her head, letting it cascade down her body.

"That is the perfume that you're smelling, my child, and that is also why it stings."

As the last bit of water hit the bottom of the tub, Orchid stood there shaking the last shivers off her body.

"Don't move."

The man went and grabbed a fresh white towel off the rack handed it to Orchid.

"Pat yourself dry with this, please."

Orchid nodded and started gently patting herself down with the fluffy white towel, and she motioned as if she was going to step out of the tub.

"No, not yet."

The man motioned for the towel, taking it from Orchid, and placed it on the floor of the bathroom, almost like a mat in front of the tub.

"Stay."

He walked into the bedroom and returned with a brown grocery bag. He set it down in front of the tub and handed Orchid a white pair of panties.

"Put these on."

"While I'm still in the tub?" Orchid asked sheepishly as she looked up to the man. The expression on his face told her the answer to her question, and slowly, carefully, one leg at a time, she slipped on the plain cotton white panties.

He then reached into the bag again and handed Orchid a light flowy white garment.

"Put this on now."

Orchid slipped the white cotton dress over her head, and let it fall nearly to her ankles. She was grateful that the water had now made its way down the drain.

The man offered Orchid his hand, and she carefully stepped out of the large claw foot tub and onto the folded white towel on the floor.

He kneeled and went back into the bag, producing a pair of heavy white pantyhose. He carefully rolled them up to the toe and motioned of Orchid to place her foot in. He helped her get both feet in, and pulled them up to her knees, allowing her to finish the task, and make them comfortable on herself.

He then produced a brand-new pair of everyday white shoes. He tenderly helped Orchid slide a foot into each, then went back into the bag and pulled out a large white headscarf.

"Hold this, please, and turn."

Orchid took the headscarf as directed and turned around, once again facing outside the window.

She could see the man's reflection in the now dark window as he turned around and walked over to the vanity, opening one of its drawers and pulling something out of it. She felt the man approach her from behind and gather up her long, wet locks of blue-black hair, high up on the crown of her head, and pulled it close to her skull.

Orchid stood frozen and let out a tight gasp as she felt and heard the sharp *Snip! Snip! Snip!* of shears cutting through her wrist-thick ponytail-worth of hair. The man quickly placed the severed locks into the brown paper bag. He then scooped up the tattered dress laying on the floor beside Orchid, and in a flash, shoved it into the bag, then crumpled it up quickly and sealed it as if it was toxic waste. The man then grabbed one of the nearly empty gallon water jugs and poured the small amount of remaining liquid onto his hands while over the tub, scrubbing veraciously while whispering in a language that Orchid didn't recognize under this breath.

The man then reached around Orchid and gently took the headscarf from her hands.

He whispered under his breath again, and he tied it tightly around her head, giving it almost the appearance of a turban. He then took Orchid lightly by her shoulders and turned her to face the mirror in the bathroom. She stood there staring at herself, although she looked nothing like . . . herself. Not only was she wearing white, but to be just wearing white, from head to toe, made her feel ugly, stripped down, and torn. It felt like when he cut off her hair, he also had cut off the last stings of identity that she had for her own.

Her eyes turned in the mirror to the man still standing behind her, he smiled warmly to her reflection and said, "There, how do you feel?"

Orchid forced a smile and nodded. The man then grabbed the paper bag off the floor and turned as he started walking out of the bathroom door.

"I am going to go bury this rubbish in the backyard. Prepare some tea. We are in for a long night."

Orchid smiled again and gave the nod as he walked out of the bathroom. She looked at the new "herself" in the mirror, and a voice, a voice somewhere in the back of her mind, echoed, just above a whisper, *You can always go home.*

Jesse reached for the volume knob and turned down Taylor Swift's "Stay, Stay, Stay" as Eastman changed lanes and started up the 5 freeway, heading over the "grapevine." She shot him a sideways dagger glance as she was forced to stop singing along to the cute-bubblegum anthem.

"So, what's the plan?"

They had been riding for the last ninety minutes in silence. Well, not really silence, but the Apple music playlist that Eastman had created for long drives she took while out in the field. Loud music always helped her think. As she would go over bridges and expressways, overpasses and tunnels, the music always helped keep her centered, focused. As the mile markers passed, her mind would be traveling also—deep into the realms of potentials and possibilities. It was almost like she was somewhere else, off in the ether, just passing through, just stopping by to say hello to the intertwining elegance of the universe.

"The plan?" She shook her head. "The plan is we go in, and hopefully make it out alive."

Jesse smirked and unzipped a little bag between his feet, pulling out his Glock 19. "This guy makes me feel a little better about our chances."

Eastman looked down at the gun that Jesse was holding between his knees and put her eyes back on the road.

"No guns."

Eastman changed lanes and merged into the carpool lane as the big black SUV stabbed northbound up the steep incline of the 5 freeway heading toward Pyramid Lake.

"What do you mean no guns? What are we supposed to do, use harsh language?"

She gave Jesse another sideways glance and sighed. "You didn't listen to anything I told you about him, did you, babe?"

Jesse placed the sleek, black, stippled Glock back into the bag with a chuckle while he zipped it back up.

"Yeah, you mean how back in the 1980's he used his Jedi mind trick superpowers to make a team of deep state government assassins kill each other? Yeah, I was listening, sounded totally tubular, dude! That was, what, thirty-five years ago? That was then, this is now. Now he's a weak old man, and I have a gun. To be honest, I'm not at all worried about some 'voodoo-hoodoo-folklore-gibberish.' He needs to worry about me."

Jesse looked over to Eastman and laughed.

She shot him back a side-eye.

"Like my man Han said, 'Hokey religions and ancient weapons are no substitute for a good blaster at your side.' Boom-boom." Jesse made his fingers into a gun and pointed them down the road and gave Eastman a sly wink. "A simple double-tap to the back of his head, then off we go to the Winchester, have a nice cold pint, and wait for this all to blow over. How's that for a slice of fried gold?"

Jesse had no time to react as Eastman pulled the steering wheel of her big black SUV hard to the right, causing the truck to swerve violently, cutting across five lanes of traffic, nearly causing two accidents before coming to a screeching, dusty halt on the dirt and rock shoulder of the freeway. Before Jesse could say *"What the fuck?"* the truck was in park, her seatbelt was off, her door was flung open, and she was on his side of the car. She threw his door open, grabbed him by his collar, and effortlessly yanked Jesse out of the SUV and using speed, strength, leverage, and technique that could only be described as a blur of gravitational elemental force, threw him onto the ground.

"Is that what you think? Because if that's what you think, let me help save you some time!"

Eastman reached into the still open passenger side of the SUV and grabbed Jesse's gun bag and threw it into the shrubs that lined the freeway.

"If you think we are going to just walk in there and handle this like some sort of Seal Team Six strike force mission, you might as well unzip that bag, shoot me in the face, and then do yourself, because I can assure you, that plan right there is going to be about as successful as your macho Han Solo bullshit. As a matter of fact, he would enjoy that. You want to really make his day? Go up to his place, kick in his door, and see what happens. Not only would he manhandle you like you were a child, but if you went in 'guns a' blaze'n,' that would be the perfect opportunity for him to eat us alive—literally."

Jesse picked himself and his bag off the ground and dusted himself off.

"We have to go in claws sharp and whisper quiet, Jesse. And we have to pray. I have a couple tricks up my sleeve that will help block him from feeling our energy, and I really hope it works. I really hope that he doesn't sense us coming. Because if he catches wind of us, if he has the slightest idea that he is being hunted, we won't stand a chance. He will kill us, Jess, and he will have a great time doing it. Then he will just disappear into the country again and go off grid. Only to pick up where he left off in a year or so, praying on a whole new batch of poor fucked up girls. Is that what you want? Or do you want to have the slightest chance of pulling this off? This is for Dani, for Judy, for Jaycee, and for Katia!"

Eastman sighed and looked off to the setting sun in the west and shook her head.

"Or did they all die for nothing?" She held up her perfectly manicured index finger. She was no longer yelling, but Jesse hung on every word.

"We only get one shot at him, Jess. One. And I don't know about you, but I want—I need—this one shot to be a fucking center mass, on target, bullseye. This didn't start with Katia. What happened to her was tragic, but she wasn't the first. I have been following his trail of dead and putting the pieces of this puzzle together for years. And I won't let him slip through my fingers this time . . .

"This could be our last chance to end this cycle of nightmares. Because, and I know you don't want to hear this, but Katia got off lucky. She wasn't brought in, consumed, and destroyed over months and years of ritual abuse. She still had light left in her when she died. I don't believe that, Jesse, I know it. Be grateful that she wasn't put through the grinder, only to be sold off to God knows who after he had squeezed every drop of goodness out of her. Before he used every spark of life left in her up to feed his own selfish motives and further his agenda. She was saved from all of that."

Eastman walked up to Jesse, and gently placed her hands on his face, staring deep into his hazel eyes.

"So please, you're going to have to trust me on this one, Jesse. I don't want to lose you, and we can't fail now. We haven't come this far to only come this far."

Jessed nodded, embraced her, and watched as the sun dipped below the jagged peaks of the mountains to the west. Eastman kissed him gently on his forehead and held his face for one more moment.

"Let's get back in the truck, we have work to do . . ."

FALL OF ROME

Sometimes even to live is an act of courage.

—Lucius Annaeus Seneca

Eastman pulled off the dark, lonely country road and parked the black SUV. They sat in the moon cast shadows of oak trees listening to the ticks and tocks of the engine as it cooled down from the long, exhaustive journey north, deep into the central valley. What the locals there proudly referred to as the "gateway to the Sequoias."

"Where the hell are we now?" Jesse asked as he opened the door to the SUV and stepped out of the car, taking a much-deserved stretch. He rolled his neck, loosening up the muscles in his back, feeling and hearing a satisfying *pop* as he flexed and exhaled deeply.

"His last location beacon is about three miles east of us."

Eastman pointed to the hills behind Jesse, and he turned to look at the darkened mountains.

"So, now we hike our way in." Eastman got out of the truck and walked around to the back of the SUV, opening the liftgate. Jesse walked around to the end of the truck, joining her, and watched as she pulled two large black duffle bags to the edge of the trunk, inspected them, handed him one, then took the other and threw it over her shoulder.

Jesse took his bag. It was heavy, but not overly so, and with a grunt, he hefted it over his shoulder and closed the SUV's lift gate.

"Lead the way, boss," Jesse said as he motioned to the dark foreboding hills. Eastman raised an eyebrow and smiled as she turned and started making her way to the base of the mountain while Jesse followed closely behind.

Orchid stood out in the pasture of the Sanctuary next to the stacked cages filled with chickens and watched as the man draped in long black robes put a torch to the massive pile of kerosene-soaked wood. Crowning the collection was a large, almost scarecrow-looking, humanoid figure crafted out of rags, branches, hay, twine, and sticks.

The man's voice boomed and echoed through the canyons of the valleys surrounding the Sanctuary as he called out, "Behold, the effigy of this, our enemy, is carried hither for our ancient rites."

The pile of deadwood immediately took lite. Wisps of fire swirled and entangled themselves in the monolithic stack of kindling. As the flames grew in strength, they reached skyward, consuming and enveloping the human-like avatar, turning it into a sparking, popping pillar of crimson.

Orchid could immediately feel the radiant heat from the bonfire warm her face as the silhouette of the man standing between her and the inferno flickered and gleamed in the darkness.

She glanced over to the goats, that were tied to a stout stake thrust into the earth. They bleated nervously as they paced back and forth, going only as far as their leashes would allow them. Orchid looked back to the man; the glow of the fire made his shadow grow long. It reached out, and touched, and danced upon her feet.

The man, shrouded in his flowing black robes, raised his head, arms, and voice to the heavens.

"The owl is in his leafy temple; let all within this place be reverent before him! Lift up your heads, O ye Trees, and be ye lift up ye ever-living spires! For behold, here is Moloch's Shrine, and holy are the pillars of this house! Weaving spiders dare come not here!"

The pyre exploded as if reacting to the man's cry.

Cinders and sparks shot up, wafted, and danced with the smoke that was arching toward the sky, only to blink out like fireflies as they succumbed to the soft breeze and darkness of the fresh night air.

The man then pulled what looked like a large piece of chalk from an inner pocket of his robe.

He knelt down a few feet from the fire and drew a circle six feet in diameter onto the hard-packed earth. Orchid watched as the man continued to etch and inscribe the design of white into the ground. He was soon finished, and he stepped back and seemed to be admiring his handiwork. Then, without so much as looking over his shoulder, he called out into the night, "Orchid, the chickens!"

The girl in white picked up two of the large wire cages that held two chickens each and deliberately, yet slowly, walked toward the man and the fire. She placed the two cages at his feet and returned to where she was initially standing to bring back the third.

By the time she had returned, the man had placed four white candles at the north, south, east, and west directions of the circle. He pulled a lighter and handed it to Orchid.

"You must light the way, my child. You are the beacon, and I am the vessel."

Orchid lit each candle, starting with the one in the east and ending with the north. She wasn't unfamiliar with the use of candles in her Pedagogue's rituals, however, this one—this ceremony already felt different from the ones she had helped him conduct in the past.

She watched as the man in black approached her, carrying a large ornately carved wooden box and placed it at her feet.

"Please, remove your shoes and hose."

Orchid slipped off the everyday white shoes and her pantyhose, placing them beside the circle.

He then took Orchid's hand, and gently directed her into the center of the sigil he had cut into the earth.

The man walked over to one of the cages where two of the six chickens huddled together silently. It was almost like the animals were hoping that if they remained quiet, they would be overlooked and forgotten. Their luck didn't hold out as the man flung the door to the cage open and reached into the cage. He grabbed the first chicken by its feet, and then the second. The two birds screeched as he ripped them from the cage, swinging them violently through the air by their taloned feet.

"Arms to your side, my child."

The girl in white held her arms to her side as the man approached her. He took care not to enter the sigil on the ground, but instead, reached over and swept the girl's body with the live, flustered chickens as if he was brushing her clean with the bird's feathers.

Orchid kept perfectly still, trying as hard as she could not to flinch from the flurry of beating wings and feathers thrashing against her. She watched the man, his lips were moving, whispering out words she couldn't understand, speaking a long-dead language that was only meant to be expressed in the dark.

He circled Orchid, still 'cleaning' her with the now thoroughly distressed birds. As he circled, his whispers grew louder, from barely audible to just below a yell, repeating the same sentence over and over. The intensity increased to a fever pitch, and as he rounded the circle for the final time, the man swung one of the chickens up to his face, catching the terrified fowl's head between his teeth.

The man bit down hard until his teeth connected, and with a savage, disgusting rip, the chicken's head was suddenly free from its body. Orchid watched as the poor animal's wings started furiously flapping and fluttering wildly with what were now, of course, strictly residual nerve impulses. The man spit the severed head at the girl's feet, and in a fluid motion repeated the same vicious procedure with the second bird.

The man in black held the two birds' bodies upright by their necks as they shook and convulsed in his grip. He looked the girl in white in her eyes and whispered to her, *"Sicut superius et inferius."*

Orchid nodded, she extended her right arm from her side and pointed her right index toward the sky, with her other arm, she pointed down and slightly out to her side.

The man turned the birds' bodies over, and like dumping out two full bottles of wine, the still-warm blood from the birds spilled, splashed, and pooled at Orchid's feet. She felt a rush of power wash over her like a wave. It started as a tingle in her toes that almost felt like the onset of pins and needles. Soon that tingle turned into a vibration, a delicious electrostatic kinetic energy that started from the earth to her pelvis. It came in from the crown of her head also, meeting in the middle of her body, surrounding, enveloping, and exploding outward from her heart. Orchid's arms started shaking. She had never felt so present, so awake, so—so alive.

"Breathe, my child."

Orchid took a deep breath in and exhaled. She felt like she was breathing in cosmos and breathing out stardust infused with the gentle feminine energy of the universe.

The man's heavy black robes fluttered as he spun and grabbed the other two cages of chickens and walked them over to the Orchid, who was still in her position, breathing deeply.

The man pulled the door open to the cage, and pulled out one of the chickens that were huddled in the far corner. Then, he reached in the cage again and grabbed the other. The two birds flapped and fought, but they never had a chance. The man muttered under his breath and cleanly took their heads off one by one with his teeth, and just as before, drained them at Orchid's feet. The rush of energy that had not surrendered nor subsided from before only became more intense as the ripples of power coursed and flowed through her veins while weaving and intertwining with her very soul.

Orchid looked down to the earth below her feet. The puddle of blood she was standing in almost had the appearance that it was bubbling, boiling. The ground was packed so hard that it was nearly stone, so not much, if any, of the blood had been soaked up by the soil. The pebbles that surrounded the blood seemed to be shimmering, quivering as if they were reacting in rhythm to the energy that was flowing from within her, from without her.

Orchid and the Pedagogue locked eyes and held each other's gaze.

"Only now are you starting to understand what is inside you, aren't you, my child?"

Orchid lowered her chin without breaking her stare, and her lips pulled back into an almost animal-like drunken grin and hissed, "Yesssssssss."

Her voice sounded primal, primitive, like steam escaping from a rusty pipe.

The man walked over to the goats that were huddled together in a tight pile, pulling against the heavy stake that anchored them to the hardened earth. He untied the largest of the four and walked it over to the woman in white. The goat was fat and black with white blotches on his back.

Orchid smiled down at the animal, reached out with one of her delicate tapered fingers, and caressed his rough, short-haired face. She let her fingers glide from between the animal's eyes and dance up to the tips his boney horns.

The man bent down and opened the ornately carved wooden box beside him and produced a large athame and held it to the animal's throat.

"Wait . . ."

The man looked up at Orchid, and she reached down again to the animal and placed her hand gently, lovingly on the side of its head.

"One last caress," Orchid whispered as the animal looked up to her with its stupid yellow eyes. At that moment, Orchid felt as though they were sharing a moment of communion. An unspoken communication. A bond. A silent pact.

Orchid giggled as the man scooped up the goat, put the athame to its throat, and in three transverse sawing motions cut so deep that it nearly decapitated the animal. He grabbed the goat's head as its eyes rolled back and pulled its chin straight up and back, breaking the goat's neck and exposing the severed arteries. The man in black then hoisted the quivering animal onto his shoulders, allowing the spurting shower of thick, red blood to soak Orchid from head to toe.

For a moment, Orchid felt nothing but a thick, sticky warmth as she was coated with a cloudburst of the bounty from the slain goat's neck. Then at once, the warm turned to a hot burn as energy erupted like a Caldera volcano inside of her. No more tingles; this was angry, violent, and shattering. Like being plugged directly into a tectonic plate or dipped into the main reactor of a power plant. This was war.

Orchid screamed and pulled the wrap off her head. She clawed and slashed at her clothes, ripping them off. They fell to her feet. The energy seemed to suck inward and destabilize as she fought her body to get it back into position, back into *Sicut superius et inferius.* As above, so below.

As soon as she locked her arms in place, the energy boomeranged back, crashing into her. Orchid had the sensation of being lifted off the ground like she was in the wave pool at the water park her and her friends would go play at when she was a kid. The waves came rolling in, bringing her up, and back down, and up, and back down. She forced her eyes open. She felt the sting of blood and taste of copper. She looked down at her nearly naked, blood-soaked body. Her feet were on pointe like a ballerina. But then again, no . . . They were off the earth, not too far, maybe an inch or two, but she was floating.

She looked up from her feet to see the man in black staring at her. His eyes were wide, and his mouth gaped open. He dropped the goat to her feet. She closed her eyes and swam deeper into the energy that surrounded her.

She let herself drown.

She was nature. She was good. She was evil. She was black. She was white. She was yin. She was yang. She was elemental.

She was.

Her body slowly floated down to earth and settled. And even though her eyes were still closed, she was awake, aware, and ready for anything. If someone were to look at her, they could have easily mistaken her for a predatory cat.

"My—My child?"

Orchid's eyes flipped open. They seem to have a faint blue glow to them, not unlike the eye shine you would see if a deer was standing by the side of the road and your headlights illuminated it.

Orchid just breathed slowly in and out, in and out, in and out. Her eyes fixated on the man in black.

She lowered her head again, and while looking at him from over under her brow, hissed, *"More."*

The man smiled and wiped the still bloody blade on his heavy vantablack robe.

Orchid cocked her head back and let out a scream that was more like the howl of an animal than that of a woman. The howl of triumph, the howl of a successful hunt. The howl of intercourse intertwining woman and nature.

Jesse and Eastman just crossed over the ridge when a howl stopped them dead in their tracks. She saw Jesse's face grimace in the pale moonlight as the haunting wail poured over the ridge above them, swept down to them, and swirled around them like a poltergeist.

"Was—Was that a wolf?"

"Let's just keep going. I hope we're not too late . . ." Eastman readjusted the large duffle bag that was over her shoulder, and they trudged along, making their way up the last switchback to the crest of the small mountain. She crouched down low, almost to a squat as they neared the precipice. She turned and whispered to Jesse,

"Okay, as soon as we get over, we don't linger on the ridge. We get the military crest as soon as we can."

"The what?"

"Just follow me, and do as I do."

Eastman crept over the ridge and immediately went down several feet and found a small plateau with good tree cover before she stood to her full height, Jesse followed and mimed her motions.

"If we stood on the ridge, we could have been seen. Now we are pretty much invisible. The Romans knew this, that's why this is called the 'military crest'; it's the only way to move over mountains or hills without being seen."

Eastman and Jesse turned as another wailing howl echoed in the cold dark air. They peered from behind a large pine and looked down into the valley below, and there between two buildings, they could see what looked like a giant bonfire and two figures silhouetted by the flames.

"We have to hurry. There isn't much time left!"

Eastman unzipped the duffle bag she had placed on the moist earth, pulled out a small flashlight, and clicked it on. The beam was red and dim. She put the small torch between her teeth and held it there, casting haunting faint purple shadows on the ground beneath her. She then pulled out a small water bottle, a Ziplock bag, and what looked like a paintbrush from the tactical kit.

Jesse watched Eastman's shoulders working in the dim red glow as she dumped a small amount of water into the plastic bag that looked to be filled with loose black powder. She then took the bamboo ink brush and started stirring the contents of the bag until it had the look of mud. Eastman turned her head and pulled the small light out from between her teeth. Without looking at the man behind her, she whispered, "Take off your shirt, Jess, now."

Jesse peeled off the black thermal he was wearing without questioning why and stood still, staring at the figures at the bottom of the valley. Eastman turned and stood in front of him, looking up to him.

"You're not worried about that light?" Jesse whispered as he looked down at Eastman dipping the brush back into the concoction and stirring it quickly.

"No, humans can't see the red wavelength from this distance, especially if it's this dim."

"Since when are we hunting humans?" Jesse said with a smirk that quickly faded as the cold, wet brush loaded with mud made contact with his bare chest.

"What are you doing?" Jesse watched as Eastman frantically, yet meticulously, painted unfamiliar designs all over his chest.

"Arms up, babe."

Jesse raised his arms over his head, and she continued to scribe sigils and symbols all over his already heavily tattooed body. She moved like music, like poetry, as she worked. Re-dipping the brush with every new design, whispering a language under her breath that Jesse couldn't identify. She circled him, anointing him, covering him from his muscular chest and soft belly, to his broad shoulders and wide tapered back, down to the belt line of his black jeans.

Eastman whispered secret incantations as she finished the circle and stood in front of the man before her.

She reached out and traced around his flesh with a fingernail as she blew on the drying, hardening mud. She smiled as Jesse's skin turned to gooseflesh under her breath and at how his muscles quivered under her touch.

"Almost done, my love. Close your eyes."

Eastman dipped the brush into the bag one last time, loading it thick with the earthy black pigment.

"This should help protect you from him, somewhat" She painted a thick vertical black line from Jesse's forehead to his chin, then a horizontal line across his eyes and the bridge of his nose, giving his face the look of a Templar. Without saying a word, Eastman embraced Jesse, kissing him deeply. She clicked off the dim red light and placed a hand on his cheek. She whispered to him, "If we don't make it out of here alive, I wanted to say thank you. Thank you for everything."

Jesse started to speak, and she raised her index finger to his lips. They stood silently for that moment in the wash of the pale moon and the shadows of the branches of the trees above them.

"The place is here. The time is now."

Without saying another word, without taking another breath, Eastman turned and put the now sealed Ziplock bag and brush back into her duffle, zipped it up, then she hoisted it over her shoulder.

She started making her way down the mountain toward the two buildings, toward the two shadowy figures, toward the screams, toward the fire.

THE RED GIRL

When life is victorious, there is birth; when it is thwarted, there is death. A warrior is always engaged in a life-and-death struggle for Peace.

—Morihei Ueshiba

Eastman stopped dead in her tracks as they reached the base of the mountain. She froze and held her hand back to Jesse in the "stop" position. She stood like a statue. Her head cocked to the side as if she was feeling, sensing every molecule of air that surrounded them. Jesse took a step forward so he was right behind the still frozen woman, and whispered, "What is it?"

"We're not alone . . ."

Eastman then ran off the path and into the woods. Jesse watched as she moved. It was as if she had turned into a shadow, a wraith. She didn't seem to make a sound; there wasn't so much as the crinkling of a leaf or a snap of a twig as she ran like a deer through the deadfall of the oaks and pines that surrounded them and doubled back the way they came. Jesse turned his attention to the two figures at the bonfire. He watched from the sheltered safety of the tree line as the man seemed to be scooping up something from the ground and holding it over the other smaller figure that Jesse could only assume was a woman standing still by the fire. Their outlines were just wavy silhouettes in the wash of heat from the fire and the darkness.

And that's when Jesse felt the barrel of a gun against the back of his head.

And in a calm, measured, almost casual speaking tone, he heard a man's voice in the darkness, "Put your hands behind your back. *Now*, asshole."

Jesse felt the clink and suffocating squeeze of handcuffs being placed on his right wrist as his arm was pulled behind his back. A moment later, his left hand was incapacitated with the bite of the chrome plated shackles, and brought behind his back also. The *click-click-clicking* sounded as the cuffs went tight and dug into the bones of his wrists.

The next thing Jesse knew, his knees were kicked out from under him, and he was on his belly face down in the dirt, a knee weighing heavy on the center of his spine.

"Where is she? What have you done with Melantha?"

The next thing Jesse heard was a heavy thud, and the pressure of dead weight as the man's body fell on top of him, nearly knocking the wind out of him. A moment later, Jesse felt the weight being rolled off, and he could sense Eastman was standing over him and the unknown gunman.

"Goddammit, Amador!" she hissed under her breath as she helped the big sheriff to his feet. The anger and frustration on her face were palpable, even in the near total darkness that the canopy of the forest provided.

"What the fuck are you doing here? And for God sakes, *keep your voice down!*"

"I'm sorry, ma'am. I have been following, following you and Jesse for weeks. I was watching your six, ma'am. I just thought that—"

"Thought what? That he killed his wife, and I was next?"

"Yes, ma'am, I thought he had taken you up here to kill you. I parked and tracked you up the hill. When I heard that scream, I thought . . ."

"Who else knows you're here?"

"Only Vic, ma'am. She knows that I'm watching over you. She is worried about you, too."

"So not even Durazo? Nobody else?"

"No, ma'am."

Another howling scream pierced through the darkness and both Amador and Eastman turned to face the direction it came from.

"What the fuck is that?"

"That's the sound of the beast, Amador. That's who we have been hunting all along."

"I'm calling this in."

Amador reached into his pocket and pulled out his cell phone. But as soon as he did, Eastman snatched it from his hands, turned it off, and slid it into the back pocket of her jeans.

"I have been working on this far too long and hard to have the LASD fuck it up for me now."

Eastman paused and considered. "You have been tailing Jesse and me for weeks?"

"Yes, ma'am."

"You're good, Amador, I'll give you that."

"Little help?" Jesse moaned as he spat leaves from his mouth and attempted to roll onto his back.

"For God sakes, get him up, and get those cuffs off of him."

Amador helped Jesse to his feet and removed the now very sore handcuffs. Jesse stretched out and rubbed his aching wrists as Amador leaned in and whispered to him, "I guess I owe you an apology, again . . . I'm sorry for all you've been through, and I'm sorry I blamed you for your wife. I can't imagine what that must have been like for you . . . And the last thing you needed was me giving you shit. Can you forgive me, Jesse?"

Amador reached out his hand, and Jesse stared at it for a moment that was longer than it needed to be before he reached out, taking Amador's hand in his, and shaking it while matching Amador's squeeze.

"Yeah, sure. Thanks. Let's see if I ever feed Leah Dog again for you."

Jesse's eyes darted from Amador to Eastman. He could tell she was trying to figure out how to finish their task with this third wheel in the mix. She was pacing back and forth silently in the dark. Her hands were on her hips, and her eyes were fixated on the bonfire in the distance—so close, yet so far. Finally, she approached the two men.

"Okay, Amador, here is the situation, full disclosure. That man there . . ."

Melantha pointed to the bonfire. "That man right there is responsible for the known murders of at least two dozen women and girls over the last fifteen years. Not to mention the kidnapping and trafficking of countless other women and children—some as young as ten—over that same period. I have been tracking him for nearly as long as I have been on the job. He is my ultimate prize."

She poked Amador hard in his chest and seethed as she whispered with venom, "And you will not fuck this up for me. So, either you walk away, go back the way you came, and forget you ever saw us here, *or* you help us finish the job my way . . . Do you copy that, Marine?"

Jesse's jaw dropped. He couldn't believe what he was hearing. He hadn't come all this way to have his revenge—Katia's revenge—slip through his fingers like sand through an hourglass. He stood there speechless in the moonlight.

Eastman picked up on the tension pouring out of him and glanced over to Jesse, then her eyes flicked back to Amador.

"But I need you to listen to me, Marine, and you listen good: this isn't about the law here. This is about justice. When you were in Afghanistan, did you do everything by the book? I expect an honest answer from you, Marine."

Amador's back stiffened as he looked over Eastman and to the bonfire as if he recalled some distant memory he had tried hard to repress. "No, ma'am, we did not . . ."

Eastman leaned in close and whispered almost sweetly to

Amador, "Why was that exactly, Marine?"

"Because we just wanted to make it out of there and make it home alive. We had to do what we had to do, ma'am . . . We had to do what we had to do . . ."

Eastman turned and stood by Amador's side, facing the fire.

"And that's where we are now, Marine. We are now at war, a spiritual war. And that over there, that is our battlefield, our Afghanistan. We have to do what we have to do . . ."

She turned to Amador and looked down to his service weapon and put out her hand. "Give me your weapon, Amador. It won't help you out there."

"Ma'am?"

"That's an order, Marine."

Amador pulled the weapon out of his holster and handed it over to her.

She dropped the magazine and slipped it into her back pocket next to Amador's phone. Eastman then quietly racked the weapon, ejecting the round that was in the chamber, and threw it into the inches deep deadfall that made up the forest floor. She presented the weapon back to Amador. He took it and slipped it back into his holster, locking it in tight.

Eastman walked over and picked up the two duffle bags. She handed one to Jesse, then threw the other over her shoulder. She looked over to Amador and gave him a wink.

"You ready to get back on the battlefield, Marine?"

Amador looked down to Eastman and smiled. "Hoorah, ma'am, Hoorah."

Eastman looked up at Jesse and threw a gentle elbow into his ribs.

"Here, you're going to need this . . ." she unzipped the duffle bag and pulled out what looked like a wrapped-up towel. She dropped to a knee and, with her eyes cast down, presented it to Jesse. Amador watched as Jesse reached down and took the item from her, and as soon as he did, he felt the weight of it.

He knew it was a sword—the same sword she had mounted in her office. He gently unwrapped it. The hilt, a simple carved figure of a woman, her head, the pommel. Jesse pulled it from its scabbard. The short double-edged blade glistened in the moonlight. It almost seemed to glow from the lunar night-fire as Jesse felt its perfectly balanced weight in his hands.

"Her name—the *sword's* name is 'Fhírinne.' She is very old and was given to me by a survivor of the Pedagogue's abuse. I promised her that one day I would catch up to him, that I would defeat him. I thought you, in this time and in this place, have more right to wield her than I do."

Jesse slid the blade back into its scabbard. It seemed to become one solid piece as it clicked into place. He held it firmly to his side.

"Are you ready to face him?"

Jesse looked from Eastman to the bonfire. He paused. The flames in the far-off distance danced and glowed, reaching to the heavens that were sprinkled with the light of a million glittering stars.

"This is for Katia."

Eastman nodded and got down low to the ground as they started making their way to the barn, to the fire, to their destiny.

Orchid swelled and soared with orgasmic, ecstatic, esoteric power.

She looked down at her feet. Around one of her ankles were the torn, plain, formally white but now red panties.

The drained lifeless bodies of three goats and six chickens littered the inside of the chalk circle, which was now just an ocean of blood.

She felt as if she was about to take off and fly, or rather, the feeling may have been more akin to feeling that, any moment, great claw-tipped leathery wings could rip through the skin of her back.

Not a patch of her milky white skin was visible anymore. She was caked, cracked, and covered from head to toe in thick, nearly dried blood.

Orchid looked down at her hands, which to her, in this state of dark euphoria, looked more like the claws of a raccoon. She flexed, chunks of the blood cracked and flaked off her fingers and fell onto the carcasses at her feet.

But as she flexed, as she squeezed, she felt the power flow. She suddenly thought of ocean waves crashing onto a rocky shore, then the water receding, pulling back, then gathering its power once again, colliding onto the beach. When she flexed her hands into fists, the tides pulled out. When she opened them, the waves crashed.

The man in black stood before her, his billowy hood and robe gently flapped in the cold, steady breeze that blew in from the west and fanned the flames of the fire, which was still burning brightly behind him and the girl.

The red girl.

"One last goat to drain, my child, and you will be ready for your assentation."

The man turned and walked over to the last remaining goat that was tethered to the stake. He paused and looked down at it. The animal was asleep, curled up in a tiny ball. It was young, just above what you could call a kid. The goat was solid white. Not a speck or fleck of color anywhere on its body. Its eyes were a pleasant light shade of pink, the same color as the inside of its ears and tummy. The man scooped up the doeling and walked back to the red girl.

The doeling goat was just starting to wake up as the man arrived in front of the red girl. Orchid looked down at it, and the animal opened its eyes and looked up to her. It almost seemed to smile at her.

Orchid reached out to the man, in a motion to hand her the

goat, and he pulled back and drew the athame from his belt. The man started chanting, and circling the red girl, with each orbit, his chanting grew louder and more intense. As the man in black circled once again, the red girl reached out for the doeling that was now bleating for her, as if it knew at a primal, instinctual level that it was in danger.

The man took half a step back and continued circling, his chant now just below a yell and reaching a manic fever pitch. As he passed behind her, the red girl looked down at her hands, her claws, and flexed them tightly. She felt the waves of power pulling, rushing back inside her and gathering strength. She was quivering with cosmic dark matter.

The man rounded the sigil for the last time and stood before Orchid. He tucked the baby under his arm and raised its head to the stars, exposing its neck to the red girl. With his other hand, he started raising the athame to the doeling's throat. He looked up to the heavens.

At that moment, the white goat and the red girl again locked eyes.

She thrust her hands toward the man in black and opened them. The rush of energy that had been pulled back—collecting and churning inside her like a whirlpool—exploded outward in a torrent of energy. The goat was pulled, catapulted from the man in black's arms, and safely into hers.

She held the animal close. It was still trembling from terror. They locked eyes again, and the red girl felt nothing but a wave of loving gratitude pouring out from the very soul of that living, breathing creature and into her. The red girl didn't see the physical animal she was holding, but rather the pure raw energy from which it was made, from which everything was made.

They bonded while standing still in those seconds that could have been a lifetime on some other planet.

The red girl looked to the man and smiled. A real smile. Probably the first genuine smile she could remember.

The man in black smiled back at her. He then raised his left hand and gently pulled.

The goat screamed in terror as it rushed back six feet through the air and into the man in black's arms. He raised the athame to the horrified animal's throat and sliced so clean, true, and strong that its head hit the ground before the goat's scream was done echoing through the canyon—before even the first drop of blood splashed on the red girl's face.

He held the once loved and cradled doeling over his head, spilling its crimson life force onto Orchid's quivering naked body. That seductive rush of drunken power washed over her again as she once more fell under its gently violent spell. She threw her head back and let out another unearthly howl. Only this time it wasn't a howl of triumph; this was a mournful howl of surrender.

Orchid looked down through a veil of tears at her feet. Her toes were once again on pointe, and she was hovering just about the ground.

The red girl's wail had subsided into a full blown sob, as if she was hoping that her tears would wash away the doeling's blood from her face.

"It is time, my child."

The red girl looked up to see the man once again wiping the blade of the athame on his heavy black robes.

"Turn and face the fire."

Orchid's body slowly turned as if she was on some sort of antiquated record player and stopped when she was staring dead into the still burning effigy on the blazing pyre. Over the crackling and popping of the old growth wood singing its song of the energy of a half millennia of growth, the red girl could hear the man in black approaching her deliberately from behind.

"You have served me well, little one, and through you, our family will be born again."

The man in black raised the athame as he reached out and wrapped his arm around the red girl's neck, he gently pulled her head back, pointing her chin to the sky.

"For you are the beacon and I am the vessel."

The man raised the blade to Orchid's throat. Her eyes rolled back and fixated on the moon that hung fat and high above her. She smiled in sweet relief that this was all about to be over. She closed her eyes.

THIS IS THE END

"Pedagogue!"

A man's voice echoed and bounced back through the canyons.

The man in black turned to see a faint shadow standing just outside the light of the bonfire.

He squinted his eyes and was able to make out the form of a man walking out of the night and into the dim glimmer of amber hues radiating from the flames. His form materialized in the night like an apparition, a specter, a ghost. The man in black slid his still clean athame into the belt of his robes and smiled. Behind him, the red girl floated to the ground, throat intact, still clutching the headless body of the white doeling.

The man in black stepped forward and called out to the ghost in the darkness.

"Who comes here?"

"I am only that which you have created, Pedagogue. I am now merely nothing more than a monster."

Jesse stepped out of the shadows and into the light, becoming visible.

"I have dreamed about this since the night I came home to find my wife and my life in pieces. I have come to collect the toll."

The man in black pulled down the hood of his robes, smiled, and stretched his arms out in a gesture that to Jesse looked almost like a greeting.

"Be careful, my boy, because sometimes even the sweetest dreams can very quickly turn into nightmares."

As he walked toward the man in black, Jesse's heart was thudding against his ribcage as if trying to escape his body as a wave of icy cold fear washed over him.

He could taste it.

He hadn't been in a real physical fight for as long as he could remember. All the cockiness he had in the car about beating up the 'old man' was gone, replaced with nothing less than that goddammed kettle drum beating of his heart and the bitter, salty burn of bile in his throat.

His daydreams about knowing some mastery of martial arts were gone. His plan of how he was going to attack was gone. All that was left was the hollowed out empty feeling of disquietude. As Jesse closed the distance to the man in black, he noticed a red woman emerging from behind him, holding the body of a white goat. She stood tall from what looked like a heaping pile of dead animals. The man in black noticed the distraction and glanced over his shoulder at the red girl.

"Don't worry, my child. Our visitor will only be here for a moment, and then we can do what needs to be done."

The man in black turned his attention back to Jesse and sighed while shaking his head.

"You're trembling, my boy. Are you sure this is what you desire?"

Jesse pulled Fhírinne from her scabbard, dropping the heavy sheath to the ground.

"It's time to finish this!"

The man in black's eyes widened when he saw the weapon. He smiled broadly, and with almost the tone of laugher, he exclaimed into the cold night air, his breath visible in the cold blue moonlight, "Now where, oh where, did you ever come across that sword, my boy?"

Jesse swallowed hard. Every muscle in his body screamed with tension. He looked down the blade that he now had pointed at the man in black, and he was right, the sword was quivering from the fear that emanated from deep inside his body.

The man in black focused his energy and raised his right hand to Jesse in a gripping motion. Jesse felt a slight tingle and burning around where Eastman had painted the ancient symbols on his body, but that was all.

The man in black lowered his hand, cocked his head, and smiled.

"Interesting. I guess we have to do this the old-fashioned way. Come at me then, my boy. Let's get this over with."

Jesse drew a deep breath through chattering teeth, raised Fhírinne, and ran full speed toward the man in the black. Jesse screamed with rage as he swiftly closed the distance between him and the beast. He watched as the man remained perfectly still; the only part of his body that moved was his mouth as it pulled back into a wide grin.

The next thing Jesse knew, he was on his back looking up at the moon. His head pounded, matching his heart as he saw the stars in the sky, and the stars that were clouding his vision. He squeezed his right hand and noticed he was still holding Fhírinne. A roar of laughter rang out in the dark night air and echoed in Jesse's ears as the man in black walked over to where he lay crumpled in the dirt.

"Get up, my boy, let's try this again."

The man in black turned and walked back to where he was standing originally beside the bonfire and the ocean of blood with the red girl holding the beheaded doeling. Orchid grinned as she bowed to the man in black before he spun to again face Jesse, who was now back on shaky legs, Fhírinne pointed towards the man in black.

Jesse dug his boots into the hard-packed soil, took in a deep breath, and attacked. He again ran full speed at the man in black. He raised Fhírinne over his head and swung hard. With a lightning-fast blur of speed that Jesse's mind couldn't even articulate, the man in black caught Jesse by the wrist with a grip that was like Iron. Jesse looked up at his hand that was still in mid-swing holding Fhírinne. The vice-like grip twisted and tightened, turning Jesse's wrist outward, compressing his radius and ulna bones nearly to the point of fracture. His whole body moved with just the grip and twist of the Pedagogue's hand.

"Now be a good boy and drop it."

Jesse screamed in pain as the man in black twisted and contorted him. Jesse's powerful muscles failed under the stress, He watched as his fist slowly opened, losing his grip, and Fhírinne fell, sticking straight out of the hard-packed earth.

Jesse's eyes darted back to the man who hadn't even broken a sweat. He was so close, so close to the beast that killed Katia that he could smell his breath, could see the pores of his skin, could see his non-elevated pulse in the veins on the side of his head.

The look on the Pedagogue's face was that of utter calm and complete serenity. He smiled at Jesse as his free right hand shot out and grabbed Jesse by the throat. Jesse tried to scream but found he was unable as that same vice-like grip that nearly broke his arm compressed his airways, cutting off the oxygen and blood supply to his brain.

Jesse couldn't speak, couldn't think, but somehow he could feel his body being lifted off the ground by that vice-like grip. The man in black looked down at Jesse's feet that were dangling four inches off the ground and smiled.

"What exactly did you think was going to happen here, my boy? Did you honestly think that you were going to run up with that sword—*my* sword—and cut me down with it?"

The man in black glanced down at the weapon stuck in the earth and loosened his grip just enough for Jesse to take a couple desperate breaths. His brain received a fresh supply of blood—just enough to keep him conscious and coherent. The man in black wanted to keep him alive for just a couple more moments.

The man took a deep breath in, as if he was tasting Jesse, reading his energy.

"It's you. You're the one that has been killing off my family."

The man in black squeezed hard again.

"Oh, you're Katia's husband, aren't you? Yes. That's why you're here . . . You *are* the monster she made you out to be. Shame about her, you know. I adored her. The real shame is, she showed potential to be my partner, my wife, the one to stand beside me while the beacon brings my family to absolute glory. Shame she didn't make it here to see this. She would be overjoyed that I finally found the true beacon."

The man in black raised Jesse a couple inches higher so he could get a clear view of the red girl that was behind him. Her eyes glowing faintly blue, her mouth twisted into a demonic giggling grin, showing off her perfect white smile. She was still cradling the headless body of the doeling, stroking its now bloodstained white fur.

"But I can sense the sweet darkness inside you, boy. I can hear that little voice that has been whispering to you your entire life . . . Oh, it whispers still."

The man in black smiled as he examined Jesse's face, his body hanging helplessly in his grip.

"You're afraid that little voice is the real you, aren't you? Your whole life you have been wearing a mask to cover it up, but it's always been there, hasn't it? Whispering dark thoughts to you in the back of your mind. That *is* your biggest fear, is it not, my boy? Becoming that voice and giving into that darkness."

The man in black's face twisted into a gargoyle-like expression of pure hate as he squeezed harder.

"No matter. Now it's time for you to die. I'd be happy to feed you to my beacon, but you stink of regret, bitterness, and hatred. I can sense it. I can sense that you don't even care if you die. I need her food to be pure . . . Pity."

Jesse's eyes rolled into the back of his head, and his hands that were grasping desperately to the hand gripped around his throat fell limply to his sides. His tongue lolled from his mouth. It was a deep shade of purple.

"What amuses me the most, my boy, is that your death will be the fault of your foolish pride thinking you could defeat me alone."

The man in black felt a tap on his shoulder and spun his head to see a big man standing beside him.

"He didn't!"

Amador swung a massive log of oak that he had found in the woodpile beside the barn and crashed it into the man's skull. The man dropped Jesse and staggered.

Jesse fell to the earth, still choking, gasping for air like a fish pulled onto dry land.

The massive piece of oak came crashing down again on the man in black's back. This time with so much force that the baseball bat-sized chunk of wood broke in two, sending splinters and debris into the earth below.

Immediately, Amador was on top of the man, securing him in the same handcuffs that were once on Jesse's wrists. As soon as he was satisfied that cuffs were secure, he leaped onto Jesse, giving him mouth to mouth resuscitation.

The red girl dropped the doeling and screamed as she tried to pounce at Amador, but her lunge was stopped in mid-air by some invisible force field that seemed to be keeping her inside the circle etched into the ground. She clawed violently at the air like some sort of rabid desperate trapped animal.

"You're okay, sweetie. We are going to get you out of here. We are going to get you safe."

The red girl snapped her neck around and hissed at the woman standing beside her circle. The red girl attacked again and bounced off the energy barrier that trapped her inside the ring. Eastman stretched her arm out, her palm facing the red girl, and she started inching toward the sigil on the ground, trying to feel the energy field that bound the red girl in the circle.

Jesse started coughing, and Amador helped him to his feet, brushing him off. Amador grabbed him by his shoulders and steadied him, looking him in his eyes.

"You okay, buddy?"

Jesse coughed once more and nodded his head, still catching his breath and getting his wits about him.

"Yeah . . . Yeah, I think so," Jesse said as he looked to the man in black laying hand-cuffed, face down in the dirt.

"Is he dead?"

Amador smiled.

"No, but when he wakes up, he's going to have one hell of a headache . . ."

But then, the man in black started laughing. That vile wet laughter echoed through the dark valley.

"Get on him!" Eastman screamed in terror as her focus was turned from the red girl and to the man in black.

Jesse and Amador in unison ran and jumped into the air, landing with a thud on top of the handcuffed man. They leaned all their weight on him as he continued to laugh.

"Holy God, he's breaking out of the cuffs!" Amador screamed as both men tried to find leverage on the man in black. The cuffs that were binding him broke and twisted off of him like some sort of prop from a child's police officer playset. He then exploded to his feet, sending Jesse and Amador flying off him. Their bodies went skidding and tumbling on the hard-packed earth, Jesse out in front of the Pedagogue, and Amador almost colliding with Eastman but landing on his head, nearly knocking him unconscious.

The red girl looked down at her claws and flexed them tight, pulling on the energy deep inside of her. She dug her nails into her skin and threw out a blast of energy that enveloped Eastman, lifting her off her feet, forcing her arms out from her sides.

She was slowly pulling Eastman into the circle.

Jesse got to his feet before Amador and watched the man in black, still laughing, drop his heavy robes to his feet, showing off his lean muscular physique that was covered with his primitive, evil tattoos. Jesse and the Pedagogue both looked to Fhírinne at the same time, without a second of hesitation, Jesse sprinted toward the sword.

The Pedagogue rushed forward with an inhuman speed, closed the distance, and made it to the sword a split second before Jesse. He pulled it from the earth and watched with a smile as Jesse skidded on the hard-packed dirt, then turn and scramble away from the now armed man.

The Pedagogue reached out, caught Jesse's throat from behind, and pulled Jesse close, at the same time thrusting the razor sharp tip of Fhírinne into Jesse's back. The blade ran true, piercing Jesse's heart, and burst through his ribcage protruding out from his chest.

The man held Jesse close as his body shivered and convulsed.

He leaned in and whispered into Jesse's ear, "What is that little voice saying now, I wonder? I hope it's screaming!"

In a clean motion, the man pulled Fhírinne from Jesse's torso and wiped the bloody blade on his pants.

Jesse fell to his knees, balanced there for just a moment, then fell flat onto the cold hard earth.

"Jesse! No!"

The man smiled when he heard Eastman's agonizing screams. He turned to see she was still fighting the pull of the red girl but was now dangerously close to the rim of the sigil that he had carved into the earth.

Amador groaned as he got to his feet and looked to see Eastman being pulled through the air toward the red girl, who was still screaming and clawing at her unseen prison. She was pacing, waiting for Eastman to enter her cage, like a tiger during feeding time at the zoo.

Amador rushed toward Eastman and tried pulling her away from the invisible energy that was tugging her like a tractor beam. Amador used all his strength and weight. He was successful in moving the now sobbing woman a couple feet back from the circle as he played tug of war with the red demon in the ring.

It was only when Eastman screamed out "Jesse!" again that Amador looked up to see the man lying dead in the field, and the beast strolling toward him, laughing, and carrying the sword.

As Amador fought and pulled against the impossible force coming from the circle, he glanced down to see the all too familiar gleam of brass in Eastman's back pocket. It was the magazine for his service weapon.

Amador pulled the heavy, fully loaded magazine from her back pocket, followed by the distinct *click* and cock of the slide as he loaded his automatic pistol.

"Amador, No!" Eastman screamed as Amador, gun leveled, started walking toward the man in black, who had now lowered his sword and was smiling at the gunman.

"You're all mine now, you creepy mother fucker!" Amador yelled as he took aim with his pistol.

Over Eastman's screams, over the red girl's hissing, Amador could hear the man say with a smile, "There is something different about you, my boy. Something you're missing that your comrade possessed."

The man raised a single hand and made a fist.

Amador lowered his weapon, and started slowly rocking from side to side.

"Oh, I see what it is now. You forgot your war paint."

The man smiled as Amador walked stupidly toward him, gun to his side, pointed harmlessly at the ground.

"Let me get a good look at you, my boy."

The man in black looked deep into Amador's eyes. He breathed in slowly and deeply, sensing everything inside Amador, looking deep into him and through him.

He saw Amador in Afghanistan, risking his own life to save children in a village under fire from the Taliban. He saw him pulling a friend out of a burning Humvee that was struck by a roadside bomb—the same bomb that threw a big piece of shrapnel into Amador's leg, nearly causing him to bleed out on the side of the hot desert road. The same piece of shrapnel that awarded Amador a Purple Heart and caused him to walk with a slight limp. He saw Amador's wedding day and felt the rush of love for his wife, Victoria. But the man in black also saw something new, something special.

The man in black smiled.

"Congratulations on the new baby, my boy. You are so very proud and so full of love. Walk with me."

The man in black put his arm around Amador's shoulder and started walking him toward the red girl in the circle.

Eastman, still floating, shrieked at the top of her lungs, "Amador! Fight him! Amador!"

Eastman's screams were drowned out by the man in black whispering in Amador's ear.

"You have led an excellent life, my boy. You have been there for your family and for your friends. You have saved countless lives while risking your own. You should be very proud of yourself. You have done well, my boy; you have done well. You have stayed . . . Pure."

"Amador, you must fight him! You have to wake up!"

The man turned Amador to face the red girl in the circle and stepped behind him.

The man stabbed Fhírinne once again into the hardened earth. He placed both his hands on Amador's shoulders as he whispered into his ear from behind, "Isn't she beautiful? She's waiting for you; she wants you to be hers. Would you like that?"

The red girl forgot about pulling Eastman into the ring and left her floating inches from the invisible barrier. Instead, the red girl slinked over to Amador. She purred and moved her beautiful body seductively. She paced and stepped on and over the corpses piled up in her circle.

Her eyes never left Amador's.

"Amador, fight!"

The man in black once more whispered into Amador's ear, "You have led a good life, my boy, a life of selflessness and sacrifice . . . Are you ready for your final offering?"

Amador's eyes didn't leave the gaze of the red girl's as he nodded his head slowly in the affirmative.

The man whispered under his breath a chant, and Amador slowly started swaying to the rhythm of it.

The chant grew louder. The man pulled the athame from his belt.

The girl in the circle's eyes opened wide, and her mouth grew into a savage fiendish grin.

The chant grew louder as the man brought the athame up to Amador's throat.

The man in black was now screaming, but somehow over the screams, over the chanting, Amador heard something—a sound off somewhere in the darkness.

"Wake up, Marine!"

Amador came back to his senses. Face to face with a smiling red devil. His eyes turned to Eastman, who was still floating helplessly just outside the circle, and for a brief second, they locked eyes.

"Ma'am?"

The man in black leaned in close and hissed into Amador's ear, the athame's blade still on his throat.

"Let's take care of her, shall we, my boy?"

Amador fought with every cell in his body as he watched his gun raise and level on Eastman, who was now screaming and pleading to him at the top of her lungs. Tears streamed down his face as he felt his finger squeeze the trigger. In slow motion, he saw an explosion of fire and felt the recoil ripple up his arm as a single round exited the barrel of his weapon.

The blonde woman fell silent into a heap just outside the circle.

The athame sliced clean around Amador's throat.

The man in black sliced again and again until he hit the vertebrae behind Amador's windpipe. A torrent of crimson showered over the girl as the man held Amador's body in position. His gaping neck, a firehose of blood, gushing with the pulsing rhythm of his still beating heart.

The girl danced and bathed in the blood. Her body convulsed with orgasmic pleasure as the blood, the life force, the energy of every good deed Amador had ever done, and all the stored potential possibilities of the lives he had still yet to save, filled her with power.

The red girl threw her head back and screamed a visceral savage howl of victory as she was once again pulled high off the earth. A bright beam of concentrated moonlight shot down like a spotlight, illuminating the soaking wet demon-possessed girl in the circle. The man threw the lifeless body of Amador into the circle as he laughed and wiped his athame clean and pointed it to the sky. Into the night, his voice bellowed triumphantly,

"Well should we know our living flame

Of Fellowship can sear

The grasping claws of Care,

Throttle his impious screams

And send his cowering carcass

From this Grove.

Begone, detested Care, begone!

Once more we banish thee!

Let the all potent spirit of this lamp

By its cleansing and ambient fire

Encircle the mystic scene!

Moloch, the demon with no reflection, come down to inhabit this beacon and claim this woman as your own!"

The red girl flexed her claws and felt all the power of the universe ebb and flow within her. She let out another gurgling primal howl as an ancient dark force swept from the dark tree line of the woods, swirled around her, and plunged inside her, taking over her body.

Eastman rolled onto her back and took a sharp breath in. The pain from the bullet wound in her shoulder radiated through her entire body.

In Amador's last gesture of heroism, he had used every ounce of strength left in his being to move the sights on the barrel of his gun just a couple centimeters to the right, taking it off Eastman's center mass, aiming it at her arm.

Eastman's mind's eye raced.

She was no longer there on the hard-packed dirt in a pool of her own blood.

She was transported back to the moment she met the only other known survivor of the Pedagogue's ritual abuse.

The scene played out like a movie.

Melantha watched herself and the woman as they sat on the couch in the small apartment in suburban Ohio. There were several deadbolt locks on the door. The windows were covered with tinfoil.

Eastman remembered the trip out there to meet her. After

months of talking on the phone, convincing the survivor that it was safe. That she was safe. It was only after Eastman sent the girl pictures of her own scars that the survivor agreed to the meeting.

Eastman watched from the corner of the room as the vision of her picked up her tea, took a sip, and looked across to the girl on the couch next to her.

The survivor sat holding a big pillow on her lap. Her arms were wrapped around it, hugging it tightly.

The survivor, a woman, was maybe only now in her mid-thirties, but her hair was already gray. Her sunken eyes stared off into an empty corner of the room. Those eyes seemed to be looking thousands of miles away. They had no spark of life left in them.

The woman rocked gently back and forth as she squeezed the pillow tightly to her chest.

"So, he found you and your sister from the foster care system?" she asked.

"Yes. I was only ten at the time. She was fourteen."

The woman closed her eyes tight, and a single tear rolled down her cheek as she muttered, "That fucking monster. He found me at the bus stop. I hitchhiked my way across to country to be an actress. He said he was an agent."

Eastman watched as her apparition scooted closer to the woman and placed a hand on her shoulder. The woman quickly pulled away and looked down at her pillow.

"But you escaped? You both escaped?"

"No. Just me. After four years of abuse, I saw him for what he was. Obsessed with finding his 'beacon.' I begged and pleaded with Andromeda, but she was lost, pulled entirely over to the darkness. She was even helping him recruit new people with social media. She is the one that taught him how to do that . . .

"By the time I woke up, there was nothing left of my sister to save. So, one night, he took us out on a yacht he rented. While everyone was sleeping, I woke my sister up and begged her to come with me, to just take the small inflatable lifeboat and go. But then she started screaming and grabbed a knife. I ran to the back of the boat . . .. She chased me, swinging that knife, slicing my back up.

"She was screaming that I was a traitor and that I had to die. I saw the lights coming on in the boat, and I panicked. I just dove into that cold black ocean. I swam. I swam for the lights on the shore . . ."

Eastman watched as the woman picked up the big pillow that was on her lap, put it over her face, and screamed into it. Her feet tapped on the floor, her hands dug and tore into the lush stuffed velour.

The woman got up from the couch, walked into her bedroom, and came out carrying an ancient looking short sword that bared resemblance to a Roman Spatha.

"This was one of his prized possessions, the sword known as 'Fhírinne.' As the story goes, the ancient British raiders stole it from Ireland; it was considered one of the most holy of Celtic treasures. When Caesar and the Roman Legions invaded Britain, it was one of the many spoils of war that was captured and taken back to Rome, and there it stayed for over 1,800 years. In 1942, Mussolini gifted it to Hitler.

"It is no secret that Hitler was obsessed with the dark arts, so he entrusted it to one of his lovers, the woman who was the head of his occult army. Because she had convinced him it was ancient and had the magical power to not only destroy life, but also to bring back the dead. To summon but also to banish. 'Fhírinne.' It means 'truth.' The Pedagogue couldn't ever learn to use it, but he kept it. It was precious to him."

The woman paused and handed Eastman the sword. She looked down at the weapon. She could feel the power coursing through it.

"I was able to make my escape only because he had left to go pick up two little girls from the foster agency. He left me alone. Alone in the house. So, I just took the sword. I wanted to feel like I could take something from him—something he loved from him. He had taken so much of me. And I just, I just ran. So, in a way, you saved me once already . . ."

Eastman watched as the two women embraced on that tiny couch and sobbed and shared a moment of strength and healing through the shared suffering and bravery that only survivors can know.

The two women got up from the couch, and Eastman watched as the woman walked the apparition of herself to the door.

"I will make him pay for what he's done to us . . . To all of us . . ." Eastman turned and started for the doorknob of the tiny apartment but paused as she felt a hand on her shoulder. She turned to the survivor, who was now standing strong and stoic.

In a calm, powerful voice, the woman whispered, "He cannot be defeated by the masculine; he will only fall to the feminine."

Eastman gasped a huge gulp of air as she was thrust back into her pain-soaked body, looking up at the night stars and the pillar of light cascading down on the howling red creature in the circle.

The man in black pointed his athame at the creature and called out, "On this night, and in the place, Moloch, the true dark owl god of the forest lives again!"

A guttural inhuman scream louder than any mortal could produce erupted from the monster in the circle.

Eastman pushed herself to her knees and then staggered to her feet.

The demon turned to her and licked its lips greedily. Savoring Amador's blood that was still caked on its soaked face.

The man turned and for the first time recognized Eastman for who she was . . .

No longer the little girl who would cower before him. She was now a woman, a lion, a warrior . . .

Eastman called out, "I am she who you gave the name 'Andraste.' As you named my sister Andromeda! I am the one who has come to break this cycle and avenge the women and children you have destroyed!"

The man laughed and pointed the athame at the bleeding woman as the beast in the circle seethed and crouched atop Amador's body, scooped up cupped hands full of his blood, and licked it off its dripping claws.

"So, it is you, my little Andraste. You've risen up from the dead?"

Eastman smiled at the man in black, took a deep breath, and raised an eyebrow.

"Honey, I do it all the time!"

Without hesitation, Eastman sprinted toward the man in black. He steadied himself, a crooked smile crept across his face. When she got close, she dove between the man's legs, sliding on the hard-packed dirt. She rolled and reached, plucking Fhírinne from the earth, and turned to face the man.

The man pulled the athame from its sheath, widened his stance, and pointed the blade at her.

"It seems the Fates have once again brought us together. The ouroboros ever spins; let us see who it favors on this night, my little one . . ."

Eastman smiled. "I am not your 'little one' anymore!"

She lunged forward with Fhírinne. With lightning speed, the Pedagogue easily parried her blow, redirecting her attack, and sending her stumbling. A red rush of pain coursed through her body. Her free hand clutched the still bleeding bullet wound in her shoulder.

The man erupted with laughter.

"Have you forgotten everything I have taught you?"

Eastman centered herself, and once again leveled Fhírinne at the man.

She false lunged, then flew forward, their two blades colliding in the moonlight. Every slash she threw at the man was blocked, every stab diverted. The man lunged at her with his athame. Eastman slid to the side. His blade found no purchase other than the cool night air. In an instant, Eastman wrapped her arm around the man's arm and swam her hand to her own bosom, attaching her grip to her own shirt, locking the man's arm in fast to her body, trapping it from moving.

With her arm, still holding Fhírinne, she drove the hilt skyward then diagonally crashed the ancient pommel into the man's jaw.

The powerful man broke the grip and pushed her away.

He looked to her and wiped his lips. A trickle of blood came from the corner of his still smiling mouth.

Eastman took a moment and flicked her eyes to the red girl that was still pacing in the circle a few feet away, then drew them back onto the man.

"There's my Andraste!"

Eastman lunged again at the man, as their blades collided in a flurry of slashes and strikes, the man once again parried her thrusts and knocked her off balance. With rapier speed, the man reached out, grabbed her by her shirt, and in a savage push-pull, drove his bald head into the bridge of Eastman's nose.

The dull blinding thud of kinetic cranial impact, and the sound of cartilage shattering as the thick bone of the man's skull broke Eastman's nose, nearly knocked her unconscious.

The man twisted his fist, balling up the fabric of her shirt, tightening the textiles, giving him more leverage.

The man then hoisted the petite woman off the ground and held her there just outside the circle.

Blood was streaming down her face. Her eyes were already swelling shut. Her hands hung loosely at her sides, fingers somehow still keeping a grip on Fhírinne.

"I think you have had enough adventure for tonight, my dear."

He dropped Eastman onto the hard earth below, Fhírinne landing right beside her.

The man looked at the ancient sword and smiled as he slid the athame back into its sheath.

"I will be taking back what is rightfully mine now, my dear."

Eastman heard a familiar sound. She opened her watering eyes and looked at the man standing over her, then beyond him, to the sky. She squinted as three shapes circled high above.

Time seemed to freeze. Nothing seemed to move except for those three circling shapes.

She heard the sound again.

"Caw-Caw!"

Eastman gasped at the dark shapes hovering in the heavens.

It's . . . It's . . . the crows.

Time came back, and the man was reaching for the blade, her blade, her Fhírinne.

In an instant, Eastman's eyes darted to Fhírinne, then to the red girl, then back to the man.

She kicked up as hard as she could, knocking the man back just a few feet, but those few feet gave the precious seconds she needed to grab Fhírinne and roll into the circle with the red girl.

As soon as she crossed the invisible boundary, the savage animal pounced and grabbed her with its claws, causing her to drop Fhírinne.

The red girl lifted Eastman's body over its head, then slammed her onto the pile or corpses.

The demon leaped on top of her and started ripping and clawing at Eastman's flesh, leaving deep gouges and lacerations all over her neck and chest. Eastman screamed as she felt the blood pour and drip from her body. The demon then paused, looked her in the eye, and held up its index finger.

Eastman watched as Moloch drove its finger deep into the bullet wound in her shoulder, pulled out its deep crimson digit, plunged it into its mouth, and slurped it clean.

Eastman screamed in agony and terror as she tried to wriggle free, but her arms were pinned helplessly to her side. The creature raised its head to the heavens and howled in victory, then dove its face into the nape of Eastman's neck.

The demon sunk its teeth into Eastman's throat.

Eastman blinked her swollen eyes hard . . . Over the red girl's shoulders, passed her blood-clotted hair, she saw a vision. Eastman saw a man . . . A kind man . . . An old man . . . Standing just outside the circle . . . He smiled at her, tipped his hat, and said, "You tell my baby girl, that her Pops says she can always come home."

Eastman blinked again and the man was gone. She felt a wave of loving energy rush into her. She screamed and struggled, her arms still pinned to her sides under the demon.

As her hands clawed and prodded, she felt something hard in the back pocket of her jeans.

She swam her hand into her pocket and pulled the cell phone free. She swung it hard, crashing it into the side of the creature's skull.

The monster shrieked and screamed in Eastman's face as she brought the phone up again, showing it to the demon.

Eastman cried out to the little girl inside the monster. She screamed aloud, not even knowing what it meant, "Pops says you can always come home!"

The demon gazed into the darkened mirror, and saw itself, saw its reflection, saw what it had become, and recoiled in revolted horror. The red demon Moloch pinned itself against the edge of the circle like a frightened animal.

Eastman held the phone out toward the monster, and while still on her back, she reached out to Fhírinne with her free left hand. For a fraction of a millisecond, the sword quivered in the earth, then flew into Eastman's outstretched hand.

She looked at Fhírinne, then down to the jagged chalk sigil that was just visible over the blood. She whispered, "His symbols will be his downfall. The power to banish . . ."

"No!" the man in black screamed and lunged toward Eastman as she swung the blade down, crashing into the etched chalk outline on the ground, breaking the circle's power.

Eastman swung the quivering sword again and pointed it at the red devil.

"By the gods and goddesses of the earth, both old and new—Moloch, I cast you out! I banish thee!"

There was a crack of thunder and the demon writhed and convulsed, vomiting blood and feathers onto the heaped pile of corpses. A dark shadow flew from the circle and crashed back into the dark tree line of the forest whence it came.

The red girl raised her head and looked at Eastman, and for the first time that night, under the blood, dirt, and filth, Eastman saw what she knew was there all along: a scared, innocent, young woman.

The sounds of the man in black's heavy footsteps sprinting toward them caught the red girl's attention. She blinked and her eyes still reflected that faint blue glow. She still had all the power from the animals inside her. The man in black reached to the girl and squeezed.

The red girl was pulled from the crouched position she was in into a contorted, shaking, unnatural, marionette-like dance three feet off the ground.

The man squeezed the life out of Orchid. He pulled the remaining power from her broken body into his.

He looked down to Eastman while laughing, feeling the power flow into him . . .

His beacon had done her job. She had no more use to him.

"No woman can stop me from doing what needs to be done! No woman can keep me from standing in my power!"

Eastman looked at the dying girl convulsing in mid-air. She then looked down to the sword in her hand.

"She—She said it could banish . . . but also . . . it had the power to *summon*."

Orchid choked and gasped as the man flexed and squeezed, draining the last bit of the beacon's energy from her body.

And over the sound of the man in black's laughing, over the sound of Orchid dying, over the sound of the crows above still circling and cawing—Eastman looked to the body of Jesse laying dead in the field. She looked down to Amador's corpse beneath her.

Eastman whispered to herself, "*He cannot be defeated by the masculine; he will only fall to the feminine . . .*"

She called forth every drop of strength she had in her broken, bloody body. She pointed Fhírinne to the heavens and called out, "Macha, the wild Goddess of the forest, who battles injustice to women and children, I summon thee!"

In that second, the only sound was the disgusting snap of Orchid's neck breaking, and the echoes of the man's laughter.

The man in black released Orchid's body from his grip.

The red girl's lifeless body fell crumbling to the ground like a paper doll.

And then there was silence.

Silence, except for a man's footsteps approaching Eastman from behind. Eastman was still frozen on top of the pile of corpses with Fhírinne still stabbing toward the sky.

The man in black whispered to Eastman as he got to the edge of the broken circle, "I thought for sure you drowned that night, little Andraste. But now, I'm going to make you wish that you had."

And at that very moment, it was as if the earth stood still. The crickets and nighttime noises of the forest stopped. Even the roaring of the bonfire went quiet. The world just stopped.

Everything was silent.

The man in black paused and looked toward the sky as a warm perfumed wind swept over the valley from the east, smelling of spring and wildflowers. The wind brought with it hundreds of crows that filled the sky and circled overhead, cawing loudly.

Eastman smiled and craned her neck to look at the man in black standing above her.

"No woman can stop you? How about a Goddess, you asshole?"

The silence was shattered by another thunderclap and deafening trumpet blast that shook the ground as a bolt of lightning arched and pierced the darkened sky. It struck Orchid's lifeless body and threw off a shockwave of kinetic energy that blasted the man in black, Eastman, and the corpses into a wide semi-circle with Orchid at its epicenter.

A moment later, Eastman raised her bloodied face from the dirt and saw Orchid standing in the pasture bathed in dazzling, brilliant amber light.

The smell of ozone and wildflowers perfumed the air.

Eastman gasped and covered her mouth with her hand, as the radiant light filled her eyes and tears streamed down her cheeks.

"Macha!" Eastman whispered, and she bowed her head to the divine Goddess of the Woods.

Every speck of blood was gone from Orchid's nude figure. Her body was healed. Her soul was cleansed, stripped clean of any of the residual darkness by the kind feminine Goddess energy that flowed through every molecule of her being. On her head sat a crown of wildflowers, held in place by what looked like velvety multi-pointed antlers.

She was the embodiment of Mother Nature.

She glowed.

The Goddess walked over to Eastman, and with every step she took, left a glowing amber footprint on the earth below her feet. She looked down to her and smiled, then glanced at Fhírinne. Eastman got to her knees and offered Macha the ancient Celtic blade. Macha smiled as she reached out and gently took the blessed weapon from Eastman's hand.

The Goddess held the blade. It seemed to take on the subtle amber glow that surrounded her.

Macha gently touched Eastman's shoulder with the tip of the blade. A warm, loving rush of power filled and flowed over Eastman's body. It felt like she was wrapped in a warm blanket, it felt like home. Eastman looked down at her wounds, and they were healed. She touched her face and her nose was no longer broken.

Eastman bowed to the deity standing before her. Macha looked down at her and smiled again, then turned her attention to the man in black, who was coughing and getting to his feet.

The Goddess's smile faded. She marched across the pasture to the man in black. She stood there, *in her power,* and confronted him.

The man in black fell to his knees before the Goddess.

Macha smiled down to the man, reached out, and placed a loving hand on his shoulder.

The man looked up to the deity with his tear-soaked eyes and whispered, "I'm sorry . . . I'm sorry for everything . . ."

Macha gave his shoulder a gentle squeeze, pulled her hand away, and nodded her head in recognition of the man's penance. Then she motioned with her index and middle finger and brought the man off his feet and into the air. She motioned again, and his arms were out from his sides, and his legs were together, toes pointing straight down.

Mid-air crucifixion.

She held Fhírinne, the pinnacle of truth, over her head and brought the blade down in two lightning-fast swipes. She severed the man's arms at the elbows, then she swept with the angelic blade horizontally, taking both of his legs below the knees.

He could never use them to harm another living creature.

The man screamed as his lifeless limbs landed on the hard dirt below, but not a drop of blood fell from the man's body, as the wounds were already healed by the blade.

Macha then reached in the man's mouth, grabbed his tongue, and ripped it out by its root.

He could never speak another evil word.

The man in black wailed to the sky in a sickening monotone exclamation of misery and confusion.

Macha then motioned with her hand, pulling the man face to face with her.

She reached out and plucked his eyes from his sockets—leaving just two empty, dried, healed holes where they had been.

He could never again see the beauty of this world.

The Goddess smiled, extended her hand, and flexed, reaching into the man's mind. She squeezed out all the knowledge he had ever had. She purged all the wisdom and secrets he had ever hoarded—removing and wiping his memories. She took his ability to use his mind for language, the alphabet—she took everything. Every piece of everything that made him who he was.

Macha took everything. Everything except the memories he had of the horrible atrocities he had committed against the countless women and children over all those dark, bloody years.

The man in black was left only with those memories. So, he could relive those, and only those memories for as long as he lived.

Just like the women and children who survived his abuse had to.

With a wave of her hand, the living torso fell to the earth and lay there squirming on its belly, shrieking incoherent inhuman noises into the dirt.

Macha then turned to see Eastman standing behind her. Eastman lowered her head into a bow and looked over to Jesse's body lying in the field. The Goddess acknowledged her and smiled. Macha approached her and took her by the arm. Together, they walked her over to the body of the fallen warrior.

Jesse's body was growing cold in the dirt where he fell. The clean wound of the blade was still visible on his back.

Eastman watched as Macha waved her hand, slowly bringing Jesse's body into the air. She turned him so he was facing them.

The Goddess looked to Eastman, who had tears running down her cheeks. Macha reached out and wiped them. She placed her index finger on Eastman's quivering lower lip, and playfully winked at her.

Eastman let out a gasp as Macha plunged Fhírinne back into the exit wound in Jesse's chest. Immediately, Jesse's body was reanimated, bathed in a warm amber glow. Jesse gasped for air as the pure loving energy of the Goddess flowed into him, reigniting the spark that had been whiffed out only minutes ago.

Macha slowly pulled Fhírinne from Jesse's body. As the tip of the blade was drawn free from the wound, it had left earlier, the gash was gone, the injury was healed.

Macha waved her delicate hand, and Jesse gently lowered to the earth below.

Jesse stood there and opened his eyes, looked around the pasture, and asked Eastman stupidly, "Did we win?"

Eastman jumped into Jesse's arms, knocking him to the ground, and covered his face with kisses.

"Okay, Mel, it's okay. You're acting like I was dead or something!"

Jesse then looked up to Macha, who was smiling down at them both with a huge toothy grin.

"Who's the chick with the cool horns?" Jesse smiled as Eastman continued painting kisses all over his face. She looked up, remembering she was in the presence of a Goddess, and pulled Jesse up to his feet.

"Jesse, this is Macha. She is a Goddess from Ireland that avenges women and children."

Macha nodded her head and smiled to Jesse. Her nose crinkled up, and her eyes flashed an amber glow.

Eastman motioned to the man standing next to her. "Macha, this is Jesse."

Jesse dropped to a knee and bowed his head.

Eastman looked over to the Goddess, who was smiling down at Jesse, and shrugged her shoulders and sighed.

"Men."

Macha giggled and took Eastman by the hand and walked her over to the bonfire, the broken circle, and the bodies of the animals. Macha grimaced and shook her head as she surveyed the scene. She looked down at her toes in the blood-soaked soil. She looked at Eastman, who was standing over the body of Amador.

Macha cleared her throat, closed her eyes, and then waved Fhírinne through the air. She turned the sword downward, and plunged it into the earth, sending out a ripple of life-giving energy in all directions.

For a moment, the night was silent, the only sound that could be heard was the perfumed breeze that blew in from the east.

Then, there was a cluck—the cluck of chickens—then the bleat of a goat. The animals started to raise up from the ground, shake off, and run out into the pasture. A tiny white goat walked up to Macha and bowed its head. The Goddess reached out, and just as Orchid had minutes ago, stroked its smooth white face. The little goat bleated and nuzzled against Macha's knees. Eastman looked down and smiled as Macha scooped up the goat and held it against her breast.

Everyone had come back.

. . . Everyone except Amador.

Macha walked over to the big man's body and looked down at him. His eyes were closed. The look on his face was peaceful. She put the goat down and touched Amador's face for a long moment. Macha turned and looked up to Eastman, who now had Jesse standing behind her, his hands resting on her shoulders. The look in Macha's eyes told them the entire story. She hadn't said a word that night; she didn't need to. The Goddess communicated through energy, and the message was clear. The warrior had fallen in battle. That was his place, this was his time. and he was already toasting in Valhalla, beside Odin, waiting for his wife and Londyn to join his side in the great hall.

Eastman smiled and nodded as a single tear ran down her cheek.

She understood.

Macha reached out for Fhírinne and opened her hand; the sword flew from the earth and into her grasp. Macha raised the blade to Eastman and Jesse, and rested it on her forehead, closed her eyes, then reopened them. They were burning with amber fire.

Macha gave a slight bow to the two humans standing before her and handed Fhírinne to Eastman.

The Goddess then turned her amber eyes up to the heavens.

There was another earth-shaking crack of thunder and a blinding flash, and Macha was gone, leaving Orchid standing there wide-eyed and confused, having no memory of the last couple hours.

"It's okay, sweetie," Eastman cooed to Orchid. "Let's get you covered up. Jesse, run into that barn over there and find a blanket or something for this girl, will ya?"

Without saying a word, Jesse turned and ran into the barn, returning a couple moments later with a large horse blanket. He handed it to Eastman, and she threw it over Orchid's shivering shoulders.

Orchid looked down and scooped up the little white goat, that was still circling around her knees, and cuddled her close.

Orchid looked up to Eastman with pleading eyes.

"She's so sweet. Is it okay if I keep her, ma'am?"

Eastman smiled sweetly back at Orchid.

"My name is Melantha, you don't need to call me, 'ma'am.' That's Jesse. You're free from the Pedagogue now. You don't have to ask permission from anyone to do anything anymore. If you want to keep her, that's your call. How's that sound to you?"

Orchid looked to Eastman, smiled, and just above a whisper replied, "A little scary to be honest."

Eastman sighed and put her hand on Orchid's shoulder. "I know what you mean, believe me. I know what you mean."

Orchid smiled and nuzzled the doeling with her nose.

"Well, if I can keep her, I need a good name for her. Any ideas?"

Eastman looked down at the little goat and patted her soft head. "How about 'Macha'?"

Orchid's eyes went big, and she smiled as she squeezed the little doeling.

"I love it. Your new name is 'Macha'!"

"Macha, the baby goat? Oh, for crying out loud," Jesse laughed as he pulled his vape out of the pocket of his jeans and took a big hit from it.

A sound started echoing through the canyon.

At first, it sounded like a faint thudding, then it grew louder. The three started turning in all directions looking for the source. It felt like it was coming from nowhere and everywhere. All at once, they all knew exactly what the sound was. It was a helicopter—and it was coming in fast.

The black helicopter screamed over the mountain and circled low overhead, blowing dust and debris everywhere, then a blinding spotlight pierced the night, drowning the three in its bright white glow.

They turned to the house and saw five sets of headlights come barrowing over the rough terrain, heading straight for them.

Five black jeeps pulled up in a screeching semi-circle and doors flew open.

Men with machine guns got out and took cover behind the steel-plated doors of the still running vehicles, while the helicopter pulled tight circle maneuvers overhead, keeping them in the wash of the blinding spotlight.

Eastman walked forward and put her hands in the air as one last car, a big black armor-plated SUV, pulled up. Two men got out and walked toward the three people in the pasture. As they got near, the helicopter pulled off, extinguishing the deafening noise. As it flew off into the distance, the men taking cover behind the Jeeps lowered their rifles.

A man with a thick Mexican accent called out to the group, "My darling, Melantha! Are you okay?"

"Who the fuck is this?" Jesse asked as the two men walked up to them, smiling.

Eastman turned to Jesse and smiled. "The Calvary."

"Mr. Perez, Jonas!" She ran and jumped into the arms of the big Mexican man who was dressed in a beautiful white suit. She then embraced the burly biker standing beside him. Melantha punched the biker playfully in his heavily tattooed arm and laughed.

"Thank you guys for getting here." Melantha looked at her watch. "And right on time, too."

"I always do what I say I'm going to do for you, my love."

Eastman gave Mr. Perez a big kiss on his cheek, making sure to avoid his thick mustache.

"Mr. Perez, Jonas, this is Jesse and Orchid."

Orchid let out a gasp and hid behind Jesse when she recognized the big, burly biker that thrashed Her Majesty's Tea House and Supply, and nearly scared her half to death.

Jonas walked over and shook Jesse's hand, turned to Orchid, and gently took her hand into his. He looked to her now with his kind eyes.

"Sorry for the show, and I'm sorry if I scared you. We had to play like that to get the Pedagogue to make a move—a dumb move. To force his hand and make him come out here, so we could take him down and rescue you."

The big burly biker looked over to Eastman and smiled.

"It was Melantha's plan, and it worked like a charm. Then again, everything she plans works out like a charm."

Orchid looked to Mr. Perez as he walked up and took her hand.

"Oh, my dear, if my husband Jonas frightened you, I sincerely apologize. I can assure you he's just a big old teddy bear!"

Mr. Perez walked over to his husband and gave him a big kiss. "Aren't you, Papi?"

Eastman scooped up Macha, handed her to Orchid, and looked her in the eyes.

"They're good men, trust me on that. They're good men. They would never harm you."

Mr. Perez smiled to Eastman, and looked over to Orchid.

"Melantha is like family to Jonas and me. My dear, let us get you home safe. We are happy to drive you anywhere, or take you to the airport, and of course, the expense is on us."

Orchid looked down at her feet, then back up to Mr. Perez and Jonas. She gave Macha a stroke and whispered, "I don't have a home. I don't . . . have anyone."

Mr. Perez and Jonas looked at each other and smiled. "Are you thinking what I'm thinking, Papi?"

Jonas smiled and looked to Mr. Perez with smiling eyes. "Same page as always, babe. Same page as always . . ."

Mr. Perez walked over to Orchid and took her by the hand.

"Orchid, how would you—you and your little friend—like to live with us for as long as you like? We have an empty *casita* on the property, and of course, you could come and go as you please. We can assure you that you will be safe, and well taken care of."

Orchid looked to Eastman, who was beaming from ear to ear.

"Melantha, what do you think?"

"I think you have a family now."

Orchid started trembling and tears streamed down her face as she squeezed Macha furiously.

"A family . . . A real family? Like, like . . ."

"Like your Pops, Orchid. Like your Pops."

Eastman laughed as Orchid squealed and jumped, Macha and all, into Jonas and Mr. Perez's arms.

"Oh . . . Ah, no. Who's that over there?"

Mr. Perez looked over to the spot where Amador's body laid on the bloody soil.

Eastman turned and looked back to Mr. Perez and Jonas.

"That's Martin Amador. He's a hero. He saved us all today . . . I need you to do me a favor. His car is on the other side of that ridge; can you make it look like he died in the line of duty, doing something heroic? Because he did. People just can't know that it was here. I want to make sure his wife, Victoria, gets the benefits. They just had a baby boy and—"

Mr. Perez put his hands up and gently cut Eastman off. She was on the verge of tears.

"Of course, my love. If he saved you, he is a hero to Jonas and I as well. We will make sure he goes down on the record as the king he is," Mr. Perez said solemnly, as Jonas put his hand on his shoulder, giving it a proud squeeze.

The moment of silence was broken by an inhuman wail coming from a dark part of the pasture.

Jonas pulled a gun from his waistband and stood in front of Mr. Perez, protecting him and Orchid from the sound coming from the dark.

Mr. Perez leaned down to Orchid and whispered in her ear, "That's why I love that man right there!"

Eastman stepped forward and started walking over to the source of the noise.

"It's safe everyone, come look."

The group huddled over the armless, legless, blind, mute monster that was still writhing in the dirt like a maggot, surrounded by his severed, bloodless limbs.

"What the fuck is that thing? Is that the Pedagogue?" Jonas said as he leveled his pistol onto the head of the hapless form laying before him. Eastman stepped in, and gently pushed the gun down, pointing it safely at the ground.

"He's stuck like that until he dies, reliving all the terrible, nasty, disgusting things he has ever done. Death would be too good for him. Let him squirm."

"So, we just leave him here?" Jesse said as he took another hit from his vape and glanced over to Eastman, who, by her smile and raised an eyebrow, clearly already had something special in mind.

"I've got a better plan for him."

Four hours and two hundred and twenty miles later, the big black SUV pulled up in front of Gladys Park in downtown Los Angeles.

Eastman and Jesse got out of the truck and were greeted by a heavily tattooed woman with bright pink hair, and a tall, handsome black man.

"Hi, Soma. Hhi, Crushow! How's it going down here?"

The tall black man smiled and nodded his head. "It is what it is, you know how it goes. Just looking after the people that society chooses to forget about. How you doing, little lady?"

Eastman gave the pair a huge hug and squeezed them tightly, almost forgetting that Jesse was there.

"Oh, guys, this is Jesse. Jesse, this is Soma and Crushow; they run the Pavement Project. It's this cool group of artists that is socially active in the houseless communities around the world. They're good people."

Jesse waved and leaned against the truck.

"So, what's up, Melantha?" Soma asked Eastman as she smiled and brushed some of her bright pink locks from her face. A face that, even in the early morning sun of Los Angeles's skid row, was still beautiful.

"We found this guy on the other side of town, and I feel just awful for him. He has no arms or legs, no eyes, and can't speak. It's unfortunate."

Jesse opened the back door of the SUV, and there was the Pedagogue, or rather, what was left of him, still writhing around, strapped in tight by a seatbelt, head looking around wildly.

"Oh, wow, that poor man!" Soma said as she reached out and stroked his perfectly manicured goatee.

"What can we do to help?"

Eastman looked into the bottomless pools of Soma's deep brown eyes. Eyes that you could tell had seen some shit, but that shit didn't fade their luster.

"Well, I was hoping if I gave you guys some money every couple months, you guys could help take care of him for me down here, you know, make sure he gets fed, gets some water, kept alive for as long as possible."

Crushow stepped forward and looked into the back of the SUV

and shook his head.

"That's a god dammed shame about that man right there. Yeah, we got you, Melantha. You came through for our community when nobody else gave a shit. When that killer was on the loose here, killing the people out here on the streets, the police acted like he was doing the city a service. So, when you caught his ass and delivered him to me and my boys for justice—yeah. We got you on this one."

Eastman reached into her purse and handed Soma a roll of hundred-dollar bills.

"Like I said, just make sure he is kept alive for as long as possible, and just call me when you need more, okay?"

Soma smiled and put the money into the back pocket of her jeans.

"You got it, sister, and thanks again for your help down here."

Eastman reached out and put her hand on Soma's shoulder.

"No, thank you for what you guys do for these people. We need more people like you and the Pavement Project."

Jesse and Eastman got back into the big black SUV and started making the long drive home to Montrose.

LAST WATCH

The funeral procession from the small church in La Cañada to the National Cemetery in Riverside was a long one, but everyone that was at the little church in the foothills made the trip to show their final respects. It took over an hour for Victoria to shake the hands of everyone who waited in line to console her and share a memory with her after Amador was lowered into the earth.

Victoria's mom and dad happily took their grandson home for a much-needed feeding and a nap. Victoria stood there alone, looking down into the casket covered with a couple handfuls of earth, whispering her goodbyes while holding a crisp, folded flag.

It was still drizzling.

"Vic, honey, there is someone I'd like you to meet."

Victoria turned around to see Eastman, Jesse, and Durazo standing there with a young girl. Her short black haircut was freshly styled into a crisp A-line bob. Her clothes were brand new, and her smile was broad yet, at the same time, full of empathy.

"Victoria, this is Orchid. She has something she wants to tell you."

As the young woman walked toward her, Victoria's eyes looked over to see two big men standing behind Melantha. She recognized one of the men, who looked like the biker she saw leading the parade of Harley's that pulled up in front of the church. The other, a tall man with dark skin and a thick black mustache, held his hat in his hands and gave her a respectful nod.

The young woman wrapped her arms around Victoria and squeezed hard, and after a long moment, she looked the mourning widow in her eyes.

"Mrs. Amador, my name is Orchid. I am the girl that your husband gave his life to save. I wanted to say thank you, but that doesn't really seem like enough. I'm not really sure what I can say other than that. But if there is anything you ever need, help with the baby . . ."

Victoria embraced the young woman and held her tight.

As they watched the women embrace, Durazo leaned over to Eastman and whispered, "I think it's bullshit that you got put on 'administrative leave' or 'downsized' or whatever they call it these days. You were the best profiler the FBI had, and they know it. If I were you, I'd sue the shit out of them for wrongful termination. So what if the trail of one killer went cold—what about the dozens of others you put behind bars?"

Eastman looked up to Durazo and smiled while she shrugged her shoulders.

"It's fine with me; the Bureau does what it does. Plus, I still have my private practice and some money saved up. I'll be fine."

Eastman gave the big man a wink. "I will miss my cool badge and windbreaker though."

Durazo laughed as he gave her a big hug and smiled.

"Well, if you ever want to join the LASD, I'm sure we could fast track you in. I'd be happy to personally vouch for you."

Eastman nodded at Durazo, then turned and looked to Jesse. "I think I'm going to take some time away from hunting bad guys for a while, and just focus on me."

She took Jesse's hand and gave him a quick peck on the cheek and looked into his eyes.

"On us."

Durazo nodded and smiled to Eastman and Jesse before looking over to the young Marines that Amador served with while in Afghanistan that were standing around, smoking cigarettes and laughing beside their cars that lined one of the countless roads along the extensive national cemetery grounds.

"I'm going to share some stories about Amador that these whippersnappers might not know about."

"Go get 'em, sergeant."

Durazo looked down to Eastman, smiled, and whispered, "Hoorah."

Mr. Perez and Jonas walked up and nodded in the direction where Orchid and Victoria were standing, sharing hushed words, tears, and smiles.

"She's really quite something, you know?" Mr. Perez said as he put his arm around Jonas, looking again to the young girl, then turning back to Eastman with a kind smile framed nicely by his mustache.

She gave the men a big hug.

"Keep her safe. I have some plans for her. She has some talents that I will need her help with."

"Of course, my love. Jonas and I will make sure that she is healthy and happy, no matter what."

"I know . . ." She sighed as she looked back to the young girl that was now saying her goodbyes to Victoria, thanking her once again for everything.

Eastman looked over to her big black SUV, and standing beside it was a dapper man with long curly hair and a beard. As they locked eyes, he gave her a little wave and motioned Eastman over.

As Victoria and Orchid got back to the group, they looked less like people who just met at the side of a grave and more like old friends. Vic was now smiling, having shared a common bond, and being able to put a face and a name to the stranger that her husband gave his life to save.

While everyone introduced each other and discussed plans for a big group lunch, Eastman excused herself to go say hi to her old friend standing beside her truck.

"Hello, Geo, to what do I owe this honor?"

Geo smiled and gave her his signature head bow.

"Always the gentleman, you."

Eastman laughed as she gave the big, burly man a hug and a kiss on his well-bearded cheek.

"Hey, Melantha, I noticed that 'our friend' hasn't been online, and his geo tag hasn't moved since I gave you his location . . . You paid him a visit?"

Eastman gave Geo a quick wink; she didn't have to say anything else.

Geo laughed then shrugged his shoulders. "I heard you got let go—something about subpar performance—so I wanted to check on you and see how you were doing."

She scoffed. "'Subpar performance,' is that what they're saying now?"

"It's all politics. If they knew half the things that I know you have done behind the scenes, you would be running the west coast region by now."

She just laughed. "Yeah, it's all politics."

Eastman watched Geo reach into the pocket of his waistcoat and produced two envelopes. One with a green plus sign on it, and one with a red 'X.' He handed them both to her.

She looked down at the two envelopes in her hands, raised an eyebrow, and looked up to Geo's smiling face.

"I know that smile. What in the devil have you been up to?"

Geo grinned and pointed to the envelope with the green plus sign on it.

"Open this one now, and then open the other one after you get some rest."

"Oh, mysterious!" She said as she ripped the corner off the one envelope and dumped the contents into her free hand. She looked down to see a flash drive and a folded-up bank statement.

"When I heard you got let go, I figured they would try to give you the shaft on any sort of severance package or pension. And being that I know all the stuff—well, a *small fraction* of the stuff you have done off the books to make the world a better place, I thought it would be only fair if I used some of my talents to . . . Maybe make the transition a little easier for you."

Eastman looked up to Geo, whose face was merely smiling a moment ago but now had a full-on shit-eating grin. She unfolded the bank statement to see an account with just over ten million dollars in it.

"The flash drive has all the information you need to access the money. The account is of course aged, meaning that it looks like it has been open for decades. The taxes have been paid for, and I have it set up so that you're getting about eleven percent a year on the interest—just under 10k a month, last time I checked."

Eastman's eyes widened. She looked back up at Geo.

"Where did you get the money for this?"

"What money? Everything nowadays is ones and zeroes. I just added some here and there. I have about a dozen of these. It's a hobby."

Eastman threw her arms around Geo's thick neck and gave him another big kiss on his cheek.

Then she remembered the other envelope. "What's in the other one, a new car?"

Geo smiled and looked back at the group that was now making their way over to the line of parked cars.

"Well, we have been friends for a long time, Melantha, a long time. And I figured now, you were going to take a little vacation, but when you're ready to get back to work, let's just say, the information in that envelope might give you some . . . inspiration."

Melantha looked down at the envelope with the red 'X' and back up to Geo.

"Would you like to know who was buying the young kids and woman the Pedagogue was selling?"

After a long moment, Geo looked off into the rows of tombstones, then asked, "Can you abide by that, Mel?"

Eastman sighed while tucking the envelope into the pocket of her purse. She looked back up to Geo and slowly shook her head.

"I didn't think so . . ." Geo sighed while he turned and looked back to Eastman, a fresh fire was now burning in her eyes.

She hugged the big man and put her head on Geo's shoulder.

"Thank you, Geo. Thank you."

"Call on me anytime you need me. You know I'm on the team."

"I know."

She gave Geo one last big squeeze before he turned and started making his way to his car. As Victoria, Jesse, Orchid, Mr. Perez, and Jonas approached, they shared with Eastman the plans they had made for lunch. They got into their cars and headed off for their first official family meal.

Then, Victoria nearly had a heart attack on the way to the restaurant when Eastman explained to her that she was going to pay off her house, car, and all of her other debts, and set up a trust fund for Londyn's college.

Sometimes there are such things as silver linings, even on the blackest days.

DOWN THE RABBIT, WHOLE

Alice: "How long is forever?"

White Rabbit: "Sometimes, just one second."

—Lewis Carroll, Alice's Adventures in Wonderland

Hours have the funny habit of turning into days, days into weeks, weeks into months, months into seasons.

Jesse and Melantha walked up Piedmont Avenue on that warm spring morning. Melantha looked back to make sure the bags of fresh vegetables they had just bought at the Montrose Farmer's Market stayed in place as she pulled the little wagon up the steep driveway leading up to the little Spanish style house.

Jesse was carrying in one arm a reusable bag that was overflowing with fresh kale. In Jesse's left hand was a heavy leash that was attached to Loki. The now fully grown puppy was nearly two years old, and although Jesse had been working on his "good boy" leash manners, Loki was still prone to a lunge now and then. Which, if you weren't ready for it, would spin you around so you were facing the wrong direction. The worst case was you would be visiting the local chiropractor for a couple weeks trying to get rid of the whiplash—or, *Wolf Lash*.

As they got to the top of the driveway to the little steps that led to the front door, Melantha parked the wagon and ran ahead of Jesse to open the unlocked front door of the little house on Piedmont.

It swung open smoothly, without even as much as a creak. A

couple short minutes later, Loki was scarfing down his breakfast while the whirr of the juicer filled the air, making fresh juice from the bounty of vegetables they got earlier that morning.

Melantha flipped the power to the juicer with the faded 'fat, sick, and nearly dead' sticker off and handed Jesse a large frothing green concoction.

"Aren't you glad we decided to go back to being healthy, babe?" Melantha asked while taking a sip from her glass, leaving a silly green mustache on her upper lip, which she immediately disposed of with her tongue.

Jesse playfully chased Melantha out of the kitchen. She ran laughing down the hallway and through the living room, where French accordion music was playing softly over the stereo—one of the many new traditions Jesse and Melantha had created together.

Sunday mornings being their favorite time of the week. They made sure that they didn't have anywhere to be, other than together.

Melantha and Jesse hadn't officially moved in together, although you couldn't tell by looking at the place. They had redecorated, rearranged, and repainted the entire house together. It was almost like a brand-new home. When they laid in bed at night, practically every night Melantha would be there, or Jesse would be over at her place in Pasadena.

They would pull out the iPad and look at houses all over the country, trying to decide on where to move. They debated the pros and cons of staying in Los Angeles, which always turned into a pile of cons and some very lonely pros.

Jesse could work nearly anywhere; that was one of the benefits of being in sales. Melantha could do the same with her practice. Everything was starting to fall back into place. Although neither of them really needed to 'work' anymore, thanks to Geo.

They discussed the money. They watched how the compounding interest rolled in every month but decided not to spend any of it. It would be a challenge to spend it even if they wanted to. In reality, the only thing they wanted to "spend" was time together.

Jesse still drove the little black Prius, and Melantha, her big black SUV. There was no need to keep the little white Ford Escape anymore, so they decided to sell it. It had gone for a steal on Craigslist and sold the same day it was posted.

Jesse finally caught up to Melantha in the hallway after chasing her playfully around the house three times. This, of course, sent Loki into a frantic tizzy as he joined in on the chase, nipping playfully at Jesse's arms as he had become very attached to and protective of Melantha the last couple months.

They both laughed as Loki kept running in circles around the house, singing the song of his people.

Jesse gave Melantha "the eyes" and whispered in her ear as he kissed her softly up the nape of her neck, "Come into the bedroom with me; I want to show you something."

Melantha grabbed Jesse by the collar and dragged him down the hall and into the bedroom. She pounced onto him like a hungry lioness on the Saharan plains taking down a gazelle. She forced Jesse to crash down onto the bed in a fit of laughter.

"Hold on, Mel, hold on. I do actually want to show you something," Jesse said between giggles as Melantha was already trying to get his shirt off.

"Yeah, I bet you do," Melantha laughed as her eyes darted from his and down to his jeans and back.

"No, really, hold on."

Jesse walked over to the big chest of drawers and slid the top right drawer open. He sat back down on the bed and turned to Melantha.

"Mel, you came into my life under the worst circumstances that anyone could ever imagine. I don't know any other way to say this, so I'm just going to say it. If it wasn't for you, I'm sure I wouldn't be here right now. I'm pretty sure I would have ended it all. You helped convert all the pain and rage I had inside me after what happened, and the pain I always had inside of me from before, into something useful, something tangible, something I could wield to not only make those motherfuckers pay, but to heal the wounds inside me that I never even knew I had. I guess what I wanted to say is: since you started helping me, since we have been a thing . . ."

Melantha smiled big. The thing about Jesse was he hardly ever shut up. Ever. So when he was tongue-tied or at a loss for words, it was adorable and endearing.

"I know what you're trying to say, babe. I appreciate it, and I love you. I'm grateful that you're in my life every day."

Jesse smiled and handed Melantha a small silk bag and waited for her to open it before he spoke.

Melantha held up a brilliant, thick, white gold necklace that shimmered in the morning sun from the bedroom's open windows.

"I figured we could go antiquing today, and I could pick out something beautiful for you to hang on it."

Melantha looked down silently at the heavy chain that snaked through her fingers.

"I guess what I'm trying to say, Mel, is that I'm in love with you, and I feel like you feel the same way. I really want us to be together for a long time, if you will have me."

Jesse looked at Melantha, who was still staring down at the heavy chain in her hands. The expression on her face was difficult to read.

Jesse reached over and gave her a playful nudge. She didn't respond. Her body was tense, it almost looked like she wasn't even breathing, a single tear rolled down Melantha's cheek.

"Babe?"

Melantha got up from the bed and walked out of the room, and then came back in and put her purse on the bed.

She slowly unzipped her bag, reached into one of the inner pockets, and took out a little pocket-sized manila envelope. Melantha took a deep breath, and slowly handed it to Jesse.

"I thought you were upset with me for a minute there," Jesse said as he casually tore open the little envelope and, without looking at the contents, dumped it into the palm of his hand.

And time stopped.

Jesse looked down in his palm, and there lying in his hand was a platinum key with a diamond set in it attached to a delicate platinum chain: Katia's necklace.

Melantha looked up to Jesse. Every ounce of color seemed to be drained from his face. His hazel eyes were fixed on that charm that he hadn't laid eyes on for just over a year.

Melantha sat frozen, waiting for Jesse to find some words, make some expression, to say anything.

Finally, after a long pregnant pause, the man closed his hand around the delicate trinket and looked up to Melantha.

"You—You found Katia's necklace. Thank you, Mel, thank you."

"I didn't find it, Jess. I took it from her."

"I don't understand, babe, I thought you said it wasn't here when you examined the scene. You told me it was missing."

Jesse looked down at the perfectly clean necklace in his hand. He studied it. The chain didn't have a hint of blood or debris on it. He looked back up to Melantha, who now had both hands covering her mouth, tears pouring out from her eyes. She looked down at the bed, unable to face him.

"Mel, what is it? I don't understand. Tell me what is going on!"

Melantha spoke through her hands, hoping that if she covered her mouth, the words wouldn't come out, "I took it off Katia after I saved her. After I killed her."

Melantha looked up to Jesse, the color had come back to his face now all right, but it was more of a deep beet red. His eyes were locked onto hers. Burning pools of hazel.

Melantha looked down through tear-soaked eyes and saw Jesse's hand curl up and ball into a fist around the platinum key.

Jesse hissed like a serpent through his teeth, "*What?* What did you just say?"

Melantha slowly started to retreat to the edge of the big California king-sized bed. Jesse sat motionlessly, but his cold eyes tracked Melantha's every movement.

Melantha was trying her best to conjure up something to say, the right words to not set this ticking time bomb off in front of her.

"Jesse, calm down. Let me explain . . ."

Jesse started moving slowly toward her, matching her speed.

"You just told me that you killed Katia. What is there left to explain?"

"Jesse, it's not what you think, please. Just calm down. I can tell you're upset right now, and you have every right to—"

"You killed her, then what? Used me to murder a bunch of innocent people?"

"No, wait, Jesse!"

Melantha turned to run out the bedroom door, but Jesse leaped through the air and caught her by her ankle, causing her to spill onto the floor of the hallway. Melantha dug her nails into the hardwood floor as Jesse dragged her back into the bedroom. He got to his feet, and yanked Melantha to hers, before pinning her to the wall.

"Why, Mel?" Jesse screamed over and over as he shook Melantha by her shoulders.

"Jesse!" Melantha looked into Jesse's eyes. He was incensed with hurt, confusion, and sorrow.

"*You* killed her? *You* did this? You lied to me! You said you would never lie to me!"

Melantha caught her breath, and called so Jesse could hear, "Follow the white rabbit!"

Immediately the shaking stopped. Melantha crumbled to the floor. The room was silent except for the sound of her chest heaving in deep breaths of oxygen.

She turned to see Loki standing in the doorway of the bedroom, his head cocked to the side, his big pale blue eyes filled with confusion and worry.

"It's okay, buddy. Go lay down . . ."

Melantha looked up from the floor to see Jesse, still standing where he was just a moment ago, gently swaying back and forth. His eyes were closed. His face was calm. The platinum chain was dangling from his closed hand, relaxed, no longer a fist.

Melantha got to her feet and took Jesse by the hand, and softly cooed to him, "C'mon now, babe, let's go sit down and relax. I'm going to explain everything to you."

Jesse let out an almost happy, pleasant sound as he allowed Melantha to guide him to the edge of the bed, where she assisted him in sitting on the corner. She sat down right beside him, on the side that was closest to the door—just in case.

"Okay, Jesse, I want you to open your eyes and look at me, but you're still mine, understand?"

Jesse's eyes opened, they were glazed over, his pupils were massively dilated.

"Okay, I'm going to tell you what happened because deep down, you have known this all along. And the more you think about it, Jess, the more relaxed you feel, my love. Because you have always wanted the truth. And the truth is, Jesse, that Katia and the Pedagogue were planning on killing you that night—the night she died. You were going to be one of the sacrifices for their ceremony. Geo has been keeping me in the loop of all his activity for years. And on that night, the night that Katia died, they were going to wait until you got home and ambush you. They were going to take you up to the Sanctuary and kill you, as tribute to their union, Jess. I couldn't let them do that.

"So, I got here first. And I tried to help Katia—I really did. I tried to turn her away from the Pedagogue and his cult, to remind her how much she was loved, and how good she had it. But just like my sister, she was too far gone. She attacked me. I defended myself. I am so, so sorry, but I killed Katia."

Melantha started weeping.

"I had to cut up her body to let out all the dark power that he had already pumped into her. So she could be free and hopefully ascend to the next level. Because that's what you would have wanted, isn't

569

it, my love?"

Jesse slowly nodded his head in the affirmative.

"I painted a warding off sigil on the door in her blood, as a protective sign, keeping her spirit safe from being pulled back into his power.

"When I got on the scene here, and I heard about how you reacted, I just had to go and see you for myself. Because I was told—it was told to me from my own methods of divination—that the one who could be the catalyst to defeat him, to bring down this plague, this scourge, would be who the spirits called, 'The Broken Redeemed.'

"So, on that night, when you were handcuffed to that hospital bed, I sat there and worked on you for hours in the hospital under the guise of interrogation. The first thing I did was to plant in you your 'trigger word' so I could activate or deactivate you at will. Remember when we talked about MK Ultra? . . . Now listen, I know how that sounds, my love, but it was the only way I could keep you safe in these situations.

"I knew you had it in you to do what we needed to do; all you needed was a little push. A little nudge. And that's what I did. You were always on the edge of the cliff. You have been your entire life, so I just gave you a little push. I set you free . . . If you think about it, my love, all of this, it was really all for you."

Jesse smiled and nodded once again. His shoulders relaxed, and his head bowed slightly as he worked over information he already knew, already had stored deep in his subconscious.

"We met several times before our first meeting you remember at my office. And now, I'm going to allow you to remember those meetings. Those times I showed up here late at night and told you everything that was going to happen. That everything was going to be okay. Do you remember that now, Jesse?"

In a hushed tone, Jesse whispered, "Yes. I remember . . ."

"Good. Every time, I took you a little bit deeper. I had to talk to that little voice that was always in your head. I had to let him know it was okay for him to take over sometimes. The time when you had to kill, I let the little voice know that he could have you only during those times . . . But you really belonged to me."

Jesse nodded.

"And now, you can finally be what you have been your whole life. You now know what you have always known your entire life: you're a survivor, Jesse. A warrior. The Broken Redeemed.

"And now, you have literally been reborn. And Macha left you with powers, Jess, powers that I will help you harness."

Melantha wiped the tears from her face.

"I am sorry about Katia. I truly am. And for Dani and Jaycee also . . . That was a shame. I didn't get any joy out of that at all, but they were too far gone.

"They were already dead inside—just like Katia. Their minds, their souls were already polluted and poisoned with the darkness. But I saved them, I saved all three of them, Jess!"

Melantha paused.

"But the Pedagogue took revenge. You remember what happened to Judy? They were able to find their way back to that house on Journeys End Drive, back to Judy . . ."

Jesse took in a deep breath as his mind processed and categorized everything Melantha was telling him.

"When I first met you, Jesse, I looked at you as nothing more than a tool—a prophesied weapon—that I could sharpen and hone to turn into a blade for my own vengeance. But as I got to see who you are, who you really are, I fell in love with every part of you, even that little oily black thing that lived inside your mind . . . I fell in love with every single broken inch of the man you are."

Melantha started crying again, and she took the man's now relaxed hand.

The precious necklace had fallen onto the floor. Melantha brought Jesse's hand up to her lips and kissed it.

"I fell in love with you because I'm broken too, and I thought, that together . . . we might make *kintsugi*. We might build something beautiful from both of our broken pieces. That we could help glue each other together with gold. Because I know that this whole time you had to have known—known that deep down—this entire thing was more than just a case I was working. That this wasn't just a job for me.

"That first night we made love, and you saw my scars, I know that you knew right then that this was more than just a job. That there was more to me—you had to have known. Because you never asked about my scars. You loved me anyway, held me, touched my scars without wincing, because you have scars too, only yours are on the inside.

"I felt them when you told me all the stories about your childhood, and I didn't run from you, so don't you dare run from me now!" Melantha hesitated and took a deep breath. She flicked her eyes to the bedroom door, and back to Jesse. She took another deep breath.

"Please don't let this be the end of us."

Melantha wiped away the tears from her bloodshot eyes, looked to the man she loved, and said, "I love you, Jesse Silver, and I hope that you always follow the white rabbit!"

Jesse's eyes immediately opened, and he looked at Melantha. For a moment, she couldn't read his expression,

She didn't have to when he grabbed her, pulled her in close, and held her tight.

Jesse and Melantha never made it out for antiquing on that spring Sunday morning.

They spent the rest of the day in bed making love, looking at homes for sale on the iPad, binge-watching their favorite series on Netflix, and ordering delivery food.

In other words, it was a perfect day.

THE END

EPILOGUE

Jesse laid on the bed like a slug trying to shake off a well-earned food coma as the last episode of "Black Mirror" finished playing. He closed the iPad and looked up to see Melantha smiling, leaning naked in the doorway, holding a white envelope with a big red 'X' on it.

ACKNOWLEDGMENTS

I want to take a moment to thank everyone that helped inspire the fictional events that you've just read.

For better or worse, thank you.

I also want to thank the friends who inspired many of the characters in this book, and the many nights you humored me by listening to me read these chapters to you, in person or over the phone. Your honest feedback and critique have been a big deal to me. I mean that.

I want to thank my family and friends again for never letting me suffer alone, the same ones that were happy to hold me and listen to the same stories, over and over and over.

And over still.

Thank you.

And finally, thank you to the real Doctor M. Eastman, who would probably listen to all this nonsense, raise an eyebrow, and say: "Drag me . . ."

Thank you, Doc.

REVERIE

ABOUT THE PUBLISHER

Di Angelo Publications was founded in 2008 by Sequoia Schmidt—at the age of seventeen. The modernized publishing firm's creative headquarters is in Los Angeles, California, with its distribution center located in Twin Falls, Idaho. In 2020, Di Angelo Publications made a conscious decision to move all printing and production for domestic distribution of its books to the United States. The firm is comprised of ten imprints, and the featured imprint, Reverie, is inspired by the long-lasting legacy of fiction and adult literature.

DAP BOOKS
DI ANGELO PUBLICATIONS

www.ingramcontent.com/pod-product-compliance
Lightning Source LLC
Chambersburg PA
CBHW030742030726
47497CB00001B/90